Of Ice & Air

By

Carlie M. A. Cullen

Credits:

Editor: Eagle Eye Editors   Cover: Blondie's Custom Book Covers

ISBN-10: 193929665X
ISBN-13: 978-1-939296-65-8

Myrddin Publishing Group

www.myrddinpublishing.com

DEDICATION

For Connie J Jasperson and Alison DeLuca, for their friendship, and having the faith in my work to bring me into Myrddin Publishing. And for my fellow authors at Myrddin, thank you for your support and encouragement. I love you guys!

ACKNOWLEDGEMENTS

As always, there are people surrounding me without whose help and support this book wouldn't have made it to publication.

First of all, I must thank my wonderful editor, Connie J Jasperson. Not only have you taken my manuscript and turned it into a novel we can both be proud of, but your support and belief in me as a writer has been invaluable. Thank you, Connie, from the bottom of my heart. You rock, woman!

To Blondie's Book Covers, aka KJ Waters and Jody Smyers, thank you so much for all your hard work and patience in creating the cover exactly as I wanted it. I love you guys!

To my BFF, Jakki Cullen (no relation), your belief in me and words of wisdom when I needed them kept me sane. The times we got together are very special and held close to my heart. You're as crazy as a box of frogs and always make me laugh! Thank you. I love you dearly.

To my very dear friends, Tracy Duncan, and Rob and Tony Cooper, thank you for the laughs, the chats, and for making sure I got out of the house and back to civilisation every now and then. Much love to you all.

To my Facebook friends, followers, and readers, thank you for making each day entertaining, for supporting me, and for taking those plastic cards from your purses to purchase my books. You have no idea how much I appreciate every one of you.

Finally, to the most special person in my life, my daughter, Maria, who makes each day special just because she's in it. Maria, your support, encouragement, care, and love know no bounds. You put your life on hold to care for me when I needed it most and now you're on the path to following your dreams, I couldn't be more proud of you. Thank you for everything, sweetheart – I love you to infinity and beyond.

Twenty Years Ago

"Hurry, Highness. They've almost reached the outer gates," Chilali cried, her skin paling.

Her mistress, who sat at a small table writing, raised her head. "Calm yourself. Time is short, but we have enough to do what we must." Her eyes moved back to the note and continued, the pen sweeping rapidly across the paper. She signed it with a flourish, folded it, and put her wax seal over the edges.

"Princess, they are coming through the outer gates..."

"Chilali, go into my bedroom and wait for me there. I'll return in time," Garalia said, snatching the two letters and a handful of small items from the table, and gathering up a bundle of cloth with her baby wrapped inside.

"Shouldn't I come with you, Highness?"

"No! Your ignorance of this matter will surely save your life, now do as I say, quickly." Chilali pouted but did as she was told, closing the bedroom door behind her. Garalia squeezed into the gap beside the bookcase and pressed the ice in a certain combination, revealing a door. As soon as she stepped through, the door closed automatically behind her. The familiar rush of air began to buffet her as it carried Garalia to her destination.

Soon she felt the fluffy floor beneath her feet and the door opened. She stepped through and to her disappointment no one was there. She rushed to the bedroom, but it too was empty. *Perhaps it's for the best that Galaxan isn't here. It would have made it even harder for me to leave.* She gently placed the baby in the centre of the huge bed and bent to kiss her sleeping daughter. "I love you with all my heart, Kailani, my child. You will be safe here." Garalia's whispered voice cracked and she stifled a sob. She laid the two letters and the items she'd grabbed next to the baby. As she turned to the door to return home, a small trickle of tears ran down her cheeks. She stepped through without turning back, knowing her resolve would weaken if she did. A sharp pain lanced across her chest, making her gasp just as the wind jostled her for her journey back home.

<<<◇>>>

Chilali waited in the bedroom as she'd been ordered when Garalia stepped through the door. The tears had frozen on her cheeks and now sparkled like diamonds.

"Highness, we must get you to the throne room, but we can't let anyone see you like this." Chilali grabbed a washcloth from beside the bowl of water and gently wiped the ice tears from the princess's face. She then grabbed a brush and pulled it softly through the platinum blonde hair. When she satisfied, Chilali removed a crown from its stand, placing it on Garalia's head. "*Now* you are fit to receive visitors," she announced with a small smile.

Garalia grinned back at her. "What would I do without you?"

"I don't know, but if we don't get you to your father's side in the next two minutes, you might just have to find out!" Chilali shuddered at the thought of what King Jaanis would say or do. She grabbed Garalia's hand, pulling her to the door and out into the corridor.

Garalia walked sedately into the throne room to find her parents and

Bellis, her brother, already seated.

"Last again. No surprise there," Bellis tutted then winked.

"Oh, be quiet, squirt!" Garalia grinned at her little brother then moved to where her parents sat and kissed each of them on the cheek. "I'm not late, am I?"

"Thankfully, no. However, another two or three minutes and you would have been. I don't think it would have gone down well with our . . . *guests* if you had been. They would have viewed it as a lack of respect," King Jaanis replied.

"I'm surprised you're wasting your precious time giving them an audience as it is."

"The only reason I'm entertaining them at all is to try and stop them attacking some of the small villages and making slaves of the populace. I want to understand what drives them to do this and what they hope to achieve. Lord Tintereq was my friend and Gengaruk is his son so I feel honour bound to see him. Besides, they asked for this meeting and I admit to being curious as to why."

"They're probably after your throne, Father," Garalia replied flippantly then in a more serious tone said, "I have a really bad feeling about this. Are all the guards on high alert?"

"Yes, my dear. Now stop worrying and try to keep your opinions to yourself when they're here. I don't want your temper to interfere with the negotiations."

She gritted her teeth. "Yes, Father." She sat on her throne at his right and peered around him at her mother. Queen Shivla smiled at her oldest child then nodded her head.

Three bangs on the door announced the arrival of the visitors. The king nodded to the guards who opened them.

A huge man with shoulders almost as wide as one of the doors stepped through. He had a bushy blonde beard and his silver eyes had a treacherous look in them. He was dressed in grubby furs and dirty boots. The six men who accompanied him looked like they hadn't had a wash in months. He strode forward and made a cursory bow before the king as if it pained him to do so.

"Welcome, Gengaruk. I trust your journey wasn't too arduous," Jaanis said in a sincere tone.

"Thank you, King Jaanis. Our trip was tiring, but we didn't encounter any trouble on route," he replied in a gruff voice.

The king snapped his fingers and chairs were brought for the visitors. Another servant carried in a tray of goblets filled with a steaming liquid and offered one to each of the visitors before attending the royal family. Gengaruk waited until Bellis had sipped his drink before trying his own.

"Is it to your liking?" Queen Shivla enquired.

"Very tasty and warming," Gengaruk replied with a nod.

The king steeled himself. "Gengaruk, you asked for this audience and I'm curious as to why. Perhaps you would care to explain."

"Your kingdom is huge and you rarely visit the far north where I and my men live. In fact, I can't remember the last time a member of the royal family came anywhere near us. The people feel you do not care about them and look to me for guidance and assistance."

"From what I have heard, you and your men have been attacking the villages in that part of my realm and making slaves of those who survive," Jaanis said with a steely undertone in his voice. "For what purpose do you treat them so harshly?"

"That is a filthy lie!" he shouted, his eyes flashing dangerously then moderated his tone and spoke with oily malice. "I have offered shelter and food to those poor citizens who were unable to look after themselves, that's all. I haven't attacked anyone!" He smiled.

"Oh, well maybe *you* don't get your hands dirty, but your men certainly do. Why do you need so many slaves?"

"I don't know what you're talking about." He gazed at the king, his eyes narrowing.

Jaanis thought for a moment before speaking again. "So what was your intention in coming here? What is it you hope to achieve?"

He took a deep breath. "What I want is to have some kind of title which will allow me to govern the northern part of the country on your behalf. I would ensure every person is treated equally and the laws of our great country are obeyed. I would collect the taxes and send them to your majesty minus a small stipend. The people already come to me so very little would change except I would have the title and your blessing."

"I see. Why do you think the people turn to you instead of someone else?"

"Perhaps because I'm well-known in the area and am seen as someone who will help them." Gengaruk shrugged his shoulders.

"So it has nothing to do with fear on the part of the citizens in that area?"

"Certainly not!"

King Jaanis nodded to one of his guards who disappeared through a doorway to the right of the thrones and re-appeared a couple of minutes later with two men and a woman, all of whom were dressed in rags and looked half starved. The king watched Gengaruk's face carefully and saw the surprise. He beckoned to the three people forward who moved forward timidly. "Do not be afraid. You are safe here." Jaanis's voice was as gentle as the expression on his face.

They came closer and stopped before the royal party, their backs to Gengaruk and his men. A growl of anger came from one of the visitors and someone hissed "Hush!"

Jaanis turned to one of the men. "Do you know who I am?"

The men bowed low and the woman curtseyed. "Of course, Sire. You are King Jaanis."

"Please relax. No harm will come to you here in the palace. I want you to speak freely and tell me what happened to you."

"His men," he gestured with his thumb over his shoulder without turning, "rode into our village one day. They told us King Gengaruk needed slaves and if we didn't go with them peaceably, we would be killed. Some of my neighbours resisted and were cut down where they stood. All the children were slaughtered. Those of us who agreed were marched off to the castle he's had built by the hands of his slaves and we were put to work. We live in cramped, dirty conditions where disease is rife, and get very little food."

The king turned to the next man. "And what about you?" he asked. The second man's story almost exactly matched the first account.

Jaanis turned to the woman. "And you, my dear? Please tell me what became of you." His voice was gentle, but the woman's eyes filled with tears and she began to shake. Garalia immediately rose and walked over to the weeping woman, placing an arm around her shoulders and whispering comforting words in her ear until she calmed down.

"I-I'm sorry, your Majesty."

"No need to apologise, my dear. Do you feel ready to continue now?"

The woman looked up at Garalia and the princess nodded as she tightened her grip a little around the woman's shoulders. "It was about six moons ago when his lot rode into my village. They rounded up the men first, killing those who refused to go with them, massacred the children including my five-year-old son and three-year-old daughter, and then I-I was... made to have... s-sex before being required to march with the men to the castle. Every night since then, one of his men has come to me at night, taken me away from the others and forced me to..." Her breathing was ragged and tears trickled down her cheeks. She paused for a long moment before continuing haltingly. "I-I'm not the only woman this happens to, Sire. One of the other women became with child as a result of these... *brutalities* and as soon as she'd given birth, th-they... they speared the infant, k-killing it instantly and left it there for her to see every day. When the c-corpse began to rot, they took it away and made her watch while they b-burnt the body." The woman's voice rose as she recalled the events.

"I see. Thank you for being so candid even though the cost you paid was huge." He turned to the soldier who had brought them in. "Take them to the kitchen and ensure they are fed. Afterwards, arrange for them to have baths, tend to any wounds, organise clean clothes, and comfortable rooms to rest in."

"At once, Sire," the soldier said and ushered them back through the same door. Garalia sat back on her throne, her face betraying her anger and loathing.

"So, despite your protestations of innocence, we have three witnesses who call you a liar." King Jaanis rose to his feet, his voice as icy as his kingdom. "You came here today to ask me to make you my representative, but you treat my citizens worse than animals. You want my blessing, but I can't give it. I hereby banish you and your men to the far West, to the area called 'The Land of No Souls', where you will remain for the rest of your days. To attempt to leave is to die."

The king raised his ice sceptre and pointed it at Gengaruk and his men; he muttered a few words under his breath and the men cried out. On each of their wrists a bangle appeared which felt burned into their skin. "Don't try and remove those bracelets, they will not come off. Even if you cut off your arm, it will transfer to another part of your body. They are bespelled and will ensure you never leave The Land of No Souls.

"My men are on their way to your 'castle' to free your slaves. All who resist them will be cut down where they stand. Any of your men who remain alive in the North will be escorted to meet you at your new home. Never again will you mistreat or cause anguish to anyone in Idenvarlis." He gestured to a knot of soldiers standing at one side of the room who immediately surrounded Gengaruk and his men.

Gengaruk shot to his feet, a mask of rage settled on his features, but one of the guards shoved him back down. "You are going to believe that low-life scum and their lies? I have served you well and this is the way you treat me? You will pay dearly for this, I promise you!"

"All you have done is brought misery and pain to the good citizens in the North of this realm. You and your men have exploited them in the worst ways humanly possible, all in the name of greed. The only person you have served well is yourself. You will be given a small meal before you set off on your journey. I pray to Xuani, Rasha, and Sylde that I never have to set eyes on your faces again. Guards, clamp them in irons then escort them to the dungeons. I want them out of my sight."

The soldiers surrounding Gengaruk and his men closed in, each one holding shackles. A scuffle ensued, but within minutes the handcuffs were on their wrists and the guards led them from the room.

Just before Gengaruk stepped through the doors, he turned. "I always keep my promises." His expression was chilling.

Queen Shivla gazed at her husband, a fierce pride in her eyes. "Dear one, I have a suggestion to make. I think we should organise a royal visit to the North. It's such a long time since we've been there and I believe our citizens would derive some comfort knowing we do still have their best interests at heart. In addition, it will give us the opportunity to see first-hand the atrocities Gengaruk perpetrated, the hardships faced by villagers, and see what we can do to help them. We need to appoint a proper governor for the region."

"An excellent suggestion, my dear. We could set off tomorrow, as soon as we are sure Gengaruk and his men are well on their way." Jaanis turned to his daughter. "Garalia, I'm happy to leave the running of the country and the palace in your care whilst we are gone. I ask that you consult Bellis on any major decisions – despite his youth, he has a sensible head on his shoulders. You may find his counsel useful although all rulings will ultimately be yours. Will you do this for us?" He placed his arm around his wife's shoulders and stared at his beloved daughter.

"Of course I will, Father. It's not as if I haven't done it before."

"I know, but this will be the farthest journey your mother and I have made without taking you both with us, so you will be running the country for much longer than before."

"Father, I would think less of you if you weren't making this journey after what we heard from those poor people. They so desperately need your help. You can leave with a light heart and mind knowing I will do everything necessary to keep the country running smoothly and, of course, consult my *baby* brother as required." She winked at Jaanis, knowing what his reaction would be. She wasn't disappointed.

Bellis leapt from his throne. "I'm only three years younger than you and I'm already a man so stop calling me a baby!" His face flushed red in his anger, as did the birthmarks on his neck.

Garalia collapsed in a fit of giggles. Even their parents couldn't keep a straight face. "You are *so* predictable!" she gasped between her chuckles.

"Bellis, my son, you need to learn when your sister is baiting you so you don't react this way. She only does it because she knows how you will respond. She's just teasing," Jaanis said, with laughter still in his eyes.

"Well two can play that game. I will bide my time though," Bellis replied thoughtfully.

"Well, if you will all excuse me, there are many arrangements which need to be made if we are to leave tomorrow. I'll see you all at lunch." Queen Shivla rose and swept from the room.

The following morning, everything was in readiness for the king and queen to begin their long journey to the north. The Blenorai, powerful, agile, armoured beasts with the head of a lion and the body of a bear, stood assembled to carry the guards and pull the sleds carrying provisions, clothing, and other necessities. The royal pennants flew proudly in the brisk breeze. The Blenorai Kai, the elite of the race who only carried the royal family, resplendent with their jewelled and bespelled armour, waited patiently for the royal family to appear.

They didn't have long to wait. King Jaanis and Queen Shivla stepped out of the Ice Palace a few minutes later accompanied by their children. After hugs and kisses were exchanged at the bottom of the steps, the party mounted their beasts and with one final wave, set off across the ice. Garalia and Bellis watched until their parents were mere specks in the distance before climbing the steps and re-entering the palace.

"What's the matter? You have a troubled expression on your face," Bellis asked.

"To be honest, I'm not sure. I just have a strong feeling something bad is going to happen."

"What? To our parents?"

"No, they will be fine, don't worry. It's something here at the palace."

"How can that be? We have a full contingent of guards to protect us and nothing has ever gone wrong before when mother and father have been away. Where has this feeling come from?"

"You know I'm rarely wrong when I get these types of feelings. I don't know what it is. I just know something is amiss."

"You look scared and that alone is enough for me to take you seriously. I'll tell the guards to be extra vigilant. Will that help give you peace of mind?"

"Maybe. I honestly don't know. We'll have to wait and see what happens, just promise me you won't leave the palace grounds alone," Garalia implored.

"I promise. Now I'm off to see Captain Karruq so he can issue instructions to his men. I'll see you at lunch." Bellis gave his sister a quick hug before striding off down the hallway.

What a fine young man my little brother is growing into. He will make a great ruler when his time comes, Garalia thought as she watched him for a few moments before heading back towards her chambers.

Suddenly she felt a pain explode in her skull and she fell to her knees. Her vision blurred and then everything went black.

Chapter 1

With her long, azure hair streaming behind her, Kailani raced along the clouds on her skipper, a round disc made with woven eagle feathers. She waved gaily to everyone she saw as she weaved through the market place, although not everyone returned her greeting. She pursed her lips at the slight, wondering if they would dare ignore her after her birthday. Turning a corner, she began to make her way back to her Cloud Castle home.

At the top of the steps, she skilfully brought the skipper to a halt and picked it up, clipping it to a belt around her waist. She walked gracefully through the doors and as soon as she was out of sight of the guards, ran down the long corridor and up the stairs to her suite of rooms, bursting through the door.

"May Savna preserve us. You scared me half to death, child!" Carina cried, with one hand over her heart. She was getting on in years, having been the nursemaid, and now the personal maid to the princess. Her hair had many silver streaks in it and her homely face was lined. Always a little on the plump side, she hadn't changed although she was now a couple of inches shorter than her charge.

"Oops, sorry Carina. I didn't know you were still in here." Kailani had a twinkle of mischief in her eyes and pressed her blue lips together to stop herself from laughing aloud.

"With the way you leave your things lying around, it's almost a full-time job picking up after you. Tomorrow you will officially be a woman and it's about time you started acting like one." Carina was the only person outside of her family who could talk to her in that manner and get away with it. She had been with Kailani since she was a baby and was like a mother figure.

"Yes, well, that's tomorrow. Today I'm still officially a child," she cheeked her nanny-come-maid as she strolled into her bedroom. "Anyway, I only came back to brush my hair before I go to see Auriga and Leda. We're going flying on our Feegles and having a picnic lunch at Lake Maradora."

"Does your father know?"

"Of course he does. He suggested the lake and has organised a lunch basket from the kitchen."

"Very well. Here, sit down and let me do that for you," Carina offered, grabbing the brush from the dressing table. Kailani obediently sat on the stool and waited while Carina's deft strokes, pulled the knots from her hair.

Does your father know? Thank the goddess I won't have to put up with that after tomorrow. I'm not the silly, impetuous girl they think I am. I'm clever, astute, and resourceful when I want to be. I can't wait to show them all, especially papa, just how grown-up I really am, Kailani thought.

When the tresses lay smooth and shining against her back, the maid replaced the brush. "You'll do, I suppose."

"Thank you. I'll see you later," Kailani said, giving the woman a quick hug before turning and rushing toward the door.

"Don't be too late back."

"I won't!" Kailani called over her shoulder mere seconds before the outer door crashed shut.

Carina tutted and shook her head. "When will that girl learn to close doors rather than slamming them?"

Kailani collected the picnic basket from the kitchen, thanked the cook, and made her way to the stables. In the fourth stall was her pure white Feegle who, upon seeing her mistress, began skittering and jumping around in excitement.

"Hello my beautiful girl," she murmured stroking the animal's furry face and head. "Shall we go out today?" Rhea, her Feegle, nodded her head. The princess placed the basket on the floor and entered the stall. She put the reins and saddle on and after checking her collar, led the stunning creature out, picking up the basket as she went. Once outside the stable, she mounted the beast and attached the basket to the saddle. A gentle flick of the reins and Rhea unfurled her large wings; within two or three flaps they were in the air.

Feegles were like small furry dragons, about a third of the size to be more accurate. They were friendly lovable creatures that didn't have a malicious bone in their bodies, could fly extremely long distances without tiring, and carry quite heavy loads (which was a blessing when you saw the size of the backsides of some of the nobles).

Guiding her Feegle gently, they landed in the small field behind Auriga's house where her two best friends were waiting with their rides all saddled up ready to go.

"Where are we off to today?" Leda asked.

"Lake Maradora. And I've got a picnic lunch from the cook."

Auriga called through the door to her mother. "We won't be home for lunch, Kailani has food."

"Alright. You girls have fun and be careful," a voice replied, swiftly followed by the woman herself. She was striking for her age and appeared much younger than she actually was.

"Yes, Mother," the girls chorused then dissolved into fits of giggles.

Ursula was used to this type of response from the girls and grinned back at them. "Hello, your Highness, it's lovely to see you again. You girls have a wonderful time and I'll see you later." Having said that, she disappeared into the house.

"Let's go!" called Kailani as she watched the others mount up. Within seconds they were in the air.

The Feegles' powerful wings made the journey in a much shorter time than expected. The girls tethered their animals and sat beside the lake.

"Wow! It's beautiful here," Auriga said looking around. The sun glistened on the lake making it appear as if it was one large diamond with a flawless cut and the light refracted in so many different directions causing rainbows of colour which bounced off the clouds.

"It certainly is," agreed Leda. "How did you find this place?"

"Father told me about it. Apparently he used to bring my mother here when they were courting. It was their favourite place."

"Have you ever found out what happened to her?" Auriga asked timidly. She didn't want to upset her friend.

"No, but I'm hoping my father will tell me tomorrow on my birthday. I'll remind him of the things that were in my blankets, which I've held onto. He can't really deny me as I'll be twenty-one and officially a woman in the eyes of everyone in our lands. As much as he might like to, he can't keep me cushioned from the world forever."

"That's true. But what if he refuses?" asked Leda.

"I'll have to force him. My grandfather will back me up. After all, I do have a right to know. I'm looking forward to being my own woman and not have to ask permission every time I want to so much as fart. Ooo I can't wait! Anyway, let's not talk about that any longer. Shall we see what delicious treats cook has packed for us?"

<<<◇>>>

Kailani woke to the sound of birds twittering outside her window. For a while she lay listening to their sweet songs, daydreaming about her birthday gala being held that evening. All the noble families from across the land had been invited as well as Auriga and Leda.

She knew that part of the celebrations was to introduce her to eligible suitors. The system seemed archaic to her, but it was a 'time honoured tradition' and one which was considered by her grandfather, King Sirris, to be 'non-negotiable'. Still, Kailani couldn't help but wonder who would be coming and if there was anyone remotely fanciable who would catch her eye. She might have to endure the attention of a few dogs along the way, but as long as there were some handsome and charming young men, it would certainly be worthwhile.

A knock at the door disturbed her musings and before she could say anything, Carina swept into the room, carrying a laden tray with a beaming smile on her face.

"Good morning, my Princess. Happy tidings for your special birthday," she sing-songed.

"Good morning, Carina, and thank you for your good wishes. What have you got there?" She pointed to the tray.

"I decided to break my own rules just for today and allow you to have your breakfast in bed."

"Really? By the Goddess Jexin, I never thought this day would come. What a treat!" Kailani shuffled into a sitting position, a genuine smile on her face.

Carina placed the tray on the princess's legs and waited for a reaction. She wasn't disappointed when Kailani squealed with delight. There was curlap juice, urples (her favourite sweet pastries filled with fruit and a creamy sauce which were very light and fluffy), and kap, the sweet tea to wash it all down.

"When you've finished and you're dressed, your grandfather, father, and aunt will be waiting for you in the king's study. I wouldn't dally too long if I were you," she warned seeing how slow Kailani was eating her pastries.

"Oh! So I can't even savour my lovely breakfast without interference?"

"Don't whine like a petulant child. You're a grown woman now and you need to start acting like one!" Carina snapped then immediately regretted her outburst. She didn't want to upset the princess, especially on her birthday.

Kailani was quiet for a few moments before she broke the silence which hung heavy in the air between them. "You're right. I'm acting like a spoilt brat. Thank you for your honesty and making me see how difficult I can be, especially when I can't get my own way. Of course, I'll hurry with my breakfast and go to see grandfather."

"I'll get your clothes laid out while you finish. Shall I pick the dress or . . .?"

"What about the lemon one with the flowers embroidered on the hem? I know the king likes me in that."

"An excellent choice, Highness," Carina responded, pulling clothes from the wardrobe and dressing table. Within a minute or two, everything was laid out on the bed, fresh water had been poured into the washing bowl, and soft white towels had been placed by its side. Kailani quickly finished her breakfast and within half an hour, was dressed and groomed in readiness.

She made her way down the long wooden-floored corridor, across the hall, and through the double arched doors into her grandfather's office. Her family was grouped around the ancient wood desk which contained gaily wrapped gifts complete with ribbons and lavish bows.

"Happy tidings for your birthday, my darling." They chorused and she received a hug and kiss from each of them.

"As I was left until last, I'm going to give you my gift to open first." Her aunt reached behind and placed a box in her niece's hands. Lying inside was a wide, bejewelled bracelet, the gems glowing with the colour of the sun.

"Thank you, Aunt Konstellia. I love it!" she said slipping the bangle onto her wrist.

"I'm pulling rank – it's my turn now," Sirris announced. He collected a box from the desk and handed it to her.

Kailani opened it excitedly and gasped. Not only was there a new coronet, he had also gifted her with a mantle denoting her official position as an heir to the throne. "Thank you, Grandpapa. They're wonderful." She leaned forward and kissed his cheek.

"You're very welcome, Kailani. Now you have reached the age of womanhood, it is appropriate you have the regalia befitting your position as a member of the royal family." Whilst his voice was gentle, a solemn undertone laced through it. The underlying message was not lost on the princess.

"Thank you again, Grandpapa. I understand," she replied, staring into his twinkling blue eyes. He leaned forward and kissed her on the forehead.

"I knew you would," he whispered.

"Well, I guess you've saved the best till last!" Galaxan said, raising his brows at his father and sister and grinning. Four presents lay on the table beside him, each in a different coloured box.

Kailani walked across to him, smiling. "Papa, you spoil me!"

"Who else do I have to treat?" he laughed handing over the first box. She opened it and inside was a necklace set with the same jewels as the bracelet given by her aunt. Kailani gasped and as she held it to her neck, her father said, "Allow me." She handed him the necklace and he fastened it.

"It's gorgeous, Papa, thank you so much."

"Let's leave all the 'thank you's till the end, shall we? That way, I get a bigger hug," he chuckled. He grabbed a smaller box and placed it in her hand. She found matching earrings inside. She placed them in her lobes and clipped the backs into place.

Galaxan smiled and handed over the largest box. Inside was a royal blue dress, an exact match to the cloak from her grandfather. However, a layer of star jewels on a delicate lace decorated the front of the dress.

"Oh, goddess. This is breath-taking." She lifted it from the box, held it up against her, and gazed down. It was a perfect length. She went to lay it back in the box, but noticed a pair of matching shoes. Kicking off her slippers, she put them on. The material was so soft, it was like wearing clouds on her feet. With the dress held up in front of her again, she began dancing around the room, a dreamy smile gracing her lips. Kailani halted as she reached Galaxan and saw the huge smile on his face. She loved to see him smile – his eyes lit up like jewels and made him even more handsome. As she replaced the dress and shoes in the box, he spoke.

"Look here," he said pointing to the shoulders and waist of the dress. Cunningly hidden, four fasteners held the jewelled lace onto the dress. He demonstrated at the shoulders only so she could see how it worked then fastened it again.

"Two dresses in one. How clever!" Konstellia said, sounding quite impressed. Kailani nodded her agreement.

The prince held the smallest box in his hand. "Besides you and the rest of my family, this is the most precious item I possess and it's only fitting that you should now have it." Emotion coloured his tone, more than Kailani had ever heard before and it puzzled her. He extended his hand and she took the box.

"Papa, are you sure you want me to have this if it's so precious to you?" she asked, needing to hear his confirmation before opening it.

"Would I be giving it to you if I was unsure?"

"I guess not." She carefully opened the box. Inside, nesting on a pad of velvet, a ring studded with what appeared to be star and moon jewels lay, but they were different to what she was used to seeing. Placing it on her middle finger, she found it was a perfect fit. As she stared at it a thought entered her head and she understood why it was so precious. "This belonged to my mother, didn't it?" Her enquiring voice was soft as she stared into her father's face.

Galaxan nodded, all traces of laughter gone to be replaced by a profound sadness. He spoke, his voice rough with emotion. "Yes, it was Garalia's. It was one of the many items I found in your blankets the night she left you in my care."

"Thank you, Papa. You have no idea how much this means to me." She took a couple of steps forward and threw her arms around his waist, leaning her head against his chest. He returned the embrace, one hand stroking her long, silky hair. Kailani released him and took a step back. "Isn't it about time I knew the full story?"

"No. I'll tell you when the time is right."

What? Surely he can't say no to me anymore, even if he is my father? "But Papa, I'm a woman now. Are you going to wait until you're on your death bed to tell me? I need to know about my mother and I think I've waited long enough!" Kailani said, her cheeks flushing and eyes flashing.

"No, I'm not going to wait that long, but I still maintain this is not the right time," Galaxan said stubbornly.

Kailani looked beseechingly to her grandfather. "Grandpapa, do you agree with Papa's decision? I've waited twenty-one years to hear the truth. All I've been told is that she was beautiful and from another world. That's not much to hold onto, apart from the few items I was given which were wrapped in my blankets with me. I really *need* to know about her." She managed to control most of the rising emotions, but her voice held more than a trace of fire.

The king was silent for a few moments then addressed his son. "Galaxan, Kailani's right. She's a woman now and deserves to know. You would wound her deeply if you deny her this knowledge." Sirris's voice was gentle yet commanding.

Galaxan looked from the king to his daughter and back again. "I just don't want Kailani to be hurt, especially on her birthday. You agree with me, don't you, Konstellia?"

"I'm sorry, brother, but on this occasion I agree with Papa." Konstellia stared at her younger brother with pity in her eyes. She understood only too well how much the telling would cost him personally. She had been his confidant all his life and knew how much pain he'd suffered when Garalia left him and Kailani and disappeared. He was going to have to relive those painful first days without any moral support – this was something he would have to do on his own.

"It seems like I'm out-voted. Very well. It goes against my better judgement, but you will have your way, Daughter. Accompany me to my rooms. I will ensure Carina collects your gifts and takes care of them." His eyes were sad and his voice defeated. Kailani quickly removed her new jewellery and replaced them in the boxes before following her father from the room.

Stopping at the threshold she turned back. "Thank you so much," she whispered before closing the door and running down the hallway to catch up to her father.

Galaxan entered his rooms with slumped shoulders, Kailani hot on his heels. She was filled with excitement and another emotion which she couldn't quite identify. He gestured for her to sit then crossed the room and opened the safe on the wall. Extracting a plain box, he left the safe door open, walked over and sat opposite his daughter. He pulled a chain hidden beneath his clothes and exposed a small key. Opening the box with it, he left it dangling in full view.

Kailani couldn't see what was inside, but her curiosity was at fever pitch. However, she kept silent and waited for her father to begin. He removed a letter and handed it to her. The wax seal was unbroken and she noticed her name written on the outside. She broke the seal and unfolded it.

My darling Kailani,

It breaks my heart to leave you in your father's care, not knowing when I'll see you again, but I have to do this for your safety. I know he will guide you well and you will grow into a beautiful, strong woman with a sense of duty.

You are part of two royal families, a princess in my world as well as your father's. One day, you may be forced to make a difficult decision between the two, but in the meantime enjoy your life in Taivass-maa.

My beautiful daughter, I love you with all my heart, please don't

ever doubt it. You will be in my thoughts every waking moment we are
apart. I can only pray to the gods and goddess that our separation will be
short.

With all my love, always,
Your mother, Garalia

Kailani looked up with tears in her eyes. She still didn't understand
why Garalia had left her in Taivass-maa, but as she read her words there
seemed to be a sense of desperation in them which tugged at Kailani's
heart. She passed the letter to her father who read it quickly and nodded.
She could see the sadness in his eyes despite the small smile which
fleetingly played across his lips. He passed the letter back to her and then
gave her another to read. The seal had been broken on this one and her
father's name was written on the outside. She looked at him questioningly
and he nodded. She unfolded it and began to read.

My darling,

I have to leave Kailani with you for her own safety. I'm not sure
what is about to happen, but I have a strong sense of danger surrounding
me. You know only too well how accurate my instincts are – I've never
been wrong yet and have no reason to think otherwise now.

I don't know when I'll see you again, but no matter what happens,
know that my love for you will never fade or disappear. You are my one
true love and I know we are meant to be together. Whatever this danger is,
I will fight with every bit of strength I have in me to return to your side as
quickly as possible.

Please bring our daughter up to be strong and independent, caring
and loving, and with a sense of duty as befits her position. In writing these

*words, I know in my heart they are not necessary as you would do it
anyway.*

> *I pray to the gods and goddesses of both our lands to reunite us as
> quickly as possible and that you will wait for me.*
> *I love you with every fibre of my being, Galaxan, and always will.*
> *Until we meet again, my love.*
> *Garalia*

Now the tears were dribbling down Kailani's cheeks and she handed
the letter back to him.

"What happened, father? What was the danger she spoke of in her
letter?"

"To be completely honest, I don't know. Since the day I found you
on my bed with these two letters, I've not seen or heard from your mother.
I have no idea what the danger was or what happened to her. I also have no
way of finding out."

"Why?"

"Your mother came from a place called Idenvarlis. It is a completely
different world to ours. It's an ice kingdom and the reason you have blue
lips, white skin, and silver eyes. You have inherited that from your mother
along with the birthmarks on your neck. The blue hair and birthmarks on
your left shoulder have come from my genes. Now you are an adult, you
will be able to perform the magics these marks identify. I don't know about
the ones on your neck, but the ones on your shoulder I can explain to you.
You have four marks which correspond to the four deities in our world and
you will now develop the art of telepathy.

"The sun means you can shoot powerful light rays from your eyes
which will burn anything or anyone who gets in the way. We call them
'Blasters'. The rest of the magic you will control through your hands, but

it's different with everyone. I think the gods and goddesses give us the weapons we need at the time we need them instead of there being any one particular gift. We can also teleport and manifest blades of fire just by thinking of it. I will teach you all of this from tomorrow.

"We also have some very useful weapons in addition to the magic which I will also teach you about. There are the Treys, five-pointed stars with whips on each point, the Panas, a slim sword which can unleash deadly lightning bolts, and Raisas which are highly dangerous in the wrong hands. If dropped or thrown, they explode on contact with Phoenix fire heated to the same temperature as the sun."

"Papa, I appreciate you telling me about the weapons, magic, and why I'm so different to everyone else in Taivass-maa, but I need to know more about mother, Idenvarlis, and anything else you can tell me about why she left." Kailani's frustration spilled into her tone.

Galaxan glared at his daughter for a long moment and then his eyes softened. "Of course you do. I'm sorry, I went off on a tangent there for a few minutes. Idenvarlis, the ice kingdom, is ruled over by your other grandparents. Your grandfather is King Jaanis and Queen Shivla is your grandmother. Prince Bellis is your uncle and younger brother of your mother. The last time I spoke to Garalia, she mentioned that a man from the north of the kingdom was coming for an audience with her father and that she was required to be present. Her plan was to see the meeting to its conclusion and then return to me here. She did mention the possibility of a dinner held in the visitor's honour if the negotiations went well, in which case she would see me the following day. You already know how this sort of thing works as we operate in the same way.

"Anyway, she made no mention at that time of anything worrying her or any bad feelings she had about the meeting. We had a wonderful few hours together with you before she returned home. We had married a few months before your conception, in Taivass-maa, as your other grandparents were vehemently opposed to our union. They never knew about our marriage – somehow the right moment to tell them never seemed to arise. I only met them twice and whilst they were courteous, it was very obvious they didn't want me in their land. I had planned to confront them the day after the meeting, but when I found you on my bed and Garalia's note, it seemed less important to tell them of our marriage and more to finding her.

"Apparently she disappeared from the ice castle. Although Jaanis has his suspicions about who was responsible, he can't see how they could have achieved it. The meeting was with a man called Gengaruk who arrived with half a dozen of his men. The man wanted to be made governor of the province where he lived, but he was treating the citizens like slaves so the king banished them to another part of the kingdom which is uninhabited. The visitors were escorted away from the castle in chains by a squad of guards and taken to their 'new home'.

"However, sometime later, Bellis went to find his sister and found her rooms empty, and her maid unconscious, tied up, and gagged. All the woman remembered was seeing two dirty-looking men enter the room and then pain exploded in her head. Her wound had bled but thankfully, had caused no long-term damage. Search parties were sent out, but she wasn't found. For the two weeks, I went to Idenvarlis every day to help with the search effort. I think maybe Jaanis warmed to me a little after seeing how much I cared for his daughter, but I still think he would have been against our marriage. At the end of that second week, he called me to him and said that whilst my efforts were greatly appreciated, I was only one man and his soldiers could cope with the search effort.

"Strangely, he never questioned how Garalia and I were able to travel between the different worlds – maybe he already knew, although somehow I doubt it. I've never seen your mother since so I can only conclude the guards never found her. And that, my dear Daughter, is about all I can tell you."

"How did you and mother travel between the two kingdoms?" Kailani asked.

Galaxan stood and beckoned her over. He showed her the panel and the order the symbols needed to be pressed to open the door.

"Thank you, Papa. I know this was difficult for you and I really appreciate your telling me. I have much to think about and digest. If you don't mind, I want to return to my room for a while. Besides, Carina will have a nagging fit if I don't rest before the gala tonight."

"That's fine. I'll see you later then." He gave his daughter a hug and kiss on the cheeks before letting her go. She picked up her letter from the table and walked from the room, deep in thought.

Chapter 2

Kailani lay on her bed re-reading her mother's letter again and again. Many unanswered questions chased through her head. Her curiosity about Idenvarlis and her other family was at fever pitch. She wanted to get to know them and resolved to talk to her father about it the following day.

Eventually she exhausted herself and dropped into a restless sleep where dreams of a mother she'd not seen in twenty years haunted her. Her dreams were vivid, showing scenes of her mother being kidnapped from the castle by two large men who looked like they needed a good long soak in a bath. She watched as Garalia was thrown in a heap on some sort of wooden platform and then dragged across the snow.

The scene then switched to her father. He wore a huge coat made of some sort of animal skin and trudged through the snow. He searched desperately, his face becoming more distraught as the day progressed.

The image changed again. This time it showed him lying on his bed, crying into the pillow. Huge wracking sobs shook his body. Another switch and it was her mother placing Kailani on her father's bed and whispering words of love before she went to the doorway and disappeared.

Everything was so real, it was as if she were actually there.

A hand gently shaking her shoulder sent the dreams away and then a familiar voice called her name.

"Kailani, wake up, you need to start getting ready." She opened her eyes and sat up feeling groggy and still tired.

"Are you alright, child?" a concerned Carina asked.

"I'm not a child any longer!" She took a couple of deep breaths. "I didn't sleep very well. I had some disturbing dreams."

"Do you want to talk about them?"

Kailani shook her head. "Not at the moment. In fact, I need to put them out of my mind altogether, at least for now, so that I can play my part as the 'belle of the ball' and charm everyone."

"And you'll do it beautifully, of that I have no doubt." Carina smiled at her.

"Thank you for the vote of confidence."

"You're welcome. Now your bath water is ready and your favourite scent of jasmine is already in the water, so up you get, my girl and let's start getting you ready."

Two hours later, Kailani was ready. Some of her hair was braided and then artfully piled on top of her head while the rest hung loose down her back, shining like stars. Her dress had been specially designed for her; layers of chiffon in pale pastel hues with beading at the edge of each layer and diamante swirls on the bodice. It was the first time she had been allowed any input when a dress for such an important occasion was being commissioned and Aunt Konstellia had approved it, much to Kailani's surprise. Her new dress was exactly as she had hoped it would be and her strappy sandals matched the dress perfectly. To finish the look, she wore the jewellery she'd been given earlier and the coronet was pinned to her hair.

She gazed at her reflection in the mirror, hardly recognising herself. "By the Goddess Denzla, I look so much more adult and...pretty."

"Even without all this regalia you are beautiful, but tonight you look so stunning it takes my breath away," Carina said, feeling quite proud of herself. "Is Prince Galaxan coming to escort you to the ball?"

"Under normal circumstances he would, but as this is such a special birthday, grandfather will accompany me. He should be here any moment." As Kailani said this, a knock sounded at the door which Carina hurried to answer.

"Good evening, your Majesty," Carina said curtseying.

King Sirris nodded to her then smiled as Kailani drifted through the door from her bedroom toward him. "My dear, you look...exquisite." His eyes were wide and filled with pride. "I will be the most envied man in the kingdom when I escort you into the ballroom."

"Thank you, Grandfather," she replied, blushing. Her eyes were lowered and a small smile hovered about her lips.

"Shall we?" He extended his curved arm for her to take. She floated forward as if walking on air and placed her hand on it.

"I hope you have a wonderful time tonight," Carina said as the royal couple walked through the door.

Kailani turned her head. "Thank you, Carina," she called back then looked forward again. She was proud to be walking with her grandfather.

When they had almost reached the ballroom, she turned to him. "Grandpapa, I'm nervous. What if I do or say the wrong thing? What if I trip going down the stairs?"

"You will be fine, I promise you. Just lift your dress a little when we descend the steps and hang on tight to me – I won't let you fall. As for doing or saying the wrong thing, I think it very unlikely. You just need to muster a little more of your normal confidence. You are a warm, intelligent woman, Kailani. Just be yourself and you'll do fine."

"Thank you." She squeezed his arm gently and he smiled down at her.

"Are you ready?" he asked just before they rounded the final corner to the grand ballroom.

She took a deep breath and let it out slowly. "As ready as I'll ever be."

He chuckled and they continued round to the huge double door where two servants dressed in their finest livery stood. As they opened the doors, the trumpeters heralded their arrival and the hall fell silent. The master of ceremonies stepped forward and cleared his throat.

"Your royal highnesses, my lords, ladies and gentlemen, I give you His Royal Majesty, King Sirris and Her Royal Highness, Princess Kailani."

As the royal couple descended, the men bowed and the women curtseyed, even the kings and queens from other countries. Kailani, for the first time in her life, truly felt like the princess she was and held her head high. When they reached the bottom and began walking across the dance floor, she had a warm smile for everyone, which endeared them to her straight away.

Soon they were across the room and ascending the few steps to the dais where their thrones stood. Sirris took Kailani to hers before seating himself. Her father leaned over to her and kissed her on the cheek.

"You look gorgeous, my darling," he said, his voice full of pride.

"Thank you, Papa."

The music began again and it wasn't long before the first suitor asked Kailani to dance. As soon as the song finished, another one appeared by her side and whisked her away across the floor, and so it continued. Each one flattered her outrageously, thinking that would be the way to melt her heart. Whilst the compliments were nice to hear, Kailani didn't appreciate them; perhaps they thought she was shallow enough to think her looks were the magic ticket to marriage and the 'happy ever after'.

About halfway through the evening, when she was grabbed by the next suitor, she waited for the over-effusive compliments. However, this one gave her quite a surprise.

"Good evening your Highness, I am Prince Dashiel from Verenfild." He bowed to her before taking her hand. "I'm guessing you're tired of all these idiots who think flattery is the way to impress you – not that I don't think you're stunningly beautiful – but I'm more interested in getting to know you as a person."

"Well, what a refreshing change. You're absolutely right about the others. In all honesty I was preparing to stifle a yawn," Kailani replied with a smile on her face.

Dashiel smiled back. "So Princess Kailani, I can see you're somewhat different from the rest of the royal family, would you care to explain?"

"I have the best of two worlds. My mother is from the ice kingdom of Idenvarlis and from her I inherited my pale complexion, silver eyes, and blue lips. My father is Prince Galaxan from here in Taivass-maa, and from him I get my hair."

"Interesting. I've never heard of Idenvarlis – can you tell me about it?"

"I wish I could, but I've never been there, well not since I was a baby. It's something I hope to rectify very soon. All I know is the little I was told earlier today, which isn't very much at all."

"Pity. Well, maybe you could tell me about it after your trip there."

"It would be my pleasure."

"So, tell me a little about yourself, the things you're passionate about, your dislikes, anything, and everything." He smiled down at her with warmth and sincerity in his eyes.

"I'm sure it would bore you, Prince Dashiel, and it would

undoubtedly take a great deal longer than one dance."

"Well, as I plan to monopolise you for the rest of the evening, or for as long as I can get away with it, you'll have plenty of time." A cheeky twinkle flashed in his eyes and Kailani couldn't help but laugh.

"Very well. It wouldn't be a hardship to spend the rest of the evening in your company. However, I'm not going to be the one doing all the talking. I want to know about you too, so let us strike a bargain, for everything I tell you about me, you must tell me something about you. Deal?" Kailani issued her challenge with a smile.

"Deal. Right. You first."

Kailani spent the majority of the rest of the evening in Prince Dashiel's company, the only exceptions being when she danced with her father and grandfather. Not only was Dashiel handsome, he really did appear to be genuinely interested in her as a person. She found him fascinating. He had travelled a fair bit and so had lots of tales about his experiences, was mildly self-deprecating, making jokes at his own expense, and surprisingly humble for a man of royal birth. He told her that being born into such a family didn't automatically make one worthy of the title and that it should be earned by ones' deeds and actions. He gave her a great deal to think about.

At the end of the evening, Prince Dashiel asked if he could call on her sometime soon, to which Kailani gave her assent. As he was about to leave, he took her hand and kissed it, his lips lingering much longer than was normal. She stared at his blonde head and wondered what it would be like to be kissed on the lips by him. As he left, her eyes followed him and just before he disappeared through the door, he turned and gave one last wave.

Soon all the guests had left and she walked to the dais where her family sat waiting.

"Have you enjoyed yourself tonight, dearest?" Konstellia asked, a knowing look on her face.

"Yes, it's been wonderful," Kailani replied in a dreamy voice.

"I'm guessing the rather dashing Prince Dashiel has something to do with it," Galaxan probed, smiling at his daughter.

"Uh-huh." She nodded.

"It would be an excellent match. I have known his father for many years and we have become firm friends in that time. They are an honourable family and I would be pleased if you decide Prince Dashiel is the man for you," Sirris said.

"It's too early to make that serious a decision yet, Grandpapa. He has asked to call on me to which I've said yes. I like him very much, but I don't want to rush into marriage, I want to get to know him first. I want to make sure I reach the right decision for the right reasons. Does that make any kind of sense?"

"Yes, it does and I think you're being very sensible and wise. You can't let your heart rule your head completely. Take your time and make sure he's what you want before committing to anything," Konstellia advised.

"Thank you, Aunt, for your counsel and understanding. Anyway, I'm pooped. Do you mind if I leave you all and retire for the night?"

"Of course not, my dear," Sirris replied.

Kailani kissed and hugged each one then floated across the floor and through the open door, not once looking back. When she arrived at her room, Carina was asleep in the armchair. If it wasn't for the fact that she looked uncomfortable, Kailani wouldn't have woken her. However, she changed into her nightgown and removed all her jewellery and coronet before doing so.

"Oh, I'm so sorry I fell asleep, Highness. Did you have a wonderful time? Did you meet anyone special?"

"Don't worry about falling asleep, Carina. It's very late and you've had a long day. Yes I had a wonderful time and I met a prince who made an impression on me, but it's too early to say whether I would call him 'special'. I wouldn't have woken you, but you didn't look very comfortable and I didn't want you to wake up in the morning all stiff and with back ache."

"That's so kind of you, Kailani. Thank you for being so thoughtful. Now, let me take your hair down so you can also have a comfortable night's sleep."

Carina's deft movements unbraided Kailani's hair quickly and painlessly then brushed it. "There you are, all done."

"Thank you, Carina. I intend to have a lie in tomorrow so there's no point in you getting up too early either. Have an extra couple of hours in bed and that's an order!"

"I suppose now you've reached an age where I can't argue when you give me a command."

"That's right, but I promise I won't abuse it, not that you'd let me, but this particular time I'm going to insist. Anyway, I'm tired, so thank you for all your help tonight, Carina. Leave and get yourself to bed." Kailani stood in the doorway to her bedroom.

"Yes, Mistress. Goodnight and sweet dreams."

"Goodnight, Carina." Kailani turned and closed her bedroom door. She walked to her bed and climbed in, snuggling into the comforting softness of the cloud and immediately fell asleep.

The next morning, Kailani awoke almost a different person. She felt stronger, more assured than she ever had before. It was almost as if some kind of magic had worked on her overnight and while the sensation was weird, she embraced it wholeheartedly. She remembered what her father had told her the previous day and decided to see if she could make her telepathy work. She closed her eyes and pictured her father's face then thought, *I want to come and talk to you after breakfast. Is that alright?* She kept her eyes closed and soon a shocked-sounding voice came back to her.

Yes, that's fine. I'm not planning on going anywhere this morning. I have to say, you're a very quick learner, Kailani. Who taught you?

No one. I just thought I'd give it a try and see what happened.

Wow. You're a natural. I'll see you after you've eaten then.

Yes, Papa. See you soon. She opened her eyes and the connection broke. She grinned widely as she thought, *Wow! I didn't expect that.* Just then a knock sounded at the door and Carina walked into the room, looking much fresher and younger than she had of late. "Did you enjoy your lay in?" Kailani asked.

"Very much, thank you. I feel a lot better for it too."

"It shows. Perhaps, now that I'm officially a woman, we can arrange it so you get more sleep. After all, I'm quite capable of brushing my own hair, dressing and undressing etcetera, I've just got so used to you doing it or helping me that I've taken it for granted. That stops right now. I will still need you a great deal, Carina, but except for special occasions, I don't see why you shouldn't finish earlier so you get more sleep. Oh, and I'll make sure you receive the same pay you do now. The reduction in hours will be our little secret. How do you feel about that?"

"Oh, Kailani, I don't know what to say. That would be wonderful. Are you sure?"

"If I wasn't I wouldn't have made the offer now, would I?"

"I suppose not. Thank you very much, my dear. I gratefully accept. I'm not as young as I used to be, and in all honesty I'm finding the long hours rather draining now. Anyway, your breakfast is set up in the other room."

"You're welcome, Carina, and thank you." Kailani wandered into her sitting room and sat at the table to eat.

As she strode down the hallways toward her father's room, Kailani tried to think of ways to phrase what she wanted to say. She fully expected a little resistance to her question, but felt confident she could overcome any objections. She reached the door and knocked. He opened it with a smile that lit up his entire face.

"Hello, my darling. And how are you this fine morning?" He ushered her in and closed the door behind her.

"I'm feeling really well, thank you, Papa," she said then leaned over to give him a kiss on the cheek before sitting down in one of the comfortable airchairs.

Galaxan sat opposite and looked at her. He noticed something different about her, but couldn't quite work out what it was. "So, what did you want to talk to me about?"

Kailani took a deep breath. "I've been thinking a great deal about what you told me yesterday and I've decided I want to visit Idenvarlis."

"Why?" His tone turned a little chilly.

"I have another family there and I want to get to know them. I want to learn more about mother, what she was like as a child and growing up, and things like that."

"What makes you think you'd be welcome in Idenvarlis?"

"Maybe I won't, but I'll have no way of knowing until I try."

"No!"

"Pardon?"

"I said no. You're not going and that's final!" His tone was cold and his eyes flashed like he was angry.

"Why not?" Her voice turned icy.

"For one thing, I know what King Jaanis and his family are like. They would reject and humiliate you. I don't want you to go through that. I don't want you to get hurt."

"You don't know for certain they would reject me, you're only surmising because they didn't accept you. Twenty years have gone by since you last saw them, they may have mellowed."

"Highly unlikely knowing Jaanis."

"As I said, you don't know with any degree of certainty so that makes your reason null and void in my opinion."

"In addition, the conditions in Idenvarlis are primitive compared to our world. The temperature alone would make you extremely uncomfortable – they live in freezing conditions, and I do mean freezing. You've never experienced cold like it and I don't believe you would cope with it."

"Primitive I can cope with and as for the cold, I could learn to adjust. I would ensure I was dressed appropriately, and besides, I don't believe for one moment my grandparents would allow the child of Garalia to suffer."

"Got an answer for everything, haven't you?" Galaxan said. His eyes were cold and angry. Kailani had never seen him this way.

"Papa, you won't lose me if I go to Idenvarlis for a visit. This is my home and where I want to stay for the rest of my life." Kailani replied, intuitively knowing some of her father's fears.

"I don't think for one moment you would want to stay in Idenvarlis."

"Yes you do. You're scared that if I go there, I won't come back, just like mother."

"Look. I've said you're not going and that's final!" he shouted at her. It was the first time he'd ever raised his voice to her and it shocked her. It also made her angry that he was being so unreasonable.

"I'm a woman now, you can't stop me!" she hollered back.

"Oh yes I can. And how *dare* you raise your voice to me? Don't forget who you're talking to."

Kailani rose from her chair as her anger flared and her silver eyes flashed dangerously. "Who am I talking to? I see my beloved father in front of me yet he has changed into a jealous and uncompromising bully. I can see right through you, Papa. You're afraid that I'll be welcomed by them and I'll learn to love them. You're scared I'll love them more than you and won't return to Taivass-maa. You won't listen when I tell you it won't happen – it's falling on deaf ears. I've never defied you before, but I'm a woman now and I have the right to make my own decisions and mistakes. I love you dearly, Papa, but I'm going whether you like it or not!"

Galaxan rose to face her. "I think not. The only way to Idenvarlis is through the secret doorway in this room. I will keep my door locked every time I leave my rooms from now on so you won't have access to it." He knew he had played his trump card and she couldn't beat it.

"I'll find a way. As the gods and goddesses are my witnesses, I *will* find a way!" Kailani turned and stalked from the room, slamming the door behind her. She needed an outlet for her anger. All she could think of was punching the life out of the pillows on her bed, but they were so soft, she doubted whether she would get much satisfaction. An idea popped into her head and she headed for the stables instead. The thing she loved to do most was flying. Perhaps if she went out with Rhea, her Feegle, it would improve her state of mind and help her think more clearly.

Within ten minutes, she was in the air. As they soared and flew at tremendous speeds, the exhilaration gradually overtook the anger and she began to feel more like herself. She and her Feegle were so in tune with each other Kailani only needed the slightest of movements on the reins to make him change direction.

When she was completely calm and didn't know or care how far Rhea had taken her, Kailani began to hatch a plan, to gain access to her father's room. She *would* find a way to that doorway. She was absolutely determined.

Chapter 3

Several days passed and it was impossible for Sirris and Konstellia not to notice the chilly atmosphere between Kailani and Galaxan. Both were stubborn and neither was willing to be the first to back down. They were polite to each other on the occasions when they were forced to speak to one another, but the usual light-hearted banter had disappeared.

Kailani had made her plans, and she was only waiting for the opportunity to arise. It came a few days later. Some sort of plague was killing the animals in the east of the kingdom and the king asked Galaxan to fly out there and find out what was happening. Kailani was eavesdropping just outside the room and when she heard this she knew her moment had come. She slipped away unheard and unseen by her father and went to a part of the castle where she could watch him go.

As he took to the air on his Feegle, Kailani's heart soared. She watched until he was out of sight, waited another few minutes to make sure he wasn't going to return then ran to her room. She scribbled a quick note, changed into her warmest clothes, put on her mother's ring, and carrying the cloak her grandfather had given her on her birthday, walked quickly to the weapons room. She gathered up four Treys, the five-pointed stars with whips on each point, two Raisas, the phoenix fire bombs, and her jewel-handled Panas, the slim sword that could unleash lightning bolts. Once she had secreted the smaller weapons about her person and her sword within the folds of her cloak, she almost ran to her father's room.

A guard stood outside looking bored. He was slumped against the door frame until he caught sight of the princess then stood to attention. Kailani nodded to him and went to try the handle.

"I'm sorry your Highness, but the door is locked," he said nervously.

"I have received a message from my father and there is something he has asked me to bring to him. He's been sent on an important mission for the king and I need to fly out to meet him immediately, so you need to unlock it for me."

"I'm not allowed to do that, Highness."

"Did you not hear what I said? It's imperative I get into my father's room *now*!"

The guard shook his head.

"Do you not realise to whom you are speaking? If you don't let me in this room right now I will have you clapped in irons for insubordination."

"I have received strict instructions from Prince Galaxan that no one is to enter his rooms under any circumstances. I'm sorry, your Highness, but I must refuse you."

"Very well. We'll see what the king has to say, shall we?"

The guard hesitated. Kailani stepped away from the door and saw where the next nearest soldier was stationed. She opened her mouth and was about to call him when the guard by the door caved and unlocked it. "Very well, your Highness, but be assured I will give a full account of this to Prince Galaxan on his return."

"I hope you do. But be aware, you might find yourself on more unpleasant duties for a while. He told me he needs this item urgently and you've kept me here for several minutes which has delayed things considerably. I won't have time to fly to him now, I'll have to teleport. Lock the door behind me when I enter."

"Yes, your Highness."

Kailani walked into her father's room and closed the door behind her. Donning her cloak and hood, she strapped her Panas around her waist, placed the note on the desk, moved to the panel her father had shown her and pressed the pattern in the order he had described. A doorway opened and without hesitation she stepped through.

It was a peculiar sensation as she travelled downwards, the air buffeting her. As she reached the bottom, she could already feel the air was much colder. A door slid open and she stepped out. The room was covered in cobwebs and all the furniture had sheets over them. She looked around the room and wondered for a moment why it had been left that way, but desire to find her family outweighed her curiosity. Dodging the silken webs, she made it to the door and cautiously opened it. She peeped out, saw no guards around, exited and began to wander down the corridor.

Her eyes swept from side to side as she walked. All the doors were pointed at the top, the picture and tapestry frames had hard edges and spiky corners, in fact everywhere she looked she saw sharp angles. It was completely at odds with the smooth, flowing curves of Taivass-maa. And the cold – her feet seemed to be like blocks of ice already – even in her warmest clothes she wasn't properly prepared and she shivered beneath her cloak.

The guards stationed along the next corridor were visibly shocked when they saw her strolling along with a regal bearing. They bowed as she passed but didn't stop her. This surprised her as she was a stranger to them, but counted her lucky stars and continued. Somehow, she found her way to the throne room after several turns, multiple corridors that were dead ends, and what seemed like more than an hour traipsing around with her now painful feet. She waited until the guards opened the door. On the thrones sat King Jaanis, Queen Shivla, and Prince Bellis, and before them were several men dressed in dark clothing. It was obviously some sort of meeting she had interrupted. The noise of the doors had alerted everyone in the room and all eyes turned to her.

"G-Garalia?" the king stammered, his eyes wide and jaw slack.

"No, your Majesty."

"Council members, please clear the room, this meeting is over," he said. All the men in black attire left the room immediately and within thirty seconds she was alone with her family.

She moved ever closer, feeling a boldness she'd never before experienced. When she was a few feet away, she stopped. She curtseyed then spoke. "Your Majesties. Please forgive my uninvited interruption to your meeting."

"Who are you? You look very much like my daughter, Garalia," said the king.

"My name is Kailani and I'm your granddaughter. Garalia is my mother."

"Impossible! We would have known if Garalia was with child."

"She must have hidden it extremely well, Majesty. When she left me in the care of my father, she also left something which you may recognise." Kailani replied moving much closer to the dais. She held out her hand and showed them the ring.

Queen Shivla gasped. "That is definitely Garalia's. I remember when we had it made for her. Does it have an inscription on it anywhere?"

She removed the ring and scrutinised every facet. "Yes, I've found one. It says 'To Garalia, on your 18th life-day, Love Mother & Father'. Is that what you expected?" She replaced the ring on her finger.

The queen nodded and tears filled her eyes. "You look so much like her when she was younger. How old are you?"

"I was twenty-one a couple of weeks ago."

"Belated life-day greetings, Kailani. Please, come closer so I can see you better. My eyesight isn't quite as good as it used to be."

Kailani nodded and walked up the steps to stand in front of the queen. "Yes, you could only be Garalia's daughter. You have all the same features as her, the same bone structure, and a similar build too. To think we've had a granddaughter all these years, Jaanis, and never known she existed."

Jaanis stared at the young woman in front of him. "The likeness is incredible." He opened his arms wide and said, "Welcome to the family, Kailani." She walked forward and was engulfed in a huge hug. She was then cuddled by her grandmother. When she stepped back, she looked at the man sitting to the right of the queen.

"Are you my uncle?"

"Yes. My name is Bellis." Obviously more reserved than his parents, he held out a hand and Kailani shook it.

"There are so many questions I need to ask you," the queen said, "and I expect you have a few of your own."

"I certainly do, Majesty." Kailani nodded.

"No, no, no. You are part of the family. You may call me Grandmother and my husband, Grandfather."

"Thank you, Grandmother. I didn't want to take it for granted and preferred to wait until I was given permission."

"You have obviously been brought up well. Come sit beside me so we may talk." Bellis moved to the next throne along, a sour expression on his face. Kailani saw it in her peripheral vision and wondered why he would look that way, but did as she was asked and the queen continued. "Now, who is your father?"

"I think you can already guess," she said and removed the hood of her cape, revealing her azure hair.

"Galaxan?" the king snapped, almost spitting out the name.

"Yes, Grandfather, your son-by-marriage." Kailani's voice turned a little chilly.

"What?" the queen cried. "Please tell me what you know of this."

Kailani revealed to her new grandmother exactly what her father had told her a couple of weeks previously. She ended with, "He still adores her to this day. My father said he could never love another woman, no matter what. He lives in hope she'll one day be found and they will be reunited."

"Did they have to get married because my daughter was already with child?" Jaanis asked.

"No. Apparently, they'd been wed around four months or so before mother found out she was carrying me."

"Why did she keep you from us?" asked Shivla with sadness in her eyes.

"Maybe for the same reason she kept her marriage from you. As I understand it, you, Grandfather, vehemently dissented to their union. I can only guess she was frightened to tell you because of the reaction she might get. My father was opposed to me coming to see you because he was scared you would reject me and I'd end up hurt. In fact, it's the only time we've ever argued and it was terrible."

"I can sort of understand why she felt she couldn't tell your grandfather, but I thought we were close enough that she could confide in me."

"I can't answer for her actions, because I don't know. I can only read between the lines of the information I've been given and try to piece it back together. What can you tell me about the day she disappeared?"

Jaanis decided to be the one to answer and he explained all about Gengaruk, his exploitation of nearby villagers and why he requested an audience. He went on to explain what happened next and the banishment. "He and his men were escorted all the way to their new home in the east and due to magic cast around them, they cannot leave the area."

"What about someone going into the area? If they belong to Gengaruk are they automatically stuck there too? What about anyone Gengaruk's men brought into their encampment who isn't one of their tribe? Wouldn't they be stuck like the others?"

"Well, yes, you see the spells on the tribe are mainly for those wearing the bracelets. However, the magic is strong enough that anyone entering the area would be stuck there too."

"I have a strong feeling that's where mother is. I am intuitive and my feelings are rarely wrong. I think there were more men with Gengaruk who didn't enter the throne room, but *did* come into the castle. I believe they somehow remained hidden until Gengaruk left the building with his escort and let them get ahead before they grabbed my mother and took her there. What do you all think?"

Surprisingly, it was Bellis who answered. "It's certainly not outside the realms of possibility. We had fewer guards in and around the palace as one battalion were escorting Gengaruk while another two battalions took much needed food, clothing, and medicine to the northern sector of the country. Anyone with enough skill to sneak into Garalia's room would certainly be able to get across the courtyard and out of the castle grounds without being seen."

"By all the gods, I think you may be onto something there," Jaanis said thoughtfully. His eyes stared at some distant thing only he could see.

When he returned from his trance, he seemed a little confused and closed his eyes, shaking his head.

Kailani knelt beside his throne and held his hand. "Grandfather?" He didn't respond. She tried again, this time shaking him. His eyes flew open wide and he looked down at her. "Grandfather, did you bespell the bangles Gengaruk and his men have to wear?"

"Yes, I did."

"Would you be able to create one to make me immune to the magic? One I could remove once I'd returned to the palace?"

"Yes of course, but why . . .? No! Absolutely not! We have only just found you, dear Granddaughter, and I will *not* allow you to put yourself in danger." Jaanis stared at Kailani with a stern expression.

"What is going on here?" Shivla asked.

"Our granddaughter has plans to go to The Land of No Souls to try and find Garalia."

"Oh, no! It's too dangerous and besides, we can't lose you as well, Kailani. It would be like losing Garalia all over again. The pain is still like an open wound and I couldn't bear it if anything happened to you." The queen's eyes had turned glassy as she fought to hold back the tears.

"Please, listen to what I have to say. One person with sufficient magic at their disposal could sneak in and at least find out if mother is there. If so, she could be rescued and brought back before Gengaruk and his men even know she's gone. There must be something in the magic you've set around the area which would prevent mother from freeing herself using her own gifts. This is where I have the advantage and the best of both worlds. Not only do I possess the magic of Idenvarlis, but Taivass-maa also. So I would assume my air magic would not be affected by whatever you have in place to keep those animals trapped in that land.

"A battalion of your men would be seen and heard from a fair distance and unless you gave them bracelets to allow them immunity from the magic, they would get stuck there and besides, I'm guessing they don't possess the full range of abilities we do, or am I wrong on that score?" Kailani's voice was commanding and self-assured.

Silence so absolute you couldn't even hear breathing suffused the throne room. Jaanis, Shivla, and Bellis looked thoughtful and Kailani breathed a sigh of relief. They were actually taking her seriously. Bellis was the first to break the silence. His voice sounded extraordinarily loud after the quiet, yet he was only speaking at his normal volume.

"You say you have all the magics from both worlds, how do you know this?"

Kailani unfastened the cape and pushed her hair to one side. Under her ear, indented into the skin, were three birthmarks: three wavy lines, a teardrop, and an icicle. Bellis bent closer to examine them and ran his finger over each one.

"Am I missing any?" she asked innocently.

"No, and they are genuine," he replied, more for his parents' benefit than Kailani's, or so she felt. "What magics do you have from the air world?" She reached up and peeled back a little of her dress to reveal her left shoulder; goosebumps smothered her skin. Four raised birthmarks could clearly be seen: a star, moon, sun, and a flash of lightning. "What can you do with them?"

"I can teleport, I'm telepathic, I can shoot light rays from my eyes which have the burning power of the sun, and I can manifest blades of fire just by thought, to name but a few." She covered her shoulder up quickly and pulled her cloak tighter around her.

Bellis turned to his parents. "Kailani must be the most powerful individual who ever came to Idenvarlis. As she said, she has the best of both worlds. I think she could stand a chance of finding Garalia if you could give her an immunity bracelet, Father." Kailani gazed at Bellis in disbelief and was surprised to see something very different in his eyes to what came from his lips. A calculating look shone there and she knew something wasn't right. Now wasn't the time to find out more, although she vowed to herself that she would on her return. Her instincts were on full alert and they told her that Bellis wanted her gone. He didn't want to share his parents' attention with her, so would support any madcap scheme she came up with to rescue his sister in the hope she wouldn't return.

Kailani felt sad that her new-found uncle wanted to be rid of her so soon after their meeting. *He isn't willing to get to know me at all. Is it only jealousy or is there more to it than that?*

Jaanis spoke, breaking into her thoughts. "I suppose you both make a good argument, but the trip to The Land of No Souls is hard. The landscape is unforgiving and treacherous, and there are many wild beasts who would view you as a meal."

"I believe I can adequately protect myself if you wouldn't mind teaching me how to access my ice powers and instruct me as to what I can do with them." Her feet felt like the ice beneath them and she worked hard not to let them see her shiver. Her warmest clothes from Taivass-maa were no match for the cold in Idenvarlis.

Quick as a blink Bellis jumped in. "I would be happy to teach my niece all she needs to know." Again, his treacherous eyes did not tally with the tone of his voice or what he was saying.

Jaanis looked at his son for a moment then shook his head. "Thank you for offering, Son, I know you would have done a fine job. However, I feel strongly this is my duty to perform and besides, I have a few tricks I've not even taught you yet."

"But father, you're so busy with the affairs of Idenvarlis, how will you find the time to instruct Kailani?"

"I will make the time. Anyway, your mother is more than capable of running the country while I'm engaged with tutoring my granddaughter. She has done it many times before and we are of like mind on all the present issues. I have no qualms about leaving the care of Idenvarlis with my wife for a few days."

Bellis knew when he was beaten. "Very well, Father. I was only trying to be helpful. If anything were to crop up that needed your urgent attention, I would be pleased to step in and help."

"I know you were, Son, and it is much appreciated, as is your offer to step in. I will certainly bear it in mind." He turned to the queen. "Dearest, am I being too presumptuous assuming you would be prepared to take over without asking you first?"

"Not at all, my dear. Under the circumstances, I am pleased to be able to take the weight off your shoulders to enable you to concentrate on teaching Kailani. She could have no better tutor," Shivla assured him, a genuine smile on her lips.

"Thank you, dearest. Let us have some lunch and then Kailani and I can make a start. Is that agreeable, Granddaughter?"

"Very much so, Grandfather. I must admit to being hungry and thirsty."

"Oh dear. What terrible hosts we are. Our poor granddaughter has been here for a considerable time already and we haven't even offered her a drink, let alone anything else. Please forgive us, Kailani. My only excuse is my excitement in meeting you and learning what you knew about your mother." Shivla was obviously mortified by what she deemed her lack of manners.

"Grandmother, please don't chastise yourself. There is nothing to forgive. I completely understand how my turning up unannounced would put you in a spin. It's not every day you find out you have a twenty-one year old grandchild, is it?"

"True. Thank you for being so gracious."

Jaanis stood and offered his arm to Kailani. She rose and placed her hand on his forearm; in her peripheral vision she noticed a brief scowl cross Bellis's face before he smiled and offered his arm to the queen. They descended the steps and walked from the throne room down a long ice corridor with torches placed every few yards the only things which marred the smoothness of the surface. There was no decoration at all and she could see her reflection as clearly as if she were looking in a mirror. The floor was the same and she was surprised at how sure-footed she was on such a slippery surface.

"Grandfather, how is it the flames on the torches don't melt the ice?"

"They are magic flames. They have no heat to them like fire does," he explained. No hint of laughter or ridicule coloured his voice, for which she was thankful.

"Oh, I see. That makes perfect sense. Thank you."

"I understand how different Idenvarlis is to your other home, so please feel free to ask as many questions as you wish."

"Thank you, Grandfather." She smiled up at him and it was returned.

By this time they had reached the dining room. It was huge with a massive, long ice table with carved legs. The chairs were also made from ice; the legs were carved to match the table and the backs were more ornate with an intricate lattice pattern. It was obvious this was also the banqueting room, similar to the one in the Cloud Castle in Taivass-maa. Jaanis pulled out a chair for her and she sat down. He sat at the head of the table and Shivla sat on his right. Kailani realised she was sitting in the place usually occupied by Bellis when she saw the scowl on his face before sitting next to his mother.

A large ice tureen was brought in on a tray along with ice bowls and cutlery. When it was placed on the table, Kailani noticed a loaf of bread beside the large pot. A servant placed cutlery and small plates beside each of them while the other lifted the lid from the tureen and began dishing up a thick steaming liquid into the bowls. Kailani's eyebrows rose. She wasn't expecting a hot lunch especially in ice bowls then she thought back to her question about the torches in the hallway and realised this was magic too. She smiled to herself and cast a sideways glance at her grandfather, finding him grinning at her, almost as if he'd read her thoughts.

The lunch was a delicious hot stew with herb bread to accompany it. She didn't realise how hungry she was, clearing her bowl long before anyone else yet still remembering her manners.

"Would you like some more, dear?" Shivla asked. "Or are you going to save some room for dessert?"

"I think I'll wait for dessert, thank you," Kailani answered, a little embarrassed.

When the main course was cleared away, another large tray was brought in. On this one was a large pie and a jug which had spirals of steam coming from it. She was served a slice of pie and asked if she would like some sauce with it, to which she said yes.

One bite of the pie with the sauce and Kailani thought she was sitting at a table with the gods and goddesses – the taste was so delicious, how could it be for mere mortals? This time she ate much slower, savouring each bite, but all too soon her bowl was empty. If she had been offered seconds, she didn't think she would have the willpower to decline.

Finally, a steaming frothy drink was placed before each of them. It was milky in colour, but had a reddish-brown powder sprinkled over the top. She took a sip. It was smooth and creamy on her tongue and the powder on top gave it a lovely, warm, spicy taste which complemented it well. As soon as she had finished, Jaanis arose from his chair and everyone else followed suit.

"I'm going to spend the afternoon training Kailani, so I will see you both later." He kissed his wife on the cheek and clapped Bellis on the shoulder. He offered his arm to Kailani once more, which she took, and they left the dining room, turning in a different direction.

Chapter 4

"Where are we going, Grandfather?" There was no fear in her voice, only excitement and wonder.

"First of all, we need you to pick your mount from the Blenorai. You need to choose one which looks strong, especially on the leg muscles. It also needs to look fearless and loyal. The Blenorai are probably unlike anything you have come across before," he said pre-empting her question. "It's better if I don't even try to describe them, but don't be afraid as they will not harm you. Ready?" Jaanis asked as they stopped in front of a door.

Kailani took a deep breath and let it out. "Yes, Grandfather." Her voice showed no fear.

He opened the door to a large stable-like room, but much more comfortable for the animals. In each stall were large fluffy blankets and individual food bowls. The centre had what appeared to be a congregation area which had matting on the floor. Some of the strange animals were sleeping in their stalls while others were in the centre appearing to be conversing in some way.

"Can they talk?" she asked as she watched them.

"In a way. They have their own language which our most talented linguists have tried to learn and translate without success. However, they do understand us and will react to anything we say to them." They descended the steps and stood on the matting. "Before you make your choice," the king continued, "I want to show you the Blenorai Kai. They are the elite of the breed and are the only ones allowed to carry members of the royal family. When a Blenorai is chosen, the Kai train them extensively until they are qualified for the title. Once you bond with a Blenorai, they are yours for life and will accept no other rider."

They walked through a door and found even more luxurious appointments for the beasts. As soon as they saw the king enter, they stopped what they were doing and stood to attention.

"Stay exactly where you are for a moment and don't move. Understand?"

"Yes, Grandfather."

He walked around the room and patted each animal on the head. One particular beast got a little more attention than the others and Kailani surmised it was the king's own mount. "Blenorai Kai, this is my granddaughter, Kailani. She must not come to any harm. She is about to choose her own mount. He or she must be trained as quickly as possible. Now, please acquaint yourself with my granddaughter." The huge, pure white beasts with the head and mane of a lion, the body of a long-haired bear, a lion's tail with wicked-looking spikes on the end, and armour on their bodies formed an orderly queue and approached her. The first one stared at her face and she was taken by the beautiful violet colour of its eyes. He then sniffed her all the way to her feet then moved away. This continued in the exact same format until each one had smelled her.

"Which one was my mother's mount?"

The king strode forward and stopped in front of the beast. "This one. His name is Yashtig."

Kailani reached forward and stroked his mane. "Hello Yashtig. I'm Princess Garalia's daughter, Kailani. I wish you could speak my language so we could talk about her. I may have need of your services soon for the benefit of my mother. Would you be prepared to help me?" The beast nodded his head. "Thank you. I will call on you as soon as my mount is ready." Again, Yashtig nodded.

"Come, Kailani. Let us choose your mount so the training may begin." She moved toward the door looking closely at the size of each, their leg muscles, and any other attributes she felt were crucial. In a way she thought it might be a test, to see if she had a good eye and could pick the best of the bunch. She didn't much care about that though, as she knew her intuition would help her.

Once back in the first room, King Jaanis cleared his throat and all the animals stood to attention. "This is my granddaughter and today she is choosing her mount," he announced. He then turned to her and said, "Feel free to wander around them, touch them, feel their muscles, look at their spikes, whatever it is that helps you decide. Take your time as your decision is probably one of the most important you will ever make in your life."

Kailani nodded and began to walk around the room, sizing up each of the beasts first. Next she went back to certain ones and asked a couple of questions, carefully watching their eyes as they either nodded or shook their heads. After that she picked certain ones and looked more carefully at their muscles and strength, touching them on occasion as if to make sure. This was all for her grandfather's benefit, she had already decided which one she wanted. She pretended to study them again then turned to the king and said,

"I have made my decision, Grandfather. This is the one I want." She placed her hand on the head of one of the beasts.

"Mishtag. An excellent choice, my dear. You have a good eye. She is probably the best one you could have picked. Now take her through to the Kai, introduce her and ask them to begin her training in earnest. Now that all the Blenorai know you it means you can venture down here to see your mount and how her training is progressing any time you want and not one of these beasts will harm you."

"Yes, Grandfather," she replied then turned to her Blenorai. "Mishtag, follow me please." The animal followed her into the room where the Kai lived and she gave them their instructions. She stayed for a couple of minutes as she watched how the Kai greeted their newest member. When she felt comfortable about leaving Mishtag, she backed out of the room and closed the door behind her. She climbed the steps to where her grandfather waited patiently. He opened the door for her and followed her through it.

"I'm impressed by your choice, Kailani. It will be interesting to see how quickly you adapt to our ways and learn your magic."

"I've always been a quick learner. When I was at school the tutors often accused me of cheating in tests because I have such a good memory."

"Well, this should be a very interesting afternoon then." Jaanis grinned and Kailani smiled back.

"I'm really looking forward to it."

They entered a large room with stuffed dummies placed around the edges in various poses and positions.

"Only those of us with the birthmarks have free access to the magic systems of our world," Jaanis said. "Others are given access to certain areas of magic as needed. They are issued with vials of water from the Sacred Wells of Rasha-Varl. The colour of the water denotes what magic they can access. Green controls the elements connected to earth and air. Red operates the element of fire. Blue influences ice and water and can move glaciers. Yellow gives the holder extra strength. White allows power over animals. Violet controls all the elements and can only be worn and activated by the royal family or the High Priest of Rasha-Varl. A spell word must be said to activate the power. You will receive your violet one later today or tomorrow when you meet the High Priest.

"Now, the vast majority of our magic is done through visualisation. What I want you to do is stand still and visualise the earth below the ice. When you have it in your mind, I want you to think of it on the floor of this room. Take your time. Hey! That was quick!"

Kailani opened her eyes and in the middle of the floor was a mound of earth. She smiled shyly, secretly pleased at what she'd achieved in such a short time.

"No one I've ever taught has been able to learn so quickly. I'm very impressed." He waved his hand over it and the dirt disappeared. "But was it a fluke or can you do it again?" Kailani grinned but said nothing. "Very well. Now I want you to visualise fire and set one of these dummies alight." She nodded but said nothing. Within seconds one of the dummies was blazing like a blow torch had set fire to it. Jaanis nodded then with another wave of his hand the fire went out.

"Right. Let's set you something a little harder then. I want you to bring a full size ice glacier into this room."

"I've never seen an ice glacier so how do I know how big a full size one is let alone what it looks like?"

The king beckoned her over to the front wall and waved his hand over it. The ice became as clear as a window. Outside she could see large glaciers. He pointed them out to her, gave her a little instruction as to how they were formed, and which were classified as full grown or full size.

"Now do you see and understand what I require of you?" Jaanis asked as the ice turned back to its normal opaque appearance.

"Yes, Grandfather, but my only worry is the damage it'll do to this room."

"Fear not, my child. This room has been built so there is nothing above or below it. In addition, I can repair any damage caused with no problem whatsoever. So, whenever you're ready . . ."

At first nothing happened. A few minutes passed and the room was completely silent. Kailani had a look of concentration on her face and the tension in her shoulders was obvious. She was starting to worry and doubt herself, but she shook it off and focused even harder. Suddenly a cracking noise echoed around the room. It became louder and louder and then the outside wall splintered into a billion pieces; each shard was as deadly as a dagger yet somehow every piece missed both Kailani and her grandfather. It was as if there was a protective but invisible wall around them. The splintering noise continued as the roof began to cave in and again, not one shard touched either of them. Suddenly a medium sized glacier sat in the middle of the room it had just demolished.

"Well, it's not quite a full size one, but I've never had such a quick student. It's nothing short of miraculous. Tell me though, how did you prevent the shards from touching us?"

"I just visualised a sort of invisible barrier around us both, sort of like a bubble. Why? Was that the wrong thing for me to do?"

"No, not at all. One of the lessons I was going to teach you was how to project a barrier around either yourself or a group of people. There are two types and you have just automatically manifested one of them. That one is probably the most useful as it's invisible to your enemies and they can't work out why their weapons are ineffective. The other type is an ice barrier which can be formed either around you and anyone with you or around your enemies."

"Like this?" Kailani asked with mock innocence as she erected an ice barrier around both of them.

"Um, yes. Exactly like this. Are you sure you've never been shown any of this before?"

"Like I said before, Grandfather, I pick things up very quickly plus my intuition leads me and I'll somehow know how to do things I've never done before. That's what happened with the barriers. I didn't really know what I was doing, I followed my instincts. However, my magic from Taivass-maa works on a similar principle of visualisation so that part wasn't exactly hard."

"You obviously have a finely-tuned instinct, that's all I can say." He waved his hand and within mere seconds, the glacier had disappeared and the room was back to normal, with no sign that half of it had been demolished. "Now there is no danger, I want you to create a barrier around yourself, and I'm going to use my Kamuk to try and get to you. I'm going to give you the count of five. Ready?"

Kailani nodded. The king counted to five and then tried to get to his granddaughter with a wicked-looking curved blade in his hand. Not only could he not get through, he was actually repelled and made to stagger back several feet every time he touched the barrier. By the third time it happened, he held his hands up in a gesture of surrender and asked her to take the barrier down. She complied immediately.

"What did you do to that barrier?"

"I placed a repelling spell on the outside of it. Shouldn't I have done that?"

"Technically, no, as I wanted to prove how effective the barrier was on its own. However, with a repelling spell on it, the barrier has double the protection for those inside as the enemy can't get close enough to even try and get to you. Well done, my dear."

"Thank you, Grandfather. I'm glad you're not upset with me over it."

"Far from it. I'm extremely proud of what you have achieved today. Are you tired? Do you want to stop and rest?"

"Not unless you do, Grandfather. I'm keen to learn as much as I can as quickly as possible," Kailani said in a determined voice.

"What is the rush?"

"As soon as you've taught me all you can, I'm going off to find my mother. I know I can do it and it's something I must do alone."

"You can't be serious, my dear. You know nothing of this country or the terrain. You have no idea what beasts are out there. It would be tantamount to suicide! I can't let you do this mad thing, not alone. We have only just found you, Granddaughter, we don't want to lose you again."

"Grandfather, I appreciate everything you've said and it makes me happier than you can ever know that you don't want to lose me, but I won't be alone. I will have Mishtag to help protect me, plus I haven't come unprepared." She began to pull the weapons from their hiding places and piled them on the floor. She explained what each one was and how it could be used. The king nodded wide-eyed as she explained. "All I will need from you is a quick lesson about the beasts and a map."

"I see you've come well-armed and you have your air magic as well as what you've learnt here, but it's still too risky. In all good conscience I cannot allow it." His face was almost stony in its seriousness.

What the hell is going on? First my father and now my maternal grandfather telling me what I can and can't do. I'm not having this! "You can't stop me. I'm a woman now and I make my own decisions. I don't want to fight with you, Grandfather, but I'm going with or without your blessing." She stood with her hands on her hips, staring back at him defiantly.

"I can have my soldiers guarding every exit with orders to prevent you from leaving," he said stubbornly.

Kailani laughed and Jaanis's forehead furrowed. He wasn't used to being laughed at and it didn't sit right. "I don't mean to be disrespectful,

Grandfather, and I apologise if you think me so, but my father tried something similar to stop me coming here to see you, yet here I am." She spread her arms wide as if to emphasise her presence.

"Perhaps my guards aren't so easily fooled. I could order them not to accept any excuse from you unless you were with your Grandmother or myself. I am vehemently opposed to you embarking on such a dangerous journey. I didn't want to say too much about it before, but as we're now alone, I feel I can be frank about my feelings."

What? Not again! What is going on with everyone? I'm still being treated like a child. I don't understand. It's not supposed to be this way. Do they think I can't be trusted to make the right decisions even though I'm a woman now? Kailani's shoulders slumped as a wave of disappointment crashed over her and for a moment her eyes became teary. She turned away from the king and quickly wiped her eyes with the back of her hand. *There's no way I'm going to give him the satisfaction of seeing me cry.* At that thought, she began to grow angry. *No! I'm not going to put up with this. I didn't take it from my father so I'll be damned if I'm going to take it from a man I've just met even if he is a king and my grandfather!*

"I'm sorry if I gave you the impression that I supported your idea of going alone and I'm sure your Grandmother will chastise me for it later, but in truth I will do everything in my power to stop you. I would be quite happy for you to go with a battalion of my best soldiers for protection, but that is the only way I would allow it."

With difficulty she held onto her temper and decided to try to work things out diplomatically and using reason. "That defeats the object. The whole idea of me going alone is that I can sneak in and out, unheard and unseen. I'm sure in the wide open expanses, the movements of a battalion of soldiers would be heard from miles away. It would give this Gengaruk and his men cause to hide my mother, if she's there, and go to great lengths to do so. This would make it much harder for me to find her."

"I can understand your reasoning, but I still maintain it's far too dangerous for you to embark on such a long journey alone. You know nothing of the dangers you could face and I would be derelict in my duty to both your parents if I were to agree to this. It would be tantamount to suicide for you to try and make the journey alone. There must be some compromise which could be reached between us so you are protected, but also so we do not alert Gengaruk and his men."

"If I have to make a concession, your soldiers can accompany me half way, but then I'm on my own from there. I think I would be much quicker travelling alone, but if that's the only way you will agree, then so be it."

"That would be a fair compromise and the soldiers would remain where they are until you got back. However, on the off chance you do find your mother there, what if she's unwell or injured? Mishtag will only be able to carry both of you for a short distance. They may be strong, but they're not built to carry more than one rider."

"We could take Yashtig with us. I'm sure if we explained it to him, he would want to accompany me and Mishtag. What do you think?"

"I'm sure Yashtig would welcome the opportunity for some exercise, especially if there's a chance of finding Garalia. Even though he has been keeping up with his training to keep himself fit, it's no real compensation for a good long run."

"Excellent. What more do you need to teach me before we can make plans to leave?"

"I need to teach you how to use the Plexan and a little about the beasts you may encounter. In addition we must see the High Priest so you can be gifted the vial."

"What's a Plexan?" Her curiosity was aroused.

"It's a bow which shoots arrows tipped with ice heads. It might not sound like much but the velocity on them is phenomenal. Their flight is completely silent and the enemy can't hear them coming."

"Sounds like fun. Is that what the rest of these dummies are for?"

"Actually, yes. Do you really want to try it now? Are you not tiring?"

"I'd love to try it now and no, I'm not tired at all." She then had a sudden thought. "Are you getting tired, Grandfather?"

"To be honest, yes. I'm far older than you might think. Allow me an hour or so to rest and then we can have some time before dinner." His eyes looked droopy and he was stifling a yawn.

"I apologise for pushing you so hard. You seem so strong and indestructible that it didn't occur to me how tiring this must be for you. Perhaps I should rest and conserve my energy also. Where should I go?" Kailani was sincerely contrite.

"Would you like to spend some time in your mother's room? No one has been in there since her disappearance, except her maid who cleans the rooms once a month."

"I would love to if you're sure you don't mind." A strange excitement began to build inside her. Maybe it was being able to touch and look through her mother's things, something she never thought she'd be allowed to do.

"Of course I don't mind. And besides, if anyone has the right to do so it's her daughter. Let me show you the way and then I'll go and rest." Kailani grabbed hold of his arm, linking it with hers to enable her to support him if necessary, and they left the training room together. However, with every step she took her brain was working overtime, trying to find a way of leaving without taking the soldiers with her, such was her determination to make the journey alone.

Chapter 5

Kailani strolled into her mother's room. It seemed almost as if she was walking into a shrine and it was the strangest feeling she'd ever had. She stood in the centre of the now cobweb-free sitting room and slowly turned around on the spot. She'd never seen a room like it. The small table with an ornately carved centre pillar and three feet, the small chair with a lattice back, the bookcase with a pointed top section, and the display cabinet holding exquisitely made ornaments of dancers and animals... All were made from ice as were the floor and the walls. She moved across the room and sat in the small chair. It was the weirdest thing, but it didn't feel cold to the touch.

She ran her fingers lightly over the table top, lovingly, and imagined her mother sitting in the very same seat, having her breakfast. After a while, Kailani rose and walked to the bookshelves. She scanned the titles, but there wasn't a single one she recognized. *Maybe all the stories I learnt as a child are completely different in this world,* she thought, *or maybe they're similar but called something else.*

After browsing the books she sat on the ice floor directly in front of the display cabinet. She opened the doors and stared at each of the figurines in turn, not daring to touch them. *They must have been made by a master craftsman.* Kailani had no idea how long she sat looking at them, but eventually she managed to drag herself away. She meandered into the bedroom. Again, all the furniture was made from ice, but the whole effect was incredible to look at.

A massive bed was the centrepiece with a coronet shape above it from which ice drapes, as delicate as fine lace, fell loosely to each side. The drapes were hooked to each side of the headboard. The headboard itself was oversized with a lacy pattern across it between the two upright pillars at each end. The linen on the bed was pure white silk with tiny blue flowers dotted around the edges and looked sumptuous.

Two wardrobes stood off to one side with a dressing table in between them. Kailani sat on the stool and peered into the mirror wondering just how much she looked like her mother. Her new found grandparents claimed she was almost identical to her yet her father had never mentioned it. She looked at the items on the surface. Pots of cream and perfume bottles sat on the embroidered cloth which covered the top. She lifted the perfume bottles and smelled them. Each had a completely difference fragrance yet Kailani liked each one for different reasons. *Perhaps that's why mother liked them too*, she thought. Carefully she put them back where they came from before examining the pots of cream. Dipping her finger in one, she rubbed it into a cheek. When the lotion was absorbed, she ran her hand over her skin, surprised by how much softer it was, so repeated the process with the rest of her face.

Kailani opened the drawer beneath the top of the dressing table and discovered tray upon tray of jewellery in myriad colours. Each one was a matching set of necklace, bracelet, earrings and ring. She was tempted to try some on yet a strange feeling flowed through her, stopping her. Closing the drawer, she resisted the temptation.

Rising from the dressing table she walked to one of the wardrobes and pulled both doors open. Inside were stunning evening gowns which shimmered and glittered, again in various colours. At the bottom were shoes to match each dress. She closed the doors and walked over to the other one. Inside were her mother's daytime clothes, a mixture of dresses and what appeared to be clothes suitable for riding on Yashtig. Looking down at her own attire, she knew she was far from suitably dressed to undertake an expedition to find her mother. *I might have to borrow some of mother's clothes, if they fit me.* At one end of the cupboard was a thick white coat. *That would be perfect for me to blend into the landscape*, she thought.

Closing the doors, she walked to the large window and looked out. Down below and off to one side were several small houses and on the other stood a market, with lots of stalls selling myriad products. A huge wall surrounded them all. Idenvarlis was a thriving centre of commerce, much like her home in Taivass-maa. She moved back into the sitting room, perched on the small chair, and thought about how and when her mother's abduction had taken place.

Something about it just didn't feel right. Perhaps it was the timing of it that bothered her and she couldn't help wondering if someone in the palace had been rather helpful. Bellis seemed rather strange, with his lips saying one thing and his eyes something else. If eyes truly were the windows to the soul then Bellis's seemed quite dark. Kailani was convinced her uncle was somehow involved, but how could she prove it? *I can't exactly go to my grandparents and accuse him outright, especially not this early in the relationship.*

Maybe she read him wrong. Perhaps he was a bit shy when he met people for the first time and what with her being family, it must have been a shock. Should she give him the benefit of the doubt until she had some proof? She wasn't sure what to do for the best. All her instincts told her he was involved somehow and she didn't trust him one iota. *I have to tread very carefully around him – the last thing I want is for him to realise I'm suspicious of him. I'll have to play my part extremely well when I'm with him. But if I get proof he's in any way responsible for mother's disappearance, I swear to the gods that he will pay!*

Kailani's thoughts were interrupted by a knock on the door. She rose and opened it to find a woman she'd not seen before.

"Oh my!" The woman's hand flew to her mouth and she took a couple of steps back, her eyes wide.

"Are you alright?" Kailani asked, concerned by the woman's behaviour.

"I-I'm sorry. You look so much like my mistress . . . I wasn't prepared."

"Don't worry about it. Won't you come in?"

"Thank you. Oh dear, I'm forgetting my manners. Please forgive me. My name is Chilali and I was . . . er, *am* Princess Garalia's maid." She closed the door behind her.

"Hello Chilali, I'm Kailani, Garalia's daughter. I'm so pleased to meet you."

"Looking at you there's no doubt whose daughter you are. I was the only one who knew of your existence here in Idenvarlis. I kept your mother's secret and looked after you when she had to be in the presence of her family. The last time I saw you was the day she disappeared. How did you get here?"

"My father let it slip how mother travelled between here and Taivass-maa, but not until my twenty-first birthday. I used the passage. I must admit I was a little nervous as to what reaction I would receive from my grandparents, but they have been most welcoming and gracious once they had recovered from the shock, of course."

"Yes, it would have come as a huge surprise for them, there's no doubt about that." Chilali nodded as she spoke, a little grin on her face.

"Well, now they know almost everything I do. I've told them about my parent's marriage, which didn't go down too well. The first thing they wanted to know was whether mother was pregnant at the time. I assured them that wasn't the case, but I got the impression grandfather still hasn't warmed toward my father, unless he's changed his mind since." Kailani had a strong feeling she could trust this woman, especially as she had kept her mother's secrets.

"And how is Galaxan? I only met him the once, but he was very charming and it was easy to see how in love he was with Garalia."

"He's well, thank you, but I imagine he'll be furious when he discovers I'm not in Taivass-maa. I don't know whether he'll come through the passage to find me or not, but I can't be here when and if he does," Kailani stated firmly, a determined look in her eyes.

"You have something planned, don't you? Your mother used to get the same expression when she was plotting and scheming. You can trust me. I swear by all the gods I won't reveal your secrets to anyone, no matter what they are." Chilali put her right hand over her breast.

"I'm going looking for my mother. I have my own Blenorai Kai now and grandfather has been teaching me how to use my magic. He only has a few more things left to show me and then I'll be as prepared as I can be. The problem is he wants to send a battalion of soldiers with me and I want to go alone with just Mishtag and Yashtig for company. I think I'll have more success finding her as I'll be able to sneak into places which will be impossible with a troop of soldiers – their armour, shields, and swords crashing and clanking with every step they take. I need to find a way to sneak out of the palace grounds with the Blenorai without being seen. Can you help me?"

Chilali stopped to think for a moment. "There is one way . . ." She hesitated before continuing. "I know of a passage which leads outside the city wall. However, not many people know of it and if I show you the way, the king will know it was me and the punishment will be severe. I-I really want to help you, but I don't think I'm strong enough to face your grandfather's wrath. And besides, if you do succeed in finding Garalia, I want to be here on her return and that won't happen if I help you with the passage."

Kailani put her arm around the woman's shoulders. "I don't want you to show me if it means you'll get in trouble. I don't want you punished on my account. Maybe . . . no, that wouldn't work either." Her brows knitted together and she pursed her lips.

"What?"

"I was wondering what the chances would be of me sort of stumbling across it on my own, if I knew roughly what part of the palace to be looking in. You could then swear quite truthfully that you didn't help me or reveal the whereabouts of the passage. But then I thought you might get into trouble just for pointing me in the right direction."

"It *is* possible for you to accidentally come across it, although unlikely unless you happened to push or lean against the exact place which opens it. However, I could tell you about various places in the palace which would be interesting to explore and give you a signal when I'm telling you about the right area. I could also give you a hint of what to look for on the ice to give you a chance, but I wouldn't be able to go any further than that," Chilali said apologetically.

"That would be wonderful. Any hints or help would be great, but promise me you won't give away so much you'd get into trouble with grandfather," Kailani urged. She desperately wanted to know exactly where the passage was, but not at the expense of her mother's maid. It wouldn't be fair or ethical.

"I promise," the servant replied, one hand over her breast. "Anyway, the main reason for coming to this room, apart from wanting to meet you, was to get you ready to attend dinner. You're not dressed for a formal dinner and as you didn't appear to bring any with you, we can only assume you have the clothes you stand up in and little else."

Kailani held both hands up and, with a grin on her face said, "Guilty as charged!"

"That's what I thought," Chilali said grinning back. "It's lucky you're about the same size as your mother, we can try some of her gowns on you. It won't be overly formal tonight. Apart from your family there will only be the council members, some of whom will either have forgotten about you or didn't get a close look. None of them have brilliant eyesight either. If it weren't for the colour of your hair, they'd think you were Garalia."

Kailani stared at her reflection in the mirror. She hardly recognised herself. Not only was she wearing one of her mother's gowns, Chilali had styled her hair very differently to how she normally wore it and it made her look much older.

"Why do I get the feeling you used to do my mother's hair like this?"

Chilali chuckled. "I can't get much past you, can I? Yes, I did. This was one of her favourite styles."

Kailani shook her head slowly. "Chilali, I'm very grateful for your hard work on this beautiful style, but I'm not my mother and you can't turn me into her. I also don't want to be responsible for scaring the older people to death. Please undo this and I will sort my hair out."

"Oh, I'm sorry, Kailani. I didn't mean to offend in any way, I just thought you might like to see how I used to do your mother's hair. I'll take it down straight away." Chilali flushed and she couldn't meet Kailani's eyes in the mirror.

"Chilali, you haven't offended me. I did enjoy seeing how mother used to wear her hair. I understand how much you must have missed her, but I'm *not* here as her replacement. I'm here to find her, remember?"

The maid nodded. Her face was still flushed and a lone tear trickled down her cheek as she pulled pins and clips from the princess's hair. She brushed it until it shone then stepped back.

"How would you like your hair done, Mistress?"

"Do you have a butterfly clip?"

"I don't know what that is. What does it look like?"

"It's difficult to describe. Show me what clips you have and we'll go from there." Chilali opened a draw in the dressing table and let Kailani rummage through. She found something similar to the clip she wanted and pulled it out. "This is similar and will do the job well." She showed the maid how she wanted it used and within a few seconds the job was done. It was a plain style yet classic and suited Kailani well.

"That really suits you," Chilali said approvingly, "but now you must hurry. It would not go down well if you're late. Do you remember the way from here?"

"To be honest, I'm not sure. Would you show me, please?"

"Of course." Chilali opened the door and stood aside to allow the princess to go ahead of her. She took her to the dining room giving her directions as they went so Kailani could find her way back. Once they were in the main corridor, it was fairly straightforward; the tricky bit was the section from the hallway to Garalia's rooms, but Kailani thought she could find it again. Soon they reached the dining room. "I'll leave you now, Mistress, but I'll be in your room on your return."

"Thank you very much, Chilali. I'm very grateful. See you later."

Kailani took a deep breath and nodded to the servants to open the door. With her back straight and head high, looking every inch the princess, she swept into the room, happy to see she wasn't the last to arrive.

Bellis sat at the table as well as the people from the meeting she'd interrupted earlier in the day. Her uncle rose and escorted her to her seat, playing the gentleman very graciously. The other guests stared at her with wide eyes and open mouths and it was all Kailani could do not to burst out laughing. Bellis made the introductions and had just finished when the king and queen entered the room. The guests rose and bowed, but as Bellis remained seated, Kailani followed his lead. The sovereigns both smiled at their son and granddaughter as they crossed the room and took their places at the table.

"Good evening to you all," King Jaanis said, looking well rested.

A chorus of "Good evening your Majesties" followed.

He turned his gaze to Kailani. "Have you been introduced to our guests, my dear?"

"Yes, thank you. My uncle was kind enough to do the honours," she said, turning to Bellis and flashing him a smile.

"Excellent." The king clapped his hands and a troop of servants walked in, each carrying a platter with a domed lid on top. They placed one before each person then removed the lids and walked away. Another three then entered with large flagons of wine. They filled the goblets on the table and also disappeared. Nobody moved until the king picked up his cutlery and began to eat, then everyone followed suit.

Dinner was a very stilted affair. Everyone ate in silence and nobody spoke in between courses. As the time stretched on, Kailani became more uncomfortable. Although the etiquette was the same as in Taivass-maa, their meal times, even with guests, was more of a jolly occasion where everyone conversed during the meal and especially between courses. *I guess this is the way they do things in Idenvarlis and I'll just have to get used to it. Besides, I'm not going to be here that long. The only things I have to organise now are food for the journey, the two Blenorai, and finding the passage. I can't wait to get started on my journey to find my mother, I just hope my father doesn't come here before I've left.*

After several courses, a frosted dessert was put in front of her. It looked too good to eat with clouds of meringue artfully piped around an open weave gate made from chocolate and icing flowers cascading down one side of it. She couldn't see what was underneath. She carefully used her spoon to pick up one of the meringues and the hidden surprise and popped it in her mouth. It was delicious and unlike anything she'd ever had before. Suddenly the bloated feeling left her as she ate the dessert, savouring every exquisite mouthful until it was gone.

Once the table had been cleared and the wine goblets refreshed, the talking began. Naturally all the guests had umpteen questions for Kailani; she answered them all truthfully and was successful in charming every one of them.

A little later, the king and queen rose, bid everyone goodnight, and left the room. Kailani was relieved as exhaustion had crept up on her and she was finding it hard to disguise the yawns. She left it a respectable five or ten minutes after her grandparents' departure before she stood and said sincerely what a pleasure it had been to meet with everyone and wished them goodnight. She bent and kissed her uncle on the cheek, much to his surprise, then swept from the room.

She remembered Chilali's directions and was soon back in her mother's room where the maid was waiting with a hot drink and a warming fire burning in the grate.

"Did you have an enjoyable evening, Mistress?" she asked as Kailani came through the door.

"Yes, thank you. Although I must admit to feeling extremely tired. It has been an exceedingly busy day."

"Allow me to help you get ready for bed then." She ushered the princess into the bedroom and helped her out of the gown and into a nightdress. Indicating the stool in front of the dressing table, Kailani sat while the maid expertly massaged a cream into her skin. When that was finished, she removed the clip from her hair and brushed it again. "Do you want your drink in bed or in the sitting room?"

"I'll have it in the sitting room, please. I wish to lock my door when you depart."

"I can do that for you. I have a key to this room."

"Very well, but I want to be awake when you leave and if I have my drink in bed, I fear I will fall asleep before finishing it and likely spill it over the bed clothes."

"If that is what you wish, Mistress," Chilali said, sounding a bit put out.

"Chilali, it's not that I don't trust you, I'm the same at home," Kailani said with fingers crossed behind her back for lying. "I can't sleep unless I know my door is securely locked."

The maid smiled looking appeased. "I understand. We all have our little quirks, don't we?" Chilali continued without waiting for an answer to her first question. "Do you need me for anything else tonight?"

"No, thank you. It's time you had some rest too. I'll see you in the morning."

"Thank you, Mistress. Goodnight."

"Goodnight." Kailani watched as Chilali left the room and turned the key, a muted thunk denoting the door was locked. She sipped her warm drink and began to feel drowsy. Rising from the chair, she moved to the door and slid the bolt across then, putting her cup back on the table, stumbled into the bedroom, climbed into bed and, before having the chance to extinguish the lights, she was asleep.

Kailani was woken by a rattling of her door. Instinct told her it wasn't morning and besides, if it was Chilali, she surely would have called out to her, wouldn't she? There were two other bolts on the door, one at the top and another at the bottom. She slipped out of bed, moved to the door, reached up, and as quietly as she could, slid the second bolt into place then did the same with the third. She put her ear against the rattling door and heard male voices whispering from the other side.

"Dammit! She must have bolted the door. We'll have to try again tomorrow," a gruff voice muttered.

"I suppose so," murmured the other voice which sounded familiar. "Let's go before we wake her up." She heard the rustle of clothing as they moved and stayed with her ear to the door until she could no longer hear it.

With the cold beginning to seep into her skin, Kailani climbed back into bed and pulled the covers up to her neck, her mind in turmoil. *What in Denzla's name is going on here? Why were those two men trying to get into my room? Whose voice sounded familiar?* She had more than a suspicion they were up to no good. Would she have disappeared like her mother? What would they gain from that? Why was she such a threat and to whom? Who else would have a key to the room other than Chilali? *I need to move up my schedule and get out of here as fast as possible.* Eventually, she wore herself out and fell into a troubled sleep.

The following morning, Kailani was up, washed, and dressed before Chilali appeared with her breakfast. The maid was surprised to find the door unlocked yet barred against her. She knocked and called out, identifying herself. The princess unbolted the door and opened it a crack to ensure the maid was alone before pulling it wide to admit her.

"Are you alright, Mistress? You look mightily troubled. Did you unlock the door?"

"No and no to answer both of your questions. Who else would have a key to this door, Chilali?"

"The king has a key to every door in the palace as does the master locksmith, but apart from them and yourself, I'm the only one with a key as far as I know."

"Send for the master locksmith. I wish to see him immediately."

"Yes, Mistress." Chilali placed the breakfast tray on the table and scurried from the room. She returned just as Kailani finished eating. With her was an elderly man who appeared quite sprightly for his age. "Princess Kailani, may I present Pirtuk, the locksmith?"

Pirtuk bowed. "Your Highness. How may I be of service?"

"Chilali, please leave us. You may return in fifteen minutes. Oh, and close the door behind you please."

"Of course, Highness." She did as she'd been asked leaving Kailani alone with the locksmith.

"Give me a moment, Pirtuk," she said and after a count of ten, rose and opened the door. The corridor was empty so she closed it again and returned to her seat. "Now, Pirtuk, I understand you hold all the keys for the palace and also make replacements, is that correct?"

"Yes, your Highness."

"Apart from King Jaanis, Chilali, and myself, does anyone else have a key to these rooms?"

"Am I right to assume you have Princess Garalia's key?" he asked.

"That is correct. Have you made a key for anyone else?"

"Yes, Highness," Pirtuk replied, but offered no further information.

This is like trying to prise teeth from a Feegle, she thought. "So, who have you made copies for?"

"I'm sorry, Highness, but I cannot tell you. I have been sworn to secrecy."

"Do you know who I am?" Kailani said haughtily, a trace of anger evident in her tone.

"By your looks, I would guess you are the daughter of Princess Garalia."

"Yes, this also makes me a member of the royal family. Now, I don't care who swore you to secrecy, I'm ordering you to tell me who you made the keys for."

"I apologise most profusely, your Highness, but I still cannot say." It was obvious he was nervous as his hands twitched and his fingers were rubbing against each other.

"I see," she replied with steel in her voice. "Well, let's see if the king can make you talk." She rose, walked over, opened the door, and called "Guards!" Within seconds, two appeared at her door. "Take this man to the king, immediately."

Pirtuk's knees began to quiver and a fine dew of perspiration appeared on his brow.

"Yes, your Highness," they answered in unison. Each grabbed an arm and they marched Pirtuk down the corridor. Kailani closed her door and walked behind them, realising she had no idea where her grandfather would be. They stopped in front of a door she'd never seen before and one of the guards knocked.

A voice from within called, "Enter." One of the guards opened the door and marched Pirtuk inside. Kailani followed.

The inside of the king's office was quite functional; his wooden desk was large but plain with papers stacked at one end. He sat in a large padded chair with two functional chairs the other side of the desk, and a cabinet was in one corner. The icy walls featured no paintings giving the room a cold and austere impression.

"Guards, please wait outside," she said. They nodded and left, closing the door behind them.

"Good morning, Grandfather. I'm sorry to disturb you, but I have requested information from this man and he refuses to tell me what I need to know." She stood with her hands on her hips, a scowl on her face.

"What information do you need?"

"I want to know who this man has cut keys to mother's bedroom for and he claims to be sworn to secrecy. He has admitted that extra keys have been cut, but other than that . . ."

"Pirtuk, you have made copies of keys to Princess Garalia's room, is that correct?"

"Yes, your Majesty, but I'm mighty scared. I was threatened with death if I were to speak of it."

King Jaanis paused a moment. "Pirtuk," he said eventually, "you have served me well for many years. If you tell me the truth, I will have you guarded night and day to ensure no harm comes to you. Now, who ordered you to make copies of the key?"

Pirtuk was visibly trembling. "I-It was Prince Bellis, your Majesty," he stammered.

"Thank you. From now on, the only order for copies of keys you will accept will be mine. Now, do you wish to be relocated for your safety?"

"Yes please, Sire. I am greatly fearful, not just for my life but that of my wife and children."

"It will be done by the end of today. Guards!" They re-entered the room. Jaanis turned to the one on the right and said, "Fetch me the Minister for Land." The guard saluted and left the room. The king turned to the other one and said "I want to see Karruq immediately." He also saluted and disappeared.

The Minister arrived first, huffing and puffing as he entered the room. Jaanis grinned, he'd always thought of him as an old windbag. "Minister, I need you to re-house master Pirtuk and his family to the other side of the palace by the end of the day."

"Yes, your Majesty. Is there anything else?"

"No, thank you. You may go." The Minister bowed and hurried from the room. A few minutes later a large uniformed man, whose shoulders only just fit through the door, entered and saluted.

"You wished to see me, your Majesty?"

"Yes, Karruq. Do you recognise this man?"

"Yes, Sire. He is Pirtuk the locksmith."

"Correct. This man's life has been threatened as well as that of his family. I want him guarded by two men day and night. I'm having him moved." The king explained the housing situation then continued. "Whoever you assign must be left under no misapprehension that these are my orders and they are not to take orders from anyone else, not even another member of my family. Under no circumstances is this man to be left unguarded until I tell you otherwise. Take him with you now and assign your men accordingly."

"Yes, Sire. Is there anything else I can assist you with?"

"There may be, later on, but for now, no thank you." The captain of the guard saluted and left Kailani alone with her grandfather. "What is all this about, my dear?"

"I had a strong instinct last night that I needed to protect myself." She then told her grandfather what had occurred. "I asked Chilali this morning who had keys to the room and also who made the keys. She gave me the information and I sent her to fetch Pirtuk. The rest you know."

"Can you describe the voices?"

"Not very well as they were talking quietly, but one of them had a gruff voice, and didn't sound like an educated man. The other was the opposite, smooth, sophisticated, and obviously in charge."

"I will make some discrete enquiries and also speak to Bellis about having extra keys cut. Now, you and I have an appointment with the High Priest of Rasha-Varl." He stood and moved to the door. "Shall we?" He offered her his arm which she took and together they walked down the corridor.

Chapter 6

Kailani and the king entered the temple. The ice cave housing the Sacred Well was filled with myriad colours and in some ways reminded Kailani of home. The light seemed to be coming from the well and as it refracted on the ice, the rainbow of colours cascaded all over the walls. It looked too magical to be real. A middle-aged man dressed in white robes stood with his back to the well as they entered.

"Welcome, your Majesty." He bowed.

To Kailani's surprise, Jaanis bowed to the High Priest. "Thank you, your Holiness." When he had straightened up, he gestured to the young woman at his side and said, "I would like to introduce you to my granddaughter, Princess Kailani."

"Welcome, your Highness. It is a pleasure to meet you." He bowed again.

Kailani bowed and replied, "Thank you, your Holiness, but the pleasure is all mine, I assure you."

The High Priest stared at Kailani for a long moment and said, "I have no doubt whose daughter this is." A note of surprise entered his voice, but he didn't ask for details. He took a deep breath then continued. "As a member and of the royal family you are entitled to a gift from the Sacred Well of Rasha-Varl. Please kneel and it will choose what power you need."

Kailani did as she was asked and bowed her head, clearing her mind. She felt a gentle probing inside her head followed by a stream of water which seemed to follow the direction of the probe. The High Priest spoke in a language she didn't recognise, but it didn't penetrate her connection with the well. It was a strange sensation as the probe seemed to access every part of her head yet it wasn't painful. She relaxed, allowing it to happen.

After a few minutes, the probe, followed by the water disappeared. The High Priest had stopped talking and was about to dip a vial into the water. His eyes met Kailani's for a moment and then she looked down again quickly, intuitively knowing she shouldn't watch. She heard a few drips and then a gasp, but tried her best to ignore it. She silently thanked the Sacred Well for the bounty it had bestowed upon her.

The High Priest held the vial before his eyes which were wide with shock. The water inside was a deep purple. Eventually, the High Priest told her to rise. She followed his instructions and saw puzzled expressions on both their faces.

"My child, you are blessed above all others. Never before has the Sacred Well bestowed this colour on anyone. It is the most powerful water and I can only conclude you are meant to do great things. To release the power you have only to say 'Rasha-Varl'. I must warn you not to take this magic for granted or use it for minor inconveniences. Do you understand?"

"Yes, your Holiness. I vow to always treat it with the greatest respect."

He walked around to where she stood and placed the chain and vial over her head. It sat comfortably in her cleavage and was oddly warm against her skin, which surprised her as she expected it to be cold.

"Thank you, your Holiness," she said and bowed. The High Priest copied her movements and they rose together.

"Go now. You still have a great deal to learn before you embark on your expedition and not much time."

She nodded to him once and backed away, thinking it would be considered rude to turn her back on him. The king and the High Priest bowed to each other and Jaanis walked backwards until he reached Kailani at the door. The High Priest disappeared from view so they turned and walked away.

The light in the corridor seemed dull after the brightness of the cave and it took a few seconds for her eyes to adjust. "Grandfather?"

"Yes?"

"Why have I been given this great power? I don't understand."

"Neither do I. Perhaps it has something to do with your journey to find Garalia. What is most important, and I cannot express this enough, is that you tell no one about the vial. There are those who would torture and kill you for the power it holds. Trust no one outside of me and your grandmother. In fact, I would urge you not to even speak to us about it unless it's too important for you not to and even then, discretion will be crucial. Do you understand?"

"Yes, Grandfather." She nodded her head, a serious expression on her face.

"Now, shall we do a little training before lunch?"

"Ooo, yes please." He smiled at her enthusiasm and led the way back to the training room.

"This morning I'm going to teach you how to use the Plexan." He picked up two thick arm guards and after placing one on his arm he did the same to Kailani. Jaanis then pulled two bows and two quivers from hooks on the wall and brought them over to where she stood.

First he showed her the proper stance then with bow in hand guided her in how to load the arrow and aim. They used the dummies as targets.

With her first arrow, she hit the dummy in the stomach area. When the king let her go and she was able to aim on her own, it was much harder. Her next few arrows sailed wide and anger surged through her. The more her frustration and impatience spilled forth, the worse her aim became. Jaanis stepped in again and, placing his hands over hers, he showed her how to line up her sight along the shaft of the arrow. They let it loose and hit the dummy in the chest. He let go and stepped back. Her next attempts hit a leg, a foot, and then a leg again. She growled and gritted her teeth, a sour expression on her face.

"You're dropping your arm as you fire. You need to keep it straight and locked," the king explained. She tried again, hitting the dummy where the genitals would be. They both laughed and the frustration she felt began to evaporate. Her next ones hit the stomach and the chest. From then on, her success rate was much higher, hitting the dummies in the heart, head, and eyes repeatedly.

"Well, I guess there's nothing more I can teach you about the Plexan. Well done, Kailani."

"Thank you. That was harder than I thought it would be. It looked so easy when I've seen others use a bow. I was frustrated at my poor performance in the beginning, but I feel better about it now. I realise it's something I'll need to practice before feeling confident." She looked at Jaanis and he smiled.

"Have you used something like this before?" he asked, pulling a curved blade from his belt.

"Not a curved one. I've used knives with straight blades though. Is there much difference between the two?"

"This is called a Kamuk. It is very sharp and has these two points on the end of the blade. However, if you slide this switch just below the hilt, the blade changes from a smooth, sharp one to a serrated edge which will hack through a man's leg in two strokes. Fighting with a Kamuk is very similar to that of a straight blade except you hold it a little differently and have the added advantage of the double points in the end and the dual blade system. This is an extremely useful weapon as it's easy to hide on your person. Do you want to get a feel for it?"

"Yes please." She walked forward and held out her hand, her eyes sparkling. He placed the hilt in her hand and watched as she felt the balance of the knife. She then held it like he had and turned away from him taking a few swipes through the air, as if fighting an imaginary opponent.

"You seem very at ease with it," Jaanis remarked.

"I am. The Kamuk has excellent balance and weight," she replied.

"You sound like quite the expert. I'm surprised."

"I've been fighting with knives of all kinds since I was thirteen," she explained. "Over time you get used to feeling what daggers are well balanced and feel comfortable in your hand. They are the ones which are well made. I'm very choosy which knives I carry."

"Do you have any on you now?"

"Yes." She seemed genuinely surprised by the question. She pulled three out. Each one was different, whether it was the length, width of the blade, or ease of concealment. She placed each one in her grandfather's hand and he could see what she meant about balance and weight. "If a knife is properly balanced, you can hold it on one finger and it will lay completely flat." She demonstrated.

He handed the knives back to her and she replaced them in their sheaths. "Now, shall we go and see how Mishtag is fairing and also to talk to Yashtig?"

"That's a good idea, besides I want to see my beautiful Blenorai Kai. However, just before we do, can I ask you something?"

"Of course. What is it?"

Kailani looked around the room to ensure they weren't overheard, but lowered her voice just in case. "When you give me the bespelled bracelet so I'm immune to the spells in the Land of No Souls, can we be completely alone please?"

"If that is what you want then yes, of course. Can I ask why?"

"It's one of my instincts and I just feel very strongly about it."

"You are so like your mother with your instincts and I learned to trust hers so I will do likewise with you, my dear. Was there anything else?"

"No, and thank you, Grandfather. I'm ready to go and see the Blenorai Kai now." She stood on tiptoe and gave the king a kiss on the cheek. He smiled and grabbed her hand.

They walked down to the room without any hesitation this time. As they entered, she could see Mishtag being put through her paces. She was a little bruised and bloody, but no more so than her colleagues. They stopped as soon as Jaanis and Kailani opened the door. The princess ran over to Mishtag and started making a fuss of her. She examined the wounds and spoke softly to her. Jaanis watched them for a while, a small smile gracing his lips, before seeking his own Blenorai. "Is Mishtag shaping up well?" The king's mount approached and nodded, "Any reservations?" The Blenorai Kai shook his head. "When will she be ready? Today? Tomorrow?" The beast nodded when Jaanis said tomorrow. "Well done all of you, and especially Mishtag."

Yashtig sat off to one side watching. Kailani approached him. "Yashtig, I'm going on a long and difficult journey to try and find Garalia. I don't believe she'll be in a good condition when I find her. Would you be prepared to come with us?" Yashtig didn't hesitate and nodded his head immediately. "Thank you. We will be leaving very soon after Mishtag is ready, alright?" He nodded again.

"Grandfather, I'm starving. When is lunch?"

He chuckled. "Now if you want. I'm actually quite hungry myself."

"Sounds good to me." She led the way out and Jaanis followed her. She remembered the way, much to her delight and was soon tucking into a bowl of delicious meat stew.

After lunch, Kailani and Jaanis went to his office. He told her all about the beasts that roamed outside the palace and what their strong and weak points were. He also told her how each of them could be killed. After they were finished, he pulled out a map and showed her the route to the Land of No Souls. The vast majority of the journey was open spaces, nothing but ice for what appeared to be hundreds of miles. However, there were two places which would save more than two days of travelling: the Silent Forest and the Lost Mire.

"What are those? It looks like they would cut off a large chunk of the journey." Kailani pointed to the relevant parts on the map.

"Believe me, you don't want to go through either of those," Jaanis said his voice serious.

"Why not?"

"The Lost Mire is one of those places where people go in and don't come back out again. The surface is still ice, but there are reeds which are so tall and thick, you can't see through them. You can get lost so easily in there and it could take months or years for someone to find you and even if they did, there's no guarantee they would be able to find the way out again with you. It would be like a vicious circle with no beginning and no end. It's also unknown what beasts, if any, lurk in those reeds."

"It does sound a bit tricky. I take it the reeds are taller than most men?"

"Yes."

"But anyone entering them would still be able to see the sky, wouldn't they?"

"They would be able to see the sky above them, but not the horizon so trying to navigate using the stars would be virtually impossible. I can understand what you're thinking, my dear, but it won't work. You'll just have to go around them, even if it does mean adding an extra day or two on the journey. Getting lost in the mire would be catastrophic and all your dreams and plans of finding your mother would come to naught."

"Yes, I see what you mean, Grandfather. It's better to get there two days later than not at all."

"Precisely!" He smiled, relief flooding his eyes that Kailani could see the risk involved.

"Now, what about the Silent Forest? Why should that be avoided?"

"It is just like any normal forest with trees, bracken, birds, and such like. However, somewhere in there is a beast that attacks and eats whatever it can lay its claws on. It's said to be huge. While the forest is full of bird song and the normal noises one would associate with it, the traveller is safe. However, when the forest goes completely silent, that's when the beast exits its lair and is on the hunt. I'm told it moves swiftly, silently, and the unwary won't hear it coming. The first they know of it is when its huge claws pierce their body."

"Does anyone know what the creature is?"

"No. The very few who have survived have just described it as extremely large and black, with claws about eight inches long, and teeth about the same size."

"Ah, but my Feegle can out-do that," Kailani said nonchalantly.

"Er, what is a Feegle?"

"I suppose you could say it's our version of the Blenorai except Feegles fly. They are small dragon-like animals with soft, almost furry pelts, very gentle, loving creatures with their own personalities and in the same way as one is bonded to a Blenorai here, so it is with Feegles too. Now I bet you're thinking a Feegle is no match for the creature in the Silent Forest, but that's where you would be wrong. Feegles are fierce fighters, have retractable claws about twelve inches long and they spit poisonous spikes. They can travel long distances at tremendous speeds and are very manoeuvrable. People make the mistake of underestimating them as they look too cute and cuddly," Kailani explained.

"Ah. Maybe you're right. I was beginning to think your Feegle was no match for the beast, but it does sound as if it could possibly defeat it. What a shame you can't get it down here," Jaanis said, thoughtfully.

"I was just trying to work out if there was any way I could get Rhea here, but even with all my magic, I'm not sure it's possible. And she's much too big to come through the passage. Pity. It would have made the journey so much quicker and less dangerous. Still, I'm completely committed to making it despite the perils."

"You are very courageous for a woman of your tender years. It is one of the qualities I admire most about you."

Kailani felt her cheeks grow hot. "Th-Thank you, Grandfather." She was unused to such compliments. People in Taivass-maa had regularly flattered her for her looks, charm, and her kind ways, but not even her father had delved beneath the surface and seen what other attributes she possessed. This admiration from a man who barely knew her meant more to her than all the servile compliments lumped together.

"Now, it looks like tomorrow will be the day for you to embark on this rescue mission. Mishtag will be ready. I have spoken to the cooks and they are busy packing food and drinks. The squad of soldiers have been hand-picked by Karruq. The only thing that remains is this." He pulled a bangle from his robes which had three gemstones in it, a clear one and two purple.

Jaanis placed it on Kailani's wrist and muttered words in a language she'd never heard before. The bracelet glowed brightly and shrank so it was a tighter fit on her arm. It grew increasingly warmer as the king continued to speak; the gems shone dazzlingly and she had to close her eyes against the glare. The heat was burning and Kailani gritted her teeth so she didn't cry out. Just when she felt she could take it no longer, it abated and her grandfather stopped speaking.

Kailani opened her eyes and looked at the bangle. It now looked ordinary yet it appeared to be welded to her skin. She tried to take it off but couldn't. It was stuck fast. Jaanis answered her unasked question.

"I'm sorry if that became somewhat unpleasant for you, my dear, but there is an excellent reason why it had to be done. We must ensure no one can take the bangle from you. Otherwise Gengaruk would undoubtedly escape. I have bespelled it so that if your mother is in the Land of No Souls and she is in physical contact with you, she too will be immune and able to leave."

"I understand, but will you be able to remove it on my return without it leaving a mark on my skin?"

"Yes, of course. You don't believe I would scar my own granddaughter, do you?"

Kailani smiled sheepishly. "No, I suppose not. Thank you for this. Changing the subject a little, one thing we haven't spoken about is why that area is called The Land of No Souls."

"Ah yes. Hundreds of years ago it was used as a burial ground for criminals. It was believed that lawbreakers didn't possess a soul and that's why they committed crimes, hence the name. In later years, the area was used to house criminals and they were left there until they died, just like

I've done with Gengaruk and his men. The land has been bespelled for at least three hundred years for that very purpose, but occasionally a criminal managed to escape and wreak havoc on the villages nearby. Eventually all the homesteads were abandoned and the people moved much closer to the palace." He pointed to the villages on the map which she would pass on her journey.

"When I became king, one of the first things I did was to strengthen the spells surrounding that land, but when it came to Gengaruk and his men I wanted to ensure there was no chance of them ever escaping which is why the bangles were placed on their arms. As soon as they crossed the invisible barrier into the land, there would be no chance of them breaking free. I believe, as countless of my ancestors did, that animals like Gengaruk cannot possess a soul otherwise they wouldn't have treated the citizens of the north so badly. He made slaves of them, killed anyone who resisted, murdered babies and young children who were no use to him, and the women were repeatedly raped. They were barely given enough food to survive, lived in deplorable conditions – much worse than we would treat our animals – and made to work extremely long hours. If any of them got sick, they were made to work until they dropped and then that person was thrown in the dungeon and left to die."

Kailani's eyes filled with horror. "I don't understand how anyone could treat another person in such an appalling way."

"Precisely, and that's why I want to ensure those animals can't escape."

"Calling them animals is an insult to the gods' creatures. They're scum, the lowest of the low." The full impact of what the king had told her suddenly hit Kailani; she moaned and her eyes filled with tears.

"What's the matter?" Jaanis rose and put his arm around her shoulders.

"I just realised something. If my mother is in the clutches of that scum, what sort of condition is she going to be in, assuming she's still alive? What deplorable acts have been inflicted on her these past twenty years? Oh, Grandfather, it's too painful to consider..." she trailed off as the tears cascaded down her face. He pulled her into his chest and held her until she was in control of her emotions again.

"Are you alright now?"

"Not completely, to be honest. But I'll tell you one thing, if they have hurt or killed mother, they won't know what's hit them. I will avenge her and they will suffer slow agonising deaths."

"That is your choice, my dear. However, don't allow your anger and hatred to blind you as that is when you're most likely to make a fatal mistake. Keep your emotions under control at all times until you are away from the Land of No Souls."

"I understand and thank you for the advice. May I have this map, please? I want to study it and ensure we take the quickest and safest route."

"Of course. I had planned to give it to you anyway." He grinned.

"Oh, and one other thing, when you spoke to the cooks about the food and drink, did you remember to tell them I would need a separate pack of my own for when I leave the soldiers?"

"No, sorry, I forgot. I will remedy that immediately."

"I can do it if you tell me which way to go. I'm heading back to my room now so I can make preparations. I can call in there on the way."

"That would be helpful. I do have some other business to attend to, one of which is making sure Pirtuk, the locksmith, is well and happy. Follow the corridor round to the left and the fifth door along on your left has stairs behind it. Take them right to the bottom and turn right. The kitchen is at the end of the corridor and the cook you need to speak to is

Aneira. She can come across as being rather abrupt, but she's a gem really."

"Alright. I've got it in my head. I'll go and speak to her right now. Actually, one question has been bouncing around my head since I arrived. How do you grow food here?"

The king chuckled. "Remember how I got you to pull earth through the ice yesterday?" Kailani nodded. "Well, that's what we do then once the seeds are planted, we use special ice panels which seem to soak up the light and any sunshine, and they project warmth onto the plants. We collect snow and rain and use those to feed the seedlings."

"Ah. Thank you. Anyway I'll let you go and attend to your other business. I'll see you at dinner, Grandfather, and thank you again for all your valuable advice and training."

King Jaanis leant forward and kissed her on the forehead. "It's been my pleasure, Kailani. Just try and get some rest. You'll need every bit of your strength over the coming days." She nodded and left the room closing the door behind her.

After speaking to Aneira, the cook, Kailani visited the provisions store and obtained everything she needed. She then returned the way she'd come until she was back in the corridor where the king's office was. This time she turned right, but instead of heading back to her room, she walked down another hallway in search of the secret passage Chilali had told her about.

The corridor lead her deeper into the palace than she'd ever been; it seemed to be never ending. There were many corridors leading from it on both sides, but from where she stood, Kailani couldn't see where she'd entered and it seemed like she'd been walking for hours. A few minutes later she noticed a strange marking within the ice itself. Moving closer she bent forward, peering at it in the dim light and stroked her hand over the surface. She was surprised to find no indents – the ice was completely smooth.

Straightening up, she began to doubt whether this was the place or not. It certainly wasn't what she expected. However, having come this far it was worth a try so she placed her hand against the mark and pushed. At first nothing happened. Kailani was about to continue walking down the corridor when she heard a small click and a large door swung open. Stepping just over the threshold, she could see very little ahead of her. The interior was unlit and as dark as night, but she could feel a slight breeze on her face. The smile on her face was jubilant as she backed out and pulled the door as closed as she could without trapping her fingers. Gravity or some mechanism inside completed the job and there was no sign a door had ever existed there.

As she returned the way she had come, Kailani counted the number of torches on the same side of the wall until she reached the end of the corridor where she had first started. Everything in her plan was slotting into place. She returned to her room to work out the rest before dinner.

Chapter 7

As soon as Chilali left for the night, Kailani bolted her door. She had already gathered her clothing, packing a bag which could be worn strapped across one's back and another for her mother, plus her weaponry from Taivass-maa. She had only to collect a Plexan, quiver, and a Kamuk from the training room on her way to collect Mishtag and Yashtig, plus two parcels of food from the kitchen and she was ready to go. She had even left a note for her grandfather to say she'd gone ahead and for the battalion to catch her up, knowing in her heart they never would.

Kailani changed into the clothes she would be travelling in – thick, fur-lined leggings under a heavy, long sleeved dress made for riding, fur-lined boots up to her knees, a thick scarf, and animal-skin gloves up to her elbows – and lay on top of the bed. She did need a little sleep before leaving and hoped her body clock would wake her at the correct hour. It took a great deal of effort to quiet her mind, but eventually she fell into a light sleep, feeling warmer than she had since arriving.

When she woke, the palace was silent. She rose and peered through the ice window at the sky. The night was clear with a crescent moon and hundreds of stars. Gathering her weapons and fastening them to her belt, she made sure she had the vial around her neck then pulled on the warm, white coat. Walking to the sitting room door, she stood with her ear to it, ensuring no one was about before unlocking it. She opened it a crack and peered into the corridor, happily discovering it was empty then slipped out and locked the door behind her.

Kailani crept along the corridors to the kitchen and slipped inside. It was easy to find all the packed food as it was lined up against one wall. She grabbed the one with her name on it plus one other and left as quietly as she had entered. Kailani stole down to the training room, grabbed the rest of the weapons plus two quivers of arrows and a leather breastplate and piled them neatly in one corner with the food before taking the short walk to the stables where the Blenorai were housed. She walked into the section where the Kai were kept and to her surprise, Mishtag and Yashtig were standing there waiting for her. She armoured and saddled them, grabbed two bags of their feed, beckoned to them, and they followed her to the training room.

She bent down and whispered to Yashtig. "Do you mind carrying the extra supplies and weapons?" The animal shook his head and after thanking him, began carefully loading and securing the items to his saddle in such a way as to not make a noise when they moved down the corridors. When she was satisfied, she strapped on her breastplate, led them through the palace and up to the hallway where her grandfather's office was. She crept to the head of the corridor and listened carefully before moving down it.

As they walked, Kailani counted the torches until they arrived at the right spot. She pressed her hand against the ice and waited for the click. The door swung open and she grabbed a torch from the wall to light their way, closing the door behind them. The pathway gradually tilted downwards for quite a way before they encountered stairs. Kailani led the way, treading carefully. At last they reached the bottom and found a door directly in front of them. She put her ear against the door and hearing nothing, pulled it open.

She stepped out into the night, relieved to see no sign of guards. The Blenorai Kai followed her out and she closed the door behind them. "Are you both ready?" she whispered. They nodded their heads. Kailani took the gloves and hat from her pockets, put them on and mounted Mishtag. "Right, let's go."

It didn't take long for Kailani to get the feel for riding Mishtag. In some ways it was quite similar to the motion of Rhea apart from the impact of her paws on the ice which made it a little less smooth. At least each footfall was not heavy so she didn't get jolted as they travelled.

The Blenorai moved at a much faster pace than she expected and she guessed they weren't running at their top speed to give her a chance to get used to riding them. She had noticed that the further they travelled the faster they ran, almost as if building her confidence bit by bit. She stroked Mishtag's head in recognition of her thoughtfulness and it was like she'd given them a signal as they suddenly ramped up the speed until they were virtually flying across the ice.

She checked their direction by the position of the moon, pleased they were going the right way. The miles seemed to melt away and Kailani felt completely invigorated, with a sense of freedom she'd never experienced before. She thought she'd achieved it with Rhea, but it paled into insignificance compared to the feeling she had right now. As she looked around at the almost barren landscape, she encountered a sensation of oneness with the ice. It was empowering and filled her with a completeness. Maybe it had something to do with her embracing the other world which was just as much a part of her as Taivass-maa was. Whatever the reason, she was grateful for it.

Before dawn they had reached the first of the villages her grandfather had shown her on the map, the ones who had relocated from the far east of the realm. Hardly anyone was around so they continued on their journey. By the time they reached the penultimate one, market traders were setting out their stalls for the day's trading and Kailani decided to stop. She bought four warm rolls with a filling called Lerin – she had no idea what it was but it smelled delicious – and a tall cup filled with a hot spiced fruit drink. She gave one each of the rolls to the Blenorai and ate the rest. It tasted as scrumptious as it smelled. The hot drink seemed to warm every part of her, right down to her toes, for which she was extremely grateful.

She offered some of the drink to Mishtag and Yashtig but they turned their noses up at it. As soon as the food and drink had been consumed they got underway again, soon racing along at the speed they were before. Dawn was not far off and Kailani hoped they had enough of a head start not to be caught up by the soldiers.

Chilali went to Kailani's room much earlier than normal. She unlocked the door and was surprised to be able to open it. She placed the breakfast tray on the table and noticed a note addressed to the king. Running into the bedroom she found it empty and was filled with fright. Without reading the letter, she snatched it up and ran from the room.

She knocked on the door and stepped back, biting her bottom lip in her nervousness. She had never disturbed the king in his chambers before. Jaanis opened the door with a scowl on his face.

Without a word, Chilali passed him the note. A puzzled expression flitted across his eyes as he opened it. He began reading.

Dearest Grandfather,

I have set off early and ahead of the soldiers. I know this will probably anger you, but I had to do it. The feeling inside me was so strong I couldn't in all good conscience ignore it.

I know I have to make this journey alone, I feel it in every fibre of my being, and it tells me what I must do. It is my destiny to find my mother and bring her safely back to the palace.

Please try to understand and not think too harshly of me.

With my love and respect

Kailani

King Jaanis pulled his robe tightly around him and took off running down the corridor as if demons were on his tail. Chilali was left standing there, mouth gaping, not knowing what to do. In the end, she closed the king's door and went back to Kailani's room to tidy up.

Jaanis crashed into Karruq's room without knocking just as the captain was getting dressed. He bowed and said, "Your Majesty. Please excuse my appearance. How can I help you?"

"It's Kailani. She's already left. You need to get the battalion after her as quickly as possible. They must catch up to her and keep her safe. I can't lose her as well."

Karruq, who had finished buttoning his plum-coloured tunic while the king explained said, "Leave it to me, your Majesty. We made a lot of preparations last night in order to leave quickly this morning so it won't take long before the men are on their way."

"Every second counts, Karruq."

The captain pulled his long black boots on and tucked his white britches inside, replying, "I understand, your Majesty. If you will excuse me, I will see to it immediately." The king stepped aside and let Karruq pass. As he reached the door, he bowed to his master and ran to the barracks where the men were housed.

Jaanis heard the captain barking orders to his men and moved onto the terrace so he could watch the preparations for himself. Less than fifteen minutes from when Jaanis burst into Karruq's room, the soldiers mounted up and left the barracks through huge double doors at one end.

The battalion all turned their heads and saluted the king then grabbed the reins and disappeared through the doors.

Karruq returned to the king's side. "I think that's the fastest we've ever gotten a battalion underway before."

"That's good but every second counts. I have no idea what time she left or how much of a lead she has on them."

"Your Majesty, I'm sure the gods will watch over her. Kailani is very skilled with weaponry, has learned all the magic from you, plus she has the skills and magic she brought with her from the sky land. She is capable and I'm sure she will cope admirably until we catch up to her."

"I hope you're right, Karruq. I hope you're right." He clapped his captain on the shoulder and walked away with slumped shoulders.

The miles disappeared beneath their feet. Kailani marvelled at the beauty of her surroundings. The occasional clump of trees broke up the barrenness of the ice yet in her mind it just added something special to the sight. The early morning sun glistened on the ice – it was like being in a magical fairyland and it took her breath away.

Suddenly, the Blenorai ground to a halt and began to growl. At once, Kailani felt the tiny hairs at the back of her neck rise and she dismounted, pulling her sword from its scabbard. She looked all around her, but couldn't see anything untoward. However, she knew by Mishtag and Yashtig's reaction that there was danger close by.

Her eyes were drawn to a clump of trees a little way ahead and slightly to their left. She studied them carefully and noticed movement between them. Moving to the other side of Yashtig and a little closer to the trees she pulled the Plexan from her shoulder and grabbed an arrow from the quiver on her back. She hooked her sword onto her belt for ease of access and cocked the arrow ready.

The Blenorai's growls became louder and without warning a beast, with the same colouring as the trunks of the trees, began hurtling toward them on all fours. Kailani aimed and fired the arrow, hitting the creature in the shoulder. She quickly reloaded and shot again, this time the arrow pierced it in the side. It let out a howl of pain as green blood began pouring from the second wound leaving a trail across the ice. She loaded another arrow, aimed carefully and let it fly. It missed the area between its eyes by a tiny margin and landed just behind the head in its neck.

The beast slowed a little as it got closer. Kailani dropped the Plexan and grabbed her sword. It rose onto its back feet and stood head and shoulders above the princess. She moved slowly toward the creature as it did to her. It swiped one of its massive paws at her, its wickedly sharp claws extended. She dodged closer to her adversary and swiped her blade across its midsection.

Blood and guts poured onto the ice and the creature shrieked in pain. Kailani pressed her advantage, cutting higher on the chest area. As it gaped, she saw the heart beating in the cavity. Without hesitation, she thrust the sword into the heart just as the beast began to move one of its paws toward her. She pulled the sword free and ducked under the paw, moving to the side of it. The creature took a step and began to fall. Kailani ran fast to the side and as it hit the ice its paw missed her by about two inches.

Adrenalin coursed through her body. She had slain the first beast they faced and she had done it all on her own. She watched it carefully for a couple of minutes to ensure it was dead, but noticed one of the paws was twitching. She moved to the side of the head, raised her sword high and brought it swiftly down on the creature, decapitating it.

She collected the arrows, pulling them from the corpse and after wiping them clean on the beasts fur, she returned to Yashtig, placing them back in the quiver. Picking up the Plexan, she slung it over her shoulder, sheathed her blade, and mounted Mishtag.

"Are we safe to continue now?" They nodded and took off again across the ice.

A few hours later, the battalion who were desperately trying to catch up to the princess came across the body of the beast she had slain. The leader dismounted and felt the creature's hide. A few of them couldn't help being impressed and one soldier voiced his opinion.

"Well, the princess can obviously look after herself if she can better this Nastiv on her own!"

The battalion leader looked at him with scorn. "This isn't the most dangerous beast she's likely to encounter. She may not fare so well with the next one. Let's press on. There is still a little warmth to the Nastiv so I think she's about three hours ahead of us. We must make every effort to catch up to her." He mounted up again and gave the signal for them to move on. Within a couple of minutes, they were back to full speed and racing away across the ice.

As the sun rose to its highest point in the sky, Kailani stopped and stretched her legs. She grabbed a small handful of food for Mishtag and Yashtig and fed them from her hands. She broke off a small chunk of bread and a little cheese and ate them slowly. When she had finished eating, Kailani took out one of the flagons of water and had a couple of swallows of water. She replaced it in the pack and fastened it.

"Are you ready to continue?" she asked the Kai who nodded their heads. She mounted Mishtag again and they set off, powering across the ice.

They kept going until dusk was upon them and the light was growing dimmer by the second. There was nowhere to shelter them; there were no trees in site, just a barren landscape of ice. She fed the Blenorai first as before then had half a small tin of cold stew, a few small mouthfuls of bread and some water to wash it down. She was careful with her provisions, knowing they had to last until she arrived back with the soldiers. Plus she had no idea how underfed her mother was going to be and she wanted to ensure she had sufficient food to keep her mother alive and strong enough for the journey.

Kailani was tired and was sure the Kai were too. She realised that apart from a small downy-soft blanket, she had brought nothing to keep her warm during the night. She unsaddled the Blenorai and removed their armour so they could rest comfortably then asked Mishtag if she could huddle up close for warmth. Mishtag agreed and lay down on her side. Kailani got down onto the ice, using her backpack of clothes as a pillow and cuddled up to her. Yashtig followed suit, but lay facing in the opposite direction so they had both ends covered while keeping the princess safe and warm. Within a few seconds they were all asleep.

Several hours later, Yashtig woke, hearing something in the far distance. Lifting his head from the ice, he listened harder. Finally he could discern what he was hearing. A flapping of huge wings closing in fast alerted him and he growled loudly. Mishtag woke instantly and got to her feet, hearing the same. Kailani slept on, blissfully unaware of the approaching danger until Mishtag nudged her and growled into her ear.

Immediately the princess was on her feet and wide awake. She still wore her sword, but not the Plexan. She grabbed it from the pile of items on the ice and positioned a quiver so she could easily grab the ice-tipped arrows. Taking one, she positioned it ready. The flapping of the wings grew closer, but she couldn't see anything and her mouth became dry.

Looking up at the sky, she could see clouds hiding the stars and moon. There was no light and they were blind to the approach of the winged creature. Kailani dropped the Plexan and arrow, took off her gloves and shoved them in her pocket, closed her eyes and brought her hands together. Mumbling some words under her breath, she opened her eyes and swept her hands apart until they were at full stretch from her body on either side. A sprinkling of light appeared in both hands which got brighter and brighter, lighting up the area. She lay her palms on the ice and an arch of light, as bright as the sun remained.

In the newly lighted sky they could now see what was approaching. A huge black winged creature was almost upon them. It was like a bird yet its head was more akin to that of a monkey. It had a beak half a foot long, four long legs with large talons on the feet, a thin monkey-like tail, and huge leathery wings with spikes running down the edges.

Kailani grabbed her Plexan and arrow and aimed at the creature's head. She fired but the beast ducked and swerved much quicker than its bulk should allow. The arrow went sailing past. She grabbed another, lined it up and shot again. This time the arrow found its mark, but not quite where she intended, hitting the wing instead of the body.

The beast yowled and veered in Kailani's direction, its eyes blazing and talons extended toward her. Knowing she didn't have time to cock another arrow, aim, and shoot before the creature was upon her, she dropped the Plexan and pulled her Panas from its scabbard, unleashing a bolt of lightning at the creature. It turned sharply and the lightning caught one of the spikes on its wing. The manoeuvrability of the animal was unexpected.

Mishtag and Yashtig rose onto their hind legs and with their sharp claws extended, swiped at the beast whenever it came within their reach, ripping holes into the wings and inflicting a couple of small cuts on the body.

It turned sharply and one of the spikes caught Kailani on the left arm, ripping through her clothes and drawing blood. Furious, she reached for her Trey and clicked the middle so the extra points with the bladed whips would extend as soon as she threw it. The beast circled and dived straight for her. Anticipating which way it would move, she threw the Trey at it; grabbing her Panas she pointed it slightly in the other direction in case it veered that way and let fly a small lightning bolt which singed a wing tip. As expected the beast turned away, straight into the Trey which embedded in its belly.

The creature crashed to the ground, but there was plenty of fight left in it. As soon as anything came near it lashed out with its wings, the lethal spikes aimed at them. Kailani took advantage of its weakened condition, firing multiple lightning bolts at the body and head. It still tried to fight back, one of its claws catching her boot, but there was insufficient strength behind the blow and it barely scratched the surface.

She walked around to the head knowing the wings would prevent her from getting too close and shot a lightning bolt from her Panas directly between the eyes. The beast was too slow to raise its wings for protection and she scored a direct hit. It slumped into a heap and stopped moving.

Creeping forward, she approached the head and in one swift strike brought her blade down, severing it from the neck.

Walking around the strange creature she was amazed at the wing span on it, even without the spikes, for what was quite a small body in contrast. She wondered how it had the strength to control the wings in such a deadly way. Grabbing one of the wings and being careful not to injure herself on the spikes, she tried to turn the body over so she could retrieve her Trey, but the weight of it was too much for her alone. Mishtag and Yashtig still on their hind legs bent to help her and between them they managed it. Kailani retrieved her Trey, wiped it on a clean part of the fur then, retracting the extra spikes and whips, replaced it on her belt. She sheathed her Panas and replaced the Plexan with the quiver.

Mishtag whimpered and pointed one paw at her arm. Blood was staining her coat where the spike had caught her. It was only when the adrenalin began to dissipate she felt the pain. She walked over to her backpack, knelt and looked inside for something she could bind it with. In the outside pocket, she found a couple of bandages and a liquid. Removing her coat, she pushed up her sleeve and poured a little of the liquid on the wound. It stung so much it was worse than the pain and she cried out. Mishtag moved up beside her and placed her head in Kailani's lap. The princess stroked the Blenorai's head in grateful thanks for the comfort. She bandaged her arm, pulled down her sleeve, and put her coat back on as she was beginning to shiver with the cold.

She moved the saddles and bags further away from the corpse, piling them neatly whilst making sure the Plexan and quiver were right on the top. Grabbing the blanket and her backpack, she placed them on the ground and waited for Mishtag to lie down again. As soon as she had, Kailani positioned the pack and blanket then walked over to where the arch of light still illuminated the night sky. Yashtig also positioned himself like before.

She picked each end up in her hands and started to bring her hands together. As she did so, the light began to diminish. By the time she reached Mishtag, it was but a small ball of light in her hands, just enough for her to see by. She sat down between her Kai's legs and brought her hands together extinguishing it.

Kailani put her gloves back on and snuggled into Mishtag. She put her head on the backpack, covered herself in the blanket and was asleep within seconds.

Chapter 8

When Kailani woke the next morning the sky was filled with dark grey clouds and a strong, biting wind had sprung up. She shivered as she moved away from the warmth of Mishtag's body. By the time she had got their food out, both the Blenorai Kai stood in front of her expectantly. Grabbing two handfuls she held them out so they could eat. They were so gentle, she barely felt them take it from her hands. When they had finished, she pulled a rudimentary bowl from the pack and poured some water in it. Mishtag and Yashtig took turns lapping from it until it was gone.

Putting the bowl away, she made a breakfast of bread and cheese, washing it down with a few mouthfuls of water. She armoured and saddled the two animals, loaded Yashtig and after putting the backpack and Plexan on her back, climbed onto Mishtag.

"Are you ready to carry on now?" she asked. Both nodded their heads. "Come on then, let's go."

They took off across the ice only to find the wind was blowing straight at them. Within a few minutes, Kailani's eyes watered and the tears instantly froze against her cheeks, her nose ran, and her face felt raw like someone had taken a file to it. She brought the Blenorai to a halt and unwound her scarf, re-positioning it so that it covered her face and only her eyes were visible. Next she pulled the hood over the hat she wore and buttoned it around her neck so it wouldn't be blown back. Only then was she ready to continue.

With a signal from Kailani, the Blenorai began to run again and were soon racing across the ice. The wind didn't seem to slow them down too much although when it really gusted, Kailani could tell they struggled a little. The miles began to disappear beneath them once more, but today she wasn't looking around at the landscape, instead she concentrated on keeping her head down and low to Mishtag's.

The glacial wind seemed to be growing in intensity. It cut through the layers of Kailani's clothes and chilled her to the bone. It was all she could do to hold onto Mishtag's reins, her fingers felt so stiff.

A few hours later, they stopped for lunch. She had great trouble as she tried to dismount, her body seemed so inflexible. Yashtig moved closer so she could access the food easier while Mishtag did what she could to shelter Kailani from the wind. After feeding the Blenorai, she plucked a piece of fruit from the bag. It was strange to her eyes, shaped like a cube and turquoise blue in colour. Still, she knew she had to eat something so took a deep breath and bit into it. The honeyed sweetness of it filled her mouth and ran down her throat; she found it one of the most delicious things she'd ever tasted. Under other circumstances, she would have eaten it slowly to savour the taste, but was aware of how far she still had to travel.

It was strange, but she didn't feel quite so cold anymore, as if the fruit had journeyed around her whole body and warmed it from the inside. She found her fingers worked properly again and she didn't feel so stiff. Quickly packing the bag away and placing it back on Yashtig's saddle, she mounted Mishtag and said "Let's go!"

As the afternoon drifted toward evening, Kailani was pleased they hadn't encountered any beasts that day. She knew there was still the possibility of another night attack, but at that moment she just felt relieved.

The clouds had lightened a little as the day wore on, but they looked heavy. Large flakes of snow began to fall quickly and with the unrelenting wind, it immediately turned into a blizzard. The Blenorai tried to battle through, but the almost hurricane strength wind and snow took its toll.

Kailani could feel Mishtag struggling beneath her and called them to a halt. She dismounted, closed her eyes and visualised an ice barrier around them, concentrating hard on what she wanted. When she could no longer feel the bite of the wind on her back she opened her eyes. Surrounding them was a large circular wall of ice more than twice the height of the princess. There was enough room for them to move around easily and stretch out. With her arms fully extended, she couldn't touch the sides. Ecstatic that she'd been able to accomplish what she had set out to do, she rubbed both of the Blenorai's heads before starting to unload Yashtig's saddle.

The Kai stared up at the princess gratefully; soldiers would have made them battle through those conditions without a single thought for how much they struggled. Once Kailani had removed both their saddles and armour, they were able to rest properly.

She saw the looks in their eyes and it appeared to be gratitude. "I wish you could talk back to me or I knew your language so I could converse with you. I've never been away from people for this long before and I miss it. I know it's a silly thing and something I need to get used to on this long journey, but a bit of chat would make the time disappear quicker." The Blenorai looked at each other for a long moment. "Please don't think for one second that I don't appreciate your company, because I do. It's just not the same when we can't talk to each other." She stroked both their heads, rubbing behind their ears and making a real fuss of them.

Outside, they could hear the wind screaming as if it were an evil spirit who was angry it couldn't get to them. Above the barrier, Kailani could see the speed of the wind, relieved not one flake was coming through the top.

Yashtig and Mishtag conversed quietly in their own language. The princess listened carefully trying to pick out any words she could make sense of, but could understand nothing. In the end, she gave up and decided to check on her wound.

She removed her coat and gloves and pushed her sleeve up. No blood had come through, which was a good sign, but when she unwound the bandage and looked at it, she was horrified to see green pus seeping from it and gasped. The Blenorai immediately stopped their conversation and moved to see what was wrong. The expression in their eyes seemed to be concern, which made Kailani more upset.

Yashtig used his claws to undo the buckle on the backpack and pushing his nose inside, re-emerged with the bottle she'd used yesterday between his teeth. "You want me to clean the wound with this?" she asked. Yashtig nodded. She reached over to the pack and found a handkerchief. Pouring some of the liquid onto it, she carefully cleaned the wound, wiping away all the disgusting-looking and smelling pus and, as much as it hurt her to do so, she dripped some into the wound and with a clean piece of the cloth, wiped the open part paying special attention to the edges of the skin. When she had finished, she cut off the soiled part of the bandage and re-wound the rest around her arm.

"Is this something for me to worry about?" she asked her companions. Yashtig shrugged and Mishtag nodded. "I'll make sure I check it every day until it's healed. Will that make you feel better about it?" They both nodded and Kailani couldn't help but smile at them. She repacked the bottle and used handkerchief as there was still plenty of clean fabric which could be utilised.

She rolled down her sleeves but left her coat off. Inside the barrier it was warmer than expected, unless the strange fruit she'd consumed for her lunch had anything to do with it. She heard one of the Blenorai's stomachs rumble and hers followed suit straight after. Kailani giggled and it sounded like they chuckled too. "Fine. I get the message," she laughed, reaching into the bag which contained their food. Grabbing two big handfuls, she fed them then pulling out the same bowl she'd used before, poured water in there for them.

The princess pulled the half empty tin of stew from the other bag and a spoon. Just before she was about to dig in, she had a brainstorm. If it worked, it meant she could have hot meals when she wanted them. She put her hands together, closed her eyes and mumbled some words. Heat began to build between her palms and she opened her eyes. Slowly pulling her hands apart she could see flames licking at her skin but they didn't burn her. She placed the fire on the ice and placed her tin of stew over the flames. It wasn't long before the contents were bubbling and as she went to pull the tin away, she scorched her fingertips on the hot metal. She grabbed a glove, removed it then extinguished the flames with her other hand. Kailani began eating the hot food, jubilant about her ideas and abilities.

When she'd finished and cleared away, a wave of tiredness swept over her and she began to yawn. She grabbed her blanket and pack, lay down on her coat and pulled the blanket around her. "I'm so tired. See you in the morning." She yawned again then closed her eyes. That was the last thing she knew until the next day.

Kailani woke to silence the next morning. The sun had not quite risen, but the sky looked clear and most importantly, the strong winds from the day before had vanished. Everything seemed so still and calm and she wanted to make up for lost time. She changed her clothes while the animals slept and managed to eat her normal breakfast of bread and cheese before either of them stirred. She pulled out their food, the smell of which woke them both instantly, and they ate with gusto. While they drank, she began to armour and saddle them and place some of the bags on Yashtig. By the time they were finished, she only had to put the bowl away and they were ready to go.

They backed up to the furthest edge away from where they were sure a great deal of snow had piled up during the storm and Kailani made the barrier disappear. Immediately the Blenorai began to growl. She looked around but could see nothing of concern. However, she trusted the Kai's instincts about such things and as they backed away from the pile of snow which had accumulated against the side of their shelter, so did she. Her hand reached down and slowly she unsheathed her Panas.

Dawn had just begun to break and the sky turned a pale purple, giving them more light to see by. Suddenly something long and white shot out from the snow aiming directly for the princess. It landed on her chest, pushing her to the ground with the velocity of its landing, winding her. She tried to bring her Panas to bear as the beast hissed in her face, but its body had trapped her arm. She struggled to kick it off her and wriggle her body, but the beast stuck firm. It opened its mouth to reveal two rows of pointed teeth, plus two large fangs at the top. It kept sniffing at her, its tongue licking its thin white lips. The eyes swivelled in all directions, constantly watching its flanks.

The princess managed to slowly move her other arm and pulled her Kamuk free. Carefully she moved her hand down until her arm was at full stretch and held the hilt tightly. When the creature seemed to be distracted by the movements of the Blenorai Kai, she struck, bringing the curved blade up and tearing into its side. It screeched and coiled in on itself before striking again, this time with fangs fully extended. She had declared war and the beast was ready to accept the challenge.

Mishtag leapt into the air and grabbed the creature just below the neck. It screeched again, its eyes fierce and ready to kill, roiling and wiggling in an effort to free itself, and Mishtag started to struggle. She clamped her teeth down harder, but it only made the beast struggle more. Yashtig joined the fight and grabbed the body several inches from where Mishtag held on tight.

The creature rose, its head making the two Blenorai stand on their hind legs and above Kailani. With her Panas already in her hand, she reached up and tried to strike the head. She was too slow and missed. She could see the black blood pouring out of the creature from where she'd cut it and from where the Kai had sunk their sharp teeth into its body. However, it showed no sign of weakening. The princess tried again to separate the head from the body without success.

She didn't know how much longer the Blenorai would be able to hold on. Some of the black blood was going in to their mouths and they couldn't spit it out without letting go. Darting under the head she stabbed the point of her Panas deep into the underbelly and ripped it open, walking back as she did so. She pulled the blade out just before she reached Yashtig's jaws. She stepped quickly to the side as the creature emitted an ear-piercing shriek of pain. Mishtag let go and spat the blood onto the ground. Yashtig followed suit.

The beast thrashed around, black blood and other fluids staining the ground as they flowed from the wounds. It stared at Kailani and made another attempt to pounce on her, but Mishtag was ready. She sprang and clamped her jaws firmly into the neck, just below the head and dragged it toward the floor. Yashtig pounced and used his paws to help force the head down. The princess realised what they were trying to do and as soon as the head was near enough to the ice, she drove the Panas into its skull, right between the eyes. Its thrashing grew weaker. Kailani put her boot on its head and pulled out the blade then removing her foot, sliced the head clean off.

Mishtag once again spat the blood out of her mouth and made a face of what could only be described as disgust.

"I'll get you some water to rinse out your mouths," Kailani said, worry lacing her tone. She had no idea how toxic it could be to them and didn't want to take the chance of either of them becoming ill. As she was about to reach into the bag, there was another hissing sound and the next thing she knew she was on the floor with another head just inches from her face. Its eyes were furious and the fangs completely extended. It slid its tongue out and licked the side of her face. It made her skin tingle and not in a pleasant way. She moved the Kamuk down and sliced into its side deeper than before.

It shrieked but didn't move. Kailani pressed the button on the hilt changing the blade to the serrated edge and cut into it again, ripping into the flesh and tearing an ugly wound in its side. This time it did move, but all it did was raise its head and open its jaws wide. Yashtig pounced and clamped its jaws around its neck. Mishtag grabbed her coat in her teeth and tried to pull the princess away, but one of Yashtig's paws was on the other side of her coat. Mishtag said something loudly in her strange language and Yashtig tried to pull the beast's head away by walking backwards on his hind paws.

Suddenly Kailani was free, but felt decidedly strange. Mishtag let her go then went to help Yashtig. Instead of clamping her jaws around the creature, she dug her claws in and starting ripping into the skin, exposing the innards within. She carried on, tearing and shredding wildly while the beast began to writhe and buck, trying to get away.

It was no match for the Blenorai Kai. Mishtag continued to drag the beast forward so she could get to more of the skin. She was out of control, furious the creature had the audacity to attack her rider, determined to make it pay with its life. The struggles grew weaker as blood flowed like a stream from all the injuries inflicted. Yashtig released the neck and as it dropped to the ground he put his paw on the head and stood on it, hearing the satisfying crunch as the bones in the skull shattered, while spitting the blood on the ground.

The Blenorai Kai waited for the princess to get up and slice the beast's head off but when they looked at her, they realised she wasn't well at all. Where the creature had licked her face, it had come up in a nasty-looking rash and she could barely move. She knew what they wanted her to do, but as hard as she tried to move, she just couldn't. Then she remembered something her grandfather had said about the animals she might encounter. He told her of a white snake-like creature with a head at each end of its body who used a toxin on their tongues to paralyse their victims before eating them. She would see and hear everything going on around her, but wouldn't be able to move. There was no known cure, but it would wear off in its own good time.

The princess knew what had happened to her, but there was nothing she could do about it. It was really frustrating. She tried to tell the Blenorai, but all that came out was garbled nonsense. Mishtag walked over to her and grabbed the sword in her front paws. She moved to the beast and holding the blade as tightly as she could, brought it down on its neck, severing the head.

Kailani so desperately wanted to get some water out to help the Blenorai clean their mouths after having that awful blood in there. She struggled against the toxin which held her in its grip and found after a few minutes of trying that she could move a finger, then another one, and then a thumb. Mishtag watched her closely and she signalled with her eyes what bag she wanted. Walking across to Yashtig, she grabbed the bag in her mouth and brought it over. The princess had trouble undoing the buckle, but after several minutes of struggling managed it. Mishtag held the flap open with one paw and watched her eyes carefully. She tried to indicate what she wanted, but it was difficult when there were so many items in there. Eventually, Mishtag pulled out the bowl and a look of relief came over Kailani's face. The Kai inched the water bottle out using her claws and rolled it over to Kailani, Mishtag also moved the bowl closer. The princess finally succeeded in getting the top off the bottle and with help from her Blenorai, poured some water into the bowl. She screwed the top on the bottle as Mishtag spoke to Yashtig. They both lapped from the bowl and spat out the first few mouthfuls, getting rid of the taste and black blood before drinking normally.

It took about four hours before Kailani had enough movement in her to rise from the ground, secure the bag to Yashtig's saddle and, with difficulty, mount Mishtag. She was stiff and walked like a wooden marionette, but at least she could move. Taking one last look at the two-headed beast they set off.

The princess was furious with herself. Admittedly she'd been caught by surprise with the first attack, but she should have remembered the lesson her grandfather gave her on the creatures they were likely to encounter and remembered it had a head at the other end. She had left herself vulnerable and if it hadn't been for the Blenorai Kai, she would have been dead by now. She owed them her life and wasn't going to forget it in a hurry.

Stupid, stupid, stupid! Why did grandfather give me the knowledge if I wasn't to use it to my advantage? If I'd been killed, the chances of the others finding my mother are probably zero – they haven't managed it in the last twenty years so probably wouldn't in the next twenty!

She continued to remonstrate with herself until a voice came into her head.

We all make mistakes or forget things. Do not be so hard on yourself.

Kailani was startled and almost dropped the reins. *Who are you?*

She heard a deep throated chuckle. *It is I, Mishtag. I did not know you were telepathic. I thought I had heard some of your thoughts before, but I was not sure, until now. Your voice appeared so clearly in my mind, but I did not know if you would be able to hear me. This is wonderful. We can communicate.*

The princess stroked Mishtag's head with one hand and what sounded like a sob escaped her lips. *Oh, Mishtag, you have no idea how much this means to me. Just to be able to share my thoughts with you and have conversations is beyond wonderful. I'd begun to feel lonely and isolated for lack of someone to talk to. Obviously having you and Yashtig were a great comfort, but I couldn't talk to you like I could another person, until now. This is perfect. I have everything with me I could possibly need.*

It was only a few minutes later when her stomach began to rumble. *Let's stop for something to eat.* Mishtag relayed the instructions to Yashtig and they both stopped. Kailani was still a bit stiff, but her movements were much more fluid than when they'd left their campsite. She quickly fed the Blenorai before pulling a piece of fruit from her bag. This one was shaped like a diamond and was orange in colour. She bit into it and found it to be sweet and thirst quenching despite its firm texture. She ate it quickly, packed away, mounted Mishtag and said, "We need to make up some of the lost time from this morning."

They took her at her word and began sprinting away. They ran faster and faster, until the ice beneath her was almost a blur. The ride was exhilarating and Kailani had never felt more alive. The weather was clear and certainly much warmer than the previous day. The sun reflected off the ice throwing prisms of light in every direction. Patches of blue in the sky matched the colour of her hair, and with the snow drifts it looked like an awe-inspiring magical kingdom.

In the distance she could see what looked like mountains. It was a welcome change from the completely flat vista, as beautiful as it had been, and she realised how far they had travelled since leaving the palace. They'd done very well, despite the occasional enforced stop to deal with 'nasties' as the princess now thought of them.

As much as she wanted to talk to Mishtag, she didn't want to distract her so kept her thoughts silent. She just continued to admire the landscape surrounding her. Even as twilight approached and the sky began to turn various shades of pink, orange, and violet, it was just as wondrous a sight to behold.

Darkness began to fall and they stopped for the night. With the small amount of light left, she gave the Blenorai a little extra food and water – they had certainly earned it – before sorting out her own. Like the previous night, she had created a small fire to heat up the contents of the tin. When she opened it she found strips of chicken with vegetables in a light gravy. Although she was starving and could easily have demolished the entire contents, the princess stopped when the can was half empty and carefully closed it again. She packed away the food lest the smell draw predators in their direction, drank a little water, and snuggled up next to Mishtag who, along with Yashtig, was already asleep. She very quickly joined them.

Chapter 9

Galaxan strode into the Cloud Castle and immediately went to his father's office. The two men embraced and he reported to King Sirris the outcome from his trip. He'd been able to find the source of the plague and eradicated it using his magic. There were still some losses, but after his actions there was a marked improvement in the animals as they began to recover. The produce hadn't been affected, which was a bonus.

"You've done well, Son. Thank you for your efforts on my behalf." The king smiled with pride in his eyes.

"You're welcome, Father. Has anything much happened while I've been away?" he asked casually.

"Nothing of any importance. However, I haven't seen Kailani for a few days." King Sirris's brow furrowed at the look of horror on his son's face. "What's the matter, Galaxan?"

"Kailani wanted to go down to Idenvarlis to meet her other grandparents, but I forbade it and ensured the door to my chambers was locked and guarded."

"Would that be so terrible?"

"Yes! They rejected me and my attempts to court Garalia. I told Kailani they would probably reject her too and that's why I didn't want her going there, but you know how tenacious and headstrong she can be when there's something she wants. I need to find out where she is. Would you please excuse me, Father?"

"Of course. Please keep me informed." His eyes showed his concern.

"I will," Galaxan replied as he rose and dashed out.

When he reached his room, he spoke to the soldier guarding the door and asked him if Kailani had entered.

"Yes, your Highness. She said she'd had a message to take something to you urgently and that's the only reason I let her in," he explained.

"There was no message, you idiot." Galaxan shouted, going red in the face. He barged past the guard, unlocked the door and entered. Immediately he saw a note propped on his desk and grabbed it. His eyes quickly scanned the contents and a heaviness settled in his stomach. He knew he had to calm down before going to Idenvarlis and took several deep breaths until he felt more in control. He walked over and pressed the keys, opening the door to the passage and stepped in. The whoosh of air buffeting him took a bit of getting used to again; he hadn't used it in twenty years and he'd forgotten how weird it felt.

Coming to a sudden halt, he stepped out into Garalia's room and a pang of heartache pierced his chest. Seeing all her things on the dressing table was a stark reminder of just how much he'd lost when she disappeared. He walked to it and ran his fingers over some of the items, surprised to find not a speck of dust. After a minute or two, he walked out of the room and stalked down the corridor, stunned when the soldiers bowed to him. It amazed him that he remembered the way to the throne room, or the great hall as it was otherwise known. The servants opened the doors and without hesitating, he walked through.

King Jaanis was just finishing a meeting with his ministers. As soon as he was done, he walked straight toward Galaxan, who moved forward to meet him halfway. They stopped a couple of feet apart and stared at each other for a long moment before Jaanis smiled and offered his hand. The prince took it warily, surprised when the king pulled him into a hug.

"Welcome, Son-in-law. Come, sit, and talk with me." Jaanis let him go and put an arm around his shoulders. The effusive greeting had more than taken Galaxan by surprise. He was truly shocked by it and moved like a child being led somewhere they're not sure about. When they reached the table, the king called for refreshments and gestured for his visitor to sit on his right.

"Thank you for your warm greeting, King Jaanis. I admit to being taken aback considering I'm not usually welcome in Idenvarlis." He chose his words very carefully.

"I know a great deal more about you and my daughter now and having met and spent time with my beautiful granddaughter, let's just say I've had my eyes opened for me. I deeply regret the way I've treated you in the past, and hope you will accept my apology."

"Of-of course," Galaxan stammered, caught unawares for the second time in the past few minutes. *Has Kailani cast some sort of spell on him?* "It's actually because of Kailani that I'm here. She disobeyed me by coming to Idenvarlis and I would have words with her about it."

"I know. She told me. With hindsight I suppose I should have sent her back to you, but it was such a joy to find out we had a granddaughter and she's so lovely, the thought never entered my head. You have done a wonderful job of raising her and she's a lot like Garalia was at that age."

"Thank you, and yes, I can see a great deal of my wife in her and not just in looks. She's definitely headstrong like her mother."

"Oh, yes. I've certainly found that out!" Jaanis nodded, his expression suddenly serious.

The tone of the king's voice and his abrupt change in demeanour made Galaxan wary and concerned. "I hope Kailani hasn't done anything to upset you since she arrived."

"Well, she disobeyed me . . . and I have something to tell you. Kailani isn't here. She said she had a very strong instinct that she knew where her mother was and set off to try and find her. She was supposed to go with a battalion of soldiers, but she decided to leave in the middle of the night on her own."

"What?" Galaxan jumped up from the chair, his face drained of colour.

"I despatched the battalion as soon as I discovered what she'd done – she could only have had about a three hour head start on them. I'm confident they'll catch up to her quickly," Jaanis said, trying to sound assured and calm.

"But she's out there all alone in a strange country. Who knows what she'll encounter on route? She's so young and defenceless." The prince paced by the side of the table, his fists clenched. "How long ago did she leave?"

"Three days. She's not as defenceless as you think. She's an excellent swordswoman, knows how to handle knives, and she's also very accurate with a bow." The king then explained what had occurred during Kailani's time there.

"I can see she put you in an impossible situation and for that I apologise on her behalf. I will be having some strong words with her when she returns...if she returns." He stopped pacing, slumped in a chair and put his head in his hands. "Oh, by the gods and goddesses, I can't lose her too, I just can't. Losing my wife nearly destroyed me, I-I..." He began to sob and Jaanis put his arm around his son-in-law's shoulders.

"I can understand only too well how you feel. But Kailani is a resourceful young woman, she's proved that already, and the circumstances are different this time. She has a battalion of my men at her disposal for one thing. And despite our private concerns, both Shivla and I believe in our hearts that Kailani will return safely."

"Y-You do?" Galaxan lifted his tear-stained face to look at his father-in-law.

"Yes," Jaanis answered in a gentle tone.

He wiped his tears away and blushed. "I feel rather embarrassed to say the least."

"Let's adjourn to my office. I know Shivla would like to see you."

The three of them sat in comfort in the king's office and chatted like they never had before. The ambiance was relaxed and Galaxan felt like part of the family for the very first time. Jaanis told him how far Kailani was going and roughly how long it would take for her to make the round trip.

"As long as that?"

"Possibly longer. It depends very much on Garalia, assuming Kailani finds and rescues her. If she is weak, it will be difficult for her to travel too far each day. You are very welcome to stay here if you wish. I can have a room made up for you."

"Thank you for your kind offer, but I cannot stay away from my kingdom for that length of time. I have duties there. However, if it's alright with you, I'll pop back every now and again to see you both and nearer the time of their return, I might come and stay for a couple of nights."

"Of course it's alright," Shivla replied with a smile. "You are welcome here anytime."

"Thank you, but if you don't mind my asking, why the sudden change of heart toward me? You were so against Garalia's and my marriage and yet now I'm suddenly being treated like one of the family. Not that I'm complaining – I always hoped you would come round and accept me."

"You have your daughter to thank in all honesty. We've now accepted your marriage and in so doing, accepted you too. Does that answer your question?" Shivla smiled at him.

"Yes, thank you, your Highness." Galaxan grinned back at her.

"Will you stay for dinner? And the night?"

"Thank you. It would be an honour."

"Oh, and one last thing, Galaxan, in private you can either call us by our first names or mother and father – whichever you feel most comfortable with."

Galaxan smiled. He came to Idenvarlis in search of his daughter and instead had acquired a second family. All he needed now was his wife and daughter back and his life would be complete.

Chapter 10

The next morning dawned crisp and cold. The sky was a pale grey with hints of violet and no sign of the sun. Kailani rose and before organising breakfast, loosened her hair. It was pleasant to feel it around her neck and she wanted to keep it down. However, it wasn't practical, especially if they ran into any more nasties, so with a sigh, she brushed and braided it.

By the time she'd finished, Mishtag and Yashtig were stirring. She put her brush away and got their food out. As always, they ate from her hands with gentleness. When they finished, she poured some water into their bowl while she ate her usual breakfast.

When she'd eaten, Kailani pulled the map from her bag, unfolded the document and studied it carefully. She was surprised and delighted by how much ground they'd covered so far. They were still heading in the right direction and as long as they kept the mountains on their left, they should reach the Lost Mire by nightfall. She folded the map and replaced it in her bag, armoured and saddled the Blenorai, and set off.

As they got closer to the mountains, Kailani could see their majesty. Their peaks were snow-capped and the bottoms were covered in ice, but the remainder was a mixture of blacks, browns, greys, and purples. The individual colours formed patterns which repeated as they passed, except for the purple. This seemed to be dotted around sporadically and the princess couldn't help but wonder why.

A breeze began to blow and she got her answer as she saw the purple swaying. It seemed strange that plants should grow there and even stranger that they would be able to survive in what was really quite a harsh environment. She studied the mountains closely. The jagged peaks resembled what she thought of as monster's teeth. From about half way up the sides appeared to be as smooth as glass and certainly not climbable. The lower half was craggy and appeared to have an occasional cave burrowed into the side. A couple of these were quite large and Kailani couldn't help fearing they were the home of some huge beast that would try and make a meal of them.

She didn't want to think about that so turned her mind to more pleasant things. Looking up at the clouds, a wave of homesickness engulfed her. As she began to think about her home in Taivass-maa, Mishtag spoke to her.

I have been very curious about the world where you grew up. Can you tell me about it?

Kailani was delighted her Kai wanted to know about it and began talking to her. By the time they stopped for lunch, she had only got as far as telling Mishtag about the Cloud Castle, her rooms, and her family. It was the first time she'd really thought about them since coming to Idenvarlis, except to hope her father didn't appear before she'd left, and it made her realise just how much she missed them and that if she wasn't careful, she might never see them again. It was a sobering thought which made her all the more determined to return alive and preferably unharmed.

After lunch was finished and they got underway, Kailani continued telling Mishtag about Taivass-maa. She spoke of the landscape, the houses, how people made their living, and the daily market in town. She continued by talking about her best friends, skippers, and her Feegle, Rhea.

Mishtag asked, *What deities are worshipped and what magic do you have? I have seen a little of what you can do and of course I know you are telepathic. I have also observed what some of your weapons can do, are there any others?*

"There are four deities we worship and each has a temple built in their honour at the end of the market square. There is Denzla, the Star Goddess; Savna, the Sun God; Jexin, the Moon Goddess; and Baelris, the Lightning God. Each temple has either priests or priestesses to maintain it, but our deities are not the sort to expect citizens to visit the temple on a regular basis to pay homage, as long as we keep them in our thoughts and pray to them occasionally, they are happy. They are benevolent and understanding dieties as long as those who follow them mark their special day each year. That is all they ask of us."

What do you mean by 'those who follow them'? Does not everyone in the land follow every deity? And what is their 'special day'?

"Not everyone in Taivass-maa has magic. Of those that do, the birthmark they are born with denotes which god or goddess they have allegiance to and what form their magic will take. Those who are born without magic can choose who they wish to follow. Each of the gods or goddesses has the equivalent of a naming day, which is celebrated in their honour each year. It is one of only four times a year when the royal family mix with the citizens and become ordinary people for a few hours. We dance, sing, talk, laugh, and dine with them. I try to be like that most of the time. I mix with local folk, shop in the markets, talk to people, and my two best friends are not of royal or noble birth. Some people shun me because I'm so different to anyone else. It used to hurt, but now I ignore it and just smile."

In what way are you so different from everyone else?

"Well, in Taivass-maa everyone has brown skin, although to varying degrees, their lips are a darkish pink and their eyes are blue. Apart from my birthmarks, the only characteristic I share with them is the colour of my hair."

The questions and answers carried on until dusk began to fall. In the distance, the princess could see a large area with high plants and realised they'd almost reached the Lost Mire. She was pleased by the progress they'd made in such a short time. Once they were on the other side of the Lost Mire, they would be halfway to their final destination.

They stopped for the night and Kailani sorted out the food and drink. She had just finished eating when the hairs on the back of her neck rose. The Blenorai hadn't picked anything up yet, but somehow she knew danger was approaching. Explaining her magic to Mishtag earlier had reminded her just what she was capable of and she intended to use her gifts when the attack came. Shoving her gloves in her pockets, she put her hands together and as before, gave them some light to see by.

Huge, hairy, ape-like beasts with a hairless, wrinkled underbelly, huge eyes that bulged from their head, pointed ears like a wolf, and paws like a bear but with opposable thumbs came closer. She wasn't sure whether to blast them or wait to see whether they were attacked. The princess was sure they only wanted food, but that was one of the few things they couldn't afford to spare, so she picked up the pack and put it on.

The first one to get close made signs that they wanted food, but Kailani shook her head, saying, "I'm sorry, but we have none to spare."

It gestured again more forcefully and Kailani shook her head again. She could feel the magic growing inside her, but held it back, signalling to the Kai to keep back. It came closer to her, ignoring the growls from the

Blenorai and made a move to snatch the pack from her. She let a little of the magic loose and a small ray flew from her eyes onto the beast's hand, making it yelp. Instead of scaring it off, all it did was make it and its gang mad.

Remembering what her father had taught her in Taivass-maa, Kailani manifested a blade of fire, hoping it would scare them off, but they ignored it and began to rush toward her. She allowed her magic full rein and the blasters flew from her eyes, cutting them down where they stood, while a couple of others were sliced in half by her flaming sword. A couple of smaller ones near the back of the mob stood still, as if not sure what to do. They appeared to be younger than the rest and by the time the entire attacking hoard had been slaughtered, they began to back away, frightened expressions on their faces.

The princess got the magic back under control and the rays from her eyes ceased, turning them back to their normal silver. She watched carefully as the younger two ran back toward the mountains before she made the blade of fire disappear too.

That was quite a display and one we could have made use of this morning, said Mishtag, her voice at first impressed and then accusing.

She answered him aloud for Yashtig's benefit. "Some of my magic is new to me as I only found out about it a couple of weeks ago. When we were talking earlier, it reminded me what I'm able to do to and was still fresh in my mind when those beasts approached us. I know we could have made use of those skills earlier today, but I'd forgotten about them. Please feel free to remind me when the need arises." Mishtag nodded her head.

The stink of singed and burnt flesh was nauseating so they moved their camp upwind. When everything was relocated, Kailani turned to the Blenorai.

"We don't know if there are more of these creatures in the

mountains or whether the young ones will try and creep back later while we sleep to steal the food then. I think it would be wise for me to put an ice barrier around us tonight. Do you agree?" They both nodded. She walked over to where the light reflected over the ice and the burnt corpses, made it smaller and brought it much closer to their new camp. She closed her eyes, visualising the barrier until it was exactly how she wanted it.

The light inside gave off some much welcome heat and as before, the ice barrier was larger than they needed so everyone was able to stretch out. It had been a very eventful day and they were all tired. Kailani took off her coat and placed it on the ground with her normal pillow. She picked up the light in her hands and brought it over to her makeshift bed. She sat on her coat, extinguished the light, pulled the blanket over her as she snuggled down and closed her eyes. She was vaguely aware of Mishtag positioning herself to keep Kailani warm, but that was the last thing she knew for a few hours.

Mishtag and Yashtig were woken by noises outside the barrier. They couldn't see out because of the thickness of the ice and the sky was still like ebony velvet above them. Then the banging began. At first it came from just one place, but then it sounded like it was all around them. Kailani woke and rubbed her eyes. The banging got louder, as the attackers attempted to break the barrier.

The princess made a small light to see by then, after placing it on the floor and clasping her hands together, closed her eyes against it and weaved lightning into the outside of the structure. The next lots of bangs were accompanied by yelps of pain. They tried again and the same thing happened, and a third and fourth time, by which they had learned their lesson, or so she thought as all became quiet. The Blenorai growled so she knew the beasts remained.

They tried to attack the barrier in different places and heights, but the same thing happened to them, the cries becoming keener. After a while they gave up and moved away. Leaving the adjustment as a permanent fixture, Kailani put out the light and snuggled down once more. She quickly fell asleep.

The next morning, when the Blenorai were saddled and ready to go, Kailani made the barrier transparent so they could check their surroundings before she took it down. There was no sign of the beasts and the bodies of those who were slain had disappeared. She wondered briefly if they were cannibals and shuddered at the thought. Removing the barrier, they set off toward the Lost Mire.

Are you sure this is wise? Have you not been cautioned about this place? Mishtag asked with concern in her voice.

"Yes, I have been warned, but my grandfather didn't know about some of the magic I possess. Besides, going around it will waste two days and I can't afford to lose the time. I have a cunning plan."

Would you care to share it with me?

"Of course. First of all, a rope will tie you and Yashtig together so we don't get separated. Secondly, I'm going to create a stream of light overhead so we have something to follow and not get lost. Finally, I will also create a fluid barrier like a kind of force field around us so nothing can get to us as we travel through. Do you see any flaws in my plan?"

Mishtag was silent for a moment as she considered it. *In theory, no, I can't see any flaws, but will you be able to sustain both lots of magic at once, especially if you are distracted?*

"Yes, it shouldn't be a problem at all. I don't want to boast, but I'm probably the most powerful being in Idenvarlis. I have all the magic from both here and Taivass-maa." Feeling Mishtag needed more reassurance she continued. "Once I set the light, it is self-sustaining. It will not falter until I pick it up at the other end. As for the force field, I can't be one hundred per cent sure, but as the barriers I've created at night don't need my concentration to keep them there, I would hope the force field is the same. I will be checking it on a regular basis to ensure it remains firm. Does that give you more confidence?"

I suppose it does, yes. Very well, we will go through the Lost Mire with you.

"Thank you, Mishtag, for your faith in me. We'll get to the edge of the Lost Mire then stop before we enter it. I'll make my preparations and once everything is in place, only then will we forge ahead."

They travelled the rest of the way in silence. Kailani was scrutinising the mountains to ensure no more of those creatures were heading their way. Thankfully there was nothing around them.

It didn't take long to reach the edge of the Lost Mire and the Blenorai stopped a few feet away. Kailani dismounted and retrieved a rope from one of the packs. She looped it through both their collars, allowing enough room for them to move freely and tied a firm knot, placing it where she could easily reach it if necessary.

Striding closer to the edge, Kailani stopped, closed her eyes, put her hands together, and began to murmur softly. She opened her eyes, peeled her hands apart and revealed the light within. She placed one hand on the floor and, muttering a few more words, threw the light over the top of all the reeds. They followed it with their eyes; it seemed to go for miles before it disappeared. An arc of yellow light now lit the direction for them.

She beckoned the Blenorai over and mounted Mishtag. "Keep very still for a moment while I put the protective force field around us. She closed her eyes once more and visualised a wall of energy surrounding them from their feet upwards and into a dome shape above their heads. As part of the deterrent, she worked in a repelling spell so anything that tried to touch the outside would be driven away.

"Everything is in place so let's go. All we need to do is follow the light and it will lead us through to the other side."

Mishtag and Yashtig complied and began to move into the reeds. Soon they were surrounded by the plants on all sides, which reached far above their heads. They were nervous, but tried not to show it.

"Do you think we can speed up a bit, please? I'd ideally like to get to the other side before nightfall. I can see the light perfectly so I can guide you through," Kailani said.

The Blenorai did as they were asked and as their confidence in their mistress grew, they sped up.

It wasn't as easy to get through the reeds as Kailani was expecting. Mishtag and Yashtig had to put their heads down to force their way through the plants and as they sprang back the princess was frequently hit by them. She lowered her body until she was almost flat to Mishtag's to avoid them, but every now and again she had to sit straight to check they still travelled in the right direction before bobbing back down again.

When they'd been travelling for a couple of hours, Kailani checked the force field and was delighted to find it was still as strong as when she'd cast it. She sat up to check their position and saw they'd gone a little off course.

"We're not in a straight line with the light. You need to move to the right a bit."

The Blenorai slowed down and began moving in that direction.

"That's it, just a little more. Now straighten up again. Perfect! The light is now directly overhead. Well done, my friends."

As they were about to start speeding up again, something to their left bounced off the force field. It happened so quickly, Kailani didn't get a chance to see what it was. She kept her eyes trained in that direction for a couple of minutes, but nothing else happened so she moved her head and looked forward.

Suddenly the Blenorai ground to a halt and began growling. The princess stared ahead, but couldn't see anything other than the reeds. She swivelled her head in all directions, but found nothing to be alarmed about. She even checked overhead and at the same time ensured they still followed the light.

"I can't see anything. What disturbs you both?"

Mishtag answered the only way she could. *Do you not see them? Look hard between the reeds. There are a dozen creatures, well camouflaged, with spears in their hands.*

She stared and as one of them moved slightly, she saw them. They were only slightly thicker than the reed stems themselves and exactly the same colour. Almost as tall as the plants with twig-like arms and legs and reddish-brown heads, they had small eyes and a mouthful of very pointed teeth. It looked like their spears had been made from the stems of the reeds with one end sharpened to a lethal-looking point.

Kailani checked the force field again and laced lightning into it. "We can safely move through them. Pay them no mind and let's continue on," she said, her voice calm and almost nonchalant.

As soon as the Blenorai began to move, there was a high pitched cry and two of the spears were thrown at them. They narrowly missed the princess. Mishtag and Yashtig began to pick up speed. As the group came into contact with the strange creatures they were repelled, screeching where they'd come into contact with the lightning. Kailani looked back and saw angry and bewildered faces as the stick creatures picked themselves up from the floor. One shook its tiny fist at them and she couldn't resist a small snicker.

A few minutes later they came across a larger group. This time, there was no hesitation on the part of the Kai and they powered through the group, watching as the creatures just bounced out of their way. Yashtig and Mishtag were much happier and full of confidence in their mistress's abilities and they raced ahead, trying to catch up some lost time.

When they had been travelling for around five hours, Kailani called them to a halt. Checking the force field yet again, she dismounted then gave Mishtag and Yashtig some food and water and grabbed a piece of fruit for herself. The strange colours and shapes of the fruit seemed almost commonplace to her now and she didn't think anything of it when she ate a pyramid shaped one which was lilac coloured.

After they'd finished eating and everything was put away, she checked the barrier and began their journey again. They were still under the light so Kailani put her head low against Mishtag's head as they powered through the reeds gathering speed.

Kailani was so comfortable with her head resting on her Kai's mane she dozed off for a little while. When she opened her eyes and sat up, she saw they had moved away from the light. Almost paranoid about the force field, she checked it again and an instinct told her to strengthen it, which she did.

"Slow down a bit," she called to the Blenorai, "we're off course again. You need to move to the left, quite a bit. That's it, keep going and I'll tell you when to stop." She put one arm up to protect her face from the reeds, the other gripped Mishtag's reins. A few minutes later, she spoke again, this time in a calmer voice. "Almost there. Just a little more. Alright now start to straighten up. That's it. Lovely. We're back under the light. Well done. Now let's crack on, please. We must be running out of time and daylight now."

The Blenorai took off again. They didn't want to stay in the Lost

Mire any longer than they had to. The whole place made them extremely uncomfortable, even with the benefits of Kailani's magic. They sped through the reeds and were grateful for the small piece of their armour which covered the top of their heads, coming down onto the forehead and with a strip running between the eyes. Without that particular piece of protection, they would not have been able to power through the reeds at such a speed and they would have suffered quite nasty headaches at the end of the day.

Kailani raised her head to check their progress. They were still under the light, but not too far ahead she could see it begin to curve downwards. She didn't say anything, preferring to wait until they got closer. She checked again about an hour later and saw the light was definitely arching down. As she was about to mention it, the Blenorai ground to a halt and began to growl. Immediately she scrutinised the shield and strengthened it further. The way the Kai were reacting she could tell it wasn't those funny stick creatures ahead. No, this was something bigger and scarier.

She closed her eyes for a moment, put her hands together and muttered quietly. When she opened her eyes and then hands, she held a thin orange line which smelled of burning. Concentrating on it, she closed her eyes again and visualised this new light running all over the force field. She threw the light to one side and watched in her mind's eye how it spread and stayed there. Opening her eyes once again, she saw the light gone from her hands.

"Can you see what is ahead of us?"

Mishtag answered. *Not yet. It is still hidden by the reeds. However, this is almost as big as the beasts we encountered last night. It smells rotten, like a carcass that has been left in the warm for a few days. It is putrid.*

"Move forward slowly until it reveals itself. We're even more protected than before so do not fear."

Yashtig snorted and turned his head to look at her with dismay in his eyes.

"What's wrong?"

The Blenorai Kai do not fear other creatures, Mishtag said haughtily. *We only fear for our riders and their safety.*

"I apologise if what I said came out wrong and I've upset you. What I was trying to get across to you is that I've strengthened the shield and added a little of my other magic into it. I will be perfectly safe."

The Kai just nodded and carried on running, but much slower than before. They stayed on the correct path under the light and Kailani lay almost flat against Mishtag again. It wasn't long before they stopped again and she could hear a deep growl. She sat up and saw the beast right in front of them, blocking their path.

It had large webbed feet, legs that were about eighteen inches long, a short snout with double rows of pointed teeth and no tail. Its belly and legs were covered in scales the same colour as the reeds, while the rest of its body had fur matching the reddish-brown of the top of the plants. It looked powerful, its legs muscular yet the princess was confident it was no match for the magic force field.

She encouraged the Blenorai to move slowly toward the beast to see how it would react. Abruptly, it put its head down and charged straight at them. As it came into contact with their shield it shook all over and almost appeared to be dancing. It roared as the pain shot through its body and then the shield repelled the creature and it landed a few feet away from them. A pitiful mewling sound emitted from it and the smell of burnt fur filled the air.

As they continued on, another beast like the first appeared and charged straight at them. This one was smaller than the other and the princess guessed it was the female, and they were a mated pair. The same thing happened to the second creature. The Kai moved on and once they passed the beasts, Kailani looked back. They attempted to crawl to each other. She felt a little pity for them, but it didn't hold her attention for long.

The sky had begun to darken a little. Twilight was on its way. The Blenorai sped up again following the curve of the light exactly although they couldn't see it. A short time later, Kailani said, "Not long now, my darlings. We're almost there." Two miles later and they came out of the reeds and carried on to where the light had landed, another half mile further on. She looked around and apart from the Lost Mire behind them and the mountains to their left there was nothing to see but an unbroken expanse of ice.

Her instincts were not warning her of anything so she took the lightning from the shield and crushed it in her hands until it had gone. She lowered the force field until it dissipated completed. Finally she dismounted then walked over and picked up the light beside them. She gave it a little tug and the huge stream of yellow they had been following all day came back into her hand, collapsing in on itself as it did so. As the other end soared over the reeds, Kailani caught it in her free hand and rested it next to its partner.

"I don't know about you, but I would feel more comfortable if we were a little further away from the Lost Mire before making camp for the night."

If that is your wish. However, you have proved beyond all doubt that you can protect yourself with your shields so why not just put up an ice barrier here? It has been a very tiring day.

"Oh, of course. I'm sorry. I should have thought about how much it's taken out of you both pushing your way through all those reeds. I apologise for my thoughtlessness. And, by the way, you have both been magnificent again today. You worked so hard to get us through the Lost Mire in one day and I sincerely thank you both for all your efforts."

She stroked each of their heads then closed her eyes, visualising an extra thick ice barrier with the repelling spell added to the outside. As soon as she opened her eyes, it was there. The first thing she did was untie the rope joining them together then unsaddled the Kai and removed their armour. She grabbed extra-large portions of their food for which they seemed to be very grateful as they ate every last bit. Pulling the bowl from the pack, she placed it on the ice and poured a healthy amount of water in it. Only then did she prepare her food for the evening.

Once all evidence of the meal had been cleared, Kailani realised just how tiring the day had been for her. She could then fully appreciate how much more it had taken out of the Blenorai. She looked at them and they were already asleep. Not wanting to disturb Mishtag, she took off her coat and placed it on the floor as usual with the pack, laid down pulling the blanket over her, extinguished the small light, and slept.

Chapter 11

The next few days were uneventful which Kailani was grateful for. No beasts attacked them which was a real bonus and although she still admired the scenery, the unbroken expanses of ice became boring. And despite her warm clothing, she struggled with the cold. They had left the mountain range behind and ice stretched as far as the eye could see in every direction, broken only by the occasional crop of trees. If it hadn't been for her talks with Mishtag, she might have gone crazy by now.

She and Mishtag had developed a real bond during their conversations. Kailani believed she could tell the Kai absolutely anything. She even admitted how she felt after turning twenty-one and still not being allowed to make her own decisions. It continued to rankle, even though she had defied everyone in making this trip alone. Nevertheless, she was prepared to face the fall-out when she returned, but if everything went as planned, she felt sure all would be forgiven and forgotten with the celebrations.

Mishtag told the princess about her parents and life in the Ice Palace. The Blenorai were kept in better conditions than some of the other animals and for that she was thankful. Occasional fights broke out between them and they were usually vicious, ending in blood being spilt, but the guards usually broke them up before any serious injuries were sustained. She had managed to stay out of any altercations by keeping to herself most of the time.

Things were entirely different when she was picked to become a Kai and not just because of the accommodations which were more luxurious in every way. The training was physically and mentally punishing, especially for Mishtag as she had to grasp everything that much quicker, but it was more than worth it. The Kai treated each other as equals, with respect, and there was no backbiting or arguments. The atmosphere was completely different; it was like belonging to an exclusive club and all of them were grateful they had been selected to become members. To be chosen to wear the jewelled collar filled them with pride.

She spoke about how she felt when her father was killed in battle by one of those two-headed snake-like things. Kailani now understood why Mishtag had fought the way she had when they were attacked by one. She talked about her mother and younger brother who had been in the pen when Kailani had come in and chosen her. She regretted being separated from them, but understood how different things became when you joined the elite ranks of the Blenorai Kai.

Kailani had told Mishtag so much about her life and way of living in Taivass-maa, she felt she knew the inner workings of the Cloud Castle and some of its members almost as well as she knew her friends at the Ice Palace. Kailani also confided her suspicions about Bellis being behind her mother's abduction and swore the Kai to secrecy.

Mishtag, in turn, told her how Bellis would disappear off for five or six weeks at a time, taking a second Blenorai with him who was fully loaded with packs and how, when they returned, the packs had all gone. She said it had been happening for many years and they were all suspicious as to where the prince went. However, both Blenorai had been sworn to secrecy on pain of death not to reveal the destination. In Kailani's mind, it seemed too much of a coincidence and she told Mishtag so.

I have to agree with you, Mistress. It does seem that way. But why would Prince Bellis do that to his sister? From all I've heard, she was wonderful to him, entertained him for hours on end and were as close as a brother and sister could be.

"Can you think of no reason at all?"

The only one I can come up with is something to do with the throne.

"Exactly! My mother was the eldest and as such would inherit the throne when my grandfather eventually goes to sit at the feet of the gods. With her out of the way, Bellis, as the next in line, would be the king's successor. However, he didn't know about me and that may have seriously affected his plans. I don't know the rules of succession in Idenvarlis, but it could be that as Garalia's daughter, I would be heir to the throne and not him."

I see what you mean. Your life could be in danger as well if that is the case. How can I help you?

"I don't know that you can except to protect me when I'm with you. Did I tell you about my first night in the Ice Palace?"

No. Why? What happened?

She recounted the event, ending with, "It was quite a while before I was able to sleep again."

Oh my. What a blessing your instincts told you to bolt the door. Did you recognise either of the voices?

"One seemed familiar, but the other I'd never heard before. It was difficult to tell as they were whispering."

Could the one that you possibly recognised have been Prince Bellis?

"Yes it could. In fact, that would make sense. I had only met a few of the ministers at dinner and I doubt it would have been any of them. And besides, I didn't converse with any one individual long enough to have been able to recognise the voice. I know it wouldn't have been my grandfather so that just leaves one person – Bellis."

Too many things point toward Prince Bellis for my liking. They cannot all be coincidences. It also makes me wonder if any of the palace guards have been subjected to some form of bribery. If that is the case, we do not know who in the battalion following us can be trusted, if any of them.

"Oh! By the Goddess Jexin, that never occurred to me. I could be walking from one beast's lair into another!" Kailani became silent, myriad thoughts tumbling around her mind as she tried to figure out what to do. Mishtag didn't interrupt; she was also trying to think of ways to help.

The silence stretched on for almost an hour when it was suddenly broken by a whoop from the princess.

"I've got it! Who is probably the most powerful person in Idenvarlis?" She didn't wait for an answer. "I've got enough magic to protect us all. Even if one of the guards could take down my ice barrier, they wouldn't be able to do anything about the lightning or whatever else I could use. That would remain so they wouldn't be able to get to us. Once we meet up with them on the return journey, I can sustain a lightning barrier around us at all times. The big question is how trustworthy is Karruq?"

Why? What does he have to do with this? Is he part of the battalion?

"Not as far as I know, but according to grandfather, Karruq handpicked the men for the journey."

Karruq is a strong but fair leader of the army. He is fiercely loyal to the royal family and was one of the last to give up searching for your mother as I understand it. I was not born then, but my mother told me all

*about Princess Garalia and what happened to her. She also told me a man
with blue hair helped in the search for a while. Was that your father?*

"Yes it was. So you deem him trustworthy then?"

Yes, I do.

"What about Yashtig? He's been around much longer than you and
has seen more of Karruq. I'll ask him and perhaps you'd be kind enough to
translate his answer?"

Of course.

"Yashtig? Can you please tell Mishtag what you know of Karruq
and whether, in your opinion, he is trustworthy?" She waited while Yashtig
spoke. To her surprise, he talked for quite a long time. Eventually he
stopped and Kailani waited until Mishtag was ready to translate.

*When Yashtig was a cub, another man was captain of the guard. He
was quite brutal and thought nothing of whipping his men, who feared him.
When Pugtak was killed, Prince Bellis chose three men, one of which was
Karruq, and interviewed them privately. Yashtig believes the prince was
trying to determine who would not be averse to looking the other way when
required. A few days later, Karruq was named captain. Yashtig saw the
prince visit Karruq a few times in the weeks following his appointment and
he did not always leave the captain's office with a smile on his face. Then
there was an extremely long period where Prince Bellis did not visit at all.
About two weeks before Princess Garalia disappeared, the prince began to
visit Karruq again. On one such occasion, he stormed out with a look of
fury on his face. The last time he entered the office was the day before your
mother disappeared. When he exited that day, he had a grin on his face.*

"This is *very* interesting. I wonder what Karruq agreed to that day to
make my uncle happy. I'd love to know."

*When your mother went missing, Karruq was horrified. He
immediately sent the men out searching, accompanying one group of them.*

Bear in mind also that due to the situation with Gengaruk, he was short of men. Every day he went out with the search parties and this went on for several weeks until finally, King Jaanis, called a halt to it. Karruq pleaded with the king to be allowed to continue searching, but he was overruled. Now whether this was a guilty conscience or because of his loyalty to the royal family only he knows. Yashtig believes Karruq would never knowingly send a traitorous guard with the battalion to protect Princess Garalia's daughter, especially if there was a chance of you succeeding.

"Thank you both. I hope you're right. However, whether I'm successful or not I'm still going to take precautions on the return journey. I can't afford to trust anyone until I'm back in the palace – present company excepted of course." The Blenorai nodded their heads.

Kailani looked at the landscape. They were approaching what looked like dense woods. The daylight was fading and she called a halt. After putting up an ice barrier and seeing to the animals, she consulted the map before eating. The trees she had seen ahead were the only ones marked on the map. It had to be the Silent Forest.

They seemed to be making good time. Once through the forest, the Land of No Souls was only one and a half days further on, but they could possibly do it in one if they pushed hard.

She hadn't really planned how to try and locate her mother or how to get her out from the Land of No Souls apart from having the bespelled bracelet. Looking at how big the area was on the map, she also had no idea how far in they'd made their camp. She had a lot of thinking to do.

Chapter 12

The sky roiled with dark purple and grey clouds as far as the eye could see. Deep rumbles of thunder seemed to make everything in Idenvarlis shudder with fear. The wind whipped around in circles turning first one way and then the other, picking up anything loose and making it dance to a tune no one could hear.

A crack of lightning ripped across the sky so loudly it woke Kailani and the Blenorai. She looked up, saw the storm clouds, and her forehead creased. "Oh Baelris, God of Lightning, I pray this storm is not a bad omen for the next part of our journey," she said in a low tone.

Hmm . . . did you say something, princess? Mishtag asked sleepily. She looked so cute when she was just waking up, Kailani had trouble holding back a giggle.

"Er, it's nothing important. I was just looking at the weather."

Mishtag lifted her large head and opened one eye. When she saw what was above, she seemed to wake in a hurry. *This does not look good. We are going to have a really bad storm, much worse than the blizzard we endured.*

"Well, we are travelling through the forest today anyway so hopefully it'll be more sheltered in there."

There is just one small flaw in your plan. This is the Silent Forest. With the noise of the thunder, lightning, wind, and rain, we will not be able to hear whether it turns silent as all the other factors will drown out the normal forest sounds.

"I've already thought of that," she said, smugly. "I will put a force field around us like we had when going through the Lost Mire."

Will the lightning not be drawn to the screen?

"I've no reason to think it would, but I can't categorically say no. I don't have to use lightning. I can just create a normal force field or one with other magic in it if you would prefer?"

Whatever you think best, Mistress, Mishtag sighed as though she had the entire weight of Idenvarlis on her shoulders.

The princess couldn't help but hear it. "Are you alright, Mishtag? What's troubling you?" Mishtag shook her head and turned away. "Please tell me, my friend." She moved closer and put her arms around her Kai.

I-I'm just a little concerned about going through the Silent Forest in this weather. I trust in you and your magical powers, but it is my job to protect you and I am worried about my ability to do that today.

"You know why I'm pushing so hard to make the journey in as short a time as possible. In addition, recognising the potential threat my uncle poses, how do we know he isn't on his way here, planning the same fate for me? I can understand your concerns though. Is this your way of telling me you don't want to make the journey through the forest today?"

I would not presume to tell you what to do. I can only say what is in my heart. I can understand all your reasons for wanting to push on and get to the Land of No Souls as quickly as possible. If you decide to go ahead, I will support your decision and do my utmost to protect you.

"Thank you, my friend. I have to go on regardless of the weather. Every single day is precious and brings me closer to my goal. I hope you understand my decision." She finished packing up, armoured and saddled the Blenorai, and mounted Mishtag. As soon as she lowered the barrier they began to run toward the forest.

They stopped just prior to entering the forest and Kailani put the domed force field around them and included lightning into it as she had when they went through the Lost Mire. Once she was satisfied, they began walking.

The forest was beautiful. Tall, majestic trees of a kind Kailani didn't know stood proudly, their tops in myriad shades of green reaching for the sky. Around the base of the trunks grew a luminous moss, glowing with a soft pale green light. Across the ground grew ferns, brackens, and a beautiful pink flower. She couldn't help wondering how all this grew on the ice when so much of her journey was barren of all but the sparsest plant life.

In between the rumbles of thunder, she could hear the sweet bird song all around her, but couldn't see any birds. They were either well camouflaged or too high up in the trees. *What a shame*, she thought. All around was an earthy smell mixed with pine and something sweet she didn't recognise. It had a calming effect on her and she breathed it in again deeply, enjoying the relaxation it induced.

Realising the scent affected her and her telepathy was weakened, the Blenorai Kai ran. It was the lure of the Silent Forest, making the beast's victims more pliable for when it attacked.

It took a while before the effects of the potent scent began to wear off, by which time the Blenorai had been running for two or three hours. Now it seemed Kailani was back to normal if her grip on the reins and Mishtag's telepathic connection to her was anything to go by.

A cloud of flying creatures swooped overhead, their thick, leathery wings making a clapping noise as they flapped. They disappeared behind them then came back as if for a second look at these strange creatures who were venturing through their forest. They flew up into the trees and Kailani could see a few of them as they perched, hanging upside down by their feet.

"What a strange breed of birds," she mused aloud staring at them with wonder.

They are not birds, Mistress, they are bats. They eat fruit and berries, but prefer mice or other small rodents, are often attracted to human blood, and will think nothing of biting you for a taste of yours. If they were given the opportunity to do so, you would be swamped and overwhelmed by them, and die from lack of blood as they could drain you almost completely.

A shudder ran down Kailani's spine at the thought. "Oh. I don't like the sound of that. Let's speed up a little, shall we?" The Kai did as she asked and they soon left the blood-thirsty bats behind them.

They stopped for lunch a couple of hours later in a pretty glade where a few pale lemon and white flowers grew in clumps between the trunks. She was about to pick one when Mishtag grabbed Kailani's sleeve between her teeth and yanked it away.

NO! she shouted in the princess's mind so loud it startled her. *You cannot touch anything in this forest, no matter how pretty it may look. There are many items here designed to attract the attention of people and even some animals, which are either poisoned or will dull your brain, anything which could make it easier for the beast to overcome you. Do you understand?*

"Yes, I do. It's a shame that items of such beauty are used in this way. Thank you for stopping me in time, Mishtag." She stroked her head in gratitude.

You are very welcome, Princess.

Kailani packed up the food bags and they got underway again. The storm had grown worse. The tree tops swayed in the wind, thunder stormed across the firmament almost continuously, and the lightning forked across the sky as if Baelris was venting his anger. In the forest they were fairly protected, the trees acting as a useful shelter against the worst of it.

The Blenorai raced through the trees, jumping over exposed roots or small rocks which were in their way. Suddenly lightning struck a tree just ahead and to the left of them. It split in half, the top crashed to the ground and burst into flames. Mishtag became nervous again and sped up, taking Yashtig by surprise who ran harder to keep up with his younger kinsman.

The noise of the thunder and lightning masked the silence which descended over the forest and the party didn't realise something was closing in on them. Another fork of lightning came down into the forest catching the edge of their force field and Mishtag's worst fears came to pass. The barrier disappeared taking the lightning with it. They were totally exposed and Kailani didn't even realise it.

Abruptly a huge creature landed directly in their path and the Blenorai ground to a halt, skidding on the floor. The beast had the face of a man and the body of a huge brown bear with massive paws. Its claws were extended and looked decidedly sharp. The paws were strange though, being a cross between hands and paws. Its legs were elongated and it had a long tail that constantly swished back and forth across the forest floor.

It wasn't until the beast began to move toward them that Kailani realised the force field was gone. It was too late to resurrect it; she wouldn't be able to before the beast was upon them. She dismounted and withdrew her Panas, the slim sword which could fire lightning bolts, and her Kamuk, the curve-bladed dagger.

It came forward on its back paws, towering above her, standing like a man, a look of anticipation on its face. It didn't appear in the least bit concerned by the weapons she held and even sneered when it saw them. Kailani held her ground and waited until it was within striking distance. The Blenorai were also standing on their hind legs, but the beast ignored them completely, intently focused on the princess as if nothing else existed around it.

It swung one of its paws as if to gather her up. Kailani ducked and struck a blow with her Panas on its wrist. It yowled as blood began to drip from the wound and the expression on its face turned to one of rage. The other paw swiped at her. This time she attacked before it got too close. Again the sword opened a deep wound on the arm. While she focussed on the one she was cutting, the other swung down. By chance she moved and it caught her on the back, its claws ripped through her clothing, leaving shallow scratches on her skin and knocking her to the floor.

She sprang to her feet like an acrobat. Now she was angry too, but her fury was concentrated, fixed on the beast and tightly controlled. Waiting to see what its next move would be, her eyes flicked back and forth. She took the opportunity to weigh up where its weak points might be. Suddenly its tail flicked around intending to knock her off her feet, but she saw it coming, jumped over it then ducked as one of the paws swiped toward her again and missed.

The princess began moving to the left, circling around the beast. It permitted her to get around to the side then lashed one of its paws backwards. Allowing it to catch her slightly, she fell forward with her blades extended and cut the tail off close to the body. Springing to her feet, she slashed at the beast's back with the serrated edge of the Kamuk and the Panas before it had the chance to turn.

The howl of pain echoed through the trees causing birds to take flight; so loud and high-pitched it could be heard over the thunder. While the creature was turning to face Kailani who had moved back out of reach of its paws, Mishtag and Yashtig moved in. The beast leapt forward on all fours, but the princess somersaulted, setting down a few feet away. As it landed, the Blenorai pounced on the creature's back, dug in their claws and started to rip into its flesh with their teeth. The beast started to turn over and the Kai jumped off and scampered back, well out of its reach.

As it rolled onto its back, Kailani pounced and landed with both feet on its stomach, sword raised. She was about to plunge it into the creature's chest when its paws grabbed her and lifted her up. It had a look of triumph in its eyes. The claws dug into her and she cried out in pain, but then she started laughing. Confusion crossed its face for a moment, but then its huge jaws opened, which were certainly not those of a man or bear. They kept going until the face could no longer be seen and its mouth was large enough to take the entirety of Kailani's head comfortably without straining.

She replaced the Kamuk on her belt then reached behind her, pulling out a Raisa, a ball of phoenix fire which, on contact, produced the heat of the sun. It fit neatly in her hand. She slashed at both arms until the claws let her go. Kailani bounced on the beast's stomach, using it as a springboard to somersault away from the body and threw the Raisa straight into its mouth.

"Take cover!" she yelled as she flipped a second time and took shelter behind the massive trunk of a tree close by. The creature shook and started to turn red and glow. It screamed in agony just before the ball exploded which cooked him from the inside out until there was nothing left but a pile of ashes.

The heat dissipated quickly, only scorching a few of the ferns and bracken on which the creature was lying. Kailani came out from behind the tree and ran over to where the Blenorai lay behind trunks.

"It's over," she said triumphantly, a big smile on her face hiding the pain of her wounds. The Kai rose and looked at her.

That is wonderful. However you are not out of danger yet, princess. You are wounded and bleeding. The smell will attract the bats and they will try to attack. You need to get a force field around us immediately as I fear they will not be so easy to despatch, Mishtag urged.

"Oh, I'd forgotten about them. You're quite right." She mounted her and immediately put the domed barrier around them. There had been no lightning since it had destroyed her previous one so she took a chance and weaved it into the shield. The thunder had quieted to a rumble and whilst the sky still roiled and the wind still blew, it seemed to be slowly moving away.

They set off again, slowly at first so Kailani could show them the ashes of the remains of the beast, before they began to pick up speed. Mishtag's assessment was spot on as it wasn't long before clouds of bats began swooping around them, trying to reach Kailani. They could smell her blood even through the force field and were slavering and determined to sink their fangs into her.

She concentrated hard on maintaining the force field surrounding and protecting them. Every bat that came too close received a shock from the lightning and spun away, only to be replaced by another. There were so many of them, it was like a black cloak draped over their barrier. The Blenorai weren't affected as the bats concentrated around Kailani. She weaved extra lightning into the barrier and noticed more bats falling away after receiving painful and near fatal shocks. She ramped up the power even more and each bat who came into contact with the shield suffered a lethal blast. Eventually the black cloud thinned as the rest finally realised they wouldn't be able to get to her, giving up after seeing so many of their kind wounded or killed by the protection surrounding the bleeding woman.

They continued through the forest, with the Blenorai running as fast as they could in the terrain, still having to jump over tree roots and rocks, but eventually the end was in sight. With relief they sped toward it and were relieved to come out the other side. The Kai knew the bats could follow them out of the forest so they kept going for at least another two hours until it was only a small blip in the distance.

Time slipped away more quickly than they realised whilst in the Silent Forest and the day was beginning to come to a close. They kept going until Kailani called them to a halt. By this time, her wounds were very painful and she was beginning to feel a little unwell. She removed the invisible force field and erected an ice barrier, weaving the remaining lightning into it. Creating a light for them to see by, larger than the one she usually made, she also put heat into it so it didn't take long before the space was quite cosy.

She fed and watered the Blenorai before thinking of herself. Stripping off her coat and top layers, she was surprised to see the extent of the injuries around her ribs where the beast dug its claws into her. The wounds were dirty, bloody, and quite deep. It was a miracle no internal organs had been damaged. She poured a little water into the now empty drinking bowl she used for the Kai and, using a clean handkerchief, began bathing the wounds and trying to get all the dirt out. It was a slow and very painful process as she had to put her finger into the deep holes. The princess winced every time she touched one of the wounds.

When she'd eventually cleaned all the dirt out, she grabbed the bottle of medicine and dabbed some on each of the wounds. The first time made her cry out and tears spring to her eyes. She gritted her teeth until all ten were done.

Just when she'd finished, she felt Mishtag behind her.

"What are you doing?" she asked curiously. The pain from the injuries she'd just been dealing with had put all thought of the ones on her back out of her mind.

You have some nasty scratches on your back which I think are out of your reach. I can clean them for you and help them heal, if you give me your permission.

"Of course you have my permission, but how . . .?"

Just please keep very still and you will see.

Kailani nodded, intrigued. Then she found out. Mishtag was licking her wounds. As soon as they were clean, she dribbled some of her spittle in each one.

You need to leave them open to the air for a while and if you need to lay down, you must do so on your stomach.

"I could feel most of what you did, but can you explain it to me, please?"

I licked them clean to get rid of all the dirt and then put some of my saliva in each of the gashes. The mucus in our mouths has healing properties. You would not have been able to do anything with them due to their position and they would have quickly become infected. We cannot afford for you to become ill so I did the only thing I could.

At first the princess felt a little repulsed, but then realised what Mishtag had done for her. "You won't become ill because of what you've done for me, will you?"

No. Our saliva protects us from infection when healing each other or a person, so do not worry.

"Thank you so much, Mishtag. I don't know what else I can say."

Your good health is thanks enough, my lady. Now you must eat and drink something. It will aid with your healing process.

"I am rather hungry and thirsty, but I also feel a little unwell." She began preparing her food anyway.

That is to be expected. You have had dirt in your wounds for some

time and they have become infected. I will check the gashes on your back
in the morning and you will need to check the ones you've been cleaning to
ensure there is no infection in them. You may have to treat them again in
the morning.

"I will. Thank you." Her food was ready and she ate it slowly, still only having half portions to ensure she had enough to give her mother a decent meal and keep her strength up for the long journey back. She drank some water then cleared up and put things away.

Reducing the heat a little, but enough to keep it warm during the cold night, she lowered the light until it was just a small ball, just big enough to cast a few shadows on the walls of the ice barrier. She laid her coat and pack on the floor and lay down on her stomach, falling into a restless sleep quite quickly.

A couple of hours later, the Blenorai were woken by a loud moaning. The princess was still lying on her stomach now covered by the blanket Mishtag and Yashtig between them had managed to pull over her. Mishtag came closer to her and saw beads of perspiration on her forehead. She put her paw on Kailani's exposed shoulder and realised she was burning with a fever. She told Yashtig the problem and together they pulled back the blanket. The gashes on her back were healing well and there was no sign of any infection. They deduced it must be from the wounds around her ribs. They turned her over extremely gently and inspected them. They noticed that whilst some were beginning to show signs of healing, others were displaying traces of infection.

There was only one thing they could do. They licked the infected ones, probing their tongues deep into the holes in the flesh until they were satisfied any remaining dirt and all signs of infection were gone. They then dribbled saliva into each of the holes they had worked on and left her uncovered for a while.

By agreement, they took turns alternately sleeping and watching Kailani. Her fever seemed to break a couple of hours before dawn and her skin returned to its normal temperature. Mishtag covered her over with the blanket again and slept.

Chapter 13

When Kailani eventually woke a couple of hours after dawn, she was surprised the Blenorai were still asleep. She felt unexpectedly weak, but didn't understand why. She ate some breakfast and drank some water, then inspected her wounds. She was astonished to see how much some of them had healed during the night while others were still extremely tender to the touch. She grabbed the cloth she'd used before and, finding a clean part, treated each of the tender ones with the same lotion as before. The pain shot through to her insides making her stomach roil and she had to grit her teeth so she didn't cry out and wake the Kai. She carefully got dressed in clean clothes, packed her bag, and left her coat on top of the packs.

The Blenorai woke a short while later and she fed them. Mishtag didn't say anything about what had happened the previous night.

How are you feeling this morning, my lady?

"In all honesty, a bit weak, but apart from that, I'm better than I expected to be."

Do you want to spend today resting to regain your strength?

"Rest? Absolutely not! Thank you for the thought, Mishtag, but we need to press on. We're so close to the Land of No Souls now. Do you and Yashtig need a rest?"

No, Princess. We are fit if you are.

"Fine. Let's get ready and go then." She pulled out the map and checked how close they were to their destination then put it away. She armoured and saddled the Blenorai, disposed of the light, mounted Mishtag and took down the barrier. The Kai didn't need telling, they ran and quickly reached their normal phenomenal speed.

Kailani looked around and up at the sky. It was such a different day; the breeze was light, the clouds were light grey and patchy, and the sun played peek-a-boo with them. The landscape was back to its normal barren self with the occasional clump of trees, but when the sun came out and glistened on the ice, she remembered why she had fallen in love with the country. The colours refracted by the ice were stunning and in other places it looked like a carpet of diamonds. It was breath-taking.

It was strange that after everything they'd gone through yesterday the weather should be so bright, almost as if it knew she needed something wonderful to gaze upon to lift her spirits and make her feel renewed.

The day seemed to whisk past and before they knew it, dusk began to fall. They carried out their normal routines, Kailani treated her wounds again, finding it almost as painful as she had that morning, and went to bed.

Just before they left the next morning, Kailani spoke to Mishtag. "We're quite close to our destination now so we must approach with care. I don't want anyone to see us as it will ruin my plans to get my mother out safely and with as little fuss as possible. If we can find a clump of trees to hide behind so I can observe them, that would be ideal, but there are none marked on the map."

Do you know where the border for the land is?

"My grandfather said I should be able to see it quite clearly. It's something to do with the magic he's put around the area to keep Gengaruk and his tribe there and prevent their escape."

So how do you wish to proceed, Princess?

"Slowly, cautiously. If my calculations are correct, we are approximately two hours away from the border. Even walking, it won't take very long to get there and we can check out the lay of the land as we approach."

That sounds a sensible way to go. If necessary, we can hold back at a safe distance so as not to give our position away.

"Absolutely. Shall we go then?"

As they moved closer, a strange mix of emotions assailed Kailani; excitement, fear, doubt, and nervousness all jockeyed for position. Her head was scrambled by it all, yet she could also be decisive. It felt completely weird and unnatural.

Mishtag had been gauging her mistress's state of mind and was not surprised to find it in such turmoil, but could do nothing to help unless she was asked. Kailani would just have to try and sort it out on her own.

When they were about half an hour away, the princess could see the outer marker of the boundary clearly. It was bright pink and like a transparent wall with the colour running through it. The camp had been set up quite close to the border and she could clearly see the most rudimentary shelters; tree branches with fabric thrown over it. Only one shelter was bigger and appeared in better condition than the others. It didn't take long for Kailani to realise what that material might be – perhaps it had come from her mother's dresses. She shivered at the thought of what Garalia might be wearing now, assuming she was still alive.

The princess was under no illusions as to what state her mother might be in, both mentally and physically. She just hoped and prayed to all her gods and goddesses that this journey had not been in vain.

Realising that if she could see the camp, they could probably see her, she lowered herself flat to the ground and gestured to the Blenorai to do the same. Wearing her mother's white coat and pulling the hood over her azure hair, she was now virtually invisible.

A clump of trees sat close to the camp. Kailani whispered to Yashtig and Mishtag, "We need to get to those trees, but it will have to be a slow process crawling on our bellies, so we don't attract attention. We'll have to move a little then stop for a few minutes and continue like that until we reach them. Alright?" The Blenorai both nodded. She began to crawl, wincing with every movement because of her injuries and once she'd covered a few feet, she stopped. The Kai were with her all the way and halted when she did.

Mishtag looked at the princess's face and saw the pain in her eyes. *Are you alright, Princess? You look rather uncomfortable.*

This time she answered with a tiny whisper, worried the sound might carry on the wind. "My wounds hurt with every movement I make," she admitted.

I already know of your courage and strength, Mistress, but you must be careful not to undo the good healing which has already begun. If that happens, it could hold you back for two or three days while they start to heal again. You will need all your strength once you enter that accursed land.

"I'm being careful. That's why I'm only moving short distances and I'm using the level of pain to tell me when to stop. I'm listening to my body and taking notice of what it tells me. Thank you for your concern, my dear friend. I really do appreciate it and your advice." She carefully reached over and stroked Mishtag's mane who flicked her eyes in Kailani's direction and saw her mistress smiling at her. She nodded her head but said nothing more.

After a few minutes of resting, they began to crawl again and when it became too much for Kailani they stopped. This continued over the next couple of hours until, at last, they reached the trees. It was a relief for the princess to be able to sit and take the pressure off her wounds. She had a quick check to ensure they hadn't gotten worse and was relieved to discover none had started bleeding again. This was a positive sign and she was extremely happy.

From where they hid, Kailani had a good view of the camp. There were a few people moving about, some carrying a few logs for the fire, a couple were skinning creatures they'd caught, and someone was stirring the huge pot hanging over the fire. This was the person the princess kept her eyes on most. The shapeless cloak hid the figure and with the hood up the hair couldn't be seen, making it difficult to tell the gender. However, cooking was considered by most men to be women's work.

Someone attracted the person's attention and as they turned the hood slipped off. Falling down the back was long, platinum-blonde hair. Kailani gasped then put her hands over her mouth. The hair was in poor condition, tangled, dull, and lifeless, but the sight of it gave the princess hope. The woman walked over to the men skinning the animals, took them and turned to go back to the pot. One look at the face and she knew it was her mother. She appeared extremely ill and it looked like every step she took was an effort. Her cheeks were sunken and she was far too thin, the rags that were once clothes nearly falling off her.

Although Kailani had prepared herself to see something like this, the reality of it shocked and horrified her. A small whine escaped Yashtig's throat as he saw his mistress in such a poor condition. The princess knew how he felt and could easily have cried an ocean of tears, but she held onto the fact that soon she would be getting her mother out of there – the first chance she had.

It seemed like it was going to come much sooner than expected. The men carrying the wood disappeared into one of the shelters and the two trappers stood and began to walk toward the rear of the camp. Only one man guarded Garalia, but he wasn't that close to her. He sat on a log and whittled at a piece of wood with a small knife, a large sword on the ground within easy reach. The bonus was the guard had his back to their position.

Kailani started to make a move. She rose and was about to slip out from behind the trees when Mishtag grabbed the hem of her coat and pulled her back. She looked questioning at her Kai who gestured with her paw. Kailani crouched down again and saw that two men had come out. She cursed under her breath as she settled down to wait.

As the smell of the food began to waft around the camp, more of them appeared with bowls in their hands. A large man exited the shelter decorated with her mother's dresses, his voice booming, "Is the food ready yet, woman?"

"Not quite. It'll only be a few minutes," she replied.

"Well, hurry up. I'm hungry!"

Garalia nodded and continued stirring the pot.

Kailani stared at the big man. *That must be Gengaruk*, she thought. *He looks evil. No wonder grandfather sent him here.*

"It's ready now." Her mother's voice drifted on the breeze. Gengaruk came over to the fire and knocked Garalia to the ground. He helped himself to the contents of the large pot and then all the others did the same. Only when all the men had taken what they wanted was she allowed to eat. She scraped the bottom of the pot and just about managed one scoop to put in her bowl. It was much less than everyone else had and Kailani's anger grew at the way her mother was being treated.

Once she had eaten her meagre dinner, she carefully removed the hot pot from over the fire. She added some logs and moved away, further into the camp. The men gathered around the fire and began singing songs, laughing, joking, and swigging from bottles which looked like wine.

If I wanted more proof that someone is supplying these animals with a few home comforts, this is it, she thought angrily. *That looks like the king's crest on those bottles, from what I can see from here. I need to get hold of one as proof.*

That might be easier than rescuing your mother, Mishtag replied.

Slowly, the men began to drift away to their shelters as the wine ran out. Gengaruk was the last to leave. Garalia was huddled on the ground with just a ratty-looking blanket over her just outside the fancy shelter. As Gengaruk passed, he grabbed her by her hair and dragged her inside. It seemed she was used to this as she didn't murmur. A great deal of grunting came from inside for quite some time and what sounded like some claps. When the noise abated, Kailani heard one loud bump as Garalia was thrown across the floor, landing just outside like a discarded toy, and told to stay there. She didn't even have the ratty blanket within reach. She gathered her cloak tightly around her and fell into an exhausted sleep.

Kailani erected a small barrier around them, making sure it didn't protrude from the trees. They couldn't afford to make a light so moved around in the darkness. It wasn't long before they'd eaten and were settled down for the night. The princess felt a rage burning in her that threatened to get out of control very quickly and it was a long time before she fell asleep.

The next morning, Kailani woke early. She treated her wounds once again, pleased to discover they were healing really well and as soon as she was dressed, dismantled the ice barrier. While she waited for the Blenorai to wake, she took the time to examine the camp more closely. It was nothing more than the most basic of tents held up by tree branches tied together and fabric draped over the top. She couldn't see how the material stayed where it was as it didn't seem to be fastened anywhere, but it was rather difficult to view from this angle.

Her mother was already up and stirring the same pot as the previous day. There were two men meandering aimlessly around the camp, bowls in hand, waiting for their breakfast. As before, when it was ready, Garalia called out and the men crowded in, almost trampling her underfoot. Gengaruk came striding from his shelter and told the others to back off a little. Again he knocked Garalia over in his haste to reach the food and fill his bowl.

The princess's portion was as pitiful as it had been the previous night. It was no wonder she was so thin and gaunt. It looked like she was eating a third or less than the others. Kailani wondered why she didn't have a little before she called out that the food was ready and then she realised what was likely to happen to her if she did. Her face appeared to be puffy around the cheekbones and lips, marks which had not been there the day before. Kailani realised what the clapping sound had been from the previous night and her rage, constantly bubbling under the surface, rose again and she hissed between her teeth. She dug her nails into the bark of the tree in front of her until her fingers began to bleed.

She hoped today would be the one where she could rescue her mother from this awful existence. It was in the lap of the gods and goddesses and she prayed to all the deities of both Taivass-maa and Idenvarlis.

A few minutes later, one of the empty wine bottles got kicked and it skidded across the ice landing just the other side of the trees. Kailani didn't dare touch it straight away in case it'd been seen and was missed. However, it could be the proof she needed for her grandfather. It was a sign the gods and goddesses were listening and trying to help her. She retrieved it after a short while and placed it in one of the packs.

As the day unfolded, she watched her mother being pulled, prodded, poked, kicked, and punched if she didn't respond quick enough to someone's request. Her heart ached so much for her mother's plight and with every cruelty Garalia suffered, tears would roll down Kailani's cheeks. The only thing that stopped her from rushing in there and breaking all their necks was the fact she was seriously outnumbered and if she got captured, it wouldn't do her mother any good at all. However, perhaps she could even things up and maybe get them distracted enough for her to grab her mother.

How would you go about evening things up?

Kailani didn't realise her thoughts were loud enough to be heard.

"Sneak into the camp at night and slit a couple of throats or stab them in the heart. They won't suspect anyone outside the camp, because as far as they know no one can enter *and* leave," she answered in a whisper.

I think we should speak telepathically. If the wind direction should change then the slightest noise from here could carry into the camp.

She agreed.

I will pass information to Yashtig, so do not worry about that. I cannot say whether your idea is a good one or possibly fraught with disaster. The fact they cannot leave would likely point the finger to someone in the camp. However, what we do not know is whether anything of this kind has happened in the last twenty years. If it has then it will not be such a shock to them. But... Mishtag paused for emphasis. *But if it has not occurred then questions are likely to be asked as to why murders are suddenly being committed now. It could well make them cautious to the point that rescuing your mother will become impossible.*

Good point. I don't want to do anything that would arouse suspicion. The only bargaining chip they have is my mother so security around her might tighten. I'll have to wait until an opportunity presents itself, but seeing how mother is being treated is tearing me apart. It's taking every bit of my self-control not to just charge into the camp, kill a few of them and get mother out of there. Kailani clenched her fists.

Yashtig and I feel the same way. We can fully understand how difficult it must be for you to watch their barbarity. You must feel quite helpless.

Helpless and guilty, she admitted with downcast eyes.

Why guilty? You have done nothing to feel guilty about.

Precisely. I have done nothing to release her from her captors – that's why I feel guilty.

Mishtag rubbed her head against her side and placed a paw on Kailani's arm, but said no more.

It took another three painful days of watching her mother suffer at the hands of the brutes before a chance came along. Kailani didn't hesitate. Without saying anything to the Blenorai, she slipped out from their hiding place and, staying low to the ground, crept up behind the guard. Quietly pulling the Kamuk from her belt, she slit the man's throat. He fell back and she wiped the blade on his clothes before hanging it back on her belt. She smoothly removed the Panas and drove it quickly through his heart.

She stood and ran over to the woman, who by now had moved a little closer, a curious look in her eyes. "Garalia?" she asked.

The woman nodded. Kailani grabbed her hand and began pulling her toward the force field. "I-I can't go through," she whispered in a defeated tone.

"You can with me. Trust me!" Garalia nodded then stumbled. Despite her injuries, Kailani scooped her mother into her arms and moved as quickly as she could toward the barrier. They were only a couple of feet away when a man came out of his shelter and saw what was happening. He shouted and then ran toward them. He was much faster than Kailani and was catching up to them rapidly. With a huge effort and burst of energy she didn't know she had in reserve, she sped up and just managed to get through the barrier before he caught them. However, he did manage to grab a lock of Garalia's hair and was pulling it hard, trying to get her back through. Kailani put her mother down, swung her blade and cut the hair very close to the man's fingers, so close that she actually nicked two of them and he began to shout obscenities at her.

By this time, everyone in the camp had crowded around the barrier looking at them. Pushing his way to the front was a large, imposing man she recognised as Gengaruk.

"You have made a very grave mistake taking our slave from us and you will pay with your life." His voice and eyes were filled with a cold fury.

She steadied her mother, putting her arm around her waist and faced him. "If anyone has made the grave mistake it is you, Gengaruk. To kidnap a member of the royal family is the most serious crime anyone could commit. I will see to it that *you* pay with *your* life and the traitor in the Ice Palace too." Her fury exceeded his and he could hear the steel core in her tone.

"Ha ha ha. That's what you think. He won't be found, he's too clever." The smug look on his face just served to fuel her fury further.

"You misguided idiot." Kailani turned her back on Gengaruk and picked her mother up again. The two Blenorai came out from behind the tree and ran up to them. She lowered her mother down in front of Yashtig and she made a big fuss of him. The Kai was just as excited to see his mistress and began lapping at her face. Garalia giggled, probably for the first time in twenty-one years.

"And who are you to say these things to me?" Gengaruk demanded.

Kailani lowered her hood and stared at him, head held high. "I am

Princess Kailani, daughter of Princess Garalia, and granddaughter of King Jaanis and Queen Shivla, not that it's any of your business. Unless my traitorous uncle has already left the Ice Palace on his way here, I wouldn't expect any more packages of food, wine, and whatever else he brings if I were you." She turned her back on Gengaruk and his men and knelt beside her mother.

"Kailani? My little Kailani all grown up?" Tears of joy cascaded down her face and she opened her arms. Her daughter slipped in and they embraced, crying. It was the moment Kailani had been waiting for all her life and she clung to her, being careful not to squeeze too hard. Eventually the tears began to dry and Kailani pulled away a little.

"Mother, we need to get you back to the Ice Palace as quickly as possible. You need medicine and things I don't have with me. Are you strong enough to travel on Yashtig?"

"I think so." She climbed on. Kailani took off her coat and put it on Garalia. "Goodness, I'd forgotten what good fabric felt like, and as for warmth . . ."

As she pulled her blue cloak from the pack and fastened it around her neck, she said, "We're only going a short way, Mother, just far enough that you don't have to look back and see this." She gestured over her shoulder. "Is that alright with you?"

"Yes, of course, my dearest. I'm happy to leave you in charge."

"As soon as we stop, you're going to eat a nutritious, hot meal, have a drink, and change out of those rags into something more fitting for the heir to the throne of Idenvarlis."

They stopped two hours away. She erected an ice barrier, filled it with warmth from the light she made and set about making her mother more comfortable. The first thing she did was heat up a can of food. She passed it to her mother who accepted it gratefully. Garalia struggled to finish the whole can because her stomach had shrunk so much, but in the end she managed it. She had a drink of water and then her daughter pulled out the clothes she'd been saving for her mother; thick underwear, her riding clothes, and boots.

Garalia caressed each item. They felt so soft unlike the rags she was wearing. Kailani helped her change, using the lotion on any injuries she had sustained and began to gently run her brush through the tangled mess her hair had become.

"Mother, I'm sure you have hundreds of questions for me and I'll do my best to answer them, but what made you think you couldn't leave the camp? You're not wearing the bangles the others did." Her voice was gentle and encouraging.

"I was told that once I crossed the barrier into the Land of No Souls, there was no way back and I believed them."

"Hmm, I thought it might be something like that."

"The one thing I can't understand is why Bellis would do this to me. I thought he and I were so close. I loved him dearly. We always spent most of our days together except when father sent him or me on official business. What made him turn on me and leave me in that dreadful place?"

"The only reason I could come up with was that he was jealous of you being the firstborn and wanted the throne for himself. That is quite a powerful motivator, if you think about it."

"Perhaps you're right." She seemed thoughtful.

"I've done the best I can for now. At least you look more like a princess now. Are you ready to continue the journey back to civilisation and home?"

"Absolutely!" Garalia smiled.

Before her mother could say anything further, Kailani said, "Before we leave, I want you to promise me something. If you're feeling tired and want a break, you say so. Promise?"

She looked into her daughter's eyes and smiled. "I promise."

Kailani nodded and packed everything back into the bags. She distributed the weight more evenly between the two Blenorai, disposed of the light, and dropped the ice barrier. The two women mounted up and set off.

It took an extra day to reach the Silent Forest due to the more regular stops, but Kailani could see the improvement already. Garalia had lost a little of the gauntness from her face and traces of her former beauty were beginning to shine through.

Due to the size of the forest and the time of day they arrived, Kailani put up the ice barrier, making the decision to stay there for the night. Because of the bats, she also constructed a lattice type top to protect them further.

"I see you have become quite adept at using your magic, my darling. What with the barriers and your light-come-warming device from Taivassmaa, I have to say I'm very impressed." Garalia smiled.

Kailani felt her cheeks grow warm. She squeezed her mother's hand but didn't reply. She prepared the food, ensuring that her mother had a full portion to herself while only having her normal half portion. She could see the food was likely to run out before they met up with the battalion.

"Mother, we will not have quite enough food to last us until we meet up with the battalion. I may have to do some hunting. As you know this land much better than I, can you point out to me what is edible and what isn't, please?"

"Of course. I'll do anything I can to help. I fear travelling through the Silent Forest. I take it you've heard the stories?"

"Well, unless there's more than one beast in the forest, we don't have to worry about that anymore. I slew him on my way through to get you! When I left, it was nothing more than a pile of ashes on the ground." She chuckled at the look of astonishment on Garalia's face.

"Was that the only creature you encountered on your journey?"

"Goodness, no. Far from it. But each was despatched to its maker without too many injuries for me. The worst of them came from the beast in the Silent Forest."

"Are you fully recovered, my dear?" Garalia's eyes mirrored the concern in her voice.

"No, but I'm well on the way. I fear I will be scarred for life. However, it is a small price to pay to have you safe and out of the clutches of that scum," Kailani replied. She smiled, the joy lighting up her face.

Garalia put her hands on Kailani's shoulders, and said, "My daughter, the warrior princess. I cannot thank you enough for rescuing me, my darling, and I'm so proud of the woman you've become."

Kailani's cheeks glowed warm and her eyes teared up. "Thank you, Mother. You don't know how much that means to me." She looked up and saw a pair of teary eyes looking back at her. They both laughed and Garalia gathered her daughter into her arms. After a few minutes, they broke apart. "Getting back to our original conversation, will you be able to guide me as to what I can hunt or pick and what I can't, please?"

"Yes. There must be quite a bit in the Silent Forest."

"Good. However, as you are wounded, the bats will come after you as they have a keen smell for blood. You will have to go through with a force field around you which I will lace with lightning for extra protection. I will have the same, but can lower it to hunt or harvest food and then put it back up again."

"Lightning? In the shield?" Her brows raised and eyes widened.

"Yes," she chuckled. "It's from father's side. I have all the magic of Taivass-maa plus that of Idenvarlis. I've learnt to combine the two when needed."

"Ingenious. Clever as well as beautiful and brave. Are there no ends to your talents?"

"Probably. Father and grandfather Jaanis will undoubtedly say I'm defiant, strong-willed, and possibly reckless."

Garalia laughed. "You get those traits from me, I'm afraid."

"That's good to know. I seem to have more of your traits than father's." She grinned.

"I'm not so sure. You certainly get your bravery from him . . ." she trailed off, stifling a yawn.

"Come, Mother. You need some rest. I suggest you snuggle up to Yashtig as he will help keep you warm. It's what I do with Mishtag. We have the rest of our lives to talk."

"It feels like there's a little role reversal going on here." Her tone was light with a hint of amusement. However, she did what her daughter said.

"There is, for now. When you're back to full strength you can boss me around, but until then . . ." She knelt beside her and kissed her cheek. "Goodnight, Mother."

"Goodnight, my darling," she said sleepily with her eyes closed. Within seconds, she was sound asleep.

Kailani dimmed the light, but kept some of the heat, curled up with Mishtag, and casting a glance at her mother, smiled as she closed her eyes.

Chapter 14

At the threshold of the Silent Forest they halted. Kailani put the force field around her mother and Yashtig, lacing in lightning, and then a separate one around herself and Mishtag. The skies were clear and the sun had come out, unlike Kailani's last foray into the forest, for which she was very grateful.

They moved at a steady walking pace. Garalia turned her head from one side to the other admiring the scenery as well as looking for edible plants. The forest looked completely different. The rays of the sun pierced the arboreal canopy causing fingers of light to dance across the carpet of ferns and bracken. All the colours were more vivid and instead of being a place to be feared, the forest became a restful haven of beauty.

Kailani was still cautious, not only because of the bats. She felt like they were being almost seduced into a false sense of security. Was it possible a second beast was hiding in the foliage? Maybe the mate of the first one? She had no way of knowing, but felt a little uneasy just the same.

Garalia pointed out some fruit and berries they could eat and some smallish creatures which could be roasted over a fire. Kailani lowered her shield, and grabbed her Plexan; she knocked an arrow, took aim, and fired at one of the creatures. It lay motionless on the ground with the arrow protruding from its body. The others scattered, but they weren't as quick as Kailani's shooting ability. She managed to get four and filled her pack with the fruit and berries. She felt a bit more confident about the food situation now and it was one less thing for her to worry about.

As she mounted Mishtag again, Kailani raised her barrier, checked both force fields, and then asked the Blenorai to start running. There was no need to dawdle any longer. She regularly checked on her mother, but she seemed to be coping fine. Earlier she had made Garalia promise to say if she needed to stop and rest, but currently she was sitting fairly tall on Yashtig and appeared to be enjoying every moment. She was gazing around and had a smile on her face that would lighten even the darkest of corners.

Looking ahead Kailani saw a dark mass flying toward them. She checked both shields, finding they held strong. She called out to Garalia. "Mother, there are a cloud of bats coming toward us. Don't be afraid, the force field will deal with them."

Her mother looked forward and saw the black shape heading straight for them. She lowered herself over Yashtig and held the reins tighter. They swooped down and smothered the pair of them, mainly concentrating on Garalia. Kailani noticed her mother's eyes grow wide and saw the fear within them.

"Don't be afraid, Mother. It'll be fine. Look what happens to them when they get too close," Kailani called, trying to reassure her.

Garalia looked at her daughter and saw a grin on her face, so she looked up a little and saw how each bat was zapped by the lightning in the shield and fell away. This happened repeatedly and slowly her shoulders relaxed a little and she sat up a bit straighter in the saddle. It didn't take long before the bats moved away and she breathed a sigh of relief.

"That was an ingenious use of both sets of magic. Well done, Kailani."

"Thank you. I came up with the idea before we went through the

Lost Mire and as that was so successful, I used the same combination coming through here last time."

"But you got injured fighting the beast so what happened?"

"The day was stormy, lightning hit the shield and it went down, taking both lots of magic out of it. I knew I wouldn't be able to get the force field back up in time so I had to fight. It was one of those strange incidents that would be unlikely to occur again. Mishtag had a bad feeling that morning and actually asked me what would happen if lightning struck the barrier.

"Looking back now, I think I was meant to fight the beast and defeat it. Maybe the gods and goddesses were testing my mettle to see whether I would face the challenge or cringe away like a coward. If that was the case, perhaps they were also testing me to see how I would react to sustaining injuries and if I would take time out to recover or press on with my goal. Despite Mishtag wanting me to take a day and rest, I refused as I was determined to continue and get to the Land of No Souls as quickly as possible."

"Maybe they were testing you, but it sounds like you acquitted yourself marvellously. Was it only me that drove you on despite everything?"

"Yes, Mother. As soon as I arrived in Idenvarlis, I had a very strong instinct of where I would find you. I knew it would be in the East and when I found out a little more about the day of your disappearance, everything came together in my mind. I puzzled out it must have been Gengaruk's men who had taken you, where you were being held prisoner, and that's when I told grandfather I intended to find you. We had a little argument, but eventually reached a compromise that I would agree to a battalion of soldiers accompanying me part of the way and then I'd go on alone. My argument was that Gengaruk and his men would hear them coming from quite a distance away and make him wary and that I would have a better chance going on alone. He agreed as he could see the sense in my argument."

"So you came part way with them?"

"Absolutely not! I snuck away in the middle of the night while everyone was sleeping and left grandfather a note. I must have had at least a four or five hour lead on them and there was no way they would close the gap unless they travelled all night. I told grandfather I wanted to go alone and that's exactly what I did."

Garalia laughed until she had tears running down her face. "Oh, you're so like me! That's exactly the sort of thing I would have done."

"You haven't heard the best of it yet," Kailani said, grinning wickedly.

"Uh-oh. Let's hear it."

She told her mother what her father had said and what she'd done, finishing with, "I left father a note though."

"Oh dear. You *are* going to be in trouble."

"I don't think so, because we will be walking into the Ice Palace side by side and when both father and grandfather see I've rescued you, I think I'll be forgiven for everything."

"You have a point there. What was my parents' reaction to seeing you?"

"At first they were shocked when I told them who I was, but after an initial wariness they welcomed me with open arms. I also had your ring which gave them more proof. Uncle Bellis was much more reserved though. I knew he was hiding something and that he was less than pleased to see me, but I didn't know why. Then I began to piece it together. What are the succession rules in Idenvarlis?"

"The oldest child takes the throne. If they cannot, for whatever reason, any offspring of that child becomes next in line. If there are no children, then the oldest sibling becomes heir. Why?"

"Well, that explains quite a lot about the way Bellis acted toward me. Having got you out of the way, he became the heir. That is, until I showed up. I wonder what plans he has in store for me? He can't dump me in the Land of No Souls – he heard grandfather say he would give me a bangle to make me immune so I could get you out. I guess the only option left open to him is to have me assassinated," she said in a disdainful tone.

"Don't underestimate him, Kailani. He and I were so close growing up and yet he did this to me. He put me through twenty years of purgatory and mocked me every time he showed up at the camp. He would have no qualms whatsoever about trying to dispose of you." There was a deep sadness in her eyes and voice, but also an edge of something else which Kailani couldn't quite make out.

"Oh, I won't. But he shouldn't underestimate me either. With the powers I have along with my exceedingly strong instincts which have never let me down yet, he doesn't stand much of a chance. Besides, when we reach the Ice Palace and present grandfather with the evidence of his betrayal, do you honestly think Bellis is going to be put in a position where he could get to either of us?"

"No, that's true, but he must have accomplices. What about them?"

"Tell me something. Am I right in thinking I get the strong instincts from you?"

"Yes, why?"

"Because when you have regained all your strength, I think between us we could weed out any accomplices in the palace. I suspect some of the guards have been coerced by him. It's possible one or more have been chosen for the battalion who were supposed to go with me and should be waiting for us at the halfway mark between the palace and the Land of No Souls.

"I understand if your instincts aren't up to their normal strength bearing in mind everything that's happened to you, but if you have the slightest inkling of something being wrong on our journey back, please tell me in case I haven't picked it up myself. I can then protect us with barriers interwoven with the powers I have from Taivass-maa." Kailani sat straighter in her saddle.

"Darling, I'm concerned by how over-confident you are. You're not invincible. You're flesh and blood just like your father and I. Yes, you have an abundance of gifts from both sides of the family, but your first journey through this forest should have taught you a valuable lesson. You thought you were safe, but you weren't and you have the wounds to prove it. Anything can suddenly interfere with our magic, as the lightning did that day with you, and if the gods and goddesses believe we are taking our gifts for granted or misusing them, they can take them away without prior notice and you won't know until you try to use it and find it's not there."

"I'm not taking my magic for granted, Mother, nor do I intend to do anything which would entice the gods and goddesses to relieve me of my gifts. Some of my confidence is bravado to be honest, but I do believe that together we have a good chance of rooting out the evil that Bellis has snaking through the palace."

"You may be right and it's certainly worth trying. I fear it's going to take quite a bit of time before I am recovered enough to even consider it. Right now I'm running on adrenalin. I'm seeing sights I've never seen before, I'm free of Gengaruk, I'm back riding my beautiful Yashtig, and best of all, I'm with my wonderful daughter who I feared I would never see again. But this adrenalin rush won't last forever – it might only last a few hours, if that – and then I'll be as weak as a new-born once again." Her voice went from happy to resigned in just a few words.

Kailani smiled gently. "I'm prepared for that, Mother. I even have things with me to help should you have trouble holding onto Yashtig's reins. They may only be rudimentary, but sometimes it's the simplest of things that make all the difference. Now, shall we stop for lunch?"

After they had eaten, they resumed their journey through the Forest. They hadn't gone far when a deathly silence descended. Kailani told the Blenorai to slow down then looked all around.

"What's the matter? Why have the birds stopped singing?"

"Don't you know about the Silent Forest, Mother?"

"Oh, yes, of course. Is there another beast then?"

"It would seem so. That's why I need to be on my guard." She checked the force fields and they were holding strong. Lacing more lightning into them for extra protection, she drew her Panas from its scabbard, just in case.

A rustling in the bushes to her left drew her attention. A creature that had dark-brown, wrinkled skin, was a bit smaller than the Blenorai with spikes on its back, a protruding snout with tusks either side, and strangely shaped hooves, charged out and headed straight for them. Garalia cried out in alarm when she saw the ugly beast barrelling toward Kailani.

"Don't worry, Mother. The shield should protect us and if not, I have a few tricks up my sleeve."

The creature hit the barrier and received a large shock for its trouble. It bounced back, landing on its rump. It squealed then rose and, putting its head down, charged again. It received the same painful payment, screeching loudly as it was repelled. Obviously an unintelligent animal, it didn't give up and tried a third, fourth, and fifth time, and each time it received a shock, its screams became louder. Kailani checked the force field again and, satisfied, told the Blenorai to speed up. She was bored with this game.

The beast chased them for a little while, but being unable to match the pace of the Kai, gave up and slinked off back into the undergrowth. A few minutes later, the birds began to sing again and the forest reverted to a calm and wondrous place. Kailani sheathed her sword and checked the sky.

"We need to reach the other side before twilight Mishtag, Yashtig, so can we go even faster, please?" The Blenorai responded immediately and increased their speed until the trees were almost a blur. She turned to her mother and saw she was coping extremely well considering how weak she was. She'd lowered her body until she was almost lying flat over Yashtig, gripping the reins tight.

Two hours later, they burst from the forest, but kept going for another mile or two at least, by which time the sky was a mixture of reds, oranges, purples, and violets. The sunset was breathtaking and while admiring it, they stopped and made camp for the night.

Garalia looked exhausted. She ate her food a little quicker than she had her previous meal, had her drink then curled up on the ground and went straight to sleep. Yashtig positioned himself around his mistress to keep her warm then closed his eyes. It wasn't too much longer before Kailani followed suit.

During the next few days, all they saw was ice as far as the horizon with the odd sparse clump of trees dotted here and there. It gave mother and daughter a chance to become more acquainted. Kailani told her what it was like growing up in Taivass-maa. Forgetting her mother had been there, she described the castle, the cloud landscape, her Feegle, the town, skippers, and told her all about her two best friends, Leda and Auriga. She spoke at length about her grandfather, Aunt Konstellia, and, of course, her father. When Garalia heard Galaxan still loved her, and had never given up hope that one day they would be reunited, tears flooded her eyes and began to cascade down her cheeks. At first Kailani thought they were tears of joy until she noticed the anguish on her face.

"Mother? What's wrong? I thought you'd be happy to know that father hasn't even looked at another woman." Her confusion was matched only by her compassion.

"The only thing that kept me going in the Land of No Souls was the hope that I would be rescued and be able to see you and your father again. But I'm sullied, dirty, damaged. Your father wouldn't want me now knowing that all this time I've been forced into fornicating with other men. Some of the disgusting things they made me do is sickening by any normal person's standards." The pain in her eyes and voice was heart-breaking. "I love you both so much, but I know my marriage to Galaxan is over. He won't take me back when he knows what I've done."

"I think you underestimate him. Listening to what you just said, the important word here is 'forced'. You did none of these things because you wanted to, you were *forced* into those acts and you did what you had to do to survive. I'm pretty sure that once father gets over the shock of what you've been through, he will welcome you back into his arms and gave you all the support you need to heal. I'm not judging you for what you've just told me."

"Thank you, darling. I truly hope you're right about your father."

"I understand, Mother, and I'll do everything I can to help. In the meantime, I've told you so much about me, it's your turn now. What was it like growing up in the Ice Palace?"

Garalia spoke at length about all the things she used to get up to as a child, usually with Bellis in tow, the tricks they used to play on members of staff, and occasionally their parents. She told Kailani about how she first discovered the passage between their worlds and used it for the first time, how startled her father was by her sudden appearance that he literally fell off his chair, how she fell for Galaxan on sight, their romance, and secret wedding. Her eyes went dreamy as if she were reliving the moment. She told of their joy when she found out she was pregnant, the plans they made, how excited they both were, and how she had to hide it from her father.

It was a very awkward situation and she prayed that if her waters broke, it happened in her room and not in front of her mother or father. As luck would have it, she went into labour when in Taivass-maa and delivered the baby there. Because she wanted to nurse Kailani herself, keeping her existence secret in the Ice Palace was difficult. She explained how supportive Chilali had been; her maid was the only one she had confided in. Garalia's eyes suddenly became hooded and her expression dark. It was such a huge and abrupt change that Kailani was immediately concerned. Her mother continued with her account.

Tears flowed from her eyes as she explained how she felt leaving Kailani behind – even though she knew it was the safest place for her to be – and the love of her life, Galaxan. It took every bit of strength she possessed to enter the passage and return to Idenvarlis. Chilali was there to dry her tears and get her ready in time.

She recalled the day of her capture with startling clarity. How she'd fought to get away, how painful and undignified the journey was, and her horrified reaction to the sight of the camp. Finally she spoke of her first encounter with Gengaruk. She'd been pushed through the barrier into his waiting arms and he'd grinned at her in a lascivious way which made her stomach churn. Gengaruk issued orders that her bag was to be taken to his quarters, spoke a few words to her captors, and then picked her up and took her to his shelter.

By now Garalia was sobbing.

"Mother, you don't have to continue. I've got a pretty good idea what happened from then onwards just by what I witnessed while we waited for the opportunity to rescue you. It was three or four days of constantly watching the camp before my chance came. I saw how you were treated and it not only made my blood boil, it also made me sick to my stomach. You don't have to say anymore."

"I know you can guess what happened, but I need to say it, to get it out of my system or it'll drive me mad. It won't make for pleasant hearing, my dear, and for that I apologise in advance, but I need to vocalise it." Garalia was fervent in her response and Kailani couldn't do anything but encourage her. If that's what her mother needed to do, she would listen and try her hardest not to be sick. She really didn't want to hear it though.

"If that's what you need to do, I'm here to listen. Just promise me that if it gets too upsetting for you you'll stop. You don't need to tell me everything today, we've still got a few days before we meet up with the battalion."

"Yes, I promise. In return I want you to realise that my tears are a release of twenty years of oppression, brutality, and abuse. I'll tell you what I can about how I was repeatedly raped on my first night." Kailani nodded her head and steeled herself for what was to come.

Garalia started talking again, slowly at first, and then it gushed out of her. She began by describing what happened to her that first day in Gengaruk's shelter. First he'd tried to kiss her, but she kept turning her face away. He grabbed her painfully around the chin and held her face. She bit his lip and drew blood. He slapped her face and threw her onto the floor. With her arms tied behind her back, the pain was excruciating and she couldn't help but cry out. He untied her feet while she was dazed and ripped her undergarments from her, leaving them in rags on the floor, and positioned himself between her legs.

Gengaruk then started to unlace her bodice, all the time grinning in a lustful way. Pulling the dress open at the top, he freed her breasts and began to squeeze them hard. He lowered his head and bit her nipples and her breasts until she was crying in pain. Loosening his britches, he freed his erect manhood, and spreading her apart rammed his penis into her, making her cry out again.

Garalia stopped to draw breath and began again haltingly. Kailani could see how upsetting it was for her to speak of it and didn't want her to continue, but she sensed her mother's need so she remained silent.

After he'd orgasmed, Garalia had thought that was the end of her ordeal, but it was only just beginning. He roughly turned her over and entered her from the rear, whipping her buttocks with a belt until she screamed for mercy. Next he put her on her side and entered again, this time squeezing her breasts so hard she thought they might explode under the pressure. Her voice was a monotone as she continued.

The nightmare continued for hours with him having short rests in between for food and water. She was given nothing. By the time he'd finished with her that first day, she was bloody, bruised, and in pain all over her body.

It wasn't until the next morning she was given anything to eat and drink and that was dry bread and a little water. After she'd eaten, Gengaruk told her what her life would be like in the Land of No Souls.

Not being allowed to change her clothes or even put any underwear on, she was put to work immediately.

Gengaruk rifled through her clothes and made her unpick the stitching on her dresses so he could use the material on his shelter. All she was allowed to keep was one set of her underwear and a cloak. He even took the blanket she was wrapped in when she arrived and gave her a rough one that was on his bedroll.

As the days continued, he used her body at nights to satisfy his perverse sexual cravings and the nights he didn't want her, she was passed around to the other men who took it in turns to add to her degradation. She was made to sleep on the ground outside Gengaruk's shelter, regardless of the weather, and if she was really lucky she would stay in the shelter of whichever man had used her that night. During the day, she made them food and was instructed by Gengaruk to serve everyone else first before eating herself. The men all wanted their bowls filled almost to the top and sometimes came back for second helpings. If she was lucky, her portion was between half and a third of what they had. Sometimes, she was left with just the dregs in the bottom of the large cooking pot and went hungry until the next meal. No matter how much extra she tried to fit in the pot to give her a bit more, it always worked out the same. She never once had a full portion of anything.

She was used as their slave in every sense of the word and if she was too slow doing something or she gave one of them a look they didn't like she would get a backhanded slap across the face or punched. The men thought it was great sport to deliberately knock into her, elbow her as she walked past, or trip her up. On those occasions, there would always be an extra couple of kicks, slaps, or punches to go with it.

The first time Bellis showed up at the camp, her heart soared. He had found her and would take her home, away from this life of misery, indignity, and pain. Her hopes were dashed within a few minutes of his arrival. Bellis's true evil came out, shattering her heart.

He turned his back on her and had a conversation with Gengaruk. "So, my friend, how are you finding your new slave?"

"It took time to whip her into shape, but she's doing alright, better in some departments than others." He made a lewd gesture which left no one in any doubt he was talking about sex. "Isn't she lads?" There were nods and shouts of agreement.

"Good. Well, although this wasn't the original plan, I told you she would be yours to do with as you wished. I'm glad you've taken me up on the offer, in every way." Bellis had smiled broadly and winked, which was met with crude laughter.

His visits were quite frequent over the years and each time he came, he taunted her about her appearance and how low she'd fallen. Every hurtful word was another wound to her heart. If she tried to avoid seeing him when he turned up, he would always ask to see her so he could torment her some more. In the end, her heart grew hardened to his painful words and she ignored him when he visited.

And so her life went on, every day virtually the same until Kailani had shown up and whisked her away.

Garalia had tears pouring from her eyes as she told her story and several times when the emotion got too much, Kailani would ask the Kai to stop and she would put her arms around her mother and comfort her. When she was calm enough to continue, they got underway again.

By the time she'd finished, her eyes were puffy and red; she kept looking over her shoulder, and was distraught.

Kailani was filled with anger and hatred for Gengaruk and his men, but most of all for Bellis. She vowed to all the gods and goddesses of both lands that she would exact revenge, one way or another, on them all, or die trying.

Chapter 15

They had camped just outside the Lost Mire and the mountains were visible on their right. Kailani had woken early and begun to organise breakfast before the others stirred. She hoped her mother didn't sleep in late as they needed all day to reach the far side of the mire.

The Blenorai rose first. Yashtig's movements woke Garalia and they were able to despatch the first meal of the day quite quickly. Kailani packed everything up and lowered the barrier.

"What is this ahead of us?" Garalia stared at the high reeds curiously.

"It's the Lost Mire."

"Please tell me we're not going through it. We'll never find our way out again." Concern and fear laced her tone.

"Mother, it's fine, don't worry. We came through the Lost Mire on our way here and it wasn't a problem. All we have to do is tie Mishtag and Yashtig together so we don't get separated. Plus I have a little trick to help us through." Kailani smiled.

"Are there any creatures in there?"

"Yes, but again, it's nothing for you to worry about. My lightning enforced shield takes care of them."

"I trust you so I suppose we'd better make a start."

They reached the edge of the Lost Mire. Kailani tied the Kai together as she had before. She closed her eyes and muttered under her breath, producing a light in her hands. Continuing to speak a spell, she threw one part over the top and when she felt it land, she placed the other part on the ground where they stood. Mounting Mishtag, she created the force field and wove the lightning into it.

"Now we're ready to go," she said, turning to smile at Garalia.

"Ingenious. I'm guessing we just follow the light to get to the other side?"

"Yes. You might want to stay quite low over Yashtig's back as the reeds tend to spring back and hit you, as I found out the hard way last time. Shall we?" Garalia nodded and they entered at a run.

They had been running for about two hours when the Blenorai slowed and began to growl. Kailani checked the force field and, satisfied it was strong enough, asked them to continue. She checked the light overhead and they were still on track. A few minutes later, their snarling got louder and they were staring straight ahead.

"What have they seen?" Garalia asked, her voice nervous.

"I don't know. I'll ask Mishtag."

"What do you mean, 'you'll ask Mishtag'? You don't speak their language do you?"

"No. Mishtag and I have a telepathic link so we can communicate with each other. It's a Taivass-maa thing – I'll explain more later."

"I've heard it all now. You never cease to amaze me, Kailani."

"In a good way I hope."

Her mother laughed and nodded.

Mishtag? What is up ahead?

We're not sure yet, but it stinks like a rotting corpse.

I would bet it's those creatures we saw on the way through last time, the ones with webbed feet and a small snout. I would guess that once they see it's us, they'll remember what happened to them last time.

I hope you're right!

We'll see in a moment.

They continued on and sure enough, they had reached the small clearing where those creatures dwelled. Immediately the larger one dropped his head and charged. As soon as he came into contact with the barrier, he bounced off. The smell of burnt fur filled the air around them and a mewling sound could be heard.

"Stupid animal! You'd think they would've learned from before."

"What is it?"

"I have no idea what it's called, but both of them tried to attack us when we came through last time. And they weren't the only ones. You'll see the others further on." Kailani was quite relaxed about it which reassured her mother even more. She checked the force field then the light, pleased to see it directly above them. She urged the Blenorai on and they increased their speed.

A couple of hours later they had a brief stop for lunch before getting underway again. The light was slightly to the side of them and Kailani guided them back. "A little more to the right... just a bit further... now straighten up... Great. Well done! We're back on course now."

The Blenorai raced away, charging through the reeds, somehow managing to stay pretty much on course. Garalia learnt the hard way to stay low over Yashtig despite Kailani's warning; it was a lesson she didn't need twice. In her frail and emaciated condition, any blow was more painful than it would normally have been, although she readily admitted it was a mere tickle compared to the treatment she'd received back at the camp.

Abruptly, the Blenorai slowed down quite considerably. Their heads moved from side to side as if looking for something. A rustle drew their attention and they began to growl. They moved forward cautiously, their ears pricked up for any sound. Kailani checked the force field once again then looked to her mother. She answered the unasked question in her eyes.

"I'm guessing it's the other ones I told you about. They're so well camouflaged, you can barely see them in the reeds, unless they move. That's what gives them away."

Kailani had just finished talking when a large gathering of the reed people, as she thought of them, came out. This time they were led by one who had a sort of crown on his thin brown head and who carried a plain wooden box. Most of them were unarmed, it was only the two either side of their leader who carried spears. All the followers held up their hands as if in surrender. Mishtag and Yashtig stopped without having to be told and waited to see what would happen.

The king, if that's what he was, approached, stopping just a few inches from the Blenorai. He held out the box and said, "Skuid glanik Jevnod a el briwhos. Den pquan tor Idenvarlis refftish yag un. El yunkil karf un mipskol prulchew cubidij zov a tengikeq lun vootif qamondik un slefgaj."

Kailani glanced at her mother. "Do you understand what he's saying? I haven't got a clue."

"It's an old language once spoken in Idenvarlis. I understand bits of it, but can't speak it. It's saying something about a sacred scroll and war in Idenvarlis." She turned to the chief and said, "I am Princess Garalia, heir to the throne of Idenvarlis. I don't speak the old language, I'm sorry."

In a raspy voice the creature said, "Me King Jevnod. Have sacred scroll, give to her." He pointed at Kailani. "She only one prevent war in Idenvarlis."

She answered him. "King Jevnod, I am Princess Kailani, second heir to the throne of Idenvarlis. If I lower our barrier of protection, will you guarantee our safety?"

"Not be harmed, oath," he replied placing one hand on his body just below his shoulders.

She lowered the barrier around herself and Mishtag, but not Garalia and Yashtig. She dismounted and slowly walked forward.

"You save Idenvarlis. Must take sacred scroll, but keep secret from all. Priest will tell, help."

"Do you mean the High Priest of Rasha-Varl will help me and tell me what I need to do?" Jevnod nodded his head. "But I can't even tell King Jaanis about this?"

"No, only priest. All be lost if told. You take now." He handed her the box, with as much ceremony as he could muster and as she took it, Kailani bowed to him. She took a couple of steps back. Secreting it inside her cape, she slowly moved back to Mishtag and mounted her.

"Thank you, King Jevnod. I will do as you say. May we go now?"

"Yes. Box will save life before reach palace. Be proof for you. Blessings." Kailani nodded to him and as one, they moved to the side. Setting off slowly, the Blenorai padded away from the gathering and when they were far enough away, began to run. They gathered speed and as soon as they were out of sight, began to race through the reeds once again.

Daylight had given way to dusk by the time they reached the other side of the Lost Mire. The Blenorai only stopped briefly for Kailani to retrieve the light then continued until they were at least a mile away. It was a good place to make camp and Kailani put up the ice barrier. She placed the warming light in the corner and removed Mishtag and Yashtig's saddles and armour before feeding them.

Once they had eaten, Garalia asked about the box given to Kailani by King Jevnod. They were both eager to discover more so Kailani opened the box and pulled out a scroll. By its shrivelled edges and yellowed colour she could tell it was old. It was wrapped around a wooden rod with polished handles at both ends. She was about to unroll it when she stopped.

"Jevnod was very clear. I'm to give this to the High Priest alone and if anyone else reads it or knows the contents, everything will be lost. I don't know about you, but I don't want to take the chance."

Garalia pouted. "I'm bursting with curiosity. Aren't you?"

"Yes, of course I am," Kailani replied, "but I'm going to follow Jevnod's instructions."

Both women remained silent for several minutes until eventually Garalia broke it. "Maybe you're right."

"This may well change my plans a little though," she said thoughtfully.

"In what way?"

"We were going to make a triumphant return at the main entrance to the Ice Palace, but if Bellis sees us coming, there's a chance we could be assassinated right on the steps and disposed of before grandfather even knows anything about it."

"So what are you thinking of doing now then?"

"I think we'll be wise to enter the palace the same way I exited. Do you know about the secret passage?"

"No! How did you find out about it? Where is it?" Garalia's eyes were wide, her mouth agape.

"Chilali told me about it under the promise I would never reveal it to anyone, or that she'd told me about it. I know she wouldn't mind me telling you. She's loyal to you and, being your daughter, she sort of transferred that loyalty to me. It's off a really long corridor close to grandfather's office. There are some markings in the ice which you press to open the passage. It comes out to the side of the palace wall where it's not overlooked by windows, guards, or anything like that. If we use that to re-enter the palace, we have more chance of getting either to grandfather's office or the throne room without being accosted by anyone. What do you think?"

"I think it sounds perfect. If we were to bump into Bellis and there was no one else around, I fear what he might do. Actually, I wonder if he knows about the prophecy. Father has never mentioned it and neither has mother so I'm not even sure *they* know about it. Still, that's not our worry at the moment. We have to get back to the palace in one piece first and if the contents of the scroll concerns you, your challenges are not yet over, my darling. Actually, thinking about that, I wonder what King Jevnod meant when he said the box would save your life?"

"I don't know. He saw me putting it under my cloak when he said it so perhaps that's where I should keep it until we get back to the palace and in the company of your parents."

Mistress? Mishtag interrupted.

"Yes, my friend. What's the matter?"

I think you may have overlooked one small detail when talking to your mother about using the secret passage to re-enter the palace.

"What might that be?" Garalia stared at her daughter in puzzlement, her head tilted to the side. Kailani didn't notice as she focused on her Blenorai.

There is a battalion of soldiers from the palace waiting for you at a pre-determined place somewhere on the route back. I presume you know roughly whereabouts they should be. How are you going to get away from the guards so you can use the passage?

"You raise a good point. Oh, gods! I'd totally forgotten about that. Thank you for reminding me." The Kai bowed her head and lay down near Kailani's feet.

"What was that all about?" Garalia asked, frowning.

"Mishtag reminded me of something I'd overlooked. There's a battalion of guards waiting to meet me part of the way back. In fact, we can't be that far from them now. I'll have to check the map. We need to find a way of skirting around them so they don't see us, or order them to proceed to the palace ahead of us. I'm not sure the latter would work as they won't go against the king's orders for anyone. So we need to find a way to bypass them."

"Thank you for letting me know what you were talking about, but I was also referring to the one-sided conversation I heard between you and Mishtag. I know they understand our language, but surely you haven't learnt theirs? And besides, Mishtag's mouth wasn't moving."

"Oh, that. Well, don't you remember what I told you when we were at the Lost Mire? What did father tell you about our skills?"

"No, I don't remember. Galaxan mentioned about the teleporting, ability to harness and manipulate the elements, about Feegles, things at . . ."

"You have just given me a brilliant idea. Thank you, Mother. Anyway, in answer to your question, I reminded you that another of our talents is telepathy. Mishtag and I can communicate directly to each other's minds. We've had some long and interesting conversations on the way to find you. I told Mishtag all about Taivass-maa and she told me what she knows of Idenvarlis. They were extremely enlightening conversations on both sides I think."

"So why can't I talk to Yashtig the same way?"

"Because you're not telepathic and I am. That's the only reason she and I can converse. It frightened me to start with, but when I realised who it was, I was relieved. We've found it a useful way of communicating, especially when we were hidden outside the camp waiting for an opportunity to rescue you. Mishtag tells Yashtig everything that's relevant on the occasions when it's safe to talk aloud. Yashtig hears what's said from her side and Mishtag fills in the gaps later."

"I see. How wonderful for you both. I wish Yashtig and I could do that." She looked a little sad for a moment then cheered up again. "So what's this wonderful idea I gave you?"

"Teleportation. If I can make us teleport far enough past the guards, it would solve quite a few problems," she replied grinning then her smile dropped. "There's just one small issue with this plan . . . er, I've never actually done it before so I don't know how successful it would be. I'm guessing I would have to be in contact with everyone to teleport us all at once, but I don't know how it works. I could take a guess that it's a visualisation sort of thing, but I won't know until I try."

"Perhaps a few small practice tries first would be a good idea. Maybe something like you being inside the barrier, teleporting outside, and then back in again. If that works well, try it with Mishtag and build up from there."

"Great idea. I'll start tomorrow. We're all tired especially Mishtag and Yashtig. Fighting their way through those reeds takes a great deal out of them. Look – they're fast asleep already."

"Now that *is* a good idea. I'm exhausted and with all the surprises today, it's added to the tiredness. I'm going to turn in." Garalia yawned.

"Me too." Kailani brought the small light and the box over to where she intended to lay, kissed her mother on the cheek then settled down before extinguishing the light.

As usual, Kailani was the first to wake. She rose silently, trying not to wake the others. There was an unusual excitement coursing through her; it was the same sort of feeling she had the first time she rode Rhea, her Feegle, and also Mishtag. She closed her eyes and visualised herself outside the barrier. A peculiar tingle radiated through her and when she opened her eyes, she was outside, looking at the vast mountains to her right and the virtually unbroken expanse of ice. A glorious sense of achievement overcame her and she punched her fist in the air. She just managed to stop herself from whooping as she did it in case she woke Garalia or the Kai.

Closing her eyes once more, she pictured the exact spot where she'd been standing inside the barrier. Again her body prickled and upon opening her eyes found she was back inside the ice barrier. She was surprised at how easy it was, but she was under no illusions that trying to do it with all four of them would likely take a great deal out of her, assuming she could do it at all. After all, she had only travelled a couple of feet – nothing compared with what she wanted to achieve. *But it's a step in the right direction*, she thought. At least she'd now proved to herself she could do it. The rest, perhaps, was a matter of self-belief and confidence, with a chunk of strength added to the mix.

Removing the map from her pack, she unfolded it as quietly as possible so she could ascertain how far they were from the battalion. By her reckoning, they were three or four days away depending on how the journey went and whether they needed to stop more often for Garalia. The other thing she needed to consider where the battalion was concerned, she wasn't exactly blending in with the surroundings anymore so wouldn't be able to slip past them. Having given her mother the warm, white coat, she was left with her royal blue cloak which, in these surroundings, would be extremely noticeable. The other consideration was food. They just about had enough to reach the battalion, and whilst she carried a surplus for the Blenorai, it was the food for Garalia and herself which was the issue. There were no more forests between here and the palace where they could obtain extra items to bolster their dwindling supplies and she knew she couldn't go totally without food for more than a couple of days before it would lessen her ability to protect them all, and her magic would possibly suffer as a result too. There had to be something she could hunt which would feed them for at least a couple of days.

Her mind drifted back to the attack by the mountain creatures and how their bodies were missing the following morning. She remembered thinking that the rest of their kind might be cannibals and that notion didn't sit well with her. *However, if they can be hunted for their meat and they are dead anyway, what would be the difference between the pack members availing themselves of the food or us?* She was so deep in thought, she didn't hear the Blenorai wake or move until Mishtag rubbed the side of her face against Kailani's leg.

She made her usual fuss of them both before feeding them, by which time her mother was awake. Excitedly, Kailani told Garalia what she'd achieved and demonstrated it so they could all see.

"That was truly wonderful, my darling," Garalia gushed. "I knew you could do it. I have every faith in you." She threw her skinny arms around her daughter and gave her a hug.

"Thank you, Mother. But trying to do it with all four of us will be quite a challenge and I don't yet know if I'm strong enough. Plus there are other considerations . . ."

"Like what?" Her eyed became hooded by her brows.

Kailani explained the food issue, told her about the mountain creatures, and her worries.

"Have you considered meeting up with the battalion and once we have acquired enough food for the remainder of the journey, we can try and teleport nearer to the palace so it would at least give us a head start on them?"

"Why, Mother, that's sneaky." She chuckled. "However, my only real concern is how many of the battalion have been corrupted already, if any. We could be walking straight into a nest of murderers."

"That's true. I can't trust my instincts at the moment so we'll have to go with yours. Are you getting anything yet?"

"No. Probably because I haven't thought about it until now. As soon as I pick anything up about that I'll let you know. But in the meantime, I do have a strong feeling that our journey back will not be as easy as mine was coming here and I did have a few nasties to deal with." Her voice was thoughtful as she delved her senses further.

"Nasties? Do you mean beasts?"

"Yes, that's what I call them. I had a bunch of the mountain creatures, a two-headed white beast, and a flying one. However, I feel there's more danger in store before we get anywhere near the battalion, and they are about three or four days ride away."

"Well, the sooner we get going, the better, I think. We'll just have to ensure we pay attention to everything around us."

"Absolutely. But before we go, how are you feeling? Are you coping with the journey? I know how frail you are." Concern was evident in her voice and eyes.

"Obviously I'm still feeling weak and sometimes I have trouble holding on to Yashtig's reins, but I've had more to eat in these few days than I have in the last month so I have noticed a little of my strength returning. It's going to take quite a while before I'm well again," she said, trying to mask how unwell she still felt.

"Why didn't you say something before about having trouble holding the reins? I can use the rope to tie you to Yashtig if it'll help?"

"Yes, it might. Let's try it today and we'll see how I cope with it. Thank you, my dearest one."

Kailani had been putting the armour and saddles on the Blenorai while she and Garalia had been talking. She'd also packed everything away so all she had to do was take down the barrier and they could leave. She pulled out the rope and was about to use it when she dropped it to the ground.

"What . . .?"

"Shhh!" Kailani made a small section of the barrier transparent for just a moment before turning it back to its normal form. She leaned in toward her mother and whispered in her ear. "There are two men outside, waiting for me to take the barrier down. They are behind us. I'm going to leave you safely in here with Yashtig while Mishtag and I go and deal with them."

Yashtig should come with us – we will have better odds that way and it also means that if one of us becomes injured, there is a third to take up the fight.

Whispering to Garalia again, she said, "Mishtag has said that Yashtig should go with us for better odds. Will you be alright here on your own?" Garalia nodded, dismounted, and put her arms around her daughter.

"Be careful, please." She then bent to Yashtig and whispered in his ear. He nodded his noble head.

"I'm not sure whether I can take both of you at once, but we'll try. My plan is to teleport us to the opposite side of the barrier to where the men wait then if you two split up and come at them from either side, I'll teleport behind them," she whispered.

They nodded and Kailani put an arm around each of their necks. She closed her eyes and visualised where she wanted them to be. The same tingle she felt before radiated through her and when she opened her eyes she found all three of them outside the barrier. A sense of elation filled her. She withdrew her Panas from its scabbard and visualised herself behind the two men. The same feeling surged through her and in the blink of an eye she was there.

She stood there for a moment watching and listening to them. Their accent was the same as Gengaruk's; at least she knew who she was dealing with now. Waiting until the Blenorai came into view, she remained silent. Suddenly one of the men spotted Yashtig and they took a couple of steps back.

"Are you waiting for someone?" Kailani said and they physically jumped before turning around and falling onto their bums. It was all she could do to keep a straight face, they looked so comical. Scrambling to their feet, they stared straight at her.

"Yes, you actually, and your whore of a mother," the taller one sneered.

Keeping her face completely neutral, she responded, "You need to keep a civil tongue in your head when addressing a member of the royal family. Well, now you've found me. What do you want?"

"It's not so much what we wants, your Highness, as what we been told to do," the smaller, chubbier one replied.

"Oh? Who has given you instructions and what are they?"

"Now that would be telling, but let's just say you're heading in the wrong direction. You will come with us to Gengaruk's camp or . . ."

"Or what?" Her voice became more challenging. The taller one drew his finger across his throat and she laughed.

"What you laughing at?" the tall one demanded, a confused expression on his face.

"The fact that only two of you were sent. You would need a battalion of men at the least to stand half a chance of making me go somewhere I don't want to."

"Really? We'll see about that!" the chubby one said and began to draw his sword. Kailani moved so fast she was almost a blur. Her Panas had pierced deep into his heart and she'd withdrawn it and turned to the tall one. His sword was already in his hand and he slashed it toward her. She blocked it and thrust toward his chest. He turned himself to the side thinking she would miss him altogether, but he didn't count on her skill. Her blade travelled up and cut into his arm.

He yelled in pain and his blade swooped toward her again. She parried and countered with a move of her own. He blocked it and tried to thrust, but she was ready for him. They parried back and forth for a few minutes. He was a better swordsman than she thought at first and she began to perspire with the effort. As she looked for an opening to end it, Kailani lost concentration for a moment and his sword nicked her shoulder drawing blood. She didn't even look at the wound; now she was angry. Her sword took on a life of its own and she slashed and thrust, driving him back and for the first time, fear flashed in his eyes.

She kept parrying, thrusting, and swinging, changing her moves to throw him off and still he walked backwards from the ferocity of her blows. She moved so fast, all he could do was try to defend himself. Her sword caught him on the stomach, the leg, and his ear before he made a mistake and Kailani thrust her Panas straight into his chest. She twisted it before withdrawing the blade. Blood bubbled up and dribbled from his lips as he fell, almost in slow motion, landing with his head on his friend's arm.

Kailani searched both bodies for anything useful, ignoring the sightless eyes staring back. She found nothing. As she straightened up she looked around and a few feet away she saw what looked like two packs. She ran over and grabbed them, searching inside for food or water. A smile came over her lips. She beckoned the Kai to her and, putting her arm around each one, visualised them inside the barrier. The now familiar tingle spread around her body and then they were back with Garalia.

She rushed to Kailani's side. "Are you alright, my darling? I heard the clashing of swords then all went quiet. I was so worried!"

"I'm fine, Mother. After I killed them, I searched them for anything useful and then found these packs. There's enough food and water in here for five or six days," she said excitedly.

"Oh, how wonderful. At least that will take the pressure off somewhat." She looked her daughter over and saw the blood on her shoulder. "You've been hurt." Garalia pointed to Kailani's wound. "Take your jacket off and I'll tend to it."

"It's only a scratch. Don't worry about it." She shrugged.

"Do as you're told!" Garalia stood there with her hands on her hips and a stern look on her face.

Kailani was taken aback. "Yes, Mother," she replied meekly and stripped her clothing off. She looked at the injury as it was cleaned with a cloth and water. As she'd said, it was only a surface wound and not deep. Still, her mother dabbed some of the ointment she'd found in her daughter's pack on it. "Ow! That stings!"

"Don't be a baby. This will help it heal and reduce the chance of infection." She dressed the wound and allowed Kailani to put her clothes on again.

This was really strange to the young princess. All her life she'd had maids or governesses to tend to cuts and scrapes, so to have her mother doing it now she was twenty-one felt peculiar, but she liked it. There had been so many times in the past when she had longed for her mother, times when there were things she couldn't tell her father. Aunt Konstellia, although she tried hard, could never take the place of Garalia. Now it really sank in, she had her mother back. She threw her arms around her and hugged her, the tears from years of pent up longing finally released as she sobbed in her mother's arms.

Garalia stroked her daughter's hair, but said nothing as she waited for Kailani to get it all out of her system. It was many minutes later before the sobbing subsided and her daughter raised her head. "Are you alright? Do you feel better now?" she asked with concern in her voice and eyes.

"Yes, thank you. I'm sorry about that. Years of longing for my mother and having to make do with someone else, finally penetrated the emotional barriers I've been carrying with me all my life."

"I know how you feel, but in a different context. I had all those years of dreaming about holding you in my arms, watching you grow up, teaching you the simple things like brushing your hair, and it was the only thing that kept me going all those years. Now my dreams have also come true." Tears streamed from her eyes and it was Kailani's turn to hold her mother and offer comfort.

Garalia recovered quicker than Kailani had and when they saw each other's puffy, red eyes they began to giggle. The Blenorai looked at each other and shrugged their large shoulders, shaking their heads which made the women laugh even harder.

Surprisingly, Kailani stopped chuckling first. She climbed onto Mishtag and made the barrier transparent so she could see outside before lowering it. The landscape surrounding them looked clear so she dropped the shield and they commenced the day's journey.

Chapter 16

The Blenorai rode hard that day. The sun popped in and out from behind the clouds giving the ice a dappled effect. Kailani found it strange yet beautiful. She'd never seen anything like it before.

She kept an eye on the mountains as they travelled, to ensure they were going in the right direction and in case any of those beasts she'd had the misfortune of coming across before were around.

As they passed below the largest peak, a low rumbling sounded and the ice under their feet began to quiver. Kailani looked at Garalia and said, "Do you have any idea what's going on?"

"No, but it doesn't feel or sound good."

They drew the Blenorai to a halt and looked up to where the noise seemed to be coming from.

All of a sudden, an almighty crack rent the air. Both women watched as, at the highest peak, a massive river of snow began sliding down. The noise set off a chain reaction as, at the apexes either side of it, the same thing happened and then again the ones either side of that until overburdened slopes along the entire range began to spill their snow down the side. The avalanche gathered speed and hurtled toward them.

Kailani said, "I think we'd better make a run for it." They set off with the Blenorai running at top speed.

"We're not going to make it," cried Garalia. Panic filled her voice as a massive wall of snow hurtled toward them.

"Don't worry. I have another plan. Let's stop here." The Blenorai ground to a halt and Kailani set a huge wall of ice, treble its normal thickness. She then guided Garalia, Mishtag, and Yashtig further away from the wall and set a double thickness barrier around them. Calling on her Taivass-maa powers by invoking the name of Savna, the Sun God, she wound stripes of sunlight around the outside of the shield, but without touching it, leaving a gap of around 6 inches between the two. She made a small light for the inside with heat so they didn't get too cold while they waited it out.

The rumble of the snow became increasingly louder the nearer it got. Garalia tried to disguise her fear, but both Kailani and Yashtig felt it coming off her in waves. As they sat on the floor, she put her arm around her mother's bony shoulders and Yashtig lay down right next to her. She unconsciously started to stroke her Kai's fur and slowly the panic started to lessen.

Kailani was also frightened although she remained calm for her mother's sake. She knew so little about Idenvarlis and its natural dangers and felt completely out of her depth. She was reacting by instinct alone and just hoped she was doing the right thing.

A loud, rumbling crash startled them all as the snow hit the wall. Kailani wasn't sure whether it would hold. She had no experience of these sorts of things; she had seen the speed in which the snow was travelling but had no idea of the power and weight it carried and did the only thing she she could think of to protect them from being buried alive.

To the side of the barrier and out of view of her mother, she made a small transparent section so she could see out. She needed to be prepared to increase the power in the stripes. One section of the wall had given way, but the momentum had slowed quite considerably. She saw the snow coming toward their barrier and waited patiently. As the snow reached the sun stripes, it immediately turned to water. Her heart soared and she breathed a sigh of relief.

"What's happened?" Garalia had taken her sigh as a sign of anxiety.

"My plan appears to be working. Do you want to see?" Her mother hesitated then nodded. Kailani pointed at the transparent 'window'. "Look, Mother." Garalia turned and saw the sun stripes melting the snow on contact. She pointed to where the wall had held on either side and looked back at her daughter with pride blazing from her eyes.

"Oh, well done, my darling. I couldn't be more proud of you." She hugged Kailani and kissed her twice on the cheek.

"Thank you, Mother. I don't know what to say . . ."

"Say nothing. Just accept the compliment with good grace as I'm sure you've been brought up to do." She smiled.

"All the time I was growing up, I often wondered what you would think of me, whether I was the young lady you wanted me to be or if I was too much of a rebel. When I did something good, I wondered if you'd be proud of me and conversely, when I was bad, would you be disappointed. After all these years of wondering, to actually hear you say the words are like a dream come true."

"I thought about you every single day pondering what you were like, whether you were a handful for your father or a prim and proper young lady. In my mind, I told you every day how much I love you and prayed to the gods to keep you safe. I also prayed for even a glimpse of the woman you'd become and then I could die in peace. I can't find the words to express how I feel."

"I understand. In some ways it's the same for me. Although I haven't suffered as you have, I often dreamed of what it would be like to finally meet you. I was never told what had happened to you and whenever I brought the subject up it was quickly diverted onto something else.

"Despite growing up without you, I treasured the things you left for me that I was allowed to have straight away or when I was old enough not to break them. I have a trinket box on my dressing table which I keep everything in except for cuddly Princess Larine who still lies beside my pillows every night."

Garalia nodded her head in understanding, a small smile on her lips. "Out of curiosity, where did you get the name Larine from?"

"I don't know. Apparently that's what I called her as soon as I was old enough to give her a name. Why?"

"Because it's my middle name, and one of yours."

"Really? How much of a coincidence is that? It's almost creepy. I didn't even know I had a middle name."

"You actually have two. Larine is from my side of the family. The one from your father's side is Arachelis."

"I can't understand why I've spent twenty-one years not knowing I had middle names, let alone what they are. Why didn't anyone tell me?" Her confusion was evident in her tone.

"I can't answer that. It's something you will have to ask your father."

"Oh, I will." Kailani glanced out of the little window she'd made with a determined expression on her face, and it appeared no more snow was coming through the wall. "I'm just going outside to see if it's safe for us to move on yet. Mishtag? Do you want to come with me?"

Mishtag rose from the floor and followed her mistress. Kailani made a doorway in the barrier and altered the bands of sun so they could safely walk through then ventured outside. They walked around to the far side of their shelter and although there was still a large pile of snow beside the barrier which was being melted by the bands of sun around it, no new snow followed it.

She walked over to the big wall and made a transparent window, but all she could see was masses of white piled against it, so strolled to one end. The avalanche had definitely stopped. Fascinated by the huge pile of snow that lay beyond the wall's edge, she picked a handful up. It was soft, powdery, and crumbled between her fingers. The pile was up to her chest and she started trying to climb over it, but found herself sinking. She gave up, stepped back, and fired a blaster from her eyes which created a pathway through. Mishtag went ahead and they continued round the end of the wall. As she came closer, Kailani noticed some dark objects buried in it. Out of curiosity she pulled one out and gasped. It was a cannon ball and she recognised several arrows, the same type she used with her Plexan. She extracted them and found ten in total.

Mistress, it looks to me like the avalanche was no accident or natural occurrence, Mishtag said.

"It certainly appears that way. We are going to have to keep our eyes sharp for the rest of the journey. Someone, and I can guess who, doesn't want us to make it back to the palace alive. If only I was sure I could teleport all of us back from here, I would do it, but I'm just not confident enough that I can achieve it. The last thing I want is to try it and land us right next to the battalion."

Have faith in yourself and remember, if all else fails, you have the pendant given to you by the High Priest. I don't know what it does, but it adds to your already large arsenal of magical workings.

"I'd forgotten all about the pendant and I don't know what it does either. Thank you for your faith in me, dear friend. I'll give serious thought to everything you've said." She bent down a little and stroked her mane, scratching behind her ears just as she liked it. "Let's go back and break the news to mother."

They returned to their shelter and Kailani showed Garalia what she'd found. Her assessment of the situation was the same as Mishtag's. "And one other thing we need to consider," Garalia said, "is that whoever shot the cannonball and those arrows could still be in the vicinity. We are not out of danger yet."

"Oh god, I didn't think of that. Let's look at this logically for a moment. The person obviously knew what would happen and wouldn't want to be trapped by the avalanche. My guess is they were positioned at the far end of the mountain range so they could escape. That means they're ahead of us somewhere. Alternatively, judging by the sheer amount of snow and how quickly it moved, he could be buried in it. He wouldn't have been able to move very fast towing a canon even with a Blenorai."

"I agree, but *if* they escaped, it could be they have doubled back to ensure our demise from the falling snow. I imagine my brother would expect no less than proof of some description. Unless . . ."

"What?"

"It could possibly be one of the soldiers was told to scout ahead to see if they could see any sign of us and it just happened to be someone who's loyal to Bellis. Perhaps he volunteered, saw your cloak in the distance, and took it upon himself to dispose of us using nature so neither he nor my brother would be implicated."

"So you believe it's possible he may have returned to the battalion rather than hang around to check on us?"

"It's possible. He could say he saw the avalanche overwhelm us."

"Hmm, there's possibly one small flaw in that idea," Kailani said, her brows knotted. "Assuming at least half the battalion, including the leader, are loyal to the king, wouldn't they come here to rescue our bodies and take them back so Jaanis and Shivla could mourn us properly?"

"Ah, yes. You're right. In that case, he's possibly waiting near the end of the mountains, in case we managed to escape the avalanche or he's returned to the battalion to say he didn't see us. But which one?"

"This is all supposition based on him surviving, of course. There's only one way of finding out. Sooner or later we're going to have to pass that area to get back to the palace. We could stay here for a couple of days to make him think he's succeeded before continuing with our journey, or we could leave now and see what happens. As you correctly pointed out, the colour of my cloak does stand out against the ice so I can be seen from far away, but there's nothing we can do about that. With our food situation as it is, I say we press on." She saw the fear in her mother's eyes, walked forward, and held her sweaty hand. "Don't worry, we'll be protected. I've become quite adept at shielding." Garalia half-smiled then nodded. "And don't forget, we'll have advance warning if anyone is ahead. Yashtig and Mishtag will let us know."

"True. My Yashtig has always protected me and I know he always will." She bent forward and stroked his head, a gentle smile on her lips. "Very well. Let's proceed then."

Kailani snuffed out the light and made the doorway a little bigger. They exited warily, but as there were no growls from the Blenorai, they felt safe to continue. After making sure her mother was wrapped in a strong force field with a repulsion spell around the outside, she wrapped a weaker one around herself and they set off, staying behind the wall so they couldn't see the mountains.

Yashtig and Mishtag ran so fast that day that one would think demons were after them. All the time they were using their senses, alert to the slightest noise or smell. No creatures prowled the ice plains and there was no hint of the person who set off the avalanche.

Once they were settled in their barrier for the night, Kailani took the map from her pack and studied it carefully. "Unless the battalion came farther than we agreed and assuming we cover as much distance per day as we did today, we'll meet up with them in three days. I can't make up my mind whether it's best to bypass them altogether or trust that they're not all assassins and meet up with them. What do you think, Mother?"

"It's a conundrum, that's for sure. I would say, let's see what happens over the next two days and make a final decision then. Of course if we catch sight of them in advance of where we're expecting them to be, we'll have to trust our instincts at the time and make a decision accordingly." Garalia had a thoughtful expression on her face.

"The thing I'm most worried about is the food situation. I think we've just about got enough for Mishtag and Yashtig, but our supplies will run out long before we reach the palace. We haven't come across anything I can kill for food nor have there been any trees with edible fruits or berries. We only have enough for about four days at most. Should we take this into consideration when we make our decision about the battalion or am I going to try and teleport us to the palace when we run out of food?" Kailani rubbed her forehead, her eyes screwed tightly shut.

Garalia moved closer and put her arm around her daughter's shoulders. "My dear child, when the time comes for us to make the decision, we'll do it together and take everything into consideration. It doesn't all fall on your shoulders anymore, you have me to lean on."

"If I lean on you, you're likely to snap in half," Kailani quipped, grinning.

"Ha ha, very funny. I'm being serious. I may be weak and under-nourished, but there's nothing wrong with my brain. Anyway, who knows what fate or the gods might drop in our laps in the meantime?"

Kailani was woken by a soft growling noise in her ear. Mishtag stood beside her and as soon as she could see her mistress open her eyes, she lifted one paw and pointed to the sky. Kailani experienced a sense of deja-vu as she heard the flapping of wings growing ever closer. She grabbed her weapons, put the armour on Mishtag, laid one hand on her, and teleported them outside the barrier. The night was bitterly cold, crisp, and clear, but even though the visibility was better than the last time one of these beasts attacked, it was still not enough to see clearly. She mumbled some words and produced an arch of bright light which she laid on the ice.

Now she could see and a familiar sight came into view. A massive, black creature with spiked, leathery wings hurtled toward them. This one was much larger than before, almost twice the size, but Kailani remained calm and focused. The beast swooped over them so low, she was forced to duck. She turned quickly to see the creature swerve and head back in their direction. This time, the princess was forced to crouch even lower to avoid it.

She quickly cocked an arrow, and as it made its third fly past, Kailani let it loose. The blade pierced its lower chest area and it screeched loudly, but didn't slow. She loaded another one and fired again, but the beast was turning and the tip lodged in one of its wings. Mishtag stood on her back legs, front paws extended so her wickedly sharp claws were ready. The creature came at them again, this time at an angle so one of its wings dipped toward them, the spikes glinting ominously in the light. Kailani quickly grabbed her Panas from its scabbard. As it came at them, Mishtag used her claws to rip into the leathery wing while the princess struck a hard blow before having to dive to one side.

As it passed, they looked back and saw the damage they'd done. One tip was completely gone and the rest of the wing was in tatters. Its flight was uneven and they could see it struggling to control its movements.

However, it was tenacious and determined to exact revenge for its fallen mate. Circling around with difficulty, it landed just in front of them and began sweeping its good wing toward them. Mishtag had moved to the other side of her mistress and as the spikes approached she stepped forward and began to slash at it with her claws. Kailani stepped in behind the Kai and opened a rent in the creature from its chest to its abdomen. The beast screeched so loud it hurt Kailani's ears. Then she heard a muffled cry from Mishtag. One of the spikes had found a gap in her armour and lodged in her side. Blood dripped onto the ice. She moved forward and carefully pulled it out.

Are you alright?

Yes. It is only a flesh wound. I can continue, Mishtag replied as she continued to tear at the wing.

Are you sure?

Yes. Let us finish this.

Kailani slipped behind Mishtag again just as the other wing came toward her. She sliced into it, almost cutting it in half. The creature shrieked again, but she ignored it. Seeing the wing couldn't be used against them again, she turned back to its body just in time to see its open beak, with what appeared to be razor sharp teeth lining the edges, coming straight at her. With the reflexes of a cat, she moved to one side at the last minute and brought her Panas down on its neck, severing the head. Blood spurted from the wound splattering both of them in equal measure, but the creature didn't stop. It continued to try and attack with one wing and now tried to use its taloned feet to inflict injury. It was easy for Kailani to lop them off using a double-handed hold on the hilt, although the vibration through her sword as she sliced through the bones shot up her arms and into her shoulders, making her gasp. She stepped closer again and thrust the blade through the heart. As she removed it, she kicked the beast and it toppled onto its back.

Immediately she moved to Mishtag who still had blood dripping from her wound. Laying her hand on her protector, she teleported them back inside their barrier where Garalia and Yashtig were awake and worriedly pacing. As soon as Yashtig saw the blood, he moved forward and licked at Mishtag's wound as the Kai lay down, exhausted and weakened from the blood loss. Garalia rushed to her daughter, looking her over as she did so and seeing her splattered with blood.

"Are you alright? Do you have any injuries?" She put her hands on Kailani's shoulders.

"I'm fine, Mother, just exhausted. It was quite a battle to take that creature down and it's the beast's blood on me so don't worry."

"Oh, thank the gods you are unharmed. But poor Mishtag – what happened to her?"

"One of the spikes on the beast's wing pierced her side. She was trying to protect me."

"Spiked wings? If it's the creature I think, it's body is edible. Take me outside so I can check."

"I will in a moment. I need to check on Mishtag first." She moved across the floor and knelt beside the Kai placing her hand on her haunch. *Are you alright, my friend?*

I will be. Yashtig is healing me and I am feeling stronger already. Once I have had some sleep I should be almost back to normal.

Thank you for protecting me. I wouldn't have been able to conquer that creature without your help and I fear the outcome might have been somewhat different. You're wonderful, Mishtag.

It is a good job I cannot blush! she chuckled.

She smiled then spoke aloud. "Mother and I are going outside for a moment. We'll be right back." She held Garalia's outstretched hand and they teleported outside.

Kailani watched as her mother inspected the bird-like body.

"Yes, this is definitely edible. If we can cut away the useless bits then chop it up into more manageable pieces, this would feed us for several days. The legs would be great for the Blenorai to gnaw on too." She grabbed the two which Kailani had already severed and placed them to one side. "Here, I'll help you."

Garalia carefully grabbed one of the wings and stretched it away from the body, indicating where they should cut. Kailani grabbed the Kamuk from her belt and began slicing away the wing. It was quite hard going, but after a while, she managed to get through it. They did the same to the other one then, using a double-handed grip, Kailani lopped off the other two legs. The first leg was easy to separate, but as her blade connected with the second, vibrations coursed through her arms and into her shoulders, making her cry out. The pain hit her like nothing she'd ever felt before and it took her breath away.

"What is it? Where are you hurt?" Her mother stretched out her hand and laid it on Kailani's arm.

"It's my shoulders, but they're alright. This creature's leg bones must be very dense. When I cut through them, the vibrations through my sword crash into my shoulders as if I'd run full pelt into the barrier. It's my own fault – I missed the joint and caught the bone instead."

"Will you be able to continue?"

"Yes."

Under Garalia's instruction, Kailani managed to cut the rest of the beast into manageable sections, discarding the pieces which were of no use. They piled them in a heap and with one hand on the raw meat and the other on her mother, Kailani teleported them back inside the barrier.

All ate well that night. Yashtig and Mishtag were overjoyed with the legs they were given and Kailani conjured a fire to roast a piece of the meat, using her sword to hold it in the flames. There was so much meat, Garalia and Kailani couldn't finish it all. As their stomachs had shrunk with the lack of food, it was hardly surprising. However, they ate until they were full to bursting, something neither of them had done in a long time.

Kailani wrapped the rest of the cooked meat and placed it in the pack with the raw meat she'd covered earlier. "Tomorrow we should cook the rest, otherwise the smell of blood might attract other beasts and it could start to go off," Garalia suggested. She yawned and stretched. The full stomach and heat from the fire had made her drowsy.

Kailani noticed Garalia's eyes drooping. "Why don't you go back to sleep, Mother? I can finish clearing up."

"Thank you, my dear." She cupped one hand on her daughter's cheek and kissed her on the forehead. She lay down and as soon as her head settled on the makeshift pillow, she was asleep. Kailani placed the blanket over her before laying down herself, extinguishing the fire as she did so.

Kailani didn't wake quite as early as normal the next morning. Upon rising, the first thing she did was examine the wound on Mishtag's side. All that was left on the surface was a red patch. The hole had completely healed over. The healing magic the Blenorai Kai possessed was special indeed.

How are you feeling, Mishtag?

Much better, thank you, she replied rising. She walked up and down in the small space inside the barrier. Kailani scrutinised her face, looking for any sign of pain or discomfort, but saw nothing to give her cause for concern.

We can stay here for the day so you can rest and heal more.

Thank you, but that will not be necessary. I feel fine and am able to continue. Mishtag spoke with a determined tone. The young princess wasn't totally convinced, but decided they would take things a little easier on their journey, for that day at least. She sensed Mishtag was uncomfortable and certainly not fully healed, but knew it would be useless to argue with her.

After a hurried breakfast, Kailani checked the map once more then placed it in her pack. As she carried the food as well as her personal things, she was concerned about the extra weight on Mishtag, but her mother wasn't strong enough to carry it, although Yashtig could. She called his name and he approached her. As she began to dress him with his armour, she whispered her thoughts in his ear ending with, "so would you be able to carry the food pack today?" The Kai nodded and rubbed his face against her arm. She stopped and stroked his mane before placing the last piece of armour on his head. When she'd fitted the saddle, Kailani strapped the food pack securely to it.

"Just before I take the barrier down, I've checked the map again and we're fast approaching the area where the battalion should be waiting. I want us to take it slower. We can't allow the soldiers to see us until Mother and I have made a final decision as to whether we're going to rendezvous with them. With the bright colour of my cloak, they will see us from quite a long way off, so at the first sighting of any of them we must stop. The sharpness of our sight is much more important than speed today." Kailani's eyes looked at each in turn and they all nodded.

She took down the barrier and they set off.

Chapter 17

The sky was dark grey with clouds so heavy it was a wonder they didn't fall to the ground. The group headed into the cold, biting wind. Kailani and Garalia had repositioned their scarves so only their eyes were showing and they had both donned gloves.

Garalia struggled to stay atop Yashtig in the fierce wind. Kailani waved to get her attention and gestured for her to almost lay on her Kai's back. She did as suggested and found it much easier.

No sooner had she got comfortable, the clouds, unable to contain the weight any longer, began to dump snow into the air. A blizzard engulfed them, the flakes so thick they could barely see. They tried to continue, but it quickly became obvious that the elements were beating them. Kailani tried to signal to Garalia, but with the thickness of the snow, her mother couldn't see her.

Kailani bent down and spoke in Mishtag's ear, who in turn mind-spoke to Yashtig, and together they drew to a halt. She had just risen when she was knocked backwards by something and her back slammed into the ice. It took her breath away at first and then she looked down. An arrow protruded from her chest and she didn't dare move, especially not knowing how bad the wound was. Pain radiated across her body and she gasped. She quickly managed to erect a barrier around them all as well as conjure a small light and a fire before she lost consciousness.

Garalia rushed to her daughter's side, a cry escaping her lips. She carefully peeled back the layers of her clothing and breathed a sigh of relief. Only the very tip had pierced the skin and she felt comfortable pulling it out without causing any further damage. She grasped the shaft which was lodged in her breastplate and pulled with all her might. She only managed to get it a few inches out, but at least it was free of the bleeding skin. She examined the wound carefully, but couldn't treat it until the arrow had been completely removed.

She saw it had pierced the box given to Kailani by the king of the reed people and it sat at the top of the shaft so she concentrated on the other end. After much pulling through each layer of clothing, it came away with the box attached. She laid it to one side and examined the wound more closely. Mishtag came closer to investigate and sniffed at the wound. She suddenly let out a loud roar making Garalia jump and fall onto her backside.

"What is it, Mishtag?"

She held her paw just above the wound and shook her head. The princess stared at her, puzzled. Mishtag pointed her paw at Garalia, then at the wound, and shook her head.

"You don't want me to touch it, is that right?" Mishtag nodded. "Why not?" she asked.

Mishtag thought for a moment then pointed to her open mouth and mimed being sick, including making the noises.

"Will it make me sick if I touch it?" Mishtag nodded. Garalia got to her knees, leaned over her daughter's body and sniffed at the wound as she'd seen Mishtag do. It had a strange smell, stronger than the odour of the blood. She straightened up and retrieved the arrow. Examining it closely, she saw the head was coated in a dark substance. The princess sniffed at it and her eyes filled with horror as she placed it back on the

225

ground, as far away as she could reach. "She's been poisoned!" she cried, tears springing to her eyes. Mishtag nodded again and whined as she gazed down at her mistress.

Garalia searched through the packs until she found the rudimentary medicine kit. She pulled everything out and stared at the items. The only thing that could be of some use was the liquid Kailani had used to clean her injuries before. She picked it up and removed the stopper. Pouring some on a piece of cloth, and being careful not to touch the wound with her skin, she cleaned it as best she could then poured a little of the liquid directly into it. She then placed a folded pad of material over the injury. The material used to clean the wound she threw into the fire; as it burned, green smoke curled upward.

"Is there any more I can do for her?" Garalia asked. Mishtag shook her head and with her paw, attempted to cover her mistress with her clothes as best she could. The princess helped and they soon had her dressed once more.

Pulling the arrow through the fabric and armour had exhausted Garalia. She had little strength despite having eaten more since leaving the camp. As she sat holding her daughter's hand, her eyelids began to droop and it wasn't long before she dozed off. Yashtig moved behind his mistress ready to catch her if she moved. Mishtag still sat beside Kailani, her eyes never leaving the princess's face. The only sound in the enclosure was the crackling of the flames.

Awake and on guard, the Blenorai discussed the situation.

She has been poisoned? Yashtig asked.

Mishtag nodded. *I have only come across this poison once before. You may be more familiar with it than I.*

Yashtig moved a bit so he could sniff the arrow tip, and his companion felt the anger rising in him. *This is a most foul concoction and is actually a blend of two potions. The effect of joining them makes it quicker acting and more deadly. Unless we can find an antidote, the chances of Princess Kailani surviving is pretty much non-existent.*

Where would we find an antidote out here? Who would we turn to?

Simply put, the assassin has chosen well. There is nowhere out here to obtain a cure and I wouldn't know what to look for anyway. The only people we could turn to for help that we know can be completely trusted is the High Priest, or the king and queen. The only one of them likely to have any idea of what to do and where to go is the High Priest, but even then unless the gods tell him, he will not know unless he has had the misfortune of coming across this poison before.

So what you're saying is that it is hopeless and she will die. Mishtag looked up, despair and pain in her eyes.

Unfortunately, yes. I'm so sorry my friend. Yashtig looked at his companion with compassion.

They drifted into silence. There was nothing more to say.

Garalia woke a couple of hours later, embarrassed that she'd fallen asleep, especially under the circumstances. She looked at Mishtag who hadn't moved at all, and spoke.

"Has she moved, made any noise, or opened her eyes?" Mishtag shook her head. The princess opened Kailani's clothes and checked under the pad. From the wound, a spider web of black lines appeared just under her skin, using every blood vessel as a transportation system. As she watched, it slowly grew further out and the lines began to get darker as the poison entered her blood stream. "Is there anything we can do?" Her voice showed her desperation.

Mishtag slowly shook her head.

Large tears coursed down her cheeks. It felt so unfair. After twenty years of being incarcerated and separated from her daughter, she'd just got her back only to lose her again. She closed her eyes and began praying to the gods to save Kailani. All she had left was her faith. The deities had answered her prayers once before, she had no reason to think they would desert her now.

As the poison spread through Kailani's body she began to moan, curling up in a ball then stretching out, tossing and turning. Garalia stroked her hair murmuring for her to fight it, but as the time passed, she became worse. She began to thrash about, her arms and legs flailing so much that Garalia had to move away from her. None of them noticed the passing of time, they were so intent on watching Kailani.

Dawn broke on the second day and Kailani grew weaker. She'd stopped moving and just lay still once more. Mishtag moved next to her again and suddenly noticed she was wearing a chain around her neck. Very carefully, she extended one claw and hooked it around the chain, pulling it gently until more of it was exposed. She made a noise in the back of her throat and caught Garalia's attention. The princess leaned forward and pulled the chain out from beneath her clothes revealing the vial given to her by the High Priest.

She gasped when she saw the colour. "I have never seen a vial like this before. I wouldn't know what words release the magic. Only Kailani and the High Priest would know and we wouldn't be able to get her to him in time."

Mishtag thought for a moment. If she could mind-speak with Kailani, she might be able to get her to say the words before it was too late. It was worth a try.

Kailani? Can you hear me? There was no response. *Kailani! Fight your way to the surface and speak to me. It is important. Your life depends on it. Come on, Kailani, talk to me. You can do it. You are one of the strongest and bravest people I have ever known and I need you to use that strength now. Fight, Kailani. Fight your way back to me. You can do it.*

Mishtag? Her voice was weak and sounded as if she were far away.

Kailani, listen carefully. We have found your vial and it is probably the only thing that will save your life. I need you to draw on every bit of strength you have left to say the magic words out loud so your mother can hear them and activate the vial. Can you do that?

I'll try.

Come on then, we don't have much time.

Mishtag put her paw on the side of Garalia's head and gently pushed it down so her ear was close to Kailani's lips.

A whisper came forth from the dying princess; only two words, but it was enough. Her mother pressed the button on the vial and said loudly, "Rasha-Varl." She laid the vial back on Kailani's chest and waited. Suddenly, a purple mist began to surround her. It curled and bubbled, engulfing her body then tendrils found their way up her nose, in her ears, and between her slightly parted lips. The thick mist continued its journey into Kailani's body until it had disappeared. All that was left behind was a purple glow which outlined her body. Nothing seemed to be happening. Garalia and the Kai looked at each other blankly, not knowing what to expect.

After about five minutes, Garalia noticed a green mist escaping from between her daughter's lips. "Get back," she ordered while moving away. The mist became thicker and had a disgusting odour to it. After another minute had passed, the same awful green mist gushed from her ears and nostrils too, drifting up and disappearing through the vent at the top of the barrier. This continued for another twenty minutes before it began to slow and a further five before it stopped altogether. The glow outlining Kailani's body began to pulse, slowly at first then speeding up until it was a blur. The glow moved over her until she was completely encased by it.

The glow became brighter and with the blurred pulsing, none of them could bear to look at it. A soft buzzing filled the enclosure which lasted for several minutes before it ceased. The glow lessened in brilliance and the pulsing slowed to the extent that Garalia and the Blenorai could watch it once more. Over the next three or four minutes the pulse slowed to a stop, the glow returned to its original level and position then disappeared completely.

The three watched Kailani intently until eventually her eyes fluttered open. She was still quite pale, but she had lost the deathly grey pallor. Looking around at them all, she managed a weak smile. Garalia gathered her daughter in her arms and hugged her as tightly as she dared.

"Oh, my darling. I thought I'd lost you! Thank the gods – I knew they wouldn't let me down."

Kailani put her arms around Garalia, resting her head on her shoulder. After a minute or so, she asked weakly, "Can I have some water, please?"

"Of course. Is there anything else you want? I can make you a little broth." Garalia laid her daughter back down and poured some water into a cup. Propping her up with one hand, while holding the cup with the other, she helped Kailani drink. Most of the cup was empty when she stopped.

"A little broth would be good, thank you."

By the time she'd consumed two small bowlfuls, her pallor was almost back to normal although she was tired. She lay down and dropped off into her own little dream world.

When Kailani eventually woke, she almost felt back to normal. The others were asleep, and the way they were placed around her looked like they'd been keeping vigil at her bedside. A rush of affection coursed through her. She stroked her mother's hair noticing the worry lines that had appeared. After everything Garalia had gone through, the last thing she needed was her daughter almost dying. She felt a momentary pang of guilt before her good sense prevailed. It was just too much to expect her to cope with.

She looked up to the vent in the top on the barrier and noticed it was still night. Snuggling down with Mishtag, she closed her eyes once more and after a few minutes she dozed off.

The next time she opened her eyes, she could see daylight through the top of the barrier. As she sat up, Mishtag opened her eyes and looked at her mistress.

How are you feeling, Kailani? she asked solicitously.

The voice startled her at first. *Much better, thank you, although I can't remember much. How long have I been asleep?*

From when you got shot by the poisoned arrow, it has been five days. We nearly lost you and felt so helpless as there was nothing we could do to stop the spread of the poison. You were dying before our eyes.

Really? So how comes I'm still here?

When you were thrashing around in agony, I spotted the chain around your neck and pointed it out to Garalia. I managed to get you lucid enough to tell her what the spell words were and she activated your pendant. That is what healed you. It drove all the poison from your body.

Wow, she said, her eyes wide and brows raised. Kailani lifted the chain and looked at the vial. It was still three-quarters full. She slipped it beneath her clothes and looked for the point where the arrow pierced her skin, seeing no mark whatsoever. *And how are you, my friend? Is your wound fully healed?*

Yes, thank you. Yashtig tells me there is only a pink mark on my flesh and I don't feel any discomfort from it at all when I move.

Oh, I'm so glad. Right, I'm going to get breakfast organised. Has my mother been eating properly while I've been ill?

To be honest, none of us have, really.

Kailani tutted, but understood. She rose and began to organise the food. When it was ready she woke her mother. As Garalia opened her eyes and saw her daughter up and well, her face lit up with joy and she threw her arms around her.

"How do you feel?"

"I'm fine, Mother." She pulled back a little. "Mishtag told me about the vial and how you activated it. Between the two of you, you saved my life." Kailani's voice was full of emotion.

"But what prevented the poisoned arrow from going deeper was the box. The arrow went straight through it and the tip only just pierced your skin. Look." She gestured to the side and on the floor it lay exactly as described.

"The king in the Lost Mire said it would save my life," she said in wonder. Picking up the box, she pushed the arrow through further and snapped the shaft, pulling both ends out, careful not to touch the poisoned tip. Her brow creased as she looked at it – the arrow was exactly the same as the ones in her quiver. She threw the pieces to the ground and kicked them away then opened the box. Miraculously, the scroll inside hadn't been damaged. She closed it again and placed it with her things. "Did any of you see the shooter?"

"Yes. I saw him briefly just before the arrow hit you," Garalia said. The anger in her voice matched her eyes.

"What . . .?"

"He was wearing the uniform of the king's guard," she interrupted.

"So our fears had substance then." Her lips pressed together in a tight line and her eyes flashed. "My guess is he was an advance scout and the fact he shot me implies he may have volunteered for the job. I think the soldiers can't be too far ahead of us now so we need to refine our plans."

"We can't risk meeting up with them now," Garalia said forcefully, "there's no way of knowing how many of them are would-be assassins."

"I agree. Let's eat while we decide what we can do." Kailani bent down and retrieved the two plates of food she'd prepared, handing one to her mother.

After a few bites, Garalia said, "Do we have enough food to take a long route around so we can pass them without their lookouts spotting us?"

"No. We are getting low again as it is. The only way I can see of getting past them safely is for me to teleport us a few miles behind them. My only worry is whether I'm strong enough to take us all far enough past so they don't see us." Her eyes crinkled as her brow hooded them.

"If you're that unsure, there must be another solution. We're missing something here . . ." her mother trailed off.

They sat in silence as they finished their meal, both wracking their brains. Suddenly Kailani let out a whoop, making all of them jump. "I've got it!" she said, punching the air.

"What?"

"I make two trips. I teleport you and Yashtig first, leaving you in a barrier so you're safe and warm, and then I return for Mishtag and the bags and make the second trip. What do you think?"

"I think it's a brilliant idea. However, it may drain your strength a little so let's take some of the bags on the first trip."

"That's a good idea. Mishtag, will you be alright if I leave you here alone inside the barrier for a short while?"

The Blenorai Kai nodded. *Get them as far past the soldiers as you possibly can.*

"I will," Kailani replied to her. "Right, let's clear everything up ready and then we can go." She pulled a piece of cloth from her pack and carefully wrapped the broken arrow inside. She wanted proof to show her grandfather. Placing it at the very bottom of her pack, she loaded everything else on top and fastened it. Once she had packed the plates away, her mother was ready to go.

Kailani did one last sweep around the barrier to ensure nothing had been forgotten then turned to her mother. "Are you and Yashtig ready?"

"Yes."

"Mishtag, I'll be back for you as soon as I possibly can – I promise you," she said staring directly into her Kai's eyes.

Kailani moved next to her mother and held her hand; the other one she placed on Yashtig's head. She closed her eyes and as Mishtag watched, they shimmered then disappeared.

Chapter 18

Teleporting was the strangest feeling any of them had encountered before. Even more peculiar was Kailani's ability to see what passed below them despite how fast they were travelling. She noticed the battalion and kept them moving for several miles past. Knowing she had to conserve some of her strength, she saw a likely spot and they re-materialised on the ice. The first thing she did was pull out her Kamuk and mark an arrow-shape in the ice to ensure they continued in the right direction.

"Are you both alright?"

Yashtig nodded.

"Yes, I'm fine. It felt rather odd though," Garalia answered, a half-smile on her lips. Her face became serious. "There's something I noticed as we flew over the battalion which concerns me. They're not riding under my father's pennant. When any of the soldiers are on official business for the king, they always ride with his flag flown high, but the ones we just passed didn't even have one with them."

Kailani erected the barrier around them while she thought for a minute. "Can we talk about this when I return?" Her mother nodded. Kailani kissed her cheek then with a wave she shimmered and disappeared, reappearing in the barrier where Mishtag waited patiently.

How are you, Kailani? Did everything go according to plan?

"I'm a little tired so just need a short rest before we make our journey," she replied, sitting down on her cloak. "And yes, everything was fine. We sailed a few miles past the battalion, far enough they wouldn't be able to see us, but not as far as I could have gone. I wanted to save some of my energy so I could come back for you. I didn't realise how much it would take out of me."

Maybe it is more the fact you have not used that particular gift for any real distance before, so you were not primed. The more you teleport, the easier it should become and the less energy you will expend.

Kailani sighed. "You're probably right. I think it's because the magic I've used up till now hasn't had any effect on me so I wasn't prepared. Anyway, I'm feeling stronger again now so let's make a move."

She had already loaded the packs on the Blenorai, so she took down the barrier, placed her hand on Mishtag's head and the same strange feeling permeated both of them as they disappeared.

They looked down as they passed the battalion. Most of the men were lounging around and sleeping, and only a couple of them were sitting, keeping watch. She looked for the pennant and found her mother was right – it wasn't there at all. Kailani grinned as they drifted away from the soldiers, but only sixty feet further on they suddenly found themselves on the ice instead of floating. She tried desperately to teleport again, but nothing happened.

A shout could be heard from behind her and she turned around. In the distance she saw one of the soldiers pointing in her direction and panic set in. She quickly mounted Mishtag and said, "Run – our lives depend on it!"

Mishtag took off and within seconds they were travelling faster than she would have believed possible. The thump, thump of arrows landing in the ice behind them faded quickly. A couple of spells came close to hitting her – she could hear and smell them – but thankfully they fell short. The scenery was nothing but a blur and Kailani's hood blew back so her hair streamed out behind her. It was exhilarating and she would have enjoyed it were it not for the band of assassins on her trail. A moment of desperation hit her as she remembered they would be riding Blenorai too, but then she relaxed a little. The Kai were far superior to anything the soldiers would have; it seemed sometimes as if they possessed a little magic of their own.

She sat forward until she was lying almost flat and said, "Tell Yashtig and mother to be ready to go as soon as we get there." Mishtag wiggled her ears so Kailani would know she'd heard. Staying in that position to make them as streamlined as possible, it seemed to the princess that they were moving even more rapidly, if that were possible.

A short while later they saw the barrier erected around Garalia and Yashtig. Kailani took it down and found her mother already mounted. Yashtig began running before they reached him and it didn't take long for him to match Mishtag's speed. As they rocketed across the ice, the Blenorai were obviously conversing, so Kailani kept quiet, checking to ensure her mother could cope with the speed. Garalia seemed to be handling it well.

Every now and then, Kailani looked behind her to see if there was any sign of their pursuers. She couldn't see the colour of their uniforms, but everything was such a blur it was difficult to see anything at all. She just had to trust that the phenomenal speed of the Kai, and the fact the battalion had to break camp and pack their belongings before setting off en masse, was enough to keep them out of harm's way. She was under no illusion that one or two soldiers had left almost immediately to chase after them though.

After several hours, she could see her mother struggling to hold on and asked the Blenorai to slow down. The light was fading fast and she didn't want to be hurtling across the ice at night unless it was absolutely necessary. Suddenly she had an epiphany. Turning to her mother she said, "If I tie you on with the rope, do you think you can manage for one more hour?"

Garalia looked at her through narrowed eyes. "Yes, I think so. Why? You've got a twinkle of mischief in your eyes."

"Just a moment, Mother. Yashtig, Mishtag, can you keep going a bit longer?" The animals nodded. "Alright. We're going to play a little game of misdirection." She coaxed them to halt and conjured a barrier, about the size of the one they would normally use. Then she tied her mother to Yashtig and placed a couple of the packs on him to even the load between the two Kai and they set off again.

Soon they were travelling at the same speed as before. As the light faded the temperature plummeted. Both women buried their faces in the shaggy manes of the Blenorai, but Garalia was better prepared, wearing gloves to keep her hands warm. Kailani hadn't had the chance to do that before they had to make their escape and it became harder to hold on. She tried shifting her grip so her hands were more protected by Mishtag's large head, but although it eased the bitter cold, it couldn't remove it completely. At the speed they were going, she didn't dare let go with even one hand to get a glove out.

Kailani felt her hands slipping on the reins. She gritted her teeth, trying desperately to hold on, but they slipped again and she cried out in frustration. Having lost track of time, she had no idea how far away they were from the barrier she'd erected.

Now Garalia looked at her daughter with concern. She noticed the red skin on the back of her hands and called them to a halt. Kailani stared behind her, but no sign of the barrier could be seen. She sighed with relief as she erected their new shield. Her hands were sore, but she untied her mother and helped her off the Kai before unloading the packs and giving Yashtig and Mishtag some well-deserved extra rations.

She could barely put the meal together as her hands stiffened, but somehow managed and they ate hungrily. As Kailani cleared up, Garalia searched through the packs until she found the medicinal items. She pulled out a small pot containing a salve; whomever had packed this had obviously tried to pick items that covered a broad spectrum of problems and the salve had just the right healing properties for her daughter's hands.

As soon as she had finished, Garalia called Kailani over and sat her down. When she looked at the skin on the back of her daughter's hands, she was mortified. The skin was so burned by the cold that it had completely dried out and split in several places so fluid mixed with blood was beginning to ooze out. Kailani hadn't complained once even though she must have been in agony. She gently smoothed the salve over the chapped, raw skin. Kailani winced a couple of times and bit her bottom lip, but didn't make a sound. By the time she had finished the application, the skin was looking better already. Some of the redness had faded and the smaller cracks appeared to be closing up.

"Thank you, Mother. It doesn't hurt so much now." The tightness around Kailani's eyes had smoothed.

"You're welcome, my darling." Garalia smiled.

"We're going to have to get an early start in the morning. We don't know how long it will take the soldiers to work out that we're not in the other shelter, so the bigger the head start we can get on them, the better. The ruse won't work a second time and we still have a long way to go before we get to the Ice Palace." Her voice was firm.

"I agree. We only have about an hour's lead on them and that could be eroded quite quickly. If the battalion leader has the power to take down the barrier, which is a distinct possibility, he could decide to do it as soon as dawn breaks and when he finds he's been duped they will set off straight away. I don't know if all of our magic system has been explained to you, has it?"

"No, not really. Grandfather told me about the birthmarks I have and what they mean. He also took me to the High Priest of Rasha-Varl who gave me the vial around my neck and explained how to use it, but that's all I know."

"Other people outside the royal family may have been born with a birthmark, but we have never come across anyone who has more than one. Whatever birthmark they have will give them power in that particular element. In addition, certain members of the royal household, for example the captain of the guard, will have been given a vial from the High Priest as well as all his lieutenants. I'm pretty sure the battalion leader, who is supposedly meant to guard you and keep you safe, will have one around his neck."

"Grandfather and the High Priest were both shocked when they saw the colour of my vial. I was told they'd never encountered one like it before."

"No, and neither have I. There are a number of different colours which come from the Sacred Wells and each controls a different element or power. All the royal family, including me, have violet ones, but the colour is nowhere near as deep a shade as yours. Ours is actually closer to lavender. It gives us extra power over all the elements. It was the one thing I managed to hold onto in that dreadful camp. "

"Oh. How did you manage that?" Kailani asked, her eyes widening.

"I sewed it into the hem of the rags I was wearing when you rescued me." Garalia replied, a note of pride in her voice.

"Why didn't you use it to try and escape?"

"Bellis told me it wouldn't work because of the spell father had put around the Land of No Souls. I don't know why I believed him, but I did and never tried to use it. I feel really stupid not even trying now I think about it, but that's all in the past. What's important is the present and getting home safely, as you said." Garalia had a sheepish look on her face. She turned away and rummaged through the bag containing the clothes, pulling out the ragged dress she had worn. Feeling around the hem, she located the vial and ripped at the seam; releasing the vial, she placed the chain around her neck. Tucking it beneath her clothing, she stuffed the clothes back in the pack and turned back to her daughter.

"I suppose the stress and fear of the situation made it all too easy to believe Bellis's and Gengaruk's lies. However, we can deal with part of that when we get back to the palace. I think we should get some sleep now so we can get that early start in the morning."

Mother and daughter hugged then settled down with their Blenorai who were already out for the count.

They woke the next morning just before dawn to a turbulent sky. Dark clouds rolled by so fast, it was as if something was chasing them. The good thing was the wind would be at their backs.

It was the first night of uninterrupted sleep she'd had since rescuing her mother and she was grateful for it. The nightmares her mother suffered were dreadful and it was going to be a long time before she would even begin to recover from her incarceration. After consuming a quick breakfast, they prepared to leave.

With the sound of the wind it was impossible to know if any of the soldiers had scouted ahead and were outside their shelter. Kailani made a row of transparent windows around the entire structure to check and was relieved to find no one out there. After putting her gloves on she took down the shelter and immediately the Kai began to run.

She looked behind her and was horrified to see a flash of colour. Someone from the guard was close, too close for comfort. How did they discover her ruse so quickly? Dawn was only just upon them – did they take the other barrier down in the night hoping to catch them asleep? After all, there would have been less chance of a struggle if the plan was to capture them, and if their intent was to dispose of them, it would have been all too easy.

Kailani bent lower and whispered into Mishtag's ear. "Run fast, my friend. The enemy is too close to us for me to feel comfortable and safe." Her voice was strained.

Within seconds, the Kai sped up and once again the scenery became a blur. They didn't know they were being fired upon until an arrow caught Garalia's sleeve. She let out a scream and Kailani turned to see the fear on her mother's colourless face.

"Mother? Are you alright? Has it pierced your skin at all?" she cried, trying to make herself heard above the rushing of the wind.

"I-I don't think so. It doesn't feel like it."

Kailani breathed a huge sigh of relief. "If you can, try and push the shaft through just enough so it's well away from your skin and I'll remove it when we next stop." It hurt the back of her throat to try and shout loudly enough to be heard, but under the circumstances, she wasn't going to complain.

Without warning the ground beneath them began to shake and rumble causing the Kai to struggle as they ran. Suddenly a large wall of ice appeared some eight feet in front of them. The Kai skidded as they desperately tried to slow down and turned their heads left and right as they frantically looked for a way out. Someone behind them had either got Ice God Xuani's birthmark on them or they had a blue vial around their necks.

Kailani reached toward her mother and shouted, "Give me your hand." Garalia held it out and her daughter grabbed it, being careful of the protruding arrow head. Suddenly they were in the air and totally invisible to the soldiers. The battalion pulled up and gaped at the area where they were. They looked around and couldn't see any sign of them. Kailani suppressed the urge to giggle – they weren't out of danger yet and still had a long way to go.

The four travelled as fast and far as Kailani had the strength to take them. Having the wind behind them was quite a boost. As her energy waned they began to descend and as gently as she could, Kailani set them on the ground. She could feel Mishtag ready to run as soon as her paws touched the ice, but she stopped her with a thought. She had no idea how much distance they had covered, she just hoped it was far enough.

Swiftly but carefully, Kailani removed the arrow from her mother's sleeve, placing it in her pack for later use. Garalia's skin was inspected thoroughly, but there was no sign of even a scratch. Satisfied, Kailani gave Yashtig and Mishtag the order to go and within a couple of seconds the scenery became like a smudge on a painting.

They didn't dare to stop for lunch, not that they had much food left anyway. Kailani managed to grab a small handful of the Kai's food, which was also running low, and by steering Mishtag closer so she was almost touching Yashtig, managed to tip the contents into her mother's hand. Immediately Garalia understood. She leant further forward and stretched her cupped hand as close to Yashtig's mouth as she could. He turned his head slightly having smelled the food and gently took it from her hand without once slowing his speed. When her hand was empty, the Blenorai nudged it. Garalia pulled it back and grabbed the reins once more, holding on tightly. Kailani fed Mishtag the same way then fastened the pack.

All day the Blenorai Kai ran, desperate to keep their precious cargo away from the murderous battalion behind them. The sky darkened, but still they didn't stop even though they felt spell-casting just a few inches from their fur.

"Do you honestly think you can fool them a second time with the barriers?" Garalia shouted over the wind.

"Not for a moment. However, it will slow them down while they investigate. They can't take the chance of picking and choosing which ones to check, they'll have to examine each one they come across, just in case we're in there. I'll have to give them a little incentive too, just to make sure they stop." She cast again and a tiny orange light inside showed just enough on the exterior to look like it was inhabited.

"If your intention is to put several of these barriers along the way, won't it drain you as you try to keep the lights glowing inside?"

"Honestly, I don't know. I've never tried to do it before. We'll soon find out," she said ruefully.

About a mile further on she erected another barrier and placed another light inside, this one slightly larger than the last. This continued for the next ten to fifteen miles. After a while she forgot how many she'd cast, but was careful to increase the light inside in increments in each one. The last one she cast had no light at all.

They continued even after the sky became a carpet of velvet black, shading toward purple. Thankfully the Kai could see in the dark because the two ladies were virtually blind. The distorted view flew past their eyes, all they could see was darkness and nothing else. They snuggled into the warm fur around the Kais' necks and closed their eyes.

Sometime later, Mishtag broke the silence as she spoke to her mistress's mind. *I am sorry to disturb you, Princess, but I see a village ahead. I believe it is the same one we stopped at on our way to rescue your mother. Do you want to stop there?*

Kailani thought for a moment. There would be safety in the village to a degree and if she could convince the innkeeper of who they were, he might even be able to find some good men who would be willing to act as bodyguards to protect them. On the downside, if the battalion did catch up to them, innocent lives could be lost and she didn't want that on her conscience. A nugget of an idea began to germinate in her brain and she answered Mishtag in the affirmative.

They soon arrived at the village. It was quite late and few people were around in the streets, but they were startled to see them and curious. Blenorai Kai were rare in their small hamlet and they knew someone important was riding them. They made their way to the inn, on one side of the street in the centre of a row of small shops. The market square opened out in front of it and the stalls were all covered for the night.

"How do the people here make a living? What do they sell apart from home-baked items?" Kailani asked, looking around at the shops and market stalls.

"Our people are industrious. Just because our kingdom is covered in ice, it doesn't mean we cannot grow fruit and vegetables or raise animals for eating. What you don't see here are the small workshops that weave material, grind grain into powder from which we make food, and the solins who carve from the bodies of trees and work with ice and metal."

"Solins? What are these things? I've never heard of them."

Garalia smiled at her daughter's confusion. "Solins are the skilled workers who have been trained to carve, mould, and shape tree bodies, ice, and metal. Here's the inn. You go and see if they have any rooms available and I'll stay here with the Blenorai Kai. I don't know if you have any money with you, but if you have to, tell them who you are. They will always make room for royalty as they know they will be paid handsomely for the accommodations."

Kailani grabbed her Plexan and quiver and gave it to her mother. "I won't leave you un-armed, even for a few minutes. Stay alert, Mother. I'll be as quick as I can." She gently squeezed Garalia's shoulder then disappeared through the door of the inn.

Approaching the bar, she saw a short, stocky man. "Are you the owner?"

"Yes."

"Good. I need two rooms for the night, plus food, and shelter for my Blenorai please. My companion is outside with them so I would appreciate it if you could send someone out to deal with the animals so she can come inside."

"Certainly, your Highness. I've known you were coming and have been holding rooms awaiting your arrival," he said, bowing.

"Really? How could you know?"

The innkeeper pointed to a hooded man who sat at a table in the corner, his face hidden. "He told me."

Chapter 19

Kailani approached the man. As she reached the table, he slipped off his hood and turned his face toward her. His hair was the same colour as hers, long and wavy, reaching well past his shoulders. She guessed him to be a similar age to her, as his face was smooth except for the tiny smile lines that appeared around his eyes. He wasn't handsome in the classical sense yet something about his face was appealing. His shoulders were broad and as he unfolded his frame to rise, Kailani was surprised by how tall he was.

"Who are you?"

"I'm Correollis, your Highness." He bowed just as she gasped. His name was legendary amongst the people of Taivass-maa. No one had ever seen him or knew where he lived, except perhaps King Sirris. Rumour had it he lived as a hermit far from any villages, but there were no reported sightings of him anywhere.

It was said he was a fearsome warrior, skilled in weaponry, who had never been bested. He was also described as a powerful wizard. The one thing documented in the history books was how loyal and protective he was toward the royal family, coming to their aid in times of strife. But how could he be the young man standing before the princess? Surely he was more likely a descendant of the famed Correollis who fought for the king so many years ago.

"The fame of that name precedes you, but what proof do you have?

Anyone could pose as the great Correollis because he's such an enigma. I'm aware of only one person who could confirm or deny your claim and he's not here. Prove to me you are who you say!" She placed her hands on her hips and stared at the stranger.

"You are Princess Kailani, born of Princess Garalia of Idenvarlis and Prince Galaxan of Taivass-maa . . ."

"Reciting my ancestry will not prove anything to me," she interrupted. "Anyone in Taivass-maa could look up that information in the Great Library. You're going to have to do better than that." Her voice was edged with scorn.

He grinned. "Very well, your Highness, allow me to do better. You carry the birthmarks of all four of our deities on your shoulder as well as those of three others on your neck. It is prophesised that one will come who will unite the two worlds, who is the most powerful being created, but the way to unity comes at a price, one which is physically arduous, fraught with danger, and will cause as much heartache as joy. You are the one the prophecy was written about." He paused to let the information sink in. "I know the Correollis of legend is written about in the history books and it is something your tutor ensured you studied. Can you tell me what happened to him during the Zannis War?"

Kailani hesitated, not so much because she didn't know the answer. Being told a prophecy had been written about her shocked her to her core. "It is written that Baelris, the Lightning God, in trying to protect Correollis made an error of judgement and the warrior was accidentally caught by the edge of one of his bolts. As a result, he carried a lightning-shaped scar across one side of his chest."

"You know the histories well, Princess," he said with a smirk.

"Don't dare to mock me." Her voice was as icy as the land she was in and her eyes flashed dangerously.

"Forgive me, Highness," he bowed, "I meant it as a compliment, nothing more. But we digress and time slowly runs against us." He lifted his shirt, something which would never normally be done in front of a lady of noble birth without first asking permission, and there, on one side of his chest, was a lightning-shaped scar burnt into the skin.

Kailani gaped. At first she was too shocked to think coherently and uttered the first thing that came into her head. "But that battle was over one hundred years ago and surely you're not the same man who fought for my grandfather in the Exul war? That was nearly fifty years ago."

He grinned. "I am he."

Kailani's eyes widened. "But you don't look any older than me," she blurted.

Correollis chuckled. "It's amazing what a little magic can do," he replied, lowering his voice. He winked and she couldn't help but smile back at him.

"Well, it's an honour to meet you, Correollis, but what are you doing in Idenvarlis? How did you get here?"

"Likewise, your Highness. When your father discovered your mission, he became extremely concerned. He spoke to your grandfather, who contacted me, asking for my help. After my audience with him, I immediately left Taivass-maa and travelled here on my Feegle."

Kailani's eyes grew wider and her brows rose. "I didn't know it was possible to travel between the two worlds on a Feegle."

"Shhh." He put his index finger to his lips then continued in a low voice. "For most people it isn't . . . but I have the ability. I can't discuss this further with you right now – we can't take the chance of being overheard."

Her face grew serious and she nodded. Before she could speak again, they were distracted by the door opening. She sensed him stiffen and turned her head to see who it was. Garalia swept through the door, her regal bearing obvious despite her weakened condition. Her mother walked directly to her side, curiosity evident in her eyes.

"Mother, may I present Correollis?" She turned to him. "This is Princess Garalia."

"I'm aware of your reputation, Correollis, and am pleased to meet you," she said with a smile.

He bowed to her. "Your Highness. It gladdens my heart that Princess Kailani was able to rescue you and I'm honoured to be in your presence."

"Thank you." She sat on one of the ice chairs next to the table and the others followed suit. "I can guess why you're here and who sent you. It's more than a blessing that you've come. Our meeting here couldn't have come at a more fortuitous time."

"I understand more than you may realise, your Highness. It won't be more than a few hours before the battalion arrives in the village and this will most likely be the first place they will come looking for you. If you don't mind my saying, you both look exhausted and in need of a hearty meal and a good night's sleep. I will ensure they cannot find you or your Blenorai – this I promise you."

"You're perceptive and no, I don't mind you voicing your observation of our condition. I won't ask how you intend to hide us. I'm grateful you have come to our aid. You need to be aware of some things, but I'm reluctant to speak of it where it can be overheard." Garalia glanced around the room noticing they were attracting more than a hint of attention from the few villagers seated across the room and the innkeeper kept peeking in their direction every so often. It was hardly surprising – they had never seen one person with azure hair, let alone two.

Correollis followed the path her eyes took. "Fear not, your Highness, we will be able to speak privately after you have eaten. As for the locals,

I'll speak with them and ensure they don't gossip about what they've seen here. I've taken the liberty of ordering food for you both and it should be arriving momentarily." He nodded to the innkeeper who brought three plates of food to the table. He returned with a plate of unleavened bread, a jug of liquid, and three goblets.

Kailani had no idea what she was eating, but was past caring. It was hot, tasted good, and filled her aching stomach. Correollis had poured each of them a drink as soon as the jug was placed on the table. She sipped it, surprised to find it was a hot and slightly spicy, fruit-flavoured beverage which seemed to warm her whole body as if she was tucked up in her own bed.

When they had finished, there was precious little left on the table save a few crumbs. The jug had been refilled twice. She wasn't the only one who found the drink delicious and moreish. It was the most Kailani and Garalia had eaten in one day since the rescue and they felt full to bursting. Despite the uncomfortable, overfull feeling, they both felt stronger, as if the food itself had worked some magic on them.

The innkeeper came over and cleared the table. He began to move away with the dirty plates, but Correollis tapped his arm. The man nodded and continued on his way.

"You'll be going up to your rooms soon. I've ordered a hot bath for each of you and you'll find clean clothes on your beds. I have things to attend to down here. When you're ready, we can meet in one of the rooms and speak freely. I hope I haven't forgotten anything that you may need."

"You've been extremely thoughtful, Correollis, and we're grateful. I'm confident you have overlooked nothing," Kailani replied, a smile on her lips.

He bowed his head in acknowledgement before speaking again. "Your rooms are ready. If you'll excuse me, I'll see you both in a short while."

"Of course," Garalia said. They rose from the table just as the innkeeper's wife appeared. She was still slim despite her advancing years, showing none of the excess fat most women of a certain age were prone to, and moved gracefully.

"If you will follow me, your Highnesses, I'll take you to your rooms now. I can assure you they are the best our humble inn can offer."

"I'm sure they will meet our needs. Please don't worry on that account," Garalia reassured her.

"Well, begging your pardon, your Highness, but it's not every day an inn such as ours would be host to not only the heir to the throne of Idenvarlis, but another member of the royal family."

"No, I suppose it isn't." They climbed the stairs, which had surprisingly even treads, and followed her down the corridor. The woman opened the doors at the far end then pressed the key in each of their hands.

"If there is anything you need, please ring the bell and I will come straight away." She curtseyed then left in a hurry.

After bathing and dressing in clean clothes, Kailani felt a great deal better. She allowed her hair to flow untethered down her back as it dried. It had been the first time in weeks since she'd been able to do so and it gave her a sense of freedom. She knew it would be short-lived, but luxuriated in the feeling while she could. It seemed almost unreal that something so simple could give her such a joyous feeling, but after everything she'd experienced since leaving the Ice Palace it was really no wonder.

The clothes were a perfect fit and were ideal for the remainder of the journey; the lightness of the fabric belied the warmth of them against her skin. After lacing her boots, she left the room and knocked on her mother's door.

Kailani was astounded at the change in Garalia and as she stood in her room, she couldn't help staring. Although her mother's skin was still pale, it now shone like a newly-glazed piece of porcelain, as if years of grime had been washed away to reveal the diamond beneath. Her hair, which appeared brown before, was now a shining platinum-blonde. It moved and the light caught it, the flowing locks appearing almost white and glistening like sunlight on fresh fallen snow.

"What are you gawping at?" Garalia's forehead wrinkled as she waited for an answer.

"You, Mother," Kailani answered with something akin to awe in her voice. "You're so beautiful."

"Thank you, my dear," she chuckled self-consciously, "as are you."

"Thank you, Mother." She lowered her eyes for a moment then raised them again. Despite how well the clothes fit, they did little to hide how thin and under-nourished her mother was. She felt heartsick at the sight.

A knock at the door interrupted Kailani's observations and she moved across the room to open it. Correollis stood in the hallway. She ushered him in closing and locking the door behind him.

"Please don't speak for a moment," he requested then pulled a gnarled stick from beneath his clothing. It was about eight inches long and made from a pale wood Kailani didn't recognise. Shaped to a point at one end, it had symbols carved into its length. He muttered some words in a language she'd never heard, "Palia des simen hosk" and watched as he pointed the stick, first at the door and then he circled it around the room. When he'd finished, he replaced it within the folds of his apparel. "Now we can speak openly without fear of being overheard. What do you need to tell me?"

Garalia began, haltingly at first then the words almost tumbled over each other as she explained her initial capture and finding out who was behind it. She left out the more personal details, like the rape, but did admit to being abused during her incarceration. She continued her story until the point where she was rescued.

Kailani took up the story, seeing how tired her mother was. She explained their theories about the members of the battalion, them not flying the king's pennant, how their journey had been sabotaged, and the chase across the ice with spells and arrows raining down on them. She ended with how they'd arrived at the village and found the inn.

Correollis listened intently to everything they had to say, absorbing the details. His face morphed through various emotions as their story unfolded, but settled on impassive by the end. He nodded his head slowly and then spoke. "I can understand your pain and anger at your brother, Princess Garalia, but we mustn't allow emotions to dictate our thoughts from here on. That also applies to you, Princess Kailani. We must be clinical, almost cold, in making our plans to get you safely to the Ice Palace and subsequently to the king so you can tell your tale without fear of interruption."

"I understand and agree, but I've been away from my home for so long, I don't know what my father's routines are anymore," Garalia said, a note of longing underlying her voice.

"Obviously I've been in the palace more recently, but I was barely there long enough to observe any particular routines. Besides," Kailani added, "I'm sure his normal habits were broken while he trained me in the use of weapons, helped me choose my Blenorai and made sure I bonded with her, and introduced me to the High Priest of Rasha-Varl. However, I do know he retired for bed at the exact same time each night."

"That's useful to know. It's likely to be the best time to reach him. Does the rest of the castle quieten down when the king retires for the night?" Correollis asked. The skin tightened around his eyes denoting his concentration and thought.

"Yes. I would say within half an hour the maids have finished their duties, the sentries change to a skeleton staff who only patrol the points of the palace which would be most likely to come under attack, plus one stationed near the king and queen's private suite of rooms. There's hardly anyone else around."

"In that case, we should aim to reach the king's rooms around forty-five minutes after he retires. The biggest problem will be getting past all the guards, especially not knowing who can and can't be trusted. Verbally walk me through the main entrance to the palace and up to the king's suite as if I were a blind man. I need to know what obstacles would be in the way, any steps and approximately how many, what areas or rooms would be passed, and any other useful information you can think of."

Garalia took up the challenge and with a little prompting from Correollis on occasions, was able to give him an excellent picture to work with.

"As I see it, the biggest problem will be gaining entry to the palace. We have to pass the entirety of the garrison's rooms as well as the area where the Blenorai are kept before we truly enter the main part of the palace. It will be a daunting task."

"Getting into the palace will be easy," Kailani announced with a grin. "The hardest part will be the final section of getting to grandfather."

"How?" Correollis's brow furrowed and confusion dulled his eyes.

She explained about the secret passage, its location, and the journey from its entrance into the corridor of the palace up to King Jaanis's room.

"That's obviously our best and safest way in and we'd only have one guard to contend with. My biggest concern is not how to get into the palace, but how we're going to get out of this village. By morning the battalion will either have this inn or the village surrounded. They'll shoot to kill and we won't hear the arrows coming. I have no idea whether they would have any regard for the villagers or if they would think of casualties as acceptable. I believe they won't worry if any innocents get injured or killed. I can't allow that to happen. I have to do something to draw them away from the village . . . in fact, that could work to our advantage." A sudden excitement danced in her eyes.

"What do you mean?" Garalia asked.

"If we could give them a false trail to follow, in a different direction to the palace, it would make our journey there much less dangerous."

"But would they fall for it? Would all of the battalion follow or would some set up camp closer to the palace? Do they have enough men to split into two groups like that? It depends on how intelligent their commanding officer is. I hate to inject doubt into your plan, Princess, but we can't assume anything. I like the thought of sending them off in the wrong direction and it's a great idea, but let's not get carried away. We must try and stay one step ahead of them because if we don't, this situation is going to end badly. I won't let that happen and it is the reason I'm here." Correollis spoke with a firm yet gentle tone.

"I can only tell you what I saw as I teleported over them. When my grandfather said about sending soldiers with me, he didn't say how many there would be. I didn't count, but at a guess I would say there's about forty or fifty of them. If there were others scouting the area, and I suspect there were, I obviously don't know how many. I think if we work on there being around fifty-four of them, we won't be far off. The only thing about my suggestion that concerns me is what direction would I go to make it believable?"

"I can help with that," Garalia answered. "There is a castle to the north, previously controlled by Gengaruk. After his banishment, my father sent a large number of troops there to take control of it and help re-build the community that had been enslaved. The battalion chasing us may think we're going there for reinforcements. Though we would both have to go to make the soldiers interested enough to follow. If you went alone, it would split their numbers and half would surely remain here."

"You raise some interesting points, Highnesses. However, my task is to ensure you arrive at the Ice Palace as soon as possible. I'm not sure how far you would need to travel in the wrong direction before returning here safely, to make the proposition viable. I'm not without skills as you've already seen. I'm confident we can slip past the battalion unnoticed, especially if we take advantage of the powers you have, Princess Kailani." Correollis turned to look at Garalia before continuing. "I know you also have powers, Highness, but you're as weak as a new-born lamb and I don't want you to exhaust yourself. I need you as strong as possible for the remainder of the journey."

Garalia nodded her agreement. She could not fault his logic.

He turned back to Kailani. "You haven't even begun to tap into the full potential of your magical abilities and once you know how, you'll find it won't drain your energy anywhere near as much as it does currently. I will show you how to do it before we leave here – we may need your skills."

She raised her eyebrows but said nothing. There had been one question burning on her tongue since she'd first met him and it wouldn't be ignored any longer, especially considering she'd already asked but received no answer. "Changing the subject for a moment, I'm dying to know how you travelled here by Feegle. You did say you would tell me later."

He took a deep breath and let it out slowly. He appeared thoughtful as he considered the question and it was several seconds before he spoke.

"Hundreds of years ago, one of my ancestors discovered a form of magic which came from the land itself. He studied it for many years, learning how to use it. Since then, each generation has acquired further knowledge and passed it to their offspring. Like you, I have birthmarks on my shoulder so I can utilise the magic the deities have bestowed upon us, but by using what my father taught me and the skills I've picked up since, I'm able to travel between worlds. That is how I arrived here on my Feegle."

"Does anyone else in Taivass-maa know of this other magic?"

"To my knowledge, I'm the only one since my father died. My family have always been tasked with protecting the royal family and I believe we were led by the gods and goddesses to learn of this. I also believe we're meant to keep it secret and teach no one except our offspring. It was and is our destiny."

Kailani stared, her eyes wide with fascination, but before she could ask anything further, Garalia spoke. "Thank you for sharing your secret with us, Correollis. However, we're digressing and need to address our precarious position here and how we're going to leave the village safely. I'm tiring quickly now. Perhaps we could adjourn and continue in the morning. It will give us all time to think about our options and between us, I'm sure we'll come up with a plan."

"Of course, your Highness. I can see how exhausted you are. With your permission, we'll take breakfast in this room so we can continue our deliberations in secret. My spell will hold until I remove it."

"An excellent idea. I will knock on your door when I'm awake. Which room are you in?"

"The one directly opposite yours, Highness."

"Very well. If there's nothing more that urgently requires my attention, I shall retire," Garalia said, her voice sounding weaker as fatigue overcame her.

"There is just one more tiny thing, Highness, and it will only take a couple of seconds." Correollis withdrew the strange stick and pointed it at the window, muttering a few words. "There. I have protected the window so no intruders can enter. I will do the same to the door once we leave the room. You can rest easy, safe in the knowledge that no one can get near you in the night. I'll do the same to Princess Kailani's room also."

"Thank you," she replied and smiled with relief in her eyes.

Kailani moved closer and gave her mother a hug and a kiss on the cheek. "Sleep well, Mother."

"You too," she replied, kissing her daughter on the forehead.

Kailani rose and walked through the door which Correollis held open. He bowed to Garalia then closed it softly behind him.

Chapter 20

When Kailani and Correollis walked into Garalia's room, a huge tray of Lerins, a jug filled with something white, and three goblets had been placed on the chest. The room looked totally different in daylight and Kailani could see just how basic it was compared to her bedroom in the Cloud Castle. Like hers, it contained a bed, a small chest of drawers, and a stool; the bath, with the now cold water, sat off to one side. The walls were rough – the ice looked like it had just been hacked with a sharp object until it was the right size and then left – as was the floor. The bed and furniture had been made from the trunks of trees and were fairly smooth to the touch, although nicks and thin ridges could be seen.

The bedding was made of some kind of fabric which had been knitted or woven; it was soft and had an immediate warm feeling to it. On top of this was an animal pelt, with fur on one side and a smooth, velvety texture on the other. It had kept her warm during the night so she assumed the same was true for her mother.

The clothes Garalia arrived in had been washed and pressed and were now in a neat pile on the chest. Kailani had found her own cleaned garments outside her door too.

Despite how much the princesses had eaten the night before, they found themselves famished and devoured several of the Lerins each. The white liquid was cold and had a creamy flavour that Kailani enjoyed. Garalia explained it was called Kelem and came from an animal.

After they'd eaten their fill, Garalia and Kailani sat on the bed while Correollis perched on the stool, and they continued their discussions of the previous evening. Being refreshed from their night's rest and strengthened from the meal, their thinking was sharper and soon came up with many ideas to avoid the battalion during their escape.

"The way I see it you have a choice between two options, Princess Kailani: disappear or fight your way out. You're torn between getting your mother out safely and making a stand. Am I right?" Correollis asked, leaning forward. A sharp intake of breath answered his question.

"How . . . ? You seem to know me quite well for someone who only met me last night. Is mind reading another of your many skills?" There was an edge to her voice. A niggle of mistrust manifested in her head.

"No, your Highness." He smiled as he continued. "When you've lived as long as I have, it doesn't take long to size people up, and one of the first things I learned was to determine a person's mettle." All frivolity vanished from his face and voice. He'd picked up on the tone of Kailani's question. "From what you told me last night, I have more than got the measure of you, Princess. I would even go so far as to surmise you want to destroy the battalion as you feel they are disloyal to King Jaanis."

"You make a good argument, Correollis, and your assessment of me is a fair one. Of course I think those soldiers are not loyal to the king. If they were, we wouldn't have had to avoid arrows and spells on our journey to this village. I can't believe the captain would allow it to happen if he were not, himself, one of Bellis's men. The apple is rotten from the stalk on down." She said the last with disgust.

"Very well. So how are we going to achieve this and still get Princess Garalia safely away from here?"

"I think I may have a plan. . ."

"Before we can leave, I need to work with you for a short while, Princess Kailani. For our plan to succeed, it's essential you can access your powers without it draining your energy. Are you agreeable?" Correollis asked. His head was tilted to one side.

"Of course. Why wouldn't I be?" she replied then continued without waiting for an answer. "I'll need access to all my magic in abundance before the whole situation is resolved so I want to learn as much as you can teach me in the time we have." Kailani's voice was resolute, her face set in a determined cast.

"Good. Would you come and sit on this stool, please?" He rose from it and she sat, looking at him expectantly. "Now, close your eyes and clearly visualise the four birthmarks on your shoulder. Concentrate on each one, look at each line, point, and curve until you feel like you know them intimately. When you've done this, please nod your head." The only sound in the room was their breathing. It took several minutes before Kailani moved. "Now do the same with the three on your neck." Her head moved quicker this time. "Now open your eyes, please. I need to test you."

Kailani acquiesced and kept her eyes on him, not sure what to expect. He held his hand up and a symbol appeared on it. Without pause, she said, "Sun." The symbol changed. "Snow." And again. "Moon." This was repeated until every birthmark had shown itself to her. She was correct on each one, speaking with confidence and no hesitation whatsoever.

"Good. Well done. Now I want you to close your eyes again and mentally reach deep inside yourself. You need to go further and deeper than you ever have before to the point where the vast chasm of power is stored. You will feel a tingle all over your body when you reach it. Nod when this happens," Correollis guided, his voice growing softer. "Reach deeper and deeper."

Her breathing slowed as she concentrated. The only sound in the room was the soft breaths of her companions. After a couple of minutes she saw, in her mind's eye, a well of energy just waiting to be drawn. She pushed herself toward it, eager to touch and feel what lay within. Suddenly she felt a prickling sensation on her skin which quickly eradiated over her entire body. It was a strange, but not unpleasant, sensation. She nodded her head as she'd been instructed.

"Well done, Highness. Now pull it up and allow it to course through your every vein and muscle. Nod again when this is done."

The power seemed almost impatient to be set free and as she began to draw on it, the energy rushed out like a torrent. A small gasp escaped from her lips as she felt it burst forth; it seemed to consume every part of her, filling her more than her lifeblood. She nodded again.

"Now open your eyes, Princess, and tell me what you see."

As she lifted her lids, Garalia gasped. Her daughter's eyes shone like polished jewels caught by the sun. They were so bright she had to turn her gaze from them.

Kailani glanced around the room, looking at objects as well as her companions. "Everything has a sort of bright haze around it, including mother and you. Is that what you were expecting?"

"Yes. Now try and do a small spell, perhaps something offensive."

Without having to concentrate, she lifted her hands and a fiery ball about the size of an apple appeared between them. Entranced she pulled her hands a little further apart and it grew accordingly. She widened them again and the fire ball expanded. Moving her hands closer together than when she'd first created it, the sphere shrank to the size of a plum. Instinctively, Kailani pressed her palms together and when she opened them again, it was gone.

"I'd like to experiment further, but I'm not sure this room would survive. My power feels like a tangible part of me, as if it's as permanent as my skin. It feels like a second skin, but one that pulses and crackles with energy," she said, wonder in her voice. Her eyes then clouded. "Would someone get hurt if they touched me?"

"Only if you willed it. You would have to call the power and layer it over your skin. You can shape it as you desire, just like when you made the fiery ball." She looked at him with doubt. "Let me prove it." He reached a hand forward. "May I?" She nodded and he laid his hand on hers. "See? I'm fine. I didn't feel a thing."

Kailani's concentration on Correollis was absolute and she didn't notice Garalia rise and place her hand on her cheek. She felt an immediate and unconscious flash of self-protection, but managed to control it before Garalia was hurt. "I see what you mean," she said, glancing at her mother before looking back at him. "The power feels almost . . . *protective*, as if it would automatically let itself loose if I didn't concentrate on keeping it reined in. That concerns me greatly. Am I going to be able to control it quickly enough when I'm caught totally unawares?" A note of panic rose in her voice.

"Fear not, your Highness. When you are in a safe environment where you feel comfortable and not threatened in any way, the power will lay almost dormant. It hibernates until it's called forth once more. Now you have tapped into it, the magical energy will never disappear or drain back to the place where you found it. It will always be instantly at your command."

"Thank you for allaying my worries. Now, is there anything else we need to discuss before we put our plan into action?"

"One small thing," Garalia said. "Provisions. The palace is still some distance away and we'll need food and water. Our packs are empty."

"I will see to that immediately, your Highness." He bowed then turned to Kailani. "I can think of nothing more."

"Good. In that case, shall we make our preparations to leave?"

Chapter 21

Kailani and Garalia descended the back stairs and passed through a door which led to the stable area. As soon as the Blenorai saw them they rose and ran forward, their tails swishing on the hay, sending it flying in all directions. Kailani placed the packs on the ground and crouched in front of them.

"Are you pleased to see us?" she crooned softly as she stroked both their heads.

Of course, Mistress, Mishtag replied. *We have missed you both.*

"Thank you. Now we must prepare to leave." Deftly, she dressed them in their armour and loaded all the packs on Yashtig. "Are you ready, Mother?" She kept her voice low, guessing there would be at least one guard outside.

"Yes, although I'm still worried."

"You have enough strength now to take down a barrier. If I haven't returned to you within three hours, set off for the palace. Yashtig knows the way to the secret entrance. Don't wait or hesitate once you've arrived. Get to grandfather as quickly as possible. You still have your vial so use it if you must. There is a small sword strapped to the outside of this pack in case you need it. I will be fine. I don't believe the gods and goddesses would allow us to reunite only to strip that from us again, do you?"

"I suppose not. But it's a mother's prerogative to worry about her children and I won't stop fretting until you're by my side once more."

Kailani rolled her eyes but didn't reply. She turned instead to their faithful Kai. "Mishtag, I'll return to you shortly."

Garalia mounted Yashtig and held her daughter's hand. There was a shimmer and they disappeared from sight.

Kailani returned to the stable a few minutes later. Mishtag stood proud in her armour with her head held high. Her mistress quickly relayed the plan and then disappeared through the door, returning to the inn.

Once back in her room, she checked all her weapons, secured the quiver, and placed the Plexan on her shoulder. She exited the room and met Correollis in the hallway. He carried two shields, one of which he handed to the princess. She looked at the design on it and saw both symbols for Idenvarlis and Taivass-maa intertwined in the centre and round the outside were runes and the icons for the deities of both worlds.

"This shield has been bespelled to protect you, Princess."

"Thank you. It's amazing. Where did you get it from?"

"I brought it with me from Taivass-maa," he replied, offering no further information.

"You bespelled it?" she asked, astutely.

"Partly," he answered cryptically, an inscrutable expression on his face.

She raised her eyebrows. "And?"

"And it's time we left, Highness. Surely you don't want your mother to worry any longer than is necessary?"

"Cleverly done." She narrowed her eyes. "This conversation isn't over."

"I didn't think it would be." His lips twitched into a semblance of a smile. Kailani huffed. "Just remember what I told you about your powers."

She nodded. "And please don't forget what I said about limiting damage to the villagers' property."

"Yes, your Highness. May the blessings of all the deities of both worlds be with you today."

"And with you," she replied, her tone and expression softening a little. She turned her back on him and they walked off in opposite directions.

Reaching the main door of the inn, Kailani paused. Using her mind she called out to her Blenorai.

Mishtag? Can you hear me?

Yes, Mistress. Are you at the door?

I am. You know what to do, right?

I do.

Promise me something, Mishtag. Promise you'll take care and we'll be reunited to go and join Mother. I can't lose you, Mishtag. Promise I won't. The Kai was touched by Kailani's concern. She never thought she'd end up with a master who cared so much about her.

I cannot make promises I may not be able to keep, Princess. What I will promise is that my spirit will always be with you and I will be careful.

I suppose that's the next best thing so I'll have to accept it. Kailani took a deep breath and let it out slowly. She could feel her power rippling beneath her skin, just waiting to be unleashed. *Ready? Let's go.* Kailani quietly inched open the door, mentally thanking the innkeeper for keeping his premises in good repair. She peeped out and saw the two soldiers guarding the door with their backs to her, chatting.

She stepped through the door and swung her sword in an arc, cutting them down where they stood. Dropping low to the ground, and using the shield to cover most of her body, she surveyed the immediate vicinity. Thankfully the wind was cold and blustery, masking the sounds. The next nearest of the guards were several feet away. Kailani stood and walked in their direction. She deliberately kept to the more open spaces as she didn't want innocent villagers caught in any crossfire. Knowing it was coming, she skirted slowly, cautiously, around the edge of the marketplace.

Not used to carrying a shield, she found it cumbersome and heavy. Although she was tempted to ditch it, something told her not too. Instincts on high alert, she knew an attack was imminent.

An arrow imbedded in the structure beside her, missing her by a fraction of an inch. She raised the shield above her head just as more arrows rained down, some striking the shield and harmlessly bouncing off, while others landed on the ground or in the building beside her. As soon as they stopped, she peeped around the edge and saw where the archers were positioned.

The magic rippling beneath her skin cried out to be freed so she let it loose a little; staring directly at the two archers with her now-fearsome eyes, a beam of light shot across the top of the market. The archers didn't have time to cry out before their bodies disintegrated and their ashes soared on the wind.

Mishtag moved quietly to the door of the stable and peered through a gap in the slats. The guards were only a few feet away, but unlike those posted at the front of the building, these two were paying more attention and stood facing the doors. She'd already been told that while she remained on the premises she was invisible, so decided to use that to her advantage. With one paw, she carefully and slowly eased back the lock. The only thing holding the door closed now was a latch.

She rattled the door with her head and made some mewling noises then peeped out again. The soldiers were now on alert and had moved closer to the door, their brows furrowed in concentration. She repeated the noises and took a couple of steps back, rising onto her back paws, her front paws positioned ready to strike.

A click sounded, the latched lifted from its cradle, and the door inched open. Part of a face could be seen peering through the space into the dimness of the stable. The gap widened considerably yet there was little change to the light inside. The guards stood on the threshold and looked around. Seeing nothing, they began to close the door when Mishtag again made the noises, this time covering her mouth with her paws and rattling the slats in one of the back corners.

The men weren't completely stupid. They looked at each for a long moment with suspicion in their eyes then one gestured with his head and the other entered while he remained at the threshold. Once the first man had passed her, she silently positioned herself between both and with claws extended lashed out at the one by the doorway. One set took the throat out while the other almost ripped him apart at the mid-section. The guard crumpled to the floor, unable to make a sound as the death throes began to twitch through his body.

Mishtag moved closer behind the soldier who had, by this time, reached the rear stall and was digging around in the hay with the tip of his sword. She didn't hesitate. Within two swipes, his head was rolling around the stall as the torso fell outside it.

First set taken care of, Mistress. I'm moving to my next position, she reported.

Well done, my friend. Let me know when you get there and especially if you encounter any problems on the way. Don't forget it's not just the two of us anymore. Correollis is here and will help us both.

I will, Princess. The proud Blenorai Kai stalked down the pathway, head held high as she travelled to her next destination.

Kailani moved herself closer to the next cache of enemies. She created an invisible barrier around herself. Then, without warning, she ran at a small knot of soldiers standing nearby just as a shout went up from another group of archers. They turned just before she reached them, but were unprepared for the ferocity of her attack, not having unsheathed their swords fully by the time she got close. Her Panas cut a swathe through the air as it arced toward the nearest man, decapitating him in one smooth move. The one next to him didn't escape the blow as the tip of her blade caught his neck and sliced neatly through his jugular. Spurts of blood flew in every direction despite his hand trying in vain to stem the flow.

By this time, the other two had their swords in their hands. One of them lunged, but she neatly side-stepped and as the momentum carried him forward, Kailani struck him on the back, severing his spinal cord. She didn't have time to watch him as she squared up to the remaining soldier. He swung his blade and she blocked it easily so he tried again with the same result. She immediately went on the offensive, her blade moving so fast he could barely keep track, yet somehow he was managing to block it until she changed tactics and suddenly lunged. Her Panas slipped below his arms, her upward thrust piercing his chest. His face registered shock as he fell to his knees, a crimson stain spreading across his tunic.

She moved away with stealth toward two more that were supposedly guarding the road out of the village at the end of the market.

Kailani's eyes swept the area as she readied for her attack. From behind some buildings, a magnificent golden Feegle with black-edged scales appeared in full battle-dress. The silent wings caused a downdraft which alerted some of the stallholders to its presence. Villagers and soldiers alike stared at it in awe, never having seen the like of such a majestic creature. Kailani seized the advantage and rushed the soldiers.

Correollis, wearing black armour and with a Panas in his hand, perched on its back, looking for all the world like some kind of god. He steered the Feegle to a rooftop where a group of six archers crouched, their arrows bouncing harmlessly off the creature's scales. When they were close enough, the Feegle opened its cavernous jaw and spit a large number of needle-thin spikes at the men before swerving away. The soldiers quickly began to convulse and as their skin turned bright green, their agonised cries filled the air. Within a minute or two, their corpses had rolled from the rooftop and landed in an untidy heap on the ground.

The Feegle swept around the entire perimeter of the market place, repeating its poisonous attack on every archer it came across before landing at the beginning of the road leading out of the village.

Stallholders and shoppers who witnessed the attacks dived for cover beneath the carts on which their wares were displayed. They peeped out where they could, still awed by the strange and fantastical creature, but now fearful of its power.

It strutted along the road, the huge head held high as its eyes searched for the next target. Correollis noticed Kailani in a fierce sword fight with two soldiers. She held her own, but appeared to be tiring.

Use your magic! his mind spoke to hers.

Immediately the air around her began to almost glisten as light rays, as hot as the sun, hit the two men, incinerating them where they stood. Their blackened corpses stood for a fraction of a second before they tumbled into a pile of ash at her feet. She turned away only to see two more soldiers running toward her, their swords raised ready to strike. This time she didn't hesitate and left more ash for the wind to carry away.

The battalion had taken heavy losses, and the survivors now resorted to desperate measures. Taking shelter behind stalls, and in some cases using the villagers as human shields, they snuck around the market.

One lone archer crouched behind a cart began firing arrows at Correollis. Despite their silent flight and deadly accuracy, the warrior was prepared and moved his shield to protect his body. All the arrows bar one hit the shield and either embedded in it or was deflected and fell to the ground. One arrow had been aimed lower than the rest and hit Correollis in the thigh.

Calmly he pulled the offending article from his leg showing no sign of pain, snapped it in half, and threw it to the ground. However, he could feel the slow progress of the poison in his body. He zeroed in on the attacker, pointed toward him, and raised his arm. As he did so, the man rose into the air, struggling like a puppet whose strings had got tangled. Correollis moved him away from the stalls then let him dangle for a long moment before clenching his fingers into a fist. The man appeared to fold in on himself before the magician lowered his hand sharply. The broken body landed in a twisted mound on the ice.

Abruptly, the Feegle took to the air and disappeared behind some buildings. Once there and out of sight, he pulled the strange pointed stick from beneath his armour. He pressed the tip into the wound, wincing; pain etched into his features as he mumbled in the same ancient language as before. He repeated the incantation several times, on each occasion speaking faster than before.

When he eventually stopped, he removed the blackened stick from the now non-existent wound and pointed it toward the ground, well away from his trusted mount. A dark, foul-smelling fluid gushed from it; as it landed on the ice a sizzling sound rent the air and the surface bubbled. By the time the wand had finished discharging its contents, it had returned to its normal colour. The ice, however, looked like acid had been poured on it. The surface was pitted and sunken leaving a hole the size of a dinner plate.

Correollis shuddered, took a few deep breaths then steered the Feegle into the air once more.

Kailani stood in the centre of the market place looking all around her. She couldn't see any of the battalion, but her instincts warned her that enemies were still close by. With eyes darting in every direction, she began to walk toward the road where Correollis had been a few minutes before. She wondered where he'd disappeared to in such a hurry.

Correollis? Are you alright? she asked.

He didn't answer at first then, after several long moments, she could hear his voice. *I am now. I was shot by a poisoned arrow.*

Are you sure? You don't sound it! When I was shot by one of them I almost died. If it hadn't been for the blessed gift from the Priest of Rasha-Varl, you and I would never have met!

I promise I'm well now, Highness.

She wasn't convinced, but let it slide.

Where are you?

I'm near the centre of the market and heading toward . . . Her voice trailed away as she was suddenly caught in a strangle hold.

"One down, one to go," a rough voice chuckled in her ear. She could feel the warmth of his breath on her neck and shuddered involuntarily.

"I wouldn't be too sure about that!" She stamped one foot down as hard as she could on his toes then swung her elbow back catching him in the midriff and winding him. He loosened his grip around her throat just enough for her to wriggle out of it and she whirled to face him. "How dare you attack a member of the royal family?"

She brought her knee up hard and fast – he screamed like a girl as his genitals were crushed. Taking a perverse pleasure in watching the soldier, as his hands tried to cup the affected area, she stood for a long moment and did nothing. Her eyes narrowed, the air began to glisten, and suddenly an almighty crack sounded from the sky as a huge lightning bolt struck the infantryman, dropping him instantly to the floor. Every piece of metal on him sparked and sizzled as he lay unmoving. His unseeing eyes were open wide, as was his now silent mouth.

She turned away from him and continued toward the road, her walk slower than before as she examined every stall and cart she passed. Suddenly, she caught sight of a soldier inching toward her using a villager as a shield. He had his hand over the poor, lady's mouth, forcing her to walk directly in front of him. Rage coursed through Kailani's veins at his cowardice as she grabbed her Plexan. She cocked an arrow and aimed it directly at the woman's head. The captive's eyes widened and abject horror filled them. The princess winked and quickly bobbed her body forward and up again. Understanding the message, the hostage abruptly bent away from her captor as Kailani shot. The arrow pierced the infantryman's eye and he fell backward onto the ice.

The woman rushed forward and bowed before the princess, kissing her hand. "Thank you, Highness, thank you."

Kailani stroked her hair once, her hand coming to rest on the lady's shoulder. "Are you alright?"

Tears ran down her face. "J-just a b-bit sore from where h-he grabbed me," she stammered – it's over now." Kailani's gentle tone soothed the woman and her tears began to subside. "Go home and rest. You've been through a shocking ordeal."

"Thank you for all your kindnesses, your Highness."

"You're welcome. Now go but keep your eyes keen. There are more of the cowards hiding in the market so get to the perimeter as quickly and safely as you can." She removed her hand from the peasant's shoulder.

"May all the deities bless you and keep you safe!"

"Thank you and you also." Kailani smiled then turned and continued her way through the stalls, another arrow ready to fire.

The princess only came across another two soldiers hiding amongst the carts and they were quickly despatched. Once she reached the road she called for her Kai.

Mishtag, what waits for us on the road out of the village? she asked as she waited for her trusty mount to reach her.

There are a line of guards forming a roadblock. They must have heard the commotion in the village and are on alert.

I'll take care of them, Correollis said.

As Mishtag reached Kailani, she saw the warrior and his Feegle appear in the air once more and head straight for the human barrier. Mounting her Blenorai, they sped after Correollis, just in time to see the men convulsing on the ground. As they drew closer, the green-skinned soldiers stopped moving; Mishtag leapt over the top of them and began running through the village.

Chapter 22

Mishtag continued sprinting over the ice with Correollis following in the air for around fifteen minutes before Kailani drew her to a halt. The Feegle landed and approached.

"I don't know if we got all of them or whether any had scouted ahead." Worry etched into Kailani's features. "In addition, we may have missed some of the cowards hiding in the market. It won't take them long to regroup, and once they've regained their bravado, they will come after us. I'm not too concerned about them – they've seen what we can do and fear is in their hearts – it's any who may be ahead of us. I have a bad feeling. We need to get to my mother, quickly."

"I agree. Why don't you teleport to her now? I can track you and be at your side within minutes of your landing."

The princess nodded. She called the power to her – it came rapidly now – and as she faded from sight, Correollis heard an urgent whisper. "Hurry."

The sight just ahead chilled her. The barrier she'd put around her mother for safety was nowhere to be seen and Garalia, sword in hand, was trying to fight two men wearing the tunics of the king's battalion. They were toying with her, laughing at her efforts as she quickly tired from the exertion.

One Blenorai laid dead or dying on the ice, blood pooling around its head. Yashtig, who was badly injured, attempted to fight off two more of his own kind (although not from the elite Kai stable) and another soldier.

As soon as she materialised on the ice, she dove into the action. Leaping off Mishtag, she slid between her mother and the two soldiers, taking the men completely by surprise. Her Panas unsheathed, she landed so as to place herself between Garalia and her attackers.

Kailani's blade sliced into one of their legs, cutting almost to the bone. As he crumpled to the ice, holding his leg and screaming, she swung her sword to block the blow headed toward her mother. The strike of metal against metal caused vibrations to sizzle all over her hand and flow up her arm.

The soldier dropped his blade and only managed to catch it with his fingertips, but not before the tip of the Panas had nicked his shoulder and the top of his sword arm. Blood began to flow down his arm, coating his hand like paint and making it hard to grip the hilt of his blade. He adopted a two-handed grip and just managed to bring it up soon enough to stop the princess from splitting his head down the centre.

But he underestimated her and as she crouched down, she twisted it away only to bring it back in a sweeping flat arc which carved into his stomach from one side to the other. His steaming entrails spilled from the wound and began to pile on the ice like sausages released from a butcher's hook. He dropped his sword as his hands flew to his stomach.

A noise to her left drew her attention. The soldier with the injured leg had struggled to his feet, swinging his blade. She rose to her full height, fury blazing from her eyes. He swung again and Kailani checked the blow, countering with one of her own. They battled, the clang of metal echoing across the icy tundra.

Despite his wound, the soldier was obviously a highly-skilled swordsman compared to his partner who was now on his knees and trying desperately to stuff his intestines back into the gaping mouth of his abdomen. However, he was no match for her. She toyed with him, as he and his friend had done to her mother. He tried every move he could think of or had ever been taught, but each time Kailani thwarted his efforts. Aware the other soldier was attacking Yashtig she decided to end the charade and whirled so fast she was a blur on the ice, the Panas gliding in a deadly arc. Her blade caught him just under his ear and continued across the neck to the other side, exiting just above the collarbone. Blood bubbled along the cut, his eyes grew wide, and his mouth dropped open as his head slid from his neck.

Mishtag went on the offensive. She launched herself at the soldier who was trying to slice into Yashtig, never going for the kill, just wounding until he couldn't put up enough of a fight to ensure survival. Her jaws clamped on his shoulder and the momentum forced him to drop his sword and fall to the ground, with the Kai landing on his chest. She didn't hesitate; her sharp teeth ripped into his throat while her long, razor-like claws pierced his chest, puncturing his lungs and aorta.

Sensing, rather than seeing, Mishtag knew one of the Blenorai had launched themselves into the air, intending to unseat her from the soldier. She knew her work with this man was done, and, timing it to perfection, leapt from the body milliseconds before the other one landed.

Mishtag turned rapidly and sized up her opponent. The Blenorai was older and a little slower, but had experience on his side. His eyes shone with a daring cunning and she knew underestimating him would be a grave mistake. She drew back and they circled each other, neither getting too close. Abruptly a paw shot out with claws extended and caught Mishtag a glancing blow across the shoulder, inflicting a small gouge wound. She immediately responded, her claws slashing the side of his face.

As if it had been choreographed, both rose onto their hind legs and launched themselves at each other with claws extended and deep growls emanating from their throats. Mishtag, with youth and speed to her advantage, stepped to the side at the last moment and swung one claw toward her opponent's face. His momentum carried him forward and he began to fall and that's when Mishtag's claw caught him across his shoulder and neck. She immediately jumped on his back and began tearing her claws into his neck and spine, ripping the fur and muscles as if it were tissue paper, while he howled in agony and rage.

She was so intent on her task she didn't see the other Blenorai racing across the ice behind her. A sudden pain in her shoulder and neck halted her attack as sharp teeth pierced her flesh. Her cry of pain joined those of her victim. Blood poured from the wound and joined the puddle already on the ice. Acting on pure instinct, she brought her fore paw up and raked her claws across the face of her attacker, catching the other's eye. It let out a muffled yelp, but didn't loosen its grip. Its body weight ensured Mishtag couldn't rise and she was totally at its mercy. She continued to do the only thing she could and kept trying to slash at its face, but then froze when she felt one of its paws begin to snake around her body.

An ear-splitting screech rent the air. The paw Mishtag had felt was gone and she saw a spray of blood arc in the air beside her. The teeth in her shoulder disappeared although the pain was only mildly less excruciating. Her victim tried to rise and squirm beneath her. She slammed her paw down on his spine, hearing a satisfying crunch. Fresh howls, higher pitched than before, echoed across the ice and he slumped back down, barely moving. Her final act was to slice through the spinal cord before she began to rise.

Behind her, Kailani was battling the other Blenorai. One of the enemy's arms hung loose at its side, held on by a couple of muscles and a bit of fur, but still it attacked. Mishtag saw the fury in the princess's face as the upright Blenorai tried to slash at her with its good forepaw. It towered above her, but Kailani ducked beneath the swinging paw and used her Panas to slice into the huge body. Blood streamed from his wounds yet he refused to give up. In a change of tactics, he suddenly began to drop down onto his good paw and with jaws open wide, aimed directly for her head.

The attack came too fast and the young princess was ill-prepared. Throwing herself onto the ice, she slid out of reach of the massive jaw and sharp teeth but not the paws. The edge of one landed on her arm and she screamed as the bone shattered.

She tried to reposition herself under the beast, but the paw held her firm, making her every movement send waves of agony through her damaged arm. She began poking his underbelly with her sword, but none of the wounds she was able to inflict were life-threatening, so she tried slashing at the leg which held her. Eventually the paw moved enough to allow her to scoot away, but as her head and torso emerged she was faced with an open jaw of razor sharp teeth.

The last thing Kailani remembered was hearing the whoosh of large wings.

Chapter 23

Kailani's eyes fluttered open, but all she could see were hazy outlines. She blinked several times, her vision clearing with each one. Her mother's tear-streaked face was the first thing she saw.

Garalia murmured a prayer of gratitude.

Kailani began to rise to a sitting position, but realised she only had one arm to do it. Her eyes darted to the arm broken by the Blenorai and found it strapped up and in a sling around her neck. She grimaced as Garalia helped her up and then gave her a cup full of a fluid with a strong smell of herbs.

"Drink this. It might not be pleasant to the taste, but it will help you heal."

Kailani sipped the warm drink and pulled a face. She looked at her mother who nodded. She took a breath and drank it all down in one go. "That has to be the foulest thing I've ever had the misfortune to drink. What was in it?"

"A mixture of herbs and a potion of my own making," a masculine voice replied. "I brought some with me in case it was needed." Correollis stepped into view, looking pleased to see her.

"He saved your life!" Garalia looked up at him.

"Thank you, Correollis. I am in your debt," Kailani said.

He nodded. "It was my pleasure and also what I was sent here to do. The bones in your arm were badly broken and the breaks were not clean.

I've healed them, but you will have to wear the strapping and the sling for the next two to three days while they finish setting. I've also healed all your cuts as well as those Princess Garalia sustained."

"Again, thank you. But if you've healed me, why did I have to drink that awful potion of yours?"

Correollis grinned. "The re-setting of bones is a painful process. Thankfully, you were unconscious and didn't feel it. However, residual pain remains and you will feel it for the rest of the day and probably tomorrow too. The potion not only aids the healing process, it's also a strong pain reliever. Hopefully, the most you will suffer is a dull ache. If it's any consolation, the tonic I gave your mother to help her regain her strength tastes only a little better."

Her eyes strayed to her mother; in comparison to the figure she saw briefly when she arrived, who could barely stand or swing a sword with any force, Garalia now looked much stronger.

"By the look of you, it must have done some good, Mother."

"I do feel better. I don't know how much longer I could have continued to defend myself. Your arrival was well-timed, although a few minutes earlier would have been even better. I know you would have returned sooner if you were able so please don't think I hold any bad feelings in that regard." Garalia removed the cup from her daughter's hand, placed it on the ground then grasped the hand and gave it a gentle squeeze.

"So what happened? The last thing I remember was a huge open jaw heading straight for me."

"My Feegle grabbed the beast in his claws and moved him a few feet away and, well let's just say we'll be dining on roast Blenorai shortly, but not the one he saved you from," he replied, a grin stretching across his face.

She ignored his attempt at humour – her mind was troubled by something else. "But what of Mishtag and Yashtig? They were both badly injured. Please tell me they have survived."

Garalia moved to one side. Lying not far behind her were their two Kais; their eyes were shut, but Kailani could see the rising and falling of their bodies as they slept. From what little she could see, there were no visible signs of injuries. She breathed a sigh of relief.

"I healed their wounds before yours, Highness. Both had lost copious amounts of blood. They are now in a spell-induced healing slumber. You have no need to fear for them. When they wake, they will be back to full health and as strong as ever."

"Now, on to more important matters." Her roving eyes lit on the bodies of the soldiers and their Blenorai. "How long can we risk staying out in the open like this, especially being so much closer to the palace? We don't know if the entire battalion in the village were dealt with, or if someone has gone ahead to warn Bellis. Surely we need to continue on while we still have some light?"

"I'll answer your questions in the order they were posed. Although it appears to you that we are in the open, it is not, in fact, the case. I've erected my own type of barrier, one that allows us to see the world around us, but not the world to see us. You're right about the village and it's entirely possible any survivors are making their way here even as we speak. Under other circumstances, you would have no way of knowing if a scout has gone ahead, but with me here..." he trailed off.

Reaching inside the folds of his cloak, he pulled out the pointed stick he'd used previously along with a small jar. He uncorked it, dipped his thumb and forefinger inside then replaced the lid. Throwing the pinch of red powder into the air, he pointed his stick at it and the substance began to whirl in a circle. A whooshing sound filled the barrier, bouncing off the walls and increasing the volume. Faster and faster it spun as it created a whirlpool effect in the air, the point moving further away from them. A strange scent filled the air with the sweetness of jasmine and the sourness of freshly dug earth.

Garalia and Kailani watched with widened eyes. Correollis uttered a few words in the archaic language he'd spoken before at the inn and a picture appeared in the centre of the opening to the circle. Abruptly, the picture, which was the same as the immediate exterior of their shelter, began to stretch as it seemingly travelled across the ice, speeding up as if it had to reach a certain point quickly. Nothing out of the ordinary was seen . . . at first. Suddenly a speck appeared and as the image extended toward it, they could see a soldier riding a Blenorai, racing across the ice. Kailani groaned as her worst fears came to life before her eyes.

"Fear not, your Highness. It will be dealt with. Princess Garalia, may I ask for your assistance for a moment?"

Garalia rose and approached the sorcerer. "What can I do to help?"

He took one of her hands and placed his strange stick into it. "Please hold this as still as you can and keep it pointed at the soldier," he replied then turned to where his Feegle lay resting. "Baelfyre!" The creature rose and quickly moved to his master's side. "Stop the traitor and his mount from reaching the Ice Palace. Bring both the bodies back here." Baelfyre nodded as Correollis reached down and pressed a button on his collar. Within the blink of an eye, he doubled in size. The sorcerer took another pinch of the red powder and sprinkled it on the Feegle then, moving his hand toward the image, Baelfyre rose into the air and as his master thrust his hand into the picture, the circle widened and the creature was sucked into it.

Garalia's hand started to tremble and Correollis placed his hand over hers to steady it. As the Feegle moved through the cone, the circle began to shrink back again then the image changed. Baelfyre had spread his wings and was now flying rapidly toward the traitor. Abruptly the man slumped over his mount who slowed before collapsing onto the ground. Baelfyre extended his huge claws and picked them up as easily as if he were carrying a baby and a cub. He turned around and began to fly back the way he'd come.

"Thank you, your Highness, but you can let go now. I've got it," Correollis said in a gentle tone. Garalia turned and stared into his eyes for a moment before she removed her hand from the stick. She went and sat beside her daughter once again, her hands trembling in her lap.

The circle began to widen again, exponentially bigger than before as it spread across the area past where the two princesses sat and had grown almost as tall as it was wide. Now Correollis's hand started to shake as he struggled to control it. He gripped it with his other hand, attempting to stabilise it. They could see the Feegle trying to get back through, but he was buffeted from all sides as the cone narrowed behind him.

Not wanting to break his concentration, Kailani whispered in Garalia's ear, "Mother, help me up, please." She rose and helped her daughter to stand. Kailani moved next to Correollis and placed her good hand over his, her fingers touching the stick. The shaking lessened then stopped altogether. The sorcerer's eyes widened and bulged in shock, but he didn't dare take his gaze from the circle. The Feegle seemed almost as if he wasn't moving at all. Correollis mumbled under his breath and the creature noticeably gained speed.

Suddenly a loud popping noise filled the structure as Baelfyre materialised before them. The circle shrank back and Kailani released her grip, stepping back to join her mother. Correollis spoke in the ancient tongue once more and the circle disappeared, taking the red powder with it. In the Feegle's huge claws were the bodies of a soldier wearing the king's tunic and a Blenorai, both peppered with spikes.

"Take them outside and dump them with the others." Baelfyre stretched his huge wings, flew straight through the barrier, and dropped his victims on top of those already spread out over the ice before returning to his master. Correollis pressed the button on the collar and the Feegle shrank to his smaller size. He returned to his corner, lay down, and closed his eyes.

"We must eat to keep up our strength before we continue on with our journey and have fresh meat at our disposal. I suggest we take advantage of it." Correollis looked at the two princesses.

"Our Blenorai Kai aren't cannibals and I don't think I could eat it. Take some for yourself and your Feegle if you want though," Garalia replied.

"Thank you, your Highness. Baelfyre will be grateful. I understand your feelings, but they aren't *your* Blenorai and we need every scrap of food we can get. There is more than enough to go around with plenty left over for another couple of meals."

"I see your point. I'll try it."

"I feel the same way, but I see the sense in grabbing whatever food we can so I'll try it too," said Kailani.

"Very well, your Highnesses. I'll go and prepare the meat."

"And I will see what food the innkeeper's wife packed for us. I'm sure there must be something to accompany our meal." Garalia walked over to where the packs had been left as Correollis moved through the barrier and across to the dead animals.

She rummaged through and found a slab of cheese, two large loaves, some vegetables, fruit, and three flasks of Kelem. By the time she had it all set out the sorcerer-warrior had returned dragging two headless, skinned carcasses behind him. He conjured a fire and made short work of chopping the meat into manageable chunks. Within a short time, the trio were sitting down to a veritable feast. He woke the Kais, knowing the food would aid in their healing, and they and the Feegle happily munched on the raw meat.

Kailani looked around as they ate, her eyes scanning for any sign of the remains of the battalion. Her instincts were strong that they hadn't eliminated all their enemies and they were regrouping – she certainly wasn't naive enough to think for one moment they'd managed to completely annihilate them. She had no doubt in her mind that the soldiers would be following as soon as possible and were probably hoping their advance scouting party had caught them by surprise. What the infantrymen were praying for was that their scouts had exterminated at least one of their targets and preferably both. A small smile graced her lips at the thought that they were in for a nasty surprise.

As soon as they'd finished eating, everything was packed away and, with the Kai now fully healed, they were able to leave. The two princesses led the way while Correollis tarried, checking the area behind them before catching up. In the far distance a small group raced across the ice toward them. They were too far away to be an immediate threat, but he kept a close eye on them. Kailani and her mother seemed to be matching the pace of their pursuers so unless the princesses had reason to stop and the soldiers didn't, it appeared unlikely that the two sides would meet. He'd taken things for granted before with disastrous outcomes, but that was when he was a young man, not even a full warrior, and still getting to grips with the ancient magic his family had access to.

The mistake he made that first time haunted him still; the loss of his own dear sister as well as friends, people he'd known all his life and grown up with, was something he would never forgive himself for. Now, with the lives of the royal family entrusted into his hands, he wasn't prepared to leave anything to chance – he would ensure they arrived at their destination unharmed or die trying.

The Feegle hovered as Correollis surveyed the area. He knew they were highly visible now that he had pressed the button on Baelfyre's collar once again; the gold and black colouring stood out starkly against the pale grey sky. He didn't want to give their direction or position away, although it seemed pretty obvious the soldiers had, by now, guessed the women were heading back to the palace, so the warrior steered his mount around and in a blur of colour streaking across the sky like a comet, he sped after his charges.

When he'd caught up with them, Correollis steered Baelfyre down so they were low enough to converse. The Feegle was forced to draw his massive claws as close to his body as possible to prevent them dragging on the ice.

"Princess Garalia?" Correollis called. "Can the battalions get messages back to the castle other than by rider?"

She thought for a moment before answering. "Riders are the most common method. However, I seem to remember hearing about them using a Tiki in times of battle."

"What's a 'Tiki'?" Kailani asked before Correollis had a chance to.

"They're intelligent creatures about as long as my forearm, low to the ground, and extremely fast over the ice. They're pure white except for a silver-grey flash on their heads. The ones used by our soldiers wear collars with a small pouch attached. The messages are placed in those pouches and the creature is told who to deliver it to. Somehow, the tikis always find their way to the right person, no matter where they are. Why do you ask?"

"I've learned not to leave anything to chance, your Highness. Although the battalion might have thought themselves more than a match for two princesses and their mounts, they might have employed another method of getting messages back to your brother. He doesn't sound like the type of man who would leave his men unprepared for any eventuality. He can't allow either of you to return to the Ice Palace alive so I can't help wondering if he is cautious enough to send one of these animals with the soldiers."

Garalia pondered for a long moment. "Bellis has a pet tiki. He calls it Hiko. He could have sent it with the men. Are you thinking that, despite all the fighting we've done to get to the castle safely and undetected, it was for naught?"

"I can't say for certain. I don't want to become complacent though, or be under any illusions that we can just stroll up to your home without a not-too-friendly welcoming committee waiting for us. We need to plan ahead for any and all contingencies. After everything you've suffered, to get this close only to be thwarted at the last would be too much for anyone to reasonably accept."

"I've already said about us using the secret passage," Kailani offered.

"And that's exactly what we intend to do, Highness, but first we need to get close enough to the entrance to use it. What if there's a cordon of soldiers around the entire palace, instructed to kill anyone who approaches on sight?"

"I'll just teleport us over them to the entrance." Kailani spoke in a matter-of-fact tone.

"If the soldiers are that close, they could hear us. Then what?" he asked scornfully, looking down at her as if she were a naïve child.

"I'm not without skills myself, Correollis," she replied sharply, glaring up at him and seeing his expression as she skilfully held Mishtag's reins with her one good hand. "I have all the magic of both Taivass-maa and Idenvarlis at my disposal and I have a vial from the High Priest of Rasha-Varl. I can attack them with lightning, burn them with the rays of the sun, or encase them in ice, to name but three methods. I also have weapons from both worlds and am skilled in their uses. Thanks to you I can access my magic much quicker and have also gained more of an understanding of how I can use each element. You already know I can fight physically, but I have a devious mind and a few thoughts have come to me as to how we can get back into the palace.

"I know I must seem like a child to you, but I was alone with these two Blenorai Kai when I made the long, arduous journey to find my mother. We had to fight off horrendous beasts, I had to use my brain to get us through various situations, and I still managed to rescue her and get us all safely back to the village. I've lost track of how long ago it was since I left, but it was over halfway out that I discovered Mishtag and I could talk telepathically. For the first part of that journey I was alone, with no one to share my thoughts and fears with. I'd embarked on what might be considered a fool's errand by some. The chances of finding my mother, and better yet discovering her alive, must have seemed a gambler's dream. It wouldn't surprise me to learn there are more than a few wagers based on the outcome of my trip. But I digress. There were times when I was terrified, days where the homesickness nearly made me ill, hours when the loneliness played on my fears like a bow on a fiddle, but I *knew* I'd find her and that alone was enough to keep me going when things were at their toughest. It's that same drive and determination which courses through my veins now. If you weren't here, I'd come up with a solution and, working together with my mother, we would succeed. You being here is an added bonus, Correollis, and one for which I'm thankful, but don't treat me like an idiot girl with nothing but clouds between her ears!" Kailani's cheeks were flushed and her eyes flashed dangerously. Her voice rose at the last and she all but spat the words at him.

Correollis looked crestfallen. His face turned crimson and nodded as he accepted the rebuke. "Please accept my apologies, your Highness. I meant no disrespect."

"No? That's not how it sounded."

"You're right. I'd forgotten all you'd endured to reach this point in time, but your comment about teleporting to the secret entrance smacked of naiveté. I should have known better than to think you didn't have some kind of plan. I'm sorry for having offended you."

Kailani stared into his eyes for a long moment before saying, "I accept your apology and I'm sorry for my rant. I didn't realise just how much emotion I'd bottled up. Now, onto more important things. Is there any sign of soldiers following us from the village?"

"Yes, Highness, a small group. They are far enough behind that if we don't stop for any reason, they won't catch up."

"We will have to stop for food and rest. However, I have a plan which will, if it works as I envisage, get them off our tail for good. After that, all we have to concentrate on is the potential for a less than welcome return at the palace, and I have a few ideas about that also. We can discuss it further when we make camp for the night. I'm sure my mother has one or two ideas of her own as well." She glanced over at Garalia, who nodded.

With a grin and a wicked glint in her eyes, she turned her face up to look at Correollis. "Oh, yes. I have one or two nasty surprises up my sleeve for my traitorous brother's men."

Chapter 24

By the time they made camp, the weak sun was about to dip below the horizon and the sky was a darkish, lilac grey. After choosing their spot for the night, Kailani walked from the preparations, back the way they'd come for more than two hundred feet. She centred herself and reached for her magic. Slipping her injured arm from the sling, she aimed both hands at the ice several feet in front of her. All at once the ground began to shake so hard it was all she could do to stay upright. She connected with her power on a deeper level and felt it course through her, steadying her on the shaking ground. Suddenly there was a loud crack and a small fissure opened in the ice. It grew larger until there was a gap of at least thirty feet between the two pieces of solid ground.

Kailani reined in the magic and the earthquake-like trembles ceased. She walked to the edge and looked down into a bottomless chasm. Taking a few steps back, she layered a paper-thin coating of ice over the crevasse. When she was finished no one would have known the crater existed and it would have stood up to serious scrutiny even in broad daylight. She dropped a small piece of raw meat on the ground and returned to the camp.

"Stop!" she commanded. He looked at her, his brow furrowed. "For my plan to work, they need to see the ice shelter I normally conjure. I believe their idea will be to surround it so when we take it down in the morning, they will attack immediately. The only way they have a chance of fulfilling their orders is to catch us unawares so it makes sense for them to think this way."

The warrior stood with a thoughtful expression for a long moment before speaking. "May I offer an alternative idea for consideration, your Highness?" She nodded so he continued. "I can see the sense in everything you're saying and it's a good plan. However, if they see the ice shelter, they will most likely approach slowly, not wanting to make any noise in case it alerts you to their presence, whereas if they see nothing, they're more likely to charge ahead and fall into your trap. If the soldiers are moving slower, there is the possibility that not all of them will succumb. This is not the outcome you want to achieve."

The princess stood silent, gazing across the ice as she mulled over his words. "I wasn't aware the shelter you conjured was invisible, so considering the circumstances your idea makes perfect sense. Please continue."

"Of course, your Highness," he said to her back as she walked over to join her mother.

Within about twenty minutes, the shelter was erected, the animals fed and watered, and the two princesses and the warrior were sitting around a conjured fire, warming themselves as they ate.

"How far are we from the palace?" Correollis asked before placing another chunk of meat in his mouth.

"Less than two days' journey. Assuming the worst and my brother is aware of our proximity, I don't think he'd have the soldiers too close to the palace as the king would want an explanation. I'm sure Bellis could come up with some plausible excuse, but he wouldn't want our father to have any knowledge of his actions. I believe the battalions will be at least fifty feet away, if not more." Garalia paused to take a sip of Kelem before continuing. "He's too clever to have the men standing in plain sight as again, he wouldn't want the king to see them and start asking questions. Therefore, I think they'll be lying on the ice with a covering over each one to disguise them. It's a trick the garrison used many years before to great effect, and Bellis is just as aware of this as I am."

"So under normal circumstances we won't know where they are until it's too late. I don't necessarily see that as a problem, Mother." Kailani turned to the warrior. "Correollis, can you make other things invisible as well as this shelter?"

"Yes, your Highness."

"Does that include yourself?"

"Yes. What are you thinking?"

"I'll answer you in a moment, but I have a few more questions first. Can you keep the invisibility in place for a prolonged period?"

"For as long as I wish."

"And others too?"

"Any number of others." He sighed softly and his eyes showed boredom.

"Are you also able to move with stealth while invisible so no one can hear your movements?"

"Yes, Princess. I can cast any number of spells on my companions and/or myself, including one for silent movement."

"If anything were to happen to you – for example if you should get injured or attacked suddenly, what could be the worst case scenario?"

"That would depend on what type of spell I cast in the first place, but it could fail if I were attacked or killed."

"Is it possible for you to cast a spell on someone and for them to be able to control it, like how long it lasts for example?"

He paused a long minute before answering. "It is possible, but only if the subject had magical ability of their own and was holding the wand with me when the spell was cast."

"Wand?" Garalia's eyes became hooded as her brows descended.

He produced the strange stick from beneath his clothes. "This is my wand. It's a magical object in its own right and, although it doesn't contain my magic, it helps me to focus it from the tiniest point to the largest expanse. Unless I bequeathed it to another, on my death the magic would drain out and into the ground or air to disperse harmlessly."

"Final question, if you were invisible and you'd made mother and I invisible too, would we be able to see each other?"

"If I worked that into the spell then yes."

"Excellent! Thank you for answering my many questions. Let me tell you my plans – I have two possible scenarios in my head . . ."

Nearly an hour passed during which time Kailani only stopped talking to lubricate her throat. It was obvious she'd given the matter a great deal of thought as her plans were very detailed, even to the point of not killing any soldiers unless it became absolutely necessary as she didn't want to weaken the king's ability to protect the palace and those residing within the walls.

The group spent the next hour asking and answering questions, refining the plans until they were as near to perfect as possible. Even Correollis seemed impressed by Kailani's thoroughness and attention to detail, admitting he couldn't have done much better himself. She'd even considered how to get them from the secret passage to the king's chambers.

By this time, they were all exhausted. It had been a long and difficult day and Kailani's arm burned like it was being consumed by fire. The sorcerer gave her another cup of the foul tasting brew which she drank, grimacing as she did so, before her mother helped her to settle down for the night. Garalia couldn't hide the small smile; it was the first time in twenty-one years she'd been able to put her daughter to bed and tuck something around her to keep her warm. It was a wonderful feeling despite the circumstances, and as she lay down and closed her eyes, the smile was still there.

Within minutes, they were all asleep.

Screams woke them the following morning. Kailani was instantly alert and as she heard the yells fade, a grin spread across her face. She pushed herself up with her good hand and peered in the direction of the trap she'd set the night before. Although it was misty outside their shelter, she could see well enough and no one stood on the other side of the crevice. She felt it was safe to assume they'd all fallen into it. Still, until Correollis could confirm it, she didn't want to get too smug.

It was later than they'd normally rise, but after the drama of the previous day, they needed the extra rest and felt better for it. If they didn't quite reach their destination that day it wouldn't matter. Besides, their plans all hinged on them getting to the king's chambers, approximately an hour after he'd retired for the night.

Before he took down their shelter, Correollis took to the skies on Baelfyre to scout around. Whilst he was out of hearing distance, Kailani turned to her mother and said, "I've got a bad feeling."

"About what?"

"I'm not sure yet, but I think it's got something to do with Correollis," she replied with a note of sadness and worry in her tone.

"Really? How can you think that after everything he's done to help us? We wouldn't have got out of the village alive if it wasn't for him, he saved your life when that Blenorai attacked, and he healed our injuries. Would he have done all that if he wasn't truly on our side?" Garalia stared at her daughter.

"Don't you think I know that? I just have this feeling we're being lulled into a false sense of security and there's something unexpected lying ahead of us. I hate the idea of thinking Correollis may somehow be involved. He's a legend in Taivass-maa and I don't believe he would willingly do anything to betray us, but I can't help what I feel, Mother. I've learned to trust my instincts, especially since setting off on this journey and they've been invaluable, as has the counsel from Mishtag."

"Do you honestly think your grandfather, King Sirris, would risk your life by sending someone who could be easily swayed to betray us? Correollis and his family before him have been protecting the royal family for hundreds of years – you said so yourself – yet now you're having doubts about him?"

"I can't explain it and I don't want to feel this way!" Kailani's voice rose.

"Shhh. I know you don't, my dear." Garalia gathered her daughter into a hug. "I know all about the instincts and senses as I get them too, but at the moment I'm not feeling anything to overly concern me. I'm not saying you shouldn't trust it, but we're all experiencing different emotions: trepidation, excitement, fear, to name but three. The adrenalin is starting to rise in each of us as we get ever closer to the palace. All I'm trying to say is that maybe you're reading it wrong because of all the other sensations coursing around your body."

Kailani moved as if to interrupt, but her mother continued, not giving her a chance. "My best advice to you is to keep your own counsel for a while. Try and calm yourself to a state where your thinking is clear and your emotions are firmly under control. Only then will you be able to more correctly interpret the senses you are being given. And, under no circumstances, should you act any different toward Correollis." Garalia stepped back, but kept her hands on Kailani's arms. She looked directly into her daughter's eyes. "I know you don't have much reason to trust the advice of a mother who has been missing since you were a baby, but I hope you know how much I love you and that I wouldn't mislead you."

"Of course, I know that, Mother, and I do trust your advice. I will take your guidance and thank you for it. Maybe, you're right. Maybe, because we've been through so much to get this far and the end is so close we can almost taste it, I *am* allowing my emotions free rein and they're clouding my judgement. I'll do as you suggest." She embraced her mother and kissed her cheek. "Thank you," she said softly as she pulled away.

Garalia stroked a hand down her daughter's cheek. "You're welcome, my sweet girl."

A whump sounded outside and the two women started. They turned to see Baelfyre had landed and was just walking into the shelter with Correollis still on his back.

"I've scouted around and can see no sign of any soldiers behind or in front of us for at least the next few miles. It was a little difficult to see too far ahead through the mist, but as we journey on, I can warn you if there's anything to worry about."

"So my trap worked?" Kailani asked excitedly, all her negative thoughts toward the sorcerer pushed to one side.

"In spectacular fashion, I would say, Princess, judging by the bodies lying at the bottom of the crevasse. Covering it over with a thin layer of ice was genius. I have to say I'm impressed, your Highness."

Kailani grinned widely. "I consider that high praise coming from a man with your reputation."

Correollis bowed his head for a moment then looked around. Everything was packed and they were ready to leave. He looked to where Kailani had stood just mere moments before to find her absent. He swivelled his body then saw her approaching the crevice she'd created. She stopped short and held the palms of her hands toward it. Almost immediately, the ground beneath their feet began to rumble and shake, the sound echoing around the almost empty land. As the quaking became more violent, enough to send Garalia sprawling on the ground, the gaping maw the young princess had created, began to close. Within no more than five minutes the crevice was gone. All that remained was a thin line in the ice. Kailani crouched and placed her hand directly onto the crack and watched, fascinated, as it filled with ice and became seamless with the terrain either side. As she stood, she looked both ways and, satisfied with her work, walked back to the others and mounted Mishtag.

"Shall we go?" she asked almost innocently.

"I'm ready now," Garalia replied.

Baelfyre had been changed back to his normal pale-honey half-size, but appeared uneasy when his master approached. Correollis sat astride him and said, "Yes, Highness." He waved his hand and the shelter vanished.

They all set off across the ice, each wrapped in their own thoughts.

Chapter 25

The journey that day was uneventful, except that Baelfire seemed nervous whenever Correollis came near. However, when the first sight of the city walls came into view, Kailani noticed tears streaming down her mother's cheeks. She pulled Mishtag and Yashtig to a halt and dismounted. Placing her arm around Garalia's shoulders, she asked, "Mother? What's the matter? Are you in pain?" Worry lines etched around her eyes.

"No, my darling. I never thought I'd see those walls again – I thought I would die in that hell-hole. These are happy tears. I'm almost home and it's all thanks to you." She turned and hugged her daughter fiercely. When she pulled away, she continued. "I'm fine to carry on. I want to keep going as every inch, every foot, brings me closer."

Kailani smiled as she mounted Mishtag. "Let's go then, shall we?"

Garalia got Yashtig moving even before she'd finished speaking. Kailani laughed and, with her mother's infectious joy touching her heart, began to give chase.

They made camp about three miles from the city walls. The view of Idenvarlis City was much clearer; the spire of the Temple of Rasha-Varl could be seen rising majestically above the walls, as could the uppermost roofs of the palace. Garalia stared, tracing each and every line of the buildings. "It's strange what you take for granted," she said, talking to no one in particular. "I lived inside those walls for almost half my life and ignored the beauty that surrounded me every day. Looking at it now, I see the intricate carvings at the top of the palace, the symbols and symmetry of the temple spire, and even the wall itself, plain though it may be, is still a wondrous sight."

Kailani moved to stand beside her and gazed at the things her mother saw. "I agree. I haven't really seen the palace and temple from the outside, so in a way this is my first proper glimpse of it. And yes, it is beautiful. The craftsmanship is inspired. I'm sure this will make me look at my home in Taivass-maa with new eyes when I return there. Speaking of which, have you given any thought as to what you'll do once you're home and had time to recover? Will you and father get back together? Will you come to Taivass-maa?"

"I want us to be a proper family, if Galaxan will agree. I've never stopped loving him," she replied tearing her eyes away from her home and looking at her daughter.

"If father will agree?" Kailani burst out incredulously. "He's never stopped loving you either – he'll be overjoyed just to know you're alive. I've never seen him show the slightest interest in any other woman, so I predict you'll be in his arms as fast as he can make it possible." She grinned, a knowing look in her eyes.

"Really? To know he still loves…I hope…It makes me more anxious than ever to return home. As much as I love my parents and can't wait to see them, it doesn't compare to my desire to see my husband again."

"I can sort of understand that. I met someone at the ball my grandfather gave for my birthday. I'm not in love with him . . . yet, but I think there may be a future for us together. He treated me so differently from all the other idiots who fawned over me and, to be honest, I'm suddenly very much looking forward to seeing him again."

A male voice behind broke into their conversation. "I don't want to ruin your thoughts of future happiness, but we need to get inside those walls and reach the king first."

Kailani was the first to turn and face Correollis. "We know that," she replied, her voice even and quiet, "but we can at least allow my mother a little time to come to terms with her feelings." Her expression brooked no argument.

"Of course, your Highness. I apologise for my thoughtlessness." He bowed his head and walked away.

"Thank you," Garalia said quietly, her eyes drawn back to the city wall. Kailani knew no words were necessary and she moved over to the Blenorai and began to strip off their armour and saddles.

It was several minutes before Garalia turned away, mainly because it became too dark to see the city clearly. By this time, a hot meal had been prepared and was ready to be consumed.

Kailani's mother had a serenity about her that hadn't been there before and she tucked into the food with gusto. Kailani began to do the same, but halfway through the meal her senses came back to the fore and she was almost overwhelmed by them. The food suddenly lost its appeal and after a couple of minutes spent pushing items around, she abandoned the effort and put the bowl on the floor.

Correollis noticed her abrupt lack of appetite. "Is the food not to your liking, Princess?"

"It's fine and tasty, but I'm not hungry anymore." She shrugged, trying hard not to let her true feelings show.

"You need to keep your strength up for tomorrow," he chided.

She glared at him. "I said, I'm not hungry anymore," she snapped. She rose and without a word walked out of the shelter into the freezing cold night. The wind had become quite brisk and began to nip at her face. Despite the layers she wore to help keep her warm, the wind seemed to cut through them as if they were made of tissue paper and chilled her to the bone in no time at all. She walked around the enclosure until she found a spot which shielded her from the worst of it and found herself looking in the direction of the palace. She longed to be inside those walls already, wishing she could somehow circumvent what her instincts were yelling at her.

Kailani knew the following day wasn't going to be easy – far from it – she just wished it could all be over. Even if she had to give up her life in the process, she'd be alright about it as long as she got her mother safely back where she belonged. She had always trusted her instincts and they'd never let her down before. But this time, despite the strength of them, part of her didn't want to acknowledge what she was feeling and that made it harder to deal with.

Deliberately, she examined the instinct like one would a bug under a microscope. It didn't make sense to her no matter how much she tried to switch things around in her head. Correollis had been wonderful so why did she doubt him now? Why was she having such negative senses about him? He'd helped them get from the village to here, hadn't he? *But I'd have been able to do it too. It was my idea to create the disguised gorge in which our pursuers fell to their deaths. I could have got us both out of the village without his help. I'd managed on my own over thousands of miles, fighting off all manner of beasts with the help of the Kai, and I could have got us into the castle safely too.* "Ah, but he saved your life from that Kai," a voice whispered in her mind. *True, but he wouldn't have had to if I'd got us out of the village my way*, her thoughts answered back.

The inner arguments raged back and forth inside her and each time the little voice came up with something in Correollis's favour, another part of her mind slapped it down. Unconsciously she'd begun to pace in the small area which sheltered her from the wind. She began to replay the day in her mind and suddenly it came to her, the thing she'd observed that hadn't registered at the time . . . Baelfyre was nervous and a bit skittish around him, and it was something unheard of.

Once a Feegle was chosen, its loyalty to its new master or mistress was almost as unswerving as the unconditional love between a mother and her child. A bond of trust was formed from the first day they rode together. The only time she'd seen a Feegle uncomfortable around its master was when the creature was being mistreated and beaten. When she witnessed the act, she'd run to her father who had dealt with it most decisively. The Feegle was given a new, gentle mistress and the cruel man had been sentenced to ten years imprisonment with hard labour. The ill-treatment of the creatures was deemed a severe offence and the penalty, as that bully had discovered to his cost, was harsh.

She'd never seen Correollis abuse or hurt Baelfyre in any way, so why would the animal act nervous around him? The only thing she could think of was that the bond between them was somehow strained, but was at a loss as to what might have caused it. She determined to keep a very close eye on them and now the seed of distrust had been planted, the princess decided to have an alternative plan, known only to her, in case it was needed. After several more minutes of thought, she retreated into the warmth of the enclosure.

As she entered, Garalia stared at her daughter, an unasked question in her eyes. Kailani shook her head almost imperceptibly and sat beside her.

"Are you alright, your Highness?" Correollis asked, his brows knitting.

"Yes, thank you. I think I'm just a little nervous about tomorrow. I'm under no illusions about what we're likely to face and, as always, my mother's safety is my primary concern."

"Indeed, and so it should be. We need to discuss our tactics. I think we should assume the worst and that there will be an unpleasant reception party awaiting our arrival. They're unlikely to be standing in plain sight and must therefore assume Bellis will have found a way of disguising them somehow, making them harder to see."

"So they could see us approaching, but we would be unable to see them lying in wait?" Garalia asked, wanting clarification.

"Precisely, your Highness. We need to even the odds or, better still, turn them in our favour."

"We spoke before about being invisible. You said you could make us, as well as yourself, unseen by them, but able to see each other. Surely that would be our best strategy. If we can slip past them, we could enter the palace by the main doors rather than sneak through a passage which may be difficult in places for my mother to negotiate, and only reveal our presence once we reach the king's chambers. I think that would be our best strategy, assuming your invisibility spell would last that length of time?"

"It will last as long as I want it to." Correollis nodded and smiled. "If it would be easier for Princess Garalia, then that is what we shall do," he replied.

"Just one question, Correollis. If we can see each other, how will we be able to tell when we're invisible and when we aren't? I just want to be prepared in case something goes wrong." Kailani worked to keep her face neutral and her eyes merely curious to hide the machinations whirling around inside her head.

"Normally there isn't a way to tell and nor should one be needed," he replied, clearly affronted.

Garalia spoke before her daughter had a chance to respond. "No insult was meant by the question, Correollis. However, my daughter was right to ask. What you will undoubtedly be unaware of is that my father regularly has drills whereby all the cannons used to protect the castle are fired to ensure they are in good working order. He doesn't ever want to be in a position where the palace could be attacked and the equipment fails. Therefore, he has the men service and fire them at least once a month and never on the same day. For all we know, tomorrow could be that day. If something were to happen to you, should you get hit when your attention is diverted elsewhere, we need to know if your invisibility spell is still active," she explained.

"Ah, I see," Correollis replied, back to his normal, charming self. "You're right, I wasn't aware he did that and can see what a valid question it is. Let me give it some thought and I'll see if I can come up with a solution."

"When we're invisible, does that mean we can't be heard?" Kailani asked. Her eyes were bright with curiosity.

"We can still communicate with each other, your Highness."

She giggled, still trying to keep up the pretence. "No, silly, that's not what I meant. Can our movements or conversations be heard by others? Would our footsteps be silent, for example?" She continued to smile, hoping he wouldn't notice anything amiss.

He smiled back, but it didn't reach his eyes. "None of our movements would be silent, nor would our voices. We would have to communicate with each other using gestures and be as silent as possible to avoid detection."

"Thank you for clarifying that. I didn't want to make a mistake and give ourselves away. It's because I value your counsel that I feel able to ask what might seem to you to be stupid or inconsequential things. I'm not a great warrior, I don't have your experience, and my magic pales next to your great workings. I admit to being worried about what tomorrow might bring, and even more worried that I'll make a mistake through ignorance."

The slight tightness around his shoulders eased and he visibly relaxed. "Of course I can understand your reasons and if you didn't ask them, I'd wonder if you belonged in the great house of D'Ara." He smiled then continued. "As your mother is still weak from her long years in captivity, I think your plan of entering through the main doors of the palace is the best one. I also understand your joint concerns should anything happen to me. I'll give some serious thought to devising a method whereby you can tell if the invisibility spell is still working to put your minds at rest. And speaking of rest, I think we should get some. Tomorrow will be a long day, one which will test our nerves to their limits. We need to be at our strongest, both physically and mentally, so if you ladies will excuse me, I'm going to retire." Correollis rose, bowed to them, and moved to the corner where his packs lay on the ground. He placed his cloak on the ice, shuffled onto it then, pulling it around him, closed his eyes.

The princesses made their own preparations, snuggling into their cloaks, but both laid awake, each busy with their own thoughts.

It wasn't until sometime later when soft snoring noises came from Correollis's side of the enclosure, that Garalia turned to face her daughter and whispered, "Why did you go outside for so long earlier?"

Kailani paused, ensuring the snoring continued before answering. "My instincts are screaming at me that something is wrong. I know you don't want to believe ill of Correollis, and neither do I, but believe me, Mother, all is not as it appears. Baelfyre is skittish around him as if the bond is missing or damaged in some way. He shouldn't be acting like that. All my life I've been told to trust my instincts, that I'd inherited this gift from my beautiful mother, and they've *never* let me down. At no time ever has an instinct been so strong."

Garalia remained silent for a moment as she digested her daughter's words. The soft noises of sleep the only sound; even the howling wind outside barely penetrated. "My first loyalty is to you, Kailani, and I trust in what you've told me. I too know how strong the instincts can be. I had one like that the day Gengaruk entered the city walls which is why I took you to Taivass-maa. I sensed you and I were both in danger, but I was expected to be present during the audience and couldn't make my excuses. My plan was to leave immediately after and join you, but I never got the chance. What are we going to do?"

"I have an idea, but I'm still working on the intricacies. We may not have the opportunity to talk without being overheard again, so please just do as I say without question when the time comes."

"Of course. Please make sure you get some sleep, my darling. Don't lie awake all night working on your idea."

"I promise I'll get some rest, Mother. Sleep well and have pleasant dreams, for if I have anything to do with it, tomorrow you'll be sleeping in your bed in the palace."

"It will be such a wonderful dream then," Garalia said sleepily. Within moments, her soft, even breathing told Kailani her mother was asleep. Wide awake, she laid staring up at the ceiling, her mind whirring with activity.

Chapter 26

Kailani was the first to wake to a grey and overcast morning. She rose and quietly began preparing food. She fed Mishtag and Yashtig then moved on to Baelfyre. As she reached him, she could see sadness in his eyes. Stroking his soft hide, he nuzzled into her as if for comfort. It was definitely odd behaviour from a Feegle who was bonded to another.

"Don't fear, little one. It will all be over soon," she whispered in his ear then rose and moved across the structure. As the food began warming, she had an idea. Perhaps something in his belongings would provide more information about him and what his true intentions were. She walked over to where Correollis's packs lie. Opening the straps on the one she'd seen him remove bottles of tonic from she began fishing around. She pulled out various vials, each with strange names on except one. As she moved to uncork it, a strong hand clasped her wrist so hard it made her cry out.

"What are you doing?" he snarled.

Kailani turned to look at him. Correollis's face was a mask of rage, his eyes flashed dangerously, and his teeth were bared like that of an animal.

"I was looking for the bottle of tonic," she replied in a sharp tone once she'd overcome her initial shock.

He snatched the bottle from her then whipped the bag away. "Don't go into my bags ever again!" he growled. He grabbed the tonic bottle and shoved it into her hands, a hateful look on his face.

The young princess became even more suspicious. She took the proffered bottle and thanked him saying, "I didn't think you'd mind me retrieving the tonic. I apologise if I over-stepped the mark." Her voice was solemn with more than a touch of sharpness as she looked pointedly down at his hand. He let go of her wrist and turned his back on her, an action that was considered the height of rudeness by the royals. Anger flared inside her.

Correoollis turned around, his face once more the pleasant and calm visage she was used to seeing. "Please accept my most humble apologies, your Highness, both for my actions and rudeness." He bowed his head then raising it again, continued. "I have potions which contain strong poisons in that bag, some of which would burn your skin to the bone at the slightest drop. Others would blind you if the vapours touched your face. I was concerned you would uncork the wrong bottle in error and harm yourself. Although my first thought was of your safety, my actions were inexcusable. I beg your forgiveness." He bowed his head again and stayed in that position awaiting her response.

Kailani hesitated as she dampened the anger within. Eventually, after a long moment, she spoke. "I can understand your fears for my safety and appreciate your concern. But I've never had anyone speak to me with such venom, or manhandle me the way you have done, especially a person who has been sent by my grandfather, King Sirris." She paused, waiting for her words to have the desired effect. His head bowed lower until his chin rested on his chest. "I'll forgive your transgression, but I won't forget it." She shoved the small bottle back into his hand. "I've changed my mind about using this. You can have it back."

He clasped his fingers around it without a word, keeping his head low then, without acknowledging it, said, "Again, I sincerely apologise for my actions, Princess Kailani. Thank you for your generosity." He raised his head, but didn't look her in the eye.

The commotion had woken Garalia, who sat up with confusion written all over her face. "What's happened? What's going on?"

Keeping an eye on Correollis, she turned slightly toward her mother. "It's nothing for you to worry about, Mother. We were just talking." In her peripheral vision she saw a look of hatred in the sorcerer's eyes and a grin which unnerved her. *What's happening to this man who has protected my family for centuries? Why would he look at me that way?*

"It sounded more than mere talking," Garalia insisted.

"We had a . . . misunderstanding. It's all resolved now, isn't it, Correollis?" She whipped her head around to face him and he quickly rearranged his features to that of the friendly servant. However, he couldn't hide the calculation in his eyes.

"Yes, your Highness." He turned to face Garalia and said, "I acted and spoke wrongly to your daughter and she quite rightly chastised me for it. She has been gracious enough to forgive me, so the episode is now at an end."

"Hmm. Perhaps all our nerves are a little on edge today," she mused aloud, "after all, we have a big day ahead where our every action could make the difference between getting into the palace safely or being caught. We need to rely on each other completely. I'm glad you've resolved your differences – we cannot afford discord between us."

"You're quite right, your Highness. Today, more than ever, even more than when we were escaping the village, we need to trust each other completely. We must assume that we're walking into some kind of trap. With my invisibility spell, we should be able to circumvent that, but all it would take is one wrong step or move and everything could start unravelling. I may be forced to act without first discussing it with you. I need to know I have your permission to do so."

Before Garalia could reply, Kailani jumped in. "You are forgetting something here, Correollis. I too have magic, double that of my evil uncle, and am fully able and capable of dealing with anything which may arise. Please don't think for one moment we don't trust you . . ." she lied convincingly, "but should matters start escalating, I will do what's best to get my mother safely to King Jaanis. I must deny you permission to do anything other than what we've discussed and agreed. Is that clear?" She looked him straight in the eyes.

He stared back at her with defiance. "Whatever you say, your Highness." The slight inflection in his tone wasn't lost on the young princess, but she chose not to mention it; instead she decided to press the point.

"Correollis, I want your promise!" she said sharply, glaring at him.

"But of course, your Highness. You have made your point most eloquently." She huffed and put both hands on her hips, her eyes narrowed, and she pursed her lips as she continued to glare at him. "Very well. It goes against my better judgement, but if it will make you happy, I promise."

"Thank you." She sighed. *I can't believe that was so hard. He was careful not to promise anything in particular even though the implication was for what I wanted. But I don't trust him anymore. It's as if Correollis has had a complete change of personality – he's gone from being warm, reassuring, and caring, to defiant, calculating, and harsh. I don't understand what's happened to him.*

Garalia interrupted her daughter's inner turmoil. "Correollis, you said yesterday you would give some thought to the problem of us knowing the invisibility spell was in place. Have you managed to come up with a solution?"

"Actually I've thought of two possible things I can do. One is to create a sort of bubble effect around you that gives off a sheen, the other is for me to bespell two cords for you to wear. While the invisibility spell works the cords will glow, but it'll fade to nothing if something goes wrong. What do you think?"

"I'm impressed." She smiled at him and he became more like the Correollis they first met. "Personally, I think I'd prefer to wear a cord around my wrist. It'll be something I'm more inclined to see clearly, so that would be my preference, please. Kailani? What about you?"

"I agree. A cord on my wrist is my choice also, please, Correollis." She worked to make her tone as pleasant as possible.

"Of course. What colour would you like?"

"I think green would be good. Kailani?" Her daughter nodded her agreement.

"Green it is." He pulled two plaited cords from one of the many hidden pockets in his cloak as well as his wand and pointing the wooden stick at them, began to mutter some words. In a few seconds he'd finished and handed one each to the princesses. They thanked him then tied them loosely around their wrists.

"They should really be a little tighter, your Highnesses. You don't want them to fall off."

"Ah, but we haven't got our gloves on yet," Garalia said grinning. "Once we have, we can pull the cords over them and they'll fit more snugly. Can you see our logic?"

"Absolutely, your Highness. However, I bespelled them to react with your skin – it won't work if there's no contact."

"Then we have a little problem. By the time we are fully dressed to go outside, we won't be able to see anything on our wrists as they'll be covered. The whole idea, as I understood it, was for us to see them and the only way that can happen is if they fit over the material. It'll be so much easier for me so can you please make that happen?" Garalia placed a hand on his arm as she spoke and looked up at him beseechingly.

"How can I deny you, your Highness, especially when you look at me like that?" he chuckled. "If you'll pass them back, I'll make the necessary adjustments to the spell." They took the cords off and handed them over. He pointed his wand at them once more and uttered a few words then gave them back. Once again, the princesses tied them on, thanking the sorcerer.

"When should we begin this last section of our journey? We don't want to wait until it's too dark in case there are complications – we'll need to be able to see what's happening and where," Garalia asked him.

"I agree with mother. We'll have to move very slowly in order not to make any noise. We need to allow for that as well."

Correollis paused and appeared thoughtful. After about a minute, he said, "You're both right, in which case we should leave in about an hour. It's difficult to tell exactly what the time is without the sun, but by my estimation it's mid-afternoon. We should begin our preparations now so we're ready to leave."

Correollis checked to ensure the women were busy then slipped outside the shelter and, positioning himself where he believed he wouldn't be seen by those left inside, stood staring toward the city walls. After a couple of minutes, he pulled his wand from inside his cloak and pointed it toward the palace. His lips moved like they were talking and suddenly a small trail of gold stars flew from the tip and into the air. After lingering in the air for a few minutes, they slowly faded away. He replaced his wand and remained in the same spot for a while until he saw a signal. Correollis grinned, thinking of the riches he'd been promised. He turned toward the enclosure, wiped the smile from his face, and entered, quickly busying himself with his packs.

Chapter 27

With Mishtag and Yashtig armoured and saddled, Baelfyre at full size, and all the packs secured, they were ready to leave. As they mounted, Kailani noticed a sparkle in Garalia's eyes. She smiled to herself. It was lovely to see her mother blossoming before her.

As Correollis mounted and took to the air, Kailani leaned over toward Garalia and, pretending to secure a pack better, whispered, "Don't ask questions now, but when I hold my hand out to you, grab it and hold on tight. And stay close to me. I'll explain later."

"Alright," Garalia whispered back.

Kailani straightened and glanced up at the sorcerer. He fiddled with his robes and she could see faint traces of green stars just in front of him in the air, just like the gold ones she'd seen earlier. Pretending she hadn't noticed anything, she called out to him, "Correollis, are we alright to proceed?"

"Yes, your Highness," he replied, his expression and voice carefully neutral. "As soon as I notice anything, I'll let you know."

"Thank you." She flicked the reins and Mishtag began to move forward; Yashtig followed and quickly caught up.

Mishtag, I believe Correollis has a hidden agenda and it's not one that bodes well for our safety. Have you noticed anything strange? she asked her Blenorai Kai using their telepathic link, and blocked it so the sorcerer couldn't hear.

Baelfyre does not seem comfortable around him at all. It is not the sort of behaviour I would expect from a creature who has supposedly been with someone a long time. Correoliis regularly checks the pack with the bottles of potions in – it is as if he is worried about losing something that is in there – and to say he overreacted when you were trying to find the tonic is putting it mildly. He is lucky I did not take his arm off for that! Mishtag replied.

Yes, I was shocked by that behaviour too. One bottle had no label. I was about to open it when he grabbed me. Perhaps the content of that particular bottle is the one he is desperate to hold on to. Have you seen anything else to concern you? she asked.

Are you referring to the gold stars he conjured earlier?

Ah, so you saw it too. Did you notice the green ones in the air a few minutes ago, just before we left? Kailani was relieved Mishtag had seen them too.

I caught a glimpse of them, yes. It makes me wonder if he is signalling someone within the palace.

Kailani glanced up at the sorcerer for a moment. He was looking straight ahead with a half-smile on his lips, so she turned her head back and continued. *That was my thought too. But Correoliis and his ancestors have been protecting my family in Taivass-maa for centuries – why would he betray me now?*

Mishtag paused for a moment. *Maybe he is not who he says he is.*

But he has a Feegle, so unless Baelfyre has been forced to come here, why would he allow himself to be brought?

I believe the clues may lie within his pack, Mishtag mused. *We have no way of getting hold of them though.*

She thought back to her prior conversation with him. *He told me earlier that some of the bottles contain poisons, one of which can kill just by inhaling the fumes. I'm not sure I believe it. We know he has potions for healing as he's used them on mother and me to good effect, but the Correollis of legend wouldn't need poisons. His magic and fighting skills are strong enough not to have to resort to using such things.*

I cannot comment on that as I have no knowledge of the stories surrounding him. But getting back to the immediate matter, do you have a plan?

Kailani almost laughed aloud and just managed to stifle it in time. *Of course I do. That's why I need you to stay close enough to Yashtig that I can grab mother's hand. Can you tell him, please?*

Certainly, Mistress. I will do it immediately. If I may offer a word of advice . . .? Mishtag paused and was rewarded by a hand stroking her mane, so she continued. *Access your magic. Keep it close to the surface at all times so you have the ability to react to any situation at a moment's notice.*

Thank you, Mishtag. It was something I'd thought about doing anyway, but having you mention it too, cements my thoughts on it. I'll need to concentrate so I'm going to be quiet now. Don't forget to tell Yashtig, please.

I will do it now, Princess.

Kailani reached deep inside herself, finding the power lying like water in a well, just waiting to be drawn. She pulled it up, cloaking herself with it so it made her skin tingle. It felt like a living organism, seemingly impatient to be unleashed, but at the same time like a close friend. She welcomed its embrace.

Glancing up at the Feegle and its passenger, she wondered if Correollis was aware of what she'd just done. She knew she was powerful, but whether it was enough to go against him if she needed to, she wasn't sure. Was her magic equal to his? The idea of battling against him wasn't something she wanted to contemplate, but if her suspicions were correct, she realised it was a distinct possibility. He looked altogether too comfortable and relaxed for her liking – surely he should be alert and ready for any eventuality. But then again, with the invisibility spell on them, did they really have anything to be concerned about? Was that why he was so calm?

Why couldn't she be as unruffled as him? Maybe it had something to do with the fact that her instincts were blaring at her, telling her something was very wrong. She looked down at the cord around her wrist; it was still glowing, but she didn't trust it. Actually she had a strong compulsion to remove it completely. She pulled at the threads, but it remained intact. Trying the other set brought the same result. Without hesitation, she pulled the Kamuk from her belt and sliced through it. The cord landed between her legs and she left it there for a moment.

Kailani leaned toward her mother and whispered, "Give me your wrist for a moment, the one with the cord on, please."

Garalia complied, but with her brows knotting together, asked, "Why? What's the matter?"

"Something is not quite right with it. Look!" She pulled the threads to show her that it wouldn't come undone.

"Oh! It's the only way for us to tell the invisibility spell is in place, but why won't it loosen?"

"Precisely my point. Here." Kailani cut through it and gave it back.

"Mother, reach for your instincts. What do they tell you?"

"That something is wrong, but I don't know what." Her brow furrowed and concern filled her eyes.

"I think these cords are a placebo, but with something else bespelled within them preventing us taking them off any other way. I'm not sure whether we should discard them completely or keep them close. What do you think?"

"Perhaps just keep one and get rid of the other. I think that's a good compromise for now. Throw your one away and I'll keep mine just here on the saddle for now."

Kailani straightened up in her saddle, took hold of the cord by one set of the threads then lay almost flat against Mishtag's back and dropped it on the ice. Using her magic, she extended her hand back toward it and covered it over with ice. She was about to sit up again when an arrow whizzed past her and embedded itself in the ground just behind them.

"Mother, get down, NOW!" she shouted then lowering her voice said, "I don't think we're invisible at all."

Garalia obeyed, her eyes widened and slowly filled with horror. She glanced up at Correollis and saw a smug-looking grin. "We've been betrayed." Her voice was filled with fury and venom.

Suddenly, from the surface of the ice, white covers rippled and soldiers emerged from them. Kailani was already drawing her Panas when the first one appeared. She didn't hesitate and stabbed him in the back before he'd even had the opportunity to get up from his knees. Grabbing a handful of Trey's, the five-pointed stars with whips on the end, she threw them at the men nearest Garalia with deadly accuracy. Those on her side were quickly cut down.

Just when she thought it was over, that they'd got through the first ambush unscathed, another group rose from the ice, this time directly in front of them and in a line. The women tried steering the Blenorai to one side, but more soldiers appeared, cutting them off.

Kailani acted instinctively and, holding out one hand, blasted them with ice, turning them into living statues. She continued along the line and across the ground as far as she could reach then directed the Kais across the ones still lying on the ice. The ground was bumpy as they stepped on the men and Garalia was almost unseated. A small whimper escaped her throat and Kailani reached over to steady her.

As they passed the line and returned to even ground, a flurry of arrows flew at them. She couldn't see or hear them, but Kailani sensed it. She pushed her mother down onto Yashtig's back, diving down a moment later, but they were too late and an arrow pierced Garalia's arm. She cried out, the force of the strike causing her to slip off the Kai. Kailani grabbed at her clothes and managed to right her just as the second wave made their way toward them.

"Hold on tight with your good hand!" Kailani said hurriedly and urged the Blenorai forward. They moved out of the way just in time, the arrows striking the ground just behind them. "We have to keep moving so we're harder to aim at. I'll put a barrier around us to try and repel the attack. Hang on, Mother. We'll soon be out of danger," she said, trying to reassure her. She conjured the barrier and laced it with lightning, the bands so close together they almost touched, hoping it would protect them. However, the next lot of arrows penetrated the barrier and two just missed her.

"It's not working! We're going to have to make a run for it. Can you hold on, Mother?"

"I'll try my best," she answered, her voice shaky. Pain was written across her face.

As the barrier was redundant, she removed it to conserve her energy. As they started to move faster across the ice, a couple of soldiers jumped up from their well-hidden position, appearing on Kailani's left side. Although she was ill-prepared for the surprise, she hadn't sheathed her Panas and as the first soldier swung his sword toward her, she was able to block the blow.

Surprising them in turn, she leapt from Mishtag's back straight at one of the attackers. He fell to the ground with her on top of him. Before he had the chance to swing his blade, she'd cut his throat. She spun around just quickly enough to counter an attack from the one still standing. As they parried, Kailani said to him, "To whom are you loyal?"

"Why? What difference does it make?" His attack became slower as he spoke.

"It makes all the difference in the world. So where does your loyalty lie?"

"With King Jaanis, of course."

"So in that case, why are you attacking his daughter and granddaughter?"

He put his sword down and gaped at her in surprised horror. "W-what?"

Kailani pointed to the Kai who had stopped just a short distance ahead. "That woman is Princess Garalia, heir to the throne of Idenvarlis, and daughter of King Jaanis. I am her daughter, Princess Kailani."

His eyes widened at the mention of Garalia's name. "We were told intruders, hoping to gain access to the palace were coming and to show no mercy. We were given the impression there were possibly as many as one-hundred. I thought you were scouting ahead for them."

"There *are* no intruders. We are just trying to return home, but someone in the palace doesn't want us to arrive alive. A faction within the King's guard is loyal to Prince Bellis and will act on his commands. Be careful who you trust with this information – you have no idea how far his reach is. I must return to my mother. She has been injured and is losing blood."

"Of course, your Highness," he said bowing. As she turned her back, an evil grin stretched across his face and he raised his sword. Just as he was about to deliver the fatal blow, Kailani spun around and lifted her blade. The clang of the metal echoed across the ice and rang in their ears. Her face was a mask of fury.

"You traitorous bastard! You dare to raise your sword against a member of the royal family? The penalty for your sedition is death," she said the last softly.

As she had planned, he leaned toward her to hear what she was saying. Quick as a flash of lightning, she grabbed the dagger from her belt with her other hand and stabbed him in the chest. His eyes grew wide and looked down at the blade. Blood stained the front of his tunic, moving outwards like a flower blossoming from a bud. His sword clattered onto the ice as his knees began to give way. Kailani shoved him so he fell onto his back and moved closer. As she bent to retrieve the Kamuk, she stared into his eyes and in a voice as cold as the ice said, "Sentence carried out." She pulled her weapon from his torso, wiped it on a clean part of his uniform and was about to replace it in its sheath when she heard her mother scream, "Look out!"

Whirling around, she saw a young soldier rushing toward her with his sword held high. He looked young, but she wasn't about to make the mistake of thinking he was inexperienced as a fighter. Acting purely on instinct she raised her left hand, palm toward him and, in a loud voice said, "Stop!" In his surprise, he did what she said. "I just have one question for you. Are you loyal to Prince Bellis or the king?"

"Why do you want to know? What difference does it make?" Confusion was evident in his voice.

"It will determine whether you live or die in the next few minutes," she replied, her voice neutral.

He studied her for a few moments then said, "My first and only fealty is to King Jaanis. Do I get to live?"

"That depends on whether you're telling the truth. What orders have you been given?" She moved closer to him, her muscles taut and ready.

"To kill anyone approaching the castle except for one that flies on the back of a great beast."

"And who issued those orders?"

"Prince Bellis himself addressed us. He said a large band of marauders were approaching, hundreds of them, and we had to stop them at all costs. The prince said not to spare a single person under any circumstances."

"It is as I suspected. What would you say if I told you that injured woman over there," she pointed to her mother, "is Princess Garalia, eldest child of King Jaanis and heir to the throne of Idenvarlis? Also, I am her daughter, Princess Kailani."

"I would say prove it," he answered, a little unsure as the strange events unfolded. She unwrapped her neck and pulled out the vial.

"Do you recognise this?"

His eyes widened a little. "It's from the Temple of Rasha-Varl," he said, "but that doesn't prove anything except you belong inside the walls rather than out here."

"Have you been taught what the colours are and what each means?"

"Of course. That's one of the first things we learned when we were inducted into the army. Why?"

"Have you ever seen one this colour, or even heard of a bright purple vial before?"

"Er... no, actually. What does it mean?"

She pulled her hood back just enough so he could see the colour of her hair. "It means I have the magics of both worlds. I have been blessed by the Gods, Xuani and Rasha, and the Goddess Sylde, as well of those from my other home. The well in the temple decreed I should have this colour."

"I remember you!" he suddenly blurted out. "I saw you when the king brought you down to pick your Blenorai."

"So, now you recognise I'm telling the truth, are you still going to attack me?"

"Of course not, your Highness. I will help you to reach the palace or die trying."

"Thank you." Kailani started to run toward her mother and the soldier followed. "What's your name?"

"Edur, your Highness."

"Well, Edur, I need to get the arrow from my mother's arm and bind it. Will you protect us while I do?"

"Of course," he replied with conviction.

They reached Garalia who was slumped over Yashtig. She could ill afford to lose any blood and weaken her already fragile body and Kailani could see how much it had affected her already. The young princess reached into one of the packs and brought out a long, clean, wide strip of cloth. Helping her mother to sit up, she grabbed the shaft and with a hard yank pulled it free. Garalia cried out, a sound that tugged on her daughter's heart. Kailani dropped the arrow and worked quickly to bind the wound, tying the bandage tightly to her arm.

"I'm sorry for hurting you, Mother, but I had to remove it," she said, her regret and sorrow heavy in her voice.

"I know and thank you." Garalia reached up and squeezed her daughter's hand.

"Can you continue on?"

"Do you think, being this close to my home for the first time in twenty years, I would allow a small injury to stop me now?"

Before Kailani could answer, a gruff voice said, "Good lad. You've captured two of the gang. I'm surprised they sent women ahead as scouts though." A large soldier walked toward the small group, five or six others trailing behind him.

"No, Sir. These women aren't with the marauders, they're part of the royal family," Edur said. Kailani walked around Yashtig and stood protecting her mother.

The older man laughed. "And you believed their lies? Ah, the inexperience of youth."

"They're not lies! I recognise the young princess and I've seen her in the palace with King Jaanis." Kailani watched the soldier's face carefully, pulling on her magic until her fingertips tingled. She knew that even with Edur's help, the two of them would struggle to fight off seven men.

He grinned. "It doesn't matter who they are. Prince Bellis said *anyone* approaching the city must die."

"I'm sure he didn't mean his sister and niece though," Edur insisted.

The man shook his head. "He meant *especially* them. Our prince doesn't want them to make it back to the palace." He began to move his sword and the men who had caught up began to fan out around them.

"You will die for your treachery!" Kailani spat, her eyes narrowed as she glared at him.

The man laughed. "At whose hand? Yours?" He chuckled again.

"Yes," she replied simply and pointed a finger at him. A bolt of lightning shot from it and hit him between the eyes. He dropped like a stone. The others began closing in. "You don't have to die. Lay down your arms and swear fealty to King Jaanis and to protect his kin." She watched them carefully; not one even hesitated and kept moving toward her, their swords ready. "Your decisions are noted." She fanned out her hand and, pointing it at the nearest group, let the lightning loose once more, each bolt finding a target. They fell to the ground, eyes unseeing. She turned her head to the last of the group who was now on his knees, quivering.

"Mercy! I beg your mercy, Highness," he cried.

"You were given a chance and made your decision. Only now when you see what I'm capable of do you bow down before me. My grandfather wouldn't want traitorous cowards in his army!" And with that, she blasted him. As she moved around the other side to where Mishtag waited sheathing her sword, she noticed the look of awe and surprise on Edur's face and giggled. "That's only a tiny fraction of what I can do."

"I've never seen anything like it!" His voice matched the expression on his face.

"We need to get moving. The sky darkens and soon it'll be difficult to see where our enemies are." Mishtag and Yashtig moved forward and Edur ran alongside them, trying to keep up. The city walls loomed ever closer. They could now see the archers poised on top of it as they let loose another flurry of arrows.

"Get down!" Kailani yelled as she pushed Mishtag to move faster. Yashtig kept pace with her. Some of the missiles sailed over their heads, while others landed in the ice around them much too close for their comfort. She sat up and pointed both hands at the top of the wall. Large stars flew from her hands and as they hit the archers, they toppled from the wall, landing inside the city. Those that remained suddenly disappeared from sight.

Edur struggled to keep up and found himself trailing behind them, but he continued running as fast as he could, his puffing breath forming misty clouds in front of him.

Suddenly a large crack appeared in the ice ahead of them and as they approached it became wider. The Blenorai Kai stopped just short of it; the chasm was too wide for them to jump across. Magic sizzled in the air and

Kailani looked up at Baelfyre. Correollis had vanished and in his place was a man with alabaster skin, a short white beard, blue lips, and piercing silver eyes.

"Oh, goddess. He must be a shape shifter of some kind," Kailani murmured. She dismounted and walked a short way behind Mishtag. As her anger rose, so did the power within. She pointed her finger at the man and a bolt of lightning shot from it. He ducked and it missed by a tiny fraction. As she prepared her next attack, she saw him raise his hand and his lips move. A ball of fire flew toward her and she dived out of the way, letting forth a flurry of stars. As they struck, he slipped on Baelfyre's back, but managed to grab hold of his neck. The Feegle bucked and writhed, unseating the changeling and he fell to the ground; Baelfyre wasted no time in flying away, landing on the ice just behind the princess. Kailani immediately mounted her next attack and sent a fireball at him. As he didn't have far to fall, he was uninjured. He rolled out of the way and jumped to his feet, firing off his own lightning strike. She jumped out of the way and sent a beam of white light at him with one hand and sharp, pointed icicles with the other. He tried to jump but couldn't – the light held his feet in place. He ducked and most of the icicles flew over his head, but one pierced his leg while another embedded itself in the top of his shoulder.

Keeping the moonbeam on him, she loosed another flurry of icicles, but as she did so, the ground beneath her began to quake so hard she fell to her knees and had to use her hands to brace herself. The shape shifter threw himself to the side, but not quite soon enough. Another icicle hit the shin of the same leg and the crack of bone could be heard above the rumbling beneath them. Another stabbed him in one side of the stomach. He screamed and the earth stopped shaking.

Kailani got to her feet and immediately set the moonbeam back on him. He sent a shower of spikes at her and she dived to one side, managing to keep the beam on him. Baelfyre took to the air, the missiles hurtling safely beneath him, but as he did so, the pack slipped and when it landed, they heard the sound of breaking glass. The changeling groaned as a golden mist rose into the air and began to form a shape. Kailani was too focused on her enemy to notice. Slowly getting to her feet, she fired several small lightning bolts from her fingers, each one finding their mark. She did it again and watched with pleasure as he writhed in agony. The third lot had the same effect. Her next assault was more of the icicles and she smiled at how many pierced his lying, treacherous body.

Abruptly she became aware of someone standing next to her. She glanced to the side and saw Correollis standing there. Her jaw dropped and eyes widened.

"Don't lose your focus," he said. "Finish this now or I will. The soldiers are closing in fast."

She turned her head back to face her foe and saw his lips moving. Without hesitating, she loosed a scorching stream as hot as the sun. It hit his ankles first and she directed it to crawl slowly up his body. He hadn't finished the spell as he was too busy screaming with the heat disintegrated his legs. A few seconds later, the shrieking stopped; all that remained was a smouldering pile of ash where his body had lain.

When she turned away, the first thing she noticed was Correollis kneeling beside Garalia. His hand was on her mother's wound and a faint white glow surrounded it. After a few seconds he removed it then took off the dressing, leaving the blood-soiled material on the ground. She walked over to them, wary of the man who had appeared so suddenly.

Correollis looked at her and said, "Do not fear me, your Highness. I promise you I'm the man you met at the inn. The shape shifter ambushed me in the stable and imprisoned me in a bottle, the same one you were about to uncork when he caught you."

"So that's why he reacted so violently," Garalia said.

"Yes. Now we haven't got time to talk as the soldiers will be upon us momentarily. I suggest we teleport straight to the entrance of the secret passage."

"How do we know you're not another shape shifter sent by Bellis? Prove you are the *real* Correollis!" Kailani demanded.

"The ring you wear is the one your mother left with you just before she was taken captive. When your father told you about her on your twenty-first birthday, he handed you a scroll containing a letter from her. He also showed you the entrance to the passageway between Taivass-maa and here, including the code to open it. He didn't want to tell you anything, but you entreated your aunt Konstellia and your grandfather to help you persuade him. Is that enough because we're running out of time?"

She looked to her mother, who nodded. "Very well. I'll accept your proof . . . for now. But I'll be watching your every move until I'm completely convinced." Her face was set in a stern cast. She looked around and saw the soldiers closing in fast. "Edur, pretend you're still one of them as it will surely save your life." He nodded and raised his sword, pointing it toward Kailani. "Let's go!" she cried. She ran to Mishtag and leapt onto her back as Correollis did the same with the Feegle. She grabbed her mother's hand, touched Baelfyre, and let her magic transport them away.

Chapter 28

Kailani's group sailed unseen over the soldiers' to the side of the great wall. A few infantrymen patrolled the area, but suddenly they fell to the ground unconscious. Kailani glanced at Correollis who smiled.

"A simple sleep spell. They will be fine when they wake in a few hours," he explained.

She nodded and set them down. Dismounting, she walked over to the wall and looked for the mark which opened the passage. It was hard to find in the dark and she removed her glove, using her hand to trace over the surface. Several minutes passed and a frisson of panic and despair began to settle inside her. She didn't want to conjure a light in case it was seen by the soldiers so she gritted her teeth and continued her search.

A sudden thought popped into her head; she stepped back and stared at the wall, allowing her magic to ripple free. Within the blink of an eye, a pale glow settled on the ice and as she moved over to it, she saw the symbol. Breathing a sigh of relief, and silently thanking the gods and goddesses, she traced it with her fingertip then placed her hand over it. After a few seconds they heard a small creaking sound as the ice slid back to reveal the entrance.

"I'll go first with Mishtag," she said. "Mother, you follow next with Yashtig and Correollis can bring up the rear with Baelfyre. You'll have to dismount though." They nodded their agreement and as she was about to slip into the tunnel, she saw the warrior press the button on the Feegle's collar, shrinking him. As she entered, Kailani threw what seemed like hundreds of stars toward the ceiling. They lit the way just enough to see by. She looked at the ice just inside the passage and, locating the symbol to close the entrance, she sprinkled some more stars around it. "Correollis, when you and Baelfyre have entered, can you place your hand on the symbol lit with stars on your right? It'll shut the door behind us."

"Of course, your Highness," he replied and nodded.

It didn't take long for her to reach the uphill section. As Kailani began to climb up the slope, she agonised over how her mother would cope, especially after all the steps. She was finding it hard enough, and if it wasn't for Mishtag behind her, she would have slipped backwards a few times.

Do not worry about your mother, Princess. Yashtig will help her, Mishtag said, trying to remove the concern from her mistress.

"Thank you, Mishtag. You always know the right thing to say. You're a great comfort to me."

I am glad, Kailani. I have seen you grow so much since we first met. You were a feisty girl determined to prove yourself, but now you are a strong, capable woman and one of the best fighters I have ever seen. Be ready when we reach the end of the passage. Bellis must know by now that you are close. He may have extra sentries in the hallways.

"Thank you. I expect to find resistance en route to the king's chambers, but I don't think we have anything to fear from the king's own guards. They are hand-picked by him and fiercely loyal to him alone."

That is true, but how do you know that Bellis won't substitute them for his own men? Mishtag asked.

"The guards won't take orders from anyone except my grandfather. I think the only way Bellis could do that would be for his men to overpower the guards, but it would make a great deal of noise and alert the king. He wouldn't want to risk that."

A simple sleeping draught would take care of them, especially if taken before reaching their posts. The prince could have one of his men put on the armour and take his place.

"It might work with one or two of the guards, but the others would notice the newcomers and become suspicious. They would attack first and ask questions later," Kailani replied in a confident tone.

I do not want you to think you are secure once you reach the king's guards. You will not be safe until you're actually in his chambers with your mother.

"You make a good point and I'll take your counsel on board. How far behind is my mother?" she asked, changing the subject. They had finished the climb and were back on a flat surface. Casting her mind back, she remembered it wasn't too far from where they were to the entrance into the castle.

Not far at all. Yashtig tells me he had to use his head to lift her from the bottom of the slope to the top. He said it felt strange her sitting on his head instead of his back. Mishtag was almost laughing as she recounted her friend's words.

"Good. Let's move just a little further on until everyone is accounted for and on the flat then we'll take the final few steps to the exit." They walked further along and stopped again, waiting for the others to catch up. Soon they were all crowded in the small space.

"We're almost at the door into the palace," Kailani whispered. "Correollis, please come up here so you can enter directly behind me, in case we run into any resistance. Mishtag you follow next, then you, Mother. Yashtig and Baelfyre, you can bring up the rear and I'm relying on you to protect and defend my mother. Mother, if we encounter trouble on the other side of the door, as soon as Baelfyre is out, press the button on his collar, please. He'll be more able to guard you in his larger form. I'm sure the corridor is wide enough for him. Is everyone ready?"

Correollis had moved as Kailani was speaking and now stood beside her. They took the final few steps to the door and stood in silence, listening. With no sounds from the other side, the young princess moved her hand toward the symbol. The warrior tapped her on the shoulder and pointed to her Panas. She nodded and silently slipped the sword from its scabbard while he did the same. Without hesitation, she placed her hand against the symbol and a few seconds later the door slid silently back.

Kailani peeped out to find the corridor empty. She stepped through and beckoned for the others to follow. Once everyone had entered the hallway, she found the symbol and placed her hand against it until the door slid shut. She led the way as far as the king's chambers, surprised not to encounter any soldiers. However, she heeded Mishtag's wise words and didn't let her guard down.

As usual, two of the king's men flanked his door and as the group approached, the guards immediately went on the offensive. They pounced forward, swords raised ready to strike. Kailani threw the hood off her head, raised her hand palm forward, and shouted, "Stop!"

The men ground to a halt within striking distance, surprised the group hadn't lifted their weapons to even protect themselves.

"Do you not recognise the king's granddaughter?" she asked in an incredulous yet regal tone.

"No," one of the guards said gruffly.

The other nudged his companion and said, "I heard something about his granddaughter having blue hair."

"It doesn't mean this is the princess. Her hair could be coloured by magic," the first one argued back.

"I can assure you I *am* Princess Kailani, granddaughter of the king. Now enough of your silly bickering, I need to see my grandfather on a matter of extreme urgency, and even though he's retired for the night, this is important enough to disturb him."

"How do you know?" the second one asked.

"Because I stayed here in the palace for a while and know his routine, of course. The lights in the hallways have dimmed and that's what happens every night when he goes into his chambers."

"You could have got that information from any of the servants at the right price," the first one said.

She pulled the vial from beneath her clothes and waved it in front of them. "Would I have this if I wasn't a member of the royal family? Now enough of your nonsense! Let me and my companions pass."

"That vial could be a cheap imitation. I heard a woman in the back streets was selling them."

"Oh for the love of Sylde! I've had enough of this, now let me pass. I've done enough killing to last me two lifetimes and believe me, I have no wish to take your lives. Besides, grandfather would probably scold me for depleting his hand-picked guards and I'm too tired to endure the lecture." She calmly walked forward and was about to move between them when she found her way blocked.

"Oh no you don't," said the gruff one. "You talk up a good tale, but nothing you've said or shown me, convinces me to let you pass."

"Prepare to die then," she whispered. He bent his head down to hear her and she rammed the hilt of her sword straight into his nose. Blood poured from the wound and he dropped his sword then sank to his knees holding both hands to his face. In a flash, the tip of her blade was digging in the other guard's throat, just enough to draw a little blood. "I haven't necessarily finished with your friend yet, and it would take me less than a second to slit your throat from ear to ear. Now back up and knock on the door."

The guard, his eyes filled with surprise and fear did her bidding. He could feel the warmth of his own blood trickling down his neck, and the speed with which she'd moved unnerved him. He rapped loudly on the door and waited.

The door was flung open and King Jaanis stood in the doorway. "You better have a good reason for . . ." he suddenly saw her and a huge smile lit his face. "Kailani! Oh, my beautiful girl, you have no idea how worried we've been!" He threw his arms around her and she dropped the Panas to hug him back.

"Grandfather, it's so wonderful to see you again. I have a surprise for you," she said warmly, pulling away from him and holding out her hand. Garalia stepped forward and when she was close enough, removed the hood. Tears streamed down her face which was lit up with a beatific smile.

"Hello Father." She could hardly get the words out.

"Garalia?" He pulled her into his embrace, hugging her fiercely as the tears flowed from his eyes. "Oh, my precious daughter. I thought we'd lost you forever."

Kailani was about to slip into the room to wake her grandmother, but there was no need. She'd heard the commotion and came to see what was happening. She hugged Kailani as soon as she saw her and was about to admonish her for worrying them, when she was interrupted. "I kept my promise, Grandmother."

Queen Shivla turned her head and saw the woman in her husband's arms. "G-Garalia?" she stammered. Her daughter turned toward her and her legs buckled. Kailani caught her and managed to hold her up enough to throw her arms around Garalia. Their tears mingled as Shivla held her cheek against Garalia's.

"Grandfather? May I present Correollis? He has been of great assistance to us and if it weren't for him, we would not have made it back here alive."

King Jaanis held out his hand and the two men shook. He laid his other hand on the warrior's shoulder and said, "I owe you a great debt."

"Thank you, your Majesty, but my reward is seeing this family reunited and home safely. If I might suggest we move this into your chambers. There are urgent matters the ladies need to discuss with you and we don't want anyone in the palace to know of the princesses' return yet. You will understand when you hear what they have to say. If I might make a recommendation?" Jaanis nodded so he continued. "You swear your guards to secrecy about everything they've seen and heard tonight. Also, our faithful creatures need taking care of. They are exhausted, in need of a good feed and plenty of rest. I would suggest my Feegle is placed somewhere more . . . private and kept under guard by one of your own men. There are certain parties who mustn't know of his existence."

The king looked puzzled but agreed. He swore his men to secrecy then arranged for the animals to be cared for as Correollis had suggested. He further ordered a tray of food and drink brought to his chambers, giving the guard a code word for when he returned with it. Jaanis ushered the women and Correollis into his suite and carefully locked and bolted the door behind him.

Chapter 29

Garalia sat with her mother on one side and her daughter on the other. Their tears had dried and refreshments had been served.

King Jaanis said, "Garalia, you've had a terribly rough time. Can you tell us what has happened since you were taken? This is the only place in the palace where we can be assured of complete secrecy."

Correollis's brow furrowed. "Sorry to interrupt, your Majesty, but are you absolutely certain because my senses are telling me otherwise?"

"What? Investigate it at once!" The king's outrage was palpable and could be felt by everyone in the room.

"Grandfather? I mean no disrespect here, but Correollis is not yours to command," Kailani said in a firm voice. Jaanis glared at her and she stared back at him, unwavering. She waited him out and after a couple of minutes, his eyes began to soften.

"You are definitely your mother's daughter," he said chuckling then turned to the sorcerer. "Correollis, please accept my apologies for the way I spoke to you. My granddaughter is quite right to rebuke me."

"Of course, your Majesty."

"Thank you. Would you please be so kind as to investigate what you suspect?"

Correollis rose and gestured toward the rooms. "May I?" The king nodded. The sorcerer muttered under his breath then walked around the rooms, looking behind furniture and drapes until he found a small glowing light in the very room they were in. On further inspection, he found a small hole, just big enough for someone to listen through. "Your Majesty, can I please ask you to come here?"

He rose and, as he approached, Correollis put one finger up to his lips. The king nodded and the warrior showed him the hole. Jaanis's face went red then puce and he gnashed his teeth. Showing a great deal of restraint, he calmly asked his wife for a handkerchief; she reached into her pocket and passed one to him. He then looked around the room and spotted the quiver on the floor beside Kailani. She had followed his eyes and handed him an arrow from it. He smiled at her and broke it over his knee then moved closer to the hole. Correollis held up a hand and walked to the door of the chambers, sliding the bolt and unlocking it silently. As he made to step through the door, he nodded to the king then disappeared.

Using the sharp, broken end, Jaanis shoved it through the hole as hard as he could. A cry of pain was heard from the other side and then another a few moments later, one of the guards poked his head through the door. "Your Majesty, Correollis asks if you could come to the door, please." The king nodded, walked across the room and stepped over the threshold. The warrior had a man in a choke hold, blood from his ear stained Correollis's sleeve.

"Do you know this man, your Majesty?"

"Yes. He's my son's manservant, or should I say was. Would you accompany my guard to the dungeons so he can put this spy in chains? I can't risk leaving this door unguarded."

"It would be my honour, Sire," Correollis replied.

The king bobbed his head toward him. He then turned to one of his guards. "Return here immediately, after this scum has been dealt with." He moved his head to look at the warrior. "Please join us again on your return."

"As you wish, your Majesty." He and the guard waited until Jaanis returned to his chambers before leaving to carry out his request. A few minutes later, Correollis returned and took the seat he'd previously vacated. Before sitting, he noticed the hole had been plugged with some fabric which was held in place by the clean end of the broken arrow. "Would you like me to make a permanent repair?" he asked, pointing to the wall.

"Yes please," Queen Shivla replied.

Correollis stood, removed his wand from beneath his clothes and walked across the room. He removed the material which he discovered was a ladies' handkerchief, pointed the stick at the hole and murmured in a strange language. Everyone watched as the hole in the ice sealed itself so completely, there was no sign it had ever been there. He waved the wand around the room, saying, "Palia des simen hosk."

"Thank you," Shivla said with a certain amount of amazement in her voice.

"You're welcome. Now nothing said in this room will be heard by anyone outside. I have bespelled it to ensure complete secrecy."

"I'm impressed," the king said then turned to Garalia. "Now, my darling, can you tell us what happened?"

She glanced at Kailani who said, "Mother, you need to tell the whole story, even the embarrassing and sordid parts. Your parents need to know and will understand."

Garalia nodded then falteringly began. She told of her instincts on that day and getting Kailani to Galaxan, her abduction, her efforts to escape during the journey, and all that happened once reaching the Land of Lost Souls. At times they could hear the venom in her voice, particularly when speaking of her brother and his taunting. Kailani watched as her grandfather's face went stony and he gritted his teeth. She saw the fury rippling through him and his struggle to contain it. As Garalia spoke of the indignities, the countless rapes, tears streamed down her face and she became so choked up, she had to stop and regain her composure before being able to continue. Two hours later, she finished with, ". . . and then Kailani arrived and rescued me." She paused for a moment then, with her face crumpling, cried out, "Bellis! My own brother did this to me...my own brother!" Garalia broke down, sobbing so hard her whole body convulsed, and was immediately gathered into her mother's embrace.

Jaanis and Shivla sat in shocked silence for several minutes before the king finally spoke in a gentle tone. "My poor child. You have endured more than any human ever should. No words of mine or your mother's could make up for, or take away, the pain you've suffered." He paused for a moment then continued in barely controlled fury. "I promise you now, those who have done this to you will pay."

He rose, walked to the bolted door and called out, "Code word." When the correct response had been given, he unlocked then opened the door. "I want the entire complement of my guards here, in full armour, within fifteen minutes, including Captain Istas. When they're assembled knock twice, pause then knock four times. Now listen carefully. It's of the utmost importance that Captain Karruq does not know about this. Warn the men as they are rounded up."

"Yes, your Majesty. I understand." The guard said as he bowed then waited for the king to close and re-lock the door.

Jaanis walked straight to the sofa and picked up one of Kailani's hands. He raised it to his lips and kissed it gently then cradled it in both of his own.

He returned to his seat, took a deep breath, and let it out slowly. "I sense your journey back has been rather eventful so can you tell us what happened? I need every scrap of information so we know how to deal with those who have betrayed us."

She began with the rescue, telling of the meeting with Jevnod, King of the Lost Mire, pulling the box containing the scroll from beneath her clothing and placing in on her lap. She ended with, "and of course, when we reached your door, the guards refused to believe who I was and I ended up besting them, causing you to make an appearance. Don't be angry with them though, Grandfather. They were doing their job just as they should and as I've not been here for quite a while, they can be forgiven for not recognising me."

"Indeed. However, if they can be bested by a girl with no military training, perhaps they should be re-trained." He chuckled. Just at that moment there were two raps at the door   followed by four as he'd instructed. He rose, moved over to it, and asked for the code word. Having been given it, Jaanis opened the door and saw the full battalion of his guards standing to attention in rows, their captain off to one side.

The king stepped over the threshold ensuring they were all indeed his hand-picked men. Satisfied, he pointed to a group of them and said, "I have an unpleasant duty for you to perform. Arrest Prince Bellis, clap him in irons, and place him in a cell in the dungeons, chained to the wall. If he isn't in his room, hunt him down. I want him guarded every minute of the day and night, so you will work in eight hour shifts. Khuno and Neige will take the first shift. Captain Istas will allocate shifts for the rest of you. The only person allowed in the cell, other than myself, will be one of you. When his food is delivered from the kitchen, you will take it in to him after inspecting the tray for any secreted weapons. Once the soldiers have returned to the barracks, I want the city gate to be locked and the keys brought to me. No one leaves without my express permission. The rest of you will remain here for the time being. Stand easy.

"Captain Istas, will you join us inside for a few minutes? Those of you who have been given your tasks may go now." The eight selected soldiers bowed their heads and marched off. Istas followed the king into his chambers and removed his helmet. If he was surprised by who was in the room he didn't show it. Jaanis pointed to a chair and said, "Please sit." Istas did as he was told and waited. "Kailani, would you briefly tell Captain Istas what you encountered on your return journey as far as the soldiers are concerned?"

"Of course, Grandfather." She repeated what she'd said previously, beginning with the avalanche and ending with them entering the castle, although she deliberately didn't mention the secret passage.

"So, we have a problem, Istas. We don't know who is loyal to Bellis and who to me," the king said in a stern tone, his brow furrowed. "Please speak freely."

"Thank you, your Majesty. I could make some enquiries down in the barracks and especially at the taverns and inns in the city. Beer does tend to loosen tongues and I know the favoured watering holes. However, all this will take time, and once word of the prince's arrest gets out, it could stir things up with the men. I doubt anyone would be brazen enough to openly admit loyalty to the prince and against their king if asked." Istas's tone bordered on outrage when he spoke of any disloyalty to his king.

Correollis had been silent while all the talking had been going on, taking everything in, and sat with a thoughtful expression on his face. "Your Majesty, may I speak?"

"Of course. You have earned the right to speak freely. I am interested to hear what you have to say."

"First if I may ask a couple of questions?" He looked at Jaanis, who nodded, so he continued. "Captain Istas, how many battalions do you have in total and how many men to a battalion?"

"There are fifty battalions with one hundred men in each. However, not all the men are here. Some have been sent up north to deal with a matter for the king."

"So roughly how many men are here at the moment?"

"His majesty sent twenty full battalions away north and the rest are here, so that's approximately three thousand men."

"Thank you, Captain. One final question, have you included the captain of the guard, the stable boys, and anyone else who works with the soldiers?"

"No, not the other workers, but the number is small, probably no more than thirty or forty."

"I see." He turned to the king and addressed him. "Your Majesty, when Princess Kailani introduced me, she didn't tell you exactly who I am. At the time it wasn't important, but now it is. I am a warrior, sworn to protect the royal family of Taivass-maa, but in addition, I'm also a skilled sorcerer. If we could get the entire garrison together, along with the sundry workers, I could cast a spell to discover the truth. It will save much time and you will know immediately who is against you. What you need to decide is what you are going to do with those loyal to Prince Bellis. Again, I can come to your assistance and bespell the men to switch loyalties, if that is what you wish, but if their minds can be so easily swayed in the first place, it could happen again in the future. If they can be persuaded to switch allegiances once more, my spell will be undone."

Jaanis sat and pondered the sorcerer's words. "I agree with your idea of the truth spell. I think it the most efficient way. As to how we handle the traitors, that needs a great deal more thought."

"I, too, am in favour of the truth spell idea," Istas said. "But if I may be so bold, what your Majesty also needs to consider is the potential number involved. It could be hundreds or more. If you decide against the sorcerer's idea of bespelling them, what would you do with that many men?"

"You raise good points. They are things to which I must give serious thought. I doubt I will get much rest tonight. Now it is very late, and we're all tired. I suggest we all retire, get some well-earned sleep, and meet again in the morning. We will all breakfast together here in my chambers and with fresh minds, decide what is to be done. I know it will be a little cramped and an unorthodox way of eating, but this is the only place in the palace where I can now be assured of complete secrecy." He winked at Correollis who smiled in response then stood.

After shaking hands with Istas and Correollis, and embracing Kailani and Garalia, he ushered them toward the door. He opened it then commanded the rest of the guard to accompany everyone to their rooms. "I want three of you men outside their rooms all night and when they are ready to return here in the morning, you will accompany them back. Istas, I leave you to work out the rest of the details with your men. Furthermore, I want the palace locked up tight, every entrance and exit. No one but the regular staff are to be admitted, with the exception of those who work with or for Prince Bellis. They are to be detained in the cells for later questioning."

"It will be as you order, your Majesty," Captain Istas replied backing from the room and replacing his helmet. "Goodnight, Sire." His men had already surrounded the two princesses and Correollis and began marching them to their rooms.

King Jaanis closed then locked and bolted the door, leaned against it, and cried.

Chapter 30

The following morning, they met in the king's chambers for breakfast as arranged. Kailani and Garalia looked brighter after a good night's sleep and were the last to arrive. Food was spread out on the small table and drinks had been placed on a long, low sideboard. When everyone was seated and had filled their plates, Jaanis spoke.

"Good morning. I trust you all slept better than I did!" He grinned half-heartedly then continued. "As I'm sure you can imagine, I've had much to ponder. Captain Istas, are you able to confirm Prince Bellis has been arrested?"

"I'm afraid not, your Majesty. He is currently missing, but I have assigned more of my men to find him. He must be in the city somewhere as the gates were locked as per your command and you are in possession of the only keys. His Blenorai Kai is still here which means he must be. Are there any secret passageways within the palace where he might hide?"

The king's eyes narrowed and he thumped his fist on the arm of his chair. "Devote every man you can spare to the task, Istas. As for secret passageways, the only one I know about is the one my granddaughter used to sneak away from the palace." He flashed Kailani a stern look.

"There is another one, although it's small," Garalia piped up. "Bellis and I used it all the time when we were children and had adjoining rooms."

"I remember where those rooms were, you Highness. Can you tell me how to open the passage, please?" Istas asked.

"Certainly. In my old room, there's a bookcase against the wall on the left as you enter, positioned in an alcove. If you count up three shelves from the bottom then press against the alcove wall in line with it, the passage will open. The same goes for his old room, but the bookcase is on the right."

The captain stood and excused himself. He disappeared through the door and returned a couple of minutes later. "I have passed the information to the guards and they are going to investigate it immediately. I've told them to ensure they have returned within an hour."

Jaanis nodded. "Now, moving on to other matters, how many young men are in the city that would possibly be willing to serve in the guard, do you think?"

"That's hard to say, Sire. Many of the right age are already gainfully employed as apprentices or work on the farms. However, if I include them, I would guess there's close to a thousand in all."

"And what about in Vendis?"

"I reckon somewhere between one hundred and one hundred and fifty, although we wouldn't want to conscript everyone, if that's what you're thinking. Some need to be left behind to ensure the prosperity of the village endures and so they can continue to supply the palace with some of their wares."

"Where's Vendis?" Kailani interrupted.

"It's the village where we first met Correollis," Garalia replied then threw her father an apologetic look.

"I see," he continued as if Kailani hadn't spoken. "First of all we need to establish how many of the guard are involved then we can base our decisions on fact and not conjecture."

"I agree, your Majesty," Istas replied.

"Correollis, you said last night about casting a truth spell. Would it work on so many men at once?"

"Yes, your Majesty. As long as they are all in the same place, it would. I have been giving the situation some thought. We'll need to separate the two factions so you know what you're dealing with. I suggest that once we've established those who are faithful to you, we send them to their barracks, thereby removing them from the equation. Then you're only left with the traitors.

"I can also cast a compulsion spell so everyone does as they are told. However they will only obey one person. I am happy to take on that responsibility and give whatever orders you direct. Alternatively, either you or Captain Istas can give the orders. I will need to know your decision prior to casting the spell as it'll be linked to the person nominated. If you don't mind my asking, have you decided what to do with the traitors yet?"

"I have one or two ideas, but it'll depend on the numbers involved. I like the idea of the compulsion spell and that a person can be nominated. Before I can make that decision, I need to know how long you intend to stay in Idenvarlis, Correollis."

"Technically my obligations have been fulfilled. I was asked to ensure Princess Kailani arrived back to this palace safely and it has been achieved. However, I don't believe either she or Princess Garalia are safe yet, so I will stay until I'm satisfied they are. How long that will take is, of course, unknown. I must admit I'm missing Taivass-maa and particularly the climate – no offense meant, but it's too cold here for my liking."

"None taken. I suppose that answers my question in a convoluted way. Captain Istas will be the one giving the orders."

"Very well. The captain and I will need a few minutes together to go through some finer points before the spell is cast, but apart from that it can be done at your command, Sire." Correollis appeared to relax a little more.

He believed the king was going to ask him to give the orders and half expected Jaanis to try and persuade him to stay.

Before the king could respond, there was a knock at the door. Istas rose and crossed the room, opening the door and stepping outside. Hushed voices could be heard then the captain returned. "I have just received word that Prince Bellis has been arrested and is now in irons in the dungeon, Sire."

"Excellent! Before you make yourself comfortable again, can you send word to Captain Karruq that I want the entire garrison, every single man without exception, assembled in the main square in forty-five minutes. That should give him enough time to round them all up."

"Yes, Sire." He returned to the door and, after relaying the instructions, returned to his seat.

Jaanis turned to the ladies. "Before I make my final decision on what is to be done with the traitors, as you two have suffered at their hands, do you have any recommendations or requests for me to take into consideration?"

The question caught both Garalia and Kailani off guard and they spent a couple of minutes thinking about it before responding. Kailani was the first to speak.

"If you just banished them, they could try to recruit others and mount an uprising against you at some time in the future. So, as I see it you have two options: you will either have to execute them all for treason, or banish them to a place where they can't mount an offensive against you." Her tone was matter-of-fact, almost to the point of being cold and clinical, but her eyes, although serious, showed a flash of irritation.

"Your voice tells me one thing, but your eyes another. How do you truly feel?" the king asked, the gentleness of his voice belying his piercing gaze.

"Truthfully, Grandfather, I have many feelings flying around inside."

"It's perfectly understandable to have mixed emotions, Kailani. You and your mother have been through an ordeal and the strain you felt must have been overwhelming at times. Can you be objective enough to make a recommendation?"

"No one will think any less of you if you can't, my dear," Queen Shivla interjected, reaching over and squeezing her granddaughter's hand.

Taking a deep breath and letting it out slowly, she answered. "I'm learning something of what it takes to be a ruler, and part of that is showing strength while tempering it with mercy where it's due. My recommendation is that the leaders be executed and the men under them banished somewhere they can never leave – but not the Land of Lost Souls. They don't deserve that. It should be somewhere where they can at least grow their own food and sustain a basic lifestyle."

"Hmm, interesting," the king replied, stroking his chin. "Garalia, what are your thoughts? Do you have any requests or recommendations?"

"I can fully understand Kailani's emotions on this matter. She put herself in danger so many times to protect me and I suffered the frustration of not being able to do anything to help her. I agree with her recommendations as far as the men are concerned. However, Bellis is another matter entirely." She paused a moment and when she continued, her voice was full of venom. "In some ways I want him to die for what he put me through, but that would be too easy. I want him to suffer as I suffered for all those years. He should be sent to the Land of Lost Souls to live out his days in the squalor I was subjected to, where he will have to hunt for his own food, build his own shelter, and stand up for himself against those savages. Nothing else would appease the hatred, the feelings of betrayal, and the need for retribution in kind." Her voice was as cold as the ice around them.

The king turned to the captain of his guard. "Istas, what are your thoughts?"

"I agree that we have a potentially dangerous situation on our hands and it needs to be dealt with quickly and decisively. I also agree with the princesses' recommendations. I would suggest they are banished to either Paavinil or the Forgotten Lands. Both places are isolated and without inhabitants, and have the means for them to grow food and sustain themselves. You can bespell whichever one you choose to stop them escaping, like you have with the Land of Lost Souls, assuming you agree with our recommendations, of course." Istas kept his face neutral, but his voice was a touch aggressive.

"Your Majesty? Please excuse the interruption, but may I ask a question?" Correollis asked.

"Yes, go ahead."

"The spell you have cast around the Land of Lost Souls, what would happen if you were to die?" Jaanis looked at him aghast, and Correollis put up his hands as if in surrender. "Please don't take my question the wrong way – I'm just concerned about the possible repercussions, especially as you are considering doing the same with the traitorous soldiers."

The king pursed his lips and seemed to stare into space for a few seconds before answering. "I've never considered it, but I suppose the spell would die with me."

"They would all become free again?" Garalia's voice showed her disbelief, panic, and fear.

"Don't worry. I can show you how to link your spell to the land itself so if anything were to happen to you, the spell would remain intact," he reassured him.

"Can you do it now? Please?" Garalia asked.

Jaanis exchanged looks with the sorcerer and, seeing him nod, said, "Of course, if that would make you happy and give you peace of mind." Garalia nodded, a haunted look in her eyes.

"Right, your Majesty. I'd like you to think of the spell you cast, close your eyes, visualise it around the Land of Lost Souls, and tell me what you see."

"I see a partition of sorts. It wraps around the land from the ground up to the height of three men. It is violet in colour."

"Good. Now I want you to look closer at it, as close as you can. Tell me what the screen is made from."

"Thousands of thin vertical lines of light."

"Excellent. Now you need to gently extend all those lines into the ice without cracking it, going as deep as you can around the entire area and as you do so, in your own tongue, say, 'I link this spell to the land and let the land maintain it always and forever. I relinquish my ties to it and pass them to Xuani, God of Ice, to ensure my spell will never be broken, even upon my death'."

King Jaanis said the words slowly, but with feeling. When he finished, he opened his eyes again. "Thank you, Correollis. You are indeed a mighty and learned sorcerer. I will do the same when I cast the next spell. Now, I think it's time to deal with the traitors." He stood and everyone rose with him. "No, ladies. I think you should remain here and rest." Garalia and Shivla sat, but not Kailani.

"I'm coming with you!" she said firmly.

"I don't think that's a good idea, Kailani."

She glared at him. "Grandfather, those men were sent to kill me. I want them to see they failed miserably. I *have* to do this. I must face them

---

353

on my own terms otherwise it will haunt me. Please understand," she implored, her eyes beseeching.

He let out a sigh. "Very well, but . . . you remain within the cordon of royal guards until Correollis has cast his spells and then stay by my side until it's done. Agreed?"

"Yes, Grandfather."

"I mean it, Kailani. If you deviate from what I've said, I will have the guards bring you back up here, forcibly if necessary." His tone brooked no argument and his eyes were as stern as his voice.

"I agree, Grandfather. I promise to do what you say."

They left the room and were immediately surrounded by the king's guards. As they descended the stairs, the captain and the sorcerer hung back, speaking in low voices. Kailani couldn't stop herself from listening in and found they were talking about the finer points of the spell Correollis would cast and how Istas would need to deal with it. After a couple of minutes she found it boring and tuned out, listening instead to the noises around the palace, muffled by their footsteps and the clanking of armour.

They approached the main square, and the mumble of voices seemed quite loud. As soon as the king appeared, silence reigned over the congregated soldiers and they all stood to attention. Jaanis nodded to Correollis who stepped forward with Istas by his side and with his hand on the sorcerer's shoulder.

The sorcerer raised his hands, extended his arms toward the men, and spoke his spell. The magic was a palpable thing; Kailani could feel it in the air around her.

Istas said, "All who are now loyal to Prince Bellis alone instead of our great king, sit on the ground. All who are loyal to both King Jaanis and

Prince Bellis, remain where you stand. Those whose loyalty remains firmly with the king alone, return to your barracks to await further instructions."

They watched as the vast majority of the men left the area. The king breathed a sigh of relief when Captain Karruq was one of those who walked away. When they had gone and after a whispered conference with the sorcerer, Istas spoke again. "I address those of you standing only. If you are willing to renounce your allegiance to Prince Bellis for all time and give your loyalty to the king alone, raise your hands." A couple of hundred did so and they were told to wait in a different area. About one thousand men now remained.

"You men are traitors and the penalty for treason is death. However, your king is merciful and you will not lose your lives. You will each be given twenty lashes with the whip, be branded on your skin, and forever banished from this city, never to return. Your families will not accompany you. Those of you still standing may join the scum seated on the ground."

The men did as they were told and Correollis held a quick conference with the king. He then returned to Istas and whispered in his ear. Stepping forward and again raising his hands over those assembled, the sorcerer said in a thunderous voice, "Am enkus des traik os zomis brak lajir."

At once, cries from the men echoed around the area, each holding their hands to their faces. It was several seconds before Kailani could see what all the fuss was about then she saw a couple of the men had a burning letter T branded into their foreheads. She grinned, thinking their biggest desire at that moment was to either put their heads against the ice or in a bucket of very cold water.

Istas told the men sitting to stand and go to the dungeons. They did as they were told, accompanied by just four of the king's guards. There were only just enough dungeons to hold them all, considering two already had occupants.

Meanwhile, Captain Karruq was summoned and Correollis removed the spells binding him. The situation was explained to him and he was genuinely horrified at how many of his men were involved. He was told the soldiers would remain under the spell until the traitors had been escorted to their new home, and he agreed. The king asked him to fetch the Minister for Justice. He then strode to the main hall, his entourage following. Sitting on his throne, he motioned for the others to sit in the seats usually occupied by the government. A few minutes later, a well-built man entered the room, bowed to the king, and took a seat.

"Kailani, I don't think you need to be present for the questioning. Please return to my chambers." It wasn't a request. She rose and left the room accompanied by three of the guards. The remainder stood around the hall with a large contingent near Jaanis; all of them stood to attention and were highly alert.

The king quickly explained to Minister Edurne what had happened and asked him to lead the questioning.

A door opened and four guards dragged a struggling man into the room and made him stand before those assembled. Dried blood could still be seen on his ear.

"Master Enir, how long have you been spying on his majesty and reporting back to Prince Bellis?" asked Minister Edurne.

"Not long," he replied, but wouldn't look anyone in the eyes.

"Come now, we know you're lying and have the means to make you tell the truth. So I'll ask you again, how long?"

Enir's eyes roved around the room. Istas twirled a dagger in his hands. Correollis stood ready to cast a truth spell. "On and off since I became his manservant, but at least twice a day since the young princess arrived."

"Your first loyalty is to the king so why would you betray him like that?"

"I didn't want to, but Prince Bellis made me. I told him I didn't want to do it and he beat me until I agreed. Often I told him there was nothing of any importance to report and he never believed me, even when it was true, and I was beaten each time until I told him exactly what was said. He told me it wasn't my place to decide what was important and what wasn't." The servant visibly trembled when he mentioned the beatings.

"I'm guessing his punishments were quite severe judging by your reaction," Edurne said, his eyes missing nothing.

"Oh yes, sir. Sometimes I could hardly move afterwards with the pain."

"So, once Princess Kailani arrived, what information did you pass to him?"

The servant told everything he'd overheard about Kailani's decision to find her mother, the direction she was planning to travel, and the king's fears for her safety.

"In summation, you gave the prince everything he needed to know about Princess Kailani's intentions and the king's plans to protect her. Is that right?"

"Yes, sir."

"Are any of the other servants under the prince's thumb like you?"

"Not as bad as me, but yes, the maid who brings the food every day – Siku. She tells him all the gossip from around the palace and he often entertains her in his room at night. She gets a different sort of beating if you know what I mean." Enir grinned lecherously.

"The prince is bedding her?"

"Yes. That's *her* reward for passing him information. I think she's in love and will do anything for him."

"So what's your reward, Enir?"

"I don't get one. I suppose it's not getting beaten."

"Any other servants?"

"None in the palace itself, but lots of the soldiers are."

"We already know about that. Has the prince's behaviour changed since Princess Kailani arrived?"

"Yes, definitely." The servant told his story. "One day, he got a message saying that a sorcerer and warrior from the sky lands had come to help the princesses. He ventured out of the castle, but I don't know where he went. There were several trips over two days and on the second day the prince took a large bag of money with him. I saw part of the message he wrote back and it said something about a shape shifter. After that, he calmed down and almost seemed jolly. He remained in a good mood until his majesty's guards came to arrest him." Enir appeared relieved, having unburdened himself of the secrets he'd been forced to keep.

"I see. Is there anything else we should know?" Edurne asked.

"Not that I can think of, my Lord."

"Very well. Now, Enir, would you be willing to give this evidence to the court at Prince Bellis's trial tomorrow?"

Enir hesitated. Everyone could see the fear in his eyes. "Er . . . can you protect me from him? You won't let him near me, will you?"

"I can assure you Prince Bellis will not be able to touch you," Edurne replied, his tone softer and reassuring.

The servant paused then said, "Alright. I'll give this evidence to the court."

"You do understand that you will face a trial yourself, don't you?"

Enir's face fell and he nodded. "Would the court take into

consideration my co-operation today and giving evidence against the prince?"

"I'm sure they would. In fact, I will tell the court myself."

"Thank you, my Lord."

"Your Majesty? Is there anything you would like to ask this man before he's returned to his cell?" The king shook his head and the servant was removed from the hall. Edurne spoke again. "Do you wish for Siku to be questioned, Sire?"

"Yes. I'd like to hear what she has to say."

A few minutes later a guard arrived dragging a girl who struggled so much, she required two guards to restrain her.

"Siku!" Edurne's voice thundered in the huge hall and echoed around its icy walls. The young woman stopped fighting and her eyes grew wide when she saw King Jaanis seated on the throne. She tried to curtsey as best she could then stood still. "Some serious allegations have been made against you, Siku. You are here to answer our questions, which will result in us deciding whether you are to be arrested. Do you understand?"

"Arrested? I haven't done nothing wrong," she replied indignantly.

"That is for us to decide. Now, we understand you passed information to Prince Bellis regarding Princess Kailani. What did you tell him?"

"Nothing that would interest you."

"On the contrary, we want to know *everything* you told him," Edurne said, his tone commanding.

"It was just girl talk, nothing important," she insisted.

"We have the means to make you tell us the truth. Don't force me to use them."

"I'm not saying anything!"

"Siku, your lover has been arrested and faces trial for treason, kidnapping, and attempted murder. The evidence against him is overwhelming and a guilty verdict on all counts is assured. He can't protect you now, so it's in your best interest to co-operate with us."

Her mouth gaped for a few seconds before her face crumpled and tears streamed down her face. "I don't care what you do to me. I won't speak against him. I won't! You can't make me!" she cried defiantly.

Istas ordered her to speak, his voice thundering.

"You don't understand," she said in a voice full of defeat. "Bellis is my life. I love him. If I'm to lose him, my life isn't worth living anyway." She paused then glared at Captain Istas. When she spoke again her eyes and tone were full of fire and venom. "Do your worst. I won't say a word against my prince, no matter what you do to me."

Edurne looked across at the sorcerer. "Correollis? I think we need your help."

Chapter 31

The great hall was full to bursting. People stood on the pedestals of statues and the carved, fluted columns, anywhere they could – they didn't want to miss a thing. Whilst public trials were part of the ethos of Idenvarlis, there had never been one which had captured the residents' interest like this. It wasn't every day a member of the royal family was on trial.

The ministers filed into the hall, each one's head covered with a red silky square, placed diamond-shaped so a point came over the forehead. They took their seats and the crowd waited expectantly. When the royal family entered, a collective gasp echoed around the walls and high ceiling, partly because some of the older people recognised Princess Garalia, and partly because there were two people with azure blue hair in the party.

"Are you sure about this?"

"Of course I am. Father not only needs to know I've returned safely, but that I've brought you back. He'll want to see you straight away."

"But I'm not the same person he fell in love with. He might end up hating me when he finds out what..." Fear shadowed her eyes.

"He's not that kind of man, and he could never hate you," Kailani said gently. "Mother, do you still love him?"

"With all my heart."

"Well, he still loves you too. The love you share is strong enough to overcome what you've endured and together you will heal. Trust me."

Garalia looked frightened, but she nodded. Kailani stepped into the passage and, with a whoosh, she disappeared.

Galaxan was sitting at his desk when he heard the familiar noise of the secret passage. He rose just as Kailani stepped out. She rushed into his waiting arms.

"You have no idea how worried I've been. I even went to speak with your... King Jaanis."

"I know. He told me. I'm sorry I worried you, Father, but there was something I had to do. I didn't know if I was right, but I had such a strong instinct about it, I just had to follow what it told me. You used to say to me that I got the instincts from my mother and to trust them, so I did."

"Jaanis mentioned something about you taking off on your own with a wild scheme of trying to find your mother. He also said you disobeyed him and went off alone when he'd told you to wait for the soldiers."

"That's all true. I had to do it on my own and I'm so glad I did. I found her, Father. I rescued mother from the worst conditions imaginable. She's malnourished, very traumatised, and so frightened you won't feel the same about her when you know what she's endured. Underneath all the pain, she's still the woman you fell in love with and she still loves you too." Her voice was passionate and earnest.

"Y-you found her?" His face paled despite his perpetual tan.

"Yes. She's waiting for us to return."

"Take me to her!" he demanded. Together they stepped into the passage and within a few blinks arrived in Idenvarlis.

Galaxan stepped out of the passage, his eyes wide as he gazed at the woman before him. "Garalia, my love," he said softly, opening his arms.

She rushed into them and burst into tears. He stroked her hair as he tried to comfort her. "My darling, I'm here now and I'm never going to let you go again. I love you so much."

She pulled her head away from his chest and gazed up into his eyes, her sight blurry from the tears. "I never stopped loving you," she whispered.

"Neither did I," he countered then gently placed his lips on hers. She kissed him back and then again with more passion and less sweetness.

Neither of them saw Kailani leave the room.

The prisoner was brought in, heavily shackled and guarded. Prince Bellis looked dishevelled and grimy with more than a day's growth of beard on his normally clean-shaven face. His eyes, though, were defiant and filled with hatred.

Minister Edurne banged a small round block of ice encased in silver on the desk in front of him until silence filled the cavernous, high-ceilinged hall. He stood and faced the prince. In an even tone, loud enough to be heard at the back of the hall, he said, "Prince Bellis, you are charged with high treason, arranging the kidnapping and incarceration of your sister, and the attempted murder of both Princess Garalia and your niece, Princess Kailani. Do you plead guilty or not guilty?"

"I don't have to answer to you, Edurne," Bellis sneered.

"You do in your present circumstances. I take it you don't wish to enter a plea then?" The prince looked down his nose at the minister and refused to speak. "Very well. Bring in the witness," he called. Enir was brought in and placed well away from his master. "Enir, you are the manservant of the prince. Is that correct?"

"Yes, my Lord."

"Will you please tell the court exactly what you told us during questioning."

Enir started to speak, slowly and hesitantly at first, feeling the prince's eyes burning into him. But after a couple of minutes, he started to relax and spoke more fluently. He not only repeated what he'd said the day before, but embellished on quite a few points which served to incriminate Bellis even more. When he finished speaking, one of the other ministers asked him a few questions, clarifying certain points.

Edurne addressed him again. "Do you have anything further you wish to tell the court?"

"Yes, my Lord. I wasn't working for Prince Bellis when he arranged the kidnapping. If I had been, I would have spoken up, told his Majesty what I knew, despite the beating which was sure to come. I didn't know anything about it, and it wasn't until Princess Kailani arrived that his behaviour changed and I got suspicious. I'd had so many beatings for the most trivial of things that I was scared to open my mouth. I want to say I'm sorry for not having the courage to come forward earlier, and for what I was forced to do. That's all," he concluded.

"Thank you, Enir." He spoke to the guards who were with him. "Take him back to his cell." When the guards and Enir were gone, Edurne said, "I call her Royal Highness, Princess Kailani to give witness." Kailani rose and walked over to where Enir had stood. A few whispers buzzed through the crowd. She suddenly felt very self-conscious and isolated standing there alone and glanced over at her parents. They smiled at her and nodded, giving her the boost she needed. Edurne said, "Your Highness, would you please give your account of your journey from the Land of Lost Souls back to here?"

"Certainly," she replied, and told the court about the avalanche, finding the arrows and cannonball, being shot with a poisoned arrow and almost losing her life, and everything up until they reached the palace, leaving out only the secret passageway and the scroll. During her testimony there were various gasps from the crowd and one or two called out comments: "Shameful", "No", and "Dreadful".

There was only one question raised by the government. "Your Highness, how did you survive the poison?" one of the ministers asked.

Kailani pulled the chain around her neck and lifted the vial so he could see it. "It was thanks to the contents of this vial, given to me by the High Priest of Rasha-Varl. This is what cured me."

With no other questions raised, Minister Edurne said, "Thank you, your Highness. That will be all." Kailani walked back to the dais and took her seat with the rest of the royal family and the crowd started to mumble amongst themselves. Once she was seated, Edurne banged the block of ice a couple of times to restore silence then spoke. "One more witness needs to testify, but she will give her evidence from where she is due to her fragility. Your Royal Highness, Princess Garalia, would you please tell the court about your kidnapping, and what has happened to you up until your return to the palace."

She nodded and Galaxan squeezed her hand. Taking care not to look at her brother, she began falteringly. It wasn't until she reached the part where Bellis turned up at the Land of Lost Souls for the first time, and the nastiness of his taunts, that her voice got stronger. There were oo's and ah's from the crowd until that point and then a gasp rolled through them. More cries rang out, "Shame on you", "Beast", "Evil", "Monster", and someone threw a rotten tomato which hit the prince squarely on the back of the head. He turned around and bared his teeth at the crowd, a look of rage on his face. Edurne banged the gavel until the crowd quietened down and the princess could continue with her story.

Garalia left out the graphic parts, but explained how she had been repeatedly violated. A couple of times during her testimony, tears rolled down her cheeks, but she ignored them and carried on. When she told of her rescue by Kailani, a cheer went up accompanied by applause and Edurne had to restore order once more. The rest of her testimony basically corroborated Kailani's.

No one raised any questions so the Minister for Justice thanked the princess and turned to the accused. "Prince Bellis, you've heard the testimony given against you. In addition, we know you turned a large number of soldiers against His Majesty, King Jaanis, and enticed them to be loyal to you alone. These men are all now in custody and will be punished tomorrow. You are charged with extremely serious offences so, before we deliberate, do you have anything to say in your defence?"

"The bitch deserved everything she got and more," he said with venom and hatred. "She stole my birth right, pretended to love me when... Since she's been gone, I've been the favourite, I've had all the attention she robbed me of, and I was the natural heir to the throne.

"I wanted to follow in my father's footsteps. I wanted to carry on the tradition of a strong country that others wouldn't dare to attack, but her," he pointed to Garalia, "that conniving, two-faced bitch was doing everything she could to undermine my efforts, while all the time pretending she was supporting me. She's a liar! She never loved me, she just said that to cover up what she was doing behind my back.

"You only have *her* word for what she said she went through. You have no proof that I was involved in any way with her disappearance. And you have no proof that I went there and taunted her on a monthly basis. The truth is more likely that she realised she'd made a terrible mistake marrying someone from a different world, and having a hybrid child was the last straw. She probably arranged her own disappearance to get away from what she'd done. She was so ashamed of it, she didn't even tell our mother and father. She hid the baby so they didn't know they were grandparents.

"She confided in me about it and I promised to keep her secret. When she disappeared, I assumed she'd gone to live in the other world with her husband and the baby. To this day, I never broke the promise I made her. Even seeing my parents' distress after she went, I didn't say anything to them about her marriage and child. They sent soldiers to every town and village in our country searching for her and when they couldn't find her, they eventually gave up looking. And all that time and every day since, I've been their special one, the person they lavished all their love and attention on, the one my father began to groom to take over as his heir.

"And now she's back, whispering her lies into their ears, getting all the attention she's missed out on all these years, and to make sure she usurped my new position as their favourite and heir, she's made up these horrendous allegations against me. It's like history repeating itself all over again. She'll do and say anything to make sure she's the favoured child. The bitch is back to steal what I've worked so hard for while she's been off enjoying herself. Well, I'm not going to let her destroy all my hard work. I'll kill her before I let her do that to me!" Bellis seemed to run out of steam at that point and stopped talking. There was a shocked hush over the crowd, all of whom looked dazed by the prince's words.

Edurne turned his back on the prince so he was facing the royal family. They also appeared to be in a state of shock, especially Garalia. "Prince Galaxan? Would you be prepared to answer a few questions for the court? You are not obliged to as you reside in a different world, but we would be grateful if you would assist us."

Galaxan rose and walked to the spot Kailani had stood in earlier. "Of course I will." He guessed what was coming and had his answers ready.

"Is it true that Princess Garalia hid your marriage from her parents?"

"Yes, it is." A few people in the crowd audibly inhaled loudly, but he ignored it and carried on. "However, it is not because she was ashamed as Bellis claims. She knew her father had a temper, and the one meeting between him and I before our marriage, when I went to ask for her hand, didn't exactly go well. He flew into a terrible rage swearing he'd never allow his daughter to marry the likes of me. He was prejudiced against me because of where I came from and I believe he was worried I'd take her away and he'd never see her again. It was obvious to me he loved her very much.

"Garalia and I were very much in love and were determined to spend the rest of our lives together. I made the suggestion of us marrying in Taivass-maa and she agreed immediately. The arrangements were made and we had a wonderful wedding in my home town. We jointly decided to keep our marriage a secret, at least until her father had calmed down and she could talk to him about how she felt. She was scared to tell him – it's as simple as that."

"And what about the baby? Is it also true she kept that from her parents?"

"Yes. Every time she tried to talk to him about me and how she felt, he became extremely angry and forbade her to see me ever again. When we discovered she was carrying my child, she tried to talk to him once more, but before she had the chance to tell him the news, he became so enraged she literally ran from the room in fear. She was frightened about what he'd do if he knew the truth so, after discussing it at length, we decided together to keep it from him and once our child was born and a couple of months old, present him with the facts, hoping that when he saw his grandchild, he would soften his attitude. However, we never got the opportunity to do so before she was kidnapped."

"When did you discover she was missing?"

The prince explained and ended with, "I returned home and concentrated on raising our child. I never lost hope of seeing her again and knew that as soon as she returned, she would want to see her child and me. I never stopped praying for her safe return and I never stopped loving her."

"Thank you for being so candid, Prince Galaxan, and for your assistance. The court has no further questions for you."

Galaxan returned to his seat and held his wife's hand, bringing it to his lips and kissing it gently.

"Your Majesty, can you corroborate what Prince Galaxan said about Princess Garalia trying to talk to you about him?" Edurne asked, showing just a touch of nervousness.

"I can. Everything he told you is the truth," Jaanis replied unruffled. He didn't even appear upset to have been asked.

"Thank you, Sire." He turned to face the group further down the line. "Princess Kailani? Would you be so kind as to answer some more questions for us?"

"Of course," she replied rising and walking to the spot her father had just vacated.

"Did you have any suspicions about Prince Bellis before rescuing your mother?"

"Yes, I did." She recounted what had happened during her first few days in Idenvarlis. "It wasn't until I'd left the palace and was journeying to find my mother that I had the time to think about it. I came to the conclusion that it was possible my uncle was somehow involved in my mother's disappearance."

"Thank you. Now could you please describe your mother's condition when you first rescued her?"

Kailani explained what she'd observed and how she rescued her mother from the camp. "Mother weighed so little, it was like picking up a child. Clad in only filthy rags, she was so undernourished and fragile that I was worried whether she would have the strength to make the long journey back. I feared she would die."

"Did you have any interaction with any of the men in the camp?"

"Yes. I had a verbal exchange with Gengaruk who demanded I give my mother back to him. He threatened me, told me she had been given to him and as such was his property. My reply was far from lady-like, I'm afraid. I was furious, not only with the way my mother had been treated, but also by the way he spoke to me. Even when I told him I was of royal birth, he showed no respect and said something about having royal connections. I honestly can't remember his exact words because my rage was so intense – I wanted nothing more than to kill him. I did strike out with my Panas and wound him, but it wasn't a life-threatening injury. Eventually I walked away with his voice ringing in my ears saying how he was going to kill my mother and make me watch before killing me slowly so I would beg for death."

"How *did* your mother survive the journey?"

"I had stockpiled food on my way to the Land of Lost Souls, only eating half portions so I would have more than enough for her. I conjured a barrier, helped her into warmer, clean clothes and made her some food. I ensured she ate a decent-sized portion of food three times a day and gradually she began to regain some of her strength. Most of the journey I had to tie her onto her Blenorai Kai to keep her from falling off. She was absolutely determined to get home and I think it was her inner strength as well as regular food that helped her."

"And my final question, did your mother tell you the circumstances of her disappearance?"

"Yes. She told me exactly what happened from the moment she was snatched from the castle until I rescued her, including the monthly visits from her brother and the way he taunted her. My mother is an incredibly brave woman to have even given evidence to this court today, but also because she was, for the most part, able to maintain her composure. She has been accused of lying. If you had been there when she first told me everything she endured, if you had seen her anguish and pain, if you had heard the horror and disgust in her voice, if you'd witnessed her almost fall apart, you would *never* doubt the truth of her words. And I can assure you she has *not* been in Taivass-maa all this time.

"Look at her!" she said, pointing to Garalia. "Does she look healthy? Does she appear well-fed? Has she got the physique of someone who has been cared for during the last twenty-one years? Mother, please expose one of your arms and hold it up as best you can." Garalia looked at Kailani for a moment then did as she was asked. It was so thin, there was no muscle tone and it looked like the skin had just been stretched over the bone. Galaxan had to support her arm so she could hold it up long enough. "I ask you, does this look like the arm of someone who has been fed and looked after?" She paused for effect and to ensure everyone got a good look before nodding to her mother. Garalia lowered her arm and covered it up once again. "I'm sure my mother won't mind me telling you, that is how she looks all over." A few women in the crowd were so distressed they were actually crying.

She crossed the floor, not to the dais as expected but into the crowd, and put her arms around one of the women who was crying. She remained like that, comforting the woman until her tears dried.

Kailani gently squeezed the woman's hand then returned to the dais and took her seat.

Edurne spoke again. "The penultimate piece of evidence is a report from a court-appointed physician. Princess Garalia agreed to undergo a humiliating examination. I will read his report. 'Having examined Her Royal Highness, Princess Garalia, I have reached the following conclusions. She has been virtually starved for a great number of years and it is a miracle she is still alive. The internal damage she has suffered as a result of sexual abuse over a long period will take just as long to heal. Further to that, it is unlikely Princess Garalia will ever be able to have more children as the damage is too extensive. There are scars on her body, arms, and legs, which tell me she has been viciously brutalised and beaten for many years'.

"The final piece of information has been received from the kitchen staff here at the palace. They have informed me that once a month, Prince Bellis would demand large quantities of food and drink to be packed up. On the prince's orders, these packages were loaded onto a number of sledges and when this was done, he would hitch them to Blenorai and disappear for several days."

It took the ministers less than two minutes to reach their decision, and when the guilty verdict was read out, the crowd went wild, cheering and clapping. More rotten tomatoes and other fruit were thrown at the disgraced prince and despite the looks he gave them, it didn't stop.

Once Minister for Justice Edurne had managed to quieten the crowd, he stood looking at the defendant. "Prince Bellis, you have been found guilty on all counts and under normal circumstances the sentence would have been death. However, after receiving recommendations from the injured parties, your sentence is that you will be taken from the palace to the Land of Lost Souls where you will live out the rest of your days in the same conditions you subjected your sister to. There will be no monthly food parcels delivered to the camp and, as of now, you are no longer considered a member of the royal family."

"NOOOOO!" Bellis roared.

"Take him back to his cell. He will be taken to his new home tomorrow," Edurne instructed. Bellis glared at the dais, but to his horror, they had all turned their backs to him.

"Father? Mother? Please? No, get off me." He struggled as the guards manhandled him back to his cell. "You can't do this to me. NOOOO!" The voice grew fainter then could be heard no more.

Chapter 32

The trial had ended. Kailani excused herself and with her bodyguards, made her way to the temple. When they reached the door she turned to them and said, "I must have a private audience with the High Priest. Please wait by the door for me."

The guards looked decidedly unhappy, but as there was only one entrance in and out, they didn't argue. The princess walked through the door and closed it behind her. Before she had taken a single step further, the High Priest appeared.

He bowed and said, "Your Highness, it is such a pleasure to see you back with us. I prayed to our deities every day for your safe return and for a successful trip."

Remembering the etiquette from her previous visit she bowed to him. "Thank you. I'm pleased to say my journey was worth all the effort as I found my mother and brought her home."

"That is joyous news indeed. We must thank our gods and goddess for their gift and blessings. Will you join me?"

"Of course," she replied and followed him to the sacred well. They knelt and silently offered up their thanks to the Gods Rasha and Xuani, and Goddess Sylde. When the High Priest rose, she did too.

"You didn't come here just to give me the news about your mother, did you?" the High Priest asked, a knowing look on his face. Kailani's eyes widened and she shook her head. "What is it, Highness?"

She pulled the box from within her clothes and, opening it, removed the scroll. "I was given this by King Jevnod in the Lost Mire. He told me to bring it straight to you upon my return."

He held out his hand and she placed the scroll in it. Unrolling the parchment, he began to read slowly. The longer he took, the more curious she became until she was almost bouncing on the balls of her feet. Eventually the High Priest spoke. "What did Jevnod say when he gave you this?"

"Something about being the chosen one and that the box would save my life."

"And did it?"

"In a way, yes. When I was shot by the poisoned arrow it went through the box before it pierced my skin. Apparently only the tip penetrated my flesh so the amount of poison entering my system was far less than it would have otherwise been," she explained, a thoughtful expression on her face.

"Hmm." He nodded sagely, his eyes drifting back to the scroll for a moment before he spoke again. "It is a prophecy which says, 'Unrest will be in the air. The king shall know not what plots are afoot and is betrayed by one he holds dear. Alliances are forged, coercion runs rife, and those once loyal become traitorous. The chain of events will begin when one of power and influence is taken, causing misery throughout the land. This is when the plan is begun.

"Twenty years shall pass. The betrayer's position has solidified and becomes the king's confidant. A war shall decimate the country of Idenvarlis, turning friend against friend, and forcing the king to abdicate. Much blood will be spilled and many lives lost. Idenvarlis, with a new king on the throne, deteriorates. His rule is harsh and greed driven. Where once the citizens were cared for and happy, they become fearful, treated as slaves, and miserable. Many die from starvation and disease.

"However, one shall come with power from two worlds. She will rescue the dear one taken so long ago. Only she can prevent the war and expose the betrayer. There will be danger around every corner and few who she can trust. There will be many obstacles for her to face and only her magic, wits, and warrior spirit will prevail.

"When twenty years have passed there will be a dispute between Idenvarlis and Daminalis. Things will quickly escalate until the two countries are on the brink of war. The chosen one will eventually work out a compromise which both parties can accept, thus preventing war. This will lead to a new understanding between the two countries which will be profitable for both sides and they become strong allies.

"The chosen one will become an ambassador for our beloved country throughout her lifetime, brokering peace and advantageous deals with neighbouring villages, towns, and countries. Eventually the chosen one will rule two worlds with strength, courage, fairness, and empathy. This ruler will be much loved and admired, not only by her subjects but by all she comes into contact with'. In short, your Highness, this twelve-hundred-year-old prophecy is all about you."

Kailani gasped, her eyes widened and jaw slackened until she was gaping like a fish. "So King Jevnod was telling the truth when he said I was the chosen one?"

The High Priest took her hand. "Yes, my child. It must seem daunting to you at the moment, but over time you will adjust to the idea and it will be less scary than it is at the moment. I will always make myself available to you if you ever need to talk to someone about it or for counsel. You cannot tell anyone about the prophecy. If your mother asks you about it, you cannot lie. I suggest you say you left the scroll with me and leave it at that. If you agree, I will hold it here for safekeeping. No one will have access to it, not even His Majesty, the king."

Kailani nodded her head mutely as she tried to take everything in. He squeezed her hand gently. "It's so much responsibility," she whispered.

"It must seem like that at the moment, but you've already fulfilled the first part of the prophecy by rescuing Princess Garalia and returning her home. I know the task was far from easy, but you came through it. You showed courage, bravery, and cunning far beyond that of your tender years. You already have most of the skills – the rest will come with age. When you think of what you have accomplished already, you will see what I mean. For now you must put it out of your mind and re-join your family. You have much to celebrate despite the betrayal of your uncle." He paused and a bright, white, glowing mist surrounded the princess. By the time she noticed it, peace stole over her and the tumult in her head ceased. Kailani smiled at him as he waved his hand and the mist vanished.

"Thank you for all your help, support, and counsel. If you'll excuse me, I need to return to my family now." She was perfectly calm and poised.

"Of course, your Highness. I look forward to seeing you again." He smiled, let go of her hand, and bowed. She bowed to him, turned and walked back to the door.

The next day was one Kailani never hoped to see again in her entire life. Shortly after breakfast, Prince Bellis left the palace on a sledge, trussed up with ropes and chains as if he were a wild animal. She stood beside King Jaanis watching as his only son, openly crying, begged his father to forgive him and not send him away. His tone was pitiful, his tear-stained face filled with desolation as he was dragged away. The soldiers accompanying him, except for one who was of the king's personal guard, were bespelled by Correollis not to pay any attention to his moans or cunning wiles. Kailani couldn't get Bellis's expression out of her mind, no matter how much she tried to distract herself.

It wasn't that she felt sorry for him, on the contrary he deserved everything that was coming his way after the manner in which he treated her mother, but it was the anguish on his face that tugged at her. Maybe that was the price she had to pay for being a decent and caring person. She couldn't help but wonder how her grandfather was feeling. After all, he heard and saw everything she did. When she looked at him, his face was a cold mask of nothingness. No emotions at all were visible, not even in his eyes; he was like one of the ice statues which decorated the forecourt of the main entrance to the palace.

The crowd that had gathered were exceedingly vocal in their condemnation and delighted in throwing rotten fruit and animal dung at him. Word had spread throughout the city of the prince's crimes and his attitude toward Princess Garalia, so a larger number of people had arrived in the town square than had been at the trial. The soldiers almost had to fight their way through, and if the officer in front hadn't been wearing the distinctive purple flash of the king's own guard on his armour, they probably would have done.

If Kailani thought that experience was hard, the next was horrendous on a different level. The crowd had stayed around to see the next lot of 'entertainment' scheduled for the day. One elderly man was heard to say, "I love to see a good whipping. There hasn't been one for many years and never as big as this is going to be!" She shuddered at his words.

How anyone could enjoy watching one of their neighbours being publicly flogged was completely alien to her.

As that thought wormed its way across the synapses of her brain, a line of forty unkempt, bare-chested men were led into the square and lined up at a newly erected scaffold. Each man's hands were tied to iron rings set in the top of the crossbar, making most of them stand on tiptoe. The audience heckled the men, but no food or faeces were thrown. Instead they had the dubious pleasure of being spat at, punched, or kicked, and called the worst names their tormentors could think of. If she hadn't been trained from a young age not to show emotions in public, she was sure some of the cussing would make her blush. She'd certainly learned a few new words.

As the last of the traitors were tied to the rings, a huge man, who was not only extremely tall but had biceps the size of a Feegle's thigh and a massive chest the like of which Kailani had never seen before, stepped out from behind the crowd. He wore a leather gilet emblazoned with the king's shield over his shoulders and chest, leaving his arms bare to the chilly day. She found the size of him mesmerising.

"That's Ijarubak," the king told her. "He doles out whatever punishments the court deems appropriate and is also our executioner." She nodded her head, not finding a single word to reply with.

As soon as the crowd saw him they erupted into spontaneous applause and cheering. Whether it was fear or not she didn't know, but as Ijarubak began walking through them, they parted. It was like something divine had come down from above the clouds to walk among them. They patted him on the back or the arm as if, by touching him, they would receive favour with the gods and goddess.

He reached the scaffold, turned to the king, and bowed low with a flourish of his arm (which looked ungainly on a man of his size). Standing upright, he looked directly at Jaanis who nodded, a solemn expression on his face. Ijarubak unhooked a thick coil from his belt and unwound it. He cracked the long snake-like shape to straighten it then turned to face the prisoners. Kailani mentally gasped when she realised what the massive man had in his hands – the longest whip she'd ever seen. Silence hung over the crowd like a canopy. Ijarubak lifted it high and with an arm movement as quick as a flash of lightning, brought it down; a thwack echoed around the walls and several of the men cried out as welts appeared on their skin, blood bubbling to the surface.

The crowd cheered, egging him on. The punisher brought his weapon down again and a fresh set of wounds set the men wailing. The whip, easily large enough to deal with twenty men at a time, lashed again and again until the sentence had been carried out. As he moved along to mete out the king's justice on the next group, a man atop the crossbar cut down the whimpering, bleeding traitors and a soldier led them away while another brought the next twenty to be tied up ready. And so it continued until every last man had tasted Ijarubak's whip.

When he had finished, the visibly tired executioner turned to the king and bowed. Jaanis nodded in acknowledgement. A man from the crowd brought a large bowl of water with some cloth draped over his arm and walked up to Ijarubak. He bowed clumsily to the royals trying hard not to spill any of the water. Kailani watched with curiosity. Small curls of steam rose from the vessel and they seemed to dance in the slight breeze before being wafted away. The crowd suddenly hushed.

Without speaking, the punisher took a cloth, dipped it in the water and wiped his sweat-drenched face. Next he curled the massive length of braided leather in the bowl and using the same cloth, washed it carefully, almost lovingly. Removing it a section at a time, he used the remaining fabric to wipe it down, discarding each piece when it became too wet. When the entirety of the whip was clean and dry, he swung it around his head and then unleashed it so it cracked harmlessly in the air.

The crowd went wild, cheering, clapping, and calling his name until it became like some sort of mantra. Ijarubak thanked the man and, with one more bow to the princess and her grandfather, he walked toward the crowd which parted for him as before. Receiving the touches of the audience, he soon disappeared from sight.

Kailani's breakfast had threatened to rise on several occasions as she saw how the skin on the men's backs had been ripped to shreds by the whip. As distasteful as the sight was, she couldn't help but admire the skill Ijarubak possessed; not one lash crossed over another, with the last batch of men's wounds as equally spaced as the first. It fascinated her in a macabre sort of way, but also repulsed her in equal measure. Her head knew the men had to be severely punished, but her heart never wanted to see such a sight ever again.

King Jaanis took her elbow and guided her to a couple of chairs placed behind them. A warm wrap had been left on each and both swaddled themselves against the chill of the breeze. Galaxan stepped through the doors, walked up behind his daughter's seat, and placed his hands on her shoulders.

"Are you holding up alright?"

"Yes, thank you, Father. There were a couple of occasions when I thought my stomach would rebel, but I'm fine now. Did you watch?"

"Yes, and I have to say, King Jaanis, that man of yours is incredibly skillful with his whip. I admire his . . . artistry."

"Thank you, Prince Galaxan. I found Ijarubak quite by chance and employed him immediately. He metes out the punishments exactly as directed every time. He's certainly earned his coin today." He paused for a moment before continuing. "On another subject, I want to thank you for the care you have administered to my daughter. She seems much happier than I expected her to be after her ordeal and can see, in just two days, a marked improvement in her condition."

"There's no need to thank me. I love her with all my heart and would do anything to make her life as comfortable and joyous as possible." He placed his hand over his heart as he spoke.

"I suppose when she's well enough, you'll take her back to Taivass-maa?" Jaanis tried to keep his tone neutral, but an undercurrent of sadness was detectable.

"That's not necessarily the case. We haven't discussed it yet, but whilst I cannot abandon certain duties at home, I have thought of various compromises so Garalia can have the best of both worlds. I'm willing to relocate to Idenvarlis if she wishes to remain here permanently, although I would have to travel back and forth on occasions. I have also considered suggesting we spend half the year in Taivass-maa and the remainder here. But whatever she wants is what I'll do. I never want to lose her again."

Jaanis let out a sigh and his shoulders visibly relaxed. "As you know I was vehemently opposed to your union. Having discovered you two are married and I have a wonderful and brave granddaughter," he glanced at Kailani and smiled, "my heart has softened. You are good for Garalia and I can see she loves you as much as you love her. You are a better, more thoughtful man than I was willing to see all those years ago and for that I apologise. I want my daughter to have nothing but happiness in her life after what she's been through, so if she decides to move to Taivass-maa, she will do so with my blessing. Eventually she'll have to return here – after all, she's heir to the throne and much as I hate to admit it, I'm not immortal – but that will be dealt with in all due time. All I ask is that you'll visit us often." He offered his hand, which Galaxan grabbed and shook.

"No apologies are necessary. I'd probably feel the same about Kailani in similar circumstances, or would have I should say." He smiled down at his daughter, but winked at the king when she lowered her head, earning him a grin. "If my wife decides she wants to live in my world, we *will* come back for regular visits and hopefully we can entice you and Queen Shivla to our home."

"An invitation we would be honoured to accept." At that moment, movement at one side of the square diverted his attention. The now clothed and heavily-shackled prisoners and their escorts began to parade through the square riding Blenorai. Jaanis rose and, holding his right hand palm uppermost, waited for Kailani. She took it and together they walked to the front of the steps. "Prince Galaxan, would you care to join us?" He walked forward and stood on the left, just behind the king's shoulder.

Kailani could see the shackled men rode five abreast with chains connecting the Blenorai both horizontally and vertically. A further chain held each prisoner to their respective mount. The execution of this journey had obviously been well planned considering the short amount of time they had. Almost as if reading her mind, Jaanis said, "This was Captain Karruq's idea."

"I was just thinking how well thought out it all was. He should be congratulated. What about when they stop to rest each night?"

"Apparently, each man will have his feet shackled and they will be chained together in groups of twenty, making it much harder for anyone to try and escape. The Blenorai will be housed separately as will the guards. The traitors are still under the spells Correollis cast, as are the guards, but Karruq didn't want to take any chances," her grandfather explained.

She noticed at least two dozen of the king's personal guard at the head and evenly spaced between the soldiers along the procession, with two at the very end. "Grandfather, aren't you putting yourself at risk by sending so many of your guards on these journeys? You sent some with Be-... the prisoner to the Land of Lost Souls and now these men going to Paavinil – how many have you got left to keep *you* safe?" Her concern was evident.

Jaanis turned his head to her and placed his hand on her shoulder. "You don't need to worry about that, dear one. I still have nearly one hundred men to guard me. Don't you remember how many there were the night you returned with your mother, and in the Great Hall during the trial?"

"To be honest, Grandfather, I didn't exactly count, but yes, I do remember there were a large number of them."

"So then you know there are still plenty remaining. I'm extremely grateful and touched that you would concern yourself with my safety though." He squeezed her shoulder gently then dropped his hand, turning his attention back to the procession.

The three royals stood silently until the last of the guards vanished from sight then they turned and walked into the palace without looking back.

Epilogue

The Grand Ballroom was resplendent with flower garlands, ribbon bows, and bubbles filled with stars. A cloud arch, sprinkled liberally with stars, stood on the dais at one end; behind it, a row of soft padded seats had been arranged in a semi-circle facing it. From the staircase to the arch was a beribboned barricade creating a walkway. Behind that, a seating area had been created for the honoured guests. In a large room just off the ballroom, huge tables groaned with platters of food and barrels of darmal, the sweet wine produced in a large village just outside the city, stood at one end with racks of shining glasses behind it. Uniformed servants began to take their places in readiness.

King Jaanis and Queen Shivla had arrived the previous day. It wasn't their first visit to the world so different from their own, so they didn't suffer the culture shock which set in on their initial visit. Thankfully, they had got on famously with King Sirris and Princess Konstellia and enjoyed every opportunity to strengthen the bonds between the two families.

Elsewhere in the Cloud Castle, Kailani sat nervously in her room while Carina fixed her hair.

"By the gods and goddesses, if you don't stop fidgeting, I'll have to start all over again and make you late – now keep still!" Carina felt under pressure to make the princess look even more stunning than she normally did.

"I'm sorry, Carina, but I can't help it. I'm so nervous and excited I could burst!"

"Well you can burst all you like after the ceremony, but right now let me finish my work," Carina said, smiling to take the edge off her stern voice.

Kailani smiled back in the mirror, watching the maid who had become so much more to her as each year passed. She concentrated on Carina's hands as she deftly curled and pinned sections of her long azure hair.

Once it was done, Carina placed a glittering row of star-shaped jewels about her charge's neck and matching bracelets on both her wrists then brought the carefully wrapped gown from a cupboard and laid it on the bed. She unwrapped it and gasped. Although it was the traditional orange hue of the sun, the dressmaker had added floaty panels of ivory and white, which glittered with tiny stars matching those on the bodice. There had never been such a glorious creation seen in Taivass-maa.

She held the dress open carefully so Kailani could step into it then pulled it up and fastened it with the long line of small buttons the exact shade of the material, which ran from the top of the gown to just above the princess's hips. The bejewelled slippers which matched the dress perfectly came next, and the final step was a circlet of flowers resplendent with small stars which was carefully placed on her head.

Kailani looked in the full-length mirror and inhaled sharply. "I look beautiful," she said in a voice filled with wonder.

"You've always been beautiful, child – you were the only one who couldn't see it," Carina replied, her eyes turning teary as she stared at the woman whom she'd cared for since she was a tiny infant.

Kailani turned and embraced her. "Thank you, Carina. Not only for today, but for everything you've ever done for me."

"It was, is, and always will be my greatest pleasure, my dear Kailani. I love you as if you were my own child," she replied with a husky voice, carefully returning the hug. "Mind your dress now. You don't want it wrinkled, do you?"

Kailani pulled away and laughed. A knock at the door interrupted the tender moment; Carina walked over and opened it, admitting Auriga and Leda, Kailani's two best friends and chosen handmaids. They were already attired in the traditional ivory-coloured dresses, but with thin, sparkling panels matching the colour of Kailani's gown. In their hands were beribboned white baskets.

They barely had time to swap compliments before another rap at the door. Carina opened it. This time Prince Galaxan stood in the doorway, looking extremely attractive in his azure outfit. After saying hello to the handmaids and complimenting them, he walked over to his daughter. He took her hands and said, "Darling, you have never looked more radiantly beautiful."

"Thank you, Father," she replied, feeling the heat of a blush in her cheeks.

He smiled. "Are you ready?" She nodded, careful not to displace the circlet.

With the handmaids leading the way, they walked through the hallways, pausing just out of sight before the main staircase. Auriga turned her head, a question in her eyes, and the prince nodded. She and Leda began to walk sedately down the stairs, sprinkling the contents of their baskets as they went. A long moment later, with her hand looped through her father's arm, Kailani and Galaxan appeared at the top of the stairs. The steps were covered with tiny stars which glittered brightly, lighting her way.

As they descended, Kailani saw all the dignitaries standing on her right and she had a smile for each. They followed the shining walkway and through the arch she could see her mother holding her contented and sleeping infant brother, both sets of grandparents, her aunt, and her soon-to-be new parents, all dressed in their best. But they were all only afforded a quick glance and smile as her eyes were drawn to the handsome ivory-clad man who stood by the arch.

Prince Dashiel gazed at Kailani with love in his eyes. As she reached him, he took the hand offered by her father. She looked at her husband-to-be with shining eyes and a radiant smile. Her future was about to begin.

The End

Books by Carlie M A Cullen

HEART SEARCH, book one: Lost

HEART SEARCH, book two: Found

HEART SEARCH, book three: Betrayal

In anthologies as a member of WriteBulb Writing Group

The Other Way is Essex

Creepy Tales for Boyz & Ghouls

Magic, Mystery, and Mayhem

Catching Santa and other festive tales

More Exciting Titles from Myrddin Publishing Group

The Tower of Bones Series by Connie J Jasperson

Billy's Revenge series by Connie J Jasperson

Tales of the Dreamtime by Connie J Jasperson

Crown Phoenix Series by Alison DeLuca

Hunted Heart by Alison DeLuca

The Ring of Lost Souls by Rachel Tsoumbakos

Emeline and the Mutants by Rachel Tsoumbakos

Metanoia by Rachel Tsoumbakos

Unremembered Things by Rachel Tsoumbakos

Silent No More by Krista Hatch

The Other Way Is Essex by Writebulb Writers Group

Magic, Mystery & Mayhem by Writebulb Writers Group

The Infinity Bridge by Ross M Kitson

The Darkness Rising Series by Ross M Kitson

Chinese Lolita by Lisa Zhang Wharton

A Simpler Guide to Gmail by Ceri Clark

A Simpler Guide to Google+ by Ceri Clark

A Simpler Guide to Calibre by Ceri Clark

A Simpler Guide to Finding Free Ebooks by Ceri Clark

Children of the Elementi by Ceri Clark

The Charm City Chronicles series by Kathleen M Barker

The Land of Nod Series by Gary Hoover

Hearts & Minds by Maria V A Johnson

After Ilium by Stephen Swartz

The Dream Land Series by Stephen Swartz

A Beautiful Chill by Stephen Swartz

A Dry Patch of Skin by Stephen Swartz

Aiko by Stephen Swartz

Brawn Stroker's Dragula by Nicole Antonia Carro

Catopia by Nicole Carro

Yum by Nicole Antonia Carson

Sons of Roland by Nicole Antonia Carson

Hired by a Demon by Gypsy Madden

The Last Guardian series by Joan Hazel

What the Heart Sees by Joan Hazel

Dark Places by Shaun Allan

Darker Places by Shaun Allan

Sax and the Suburbs by Marilyn Rucker

Girls Can't be Knights by Lee French

Al-Kabar by Lee French

Heart Search trilogy by Carlie M A Cullen

Of Ice & Air by Carlie M A Cullen

Check www.myrddinpublishing.com for new titles coming soon.

www.ingramcontent.com/pod-product-compliance
Lightning Source LLC
Chambersburg PA
CBHW051519250626
47156CB00001B/153